The Unnatura of the Three-Eyed Skull's Field Guide
to
Cryptids, Creatures, Creeps, Demons, Horrors, Haunts, Haints, Hags, Ghosts, Monsters, Mutants and Madmen

Volume 2

First edition.

Illustrations by:
ANDREW P. BARR

Copyright © 2020 Andrew P. Barr all rights reserved.
No portion of the contents of this book may be reproduced or transmitted in any form or by any electronic, mechanical, physical, psychical, or interdimensional means without express permission from the author.

APB-art.com   moviemonstars.blogspot.com

Shortly after the publication of the first volume of *Unnatural Order of the Three Eyed Skull's Field Guide, etc.*, Archduke G. Philo Esterscott, sent me a message expressing concern that vast majority (more than 95%) of creatures represented in that volume were located not just in Canada but predominantly within the province of Ontario. I explained to him that since I was living in that province it was easier for me to document the creatures found in that area. He was not impressed and demanded that I rectify that in this volume.

As with the last volume it would be remiss of me to not warn you that the information contained herein is true and can be considered dangerous to your mental and psychic well being.

Please, if you encounter one of these creatures, even the more benign ones, do not attempt to communicate with them. At least 20 people have gone missing after attempting to make contact with "The Blue Bird" of eastern Ontario and I know of someone in Sweden has been menaced by what appears to be the "Montcleary's Monster." They claim it is friendly, but that might just be what the Monster is making them say.

Once again the entries in this book are not organized in any specific way. Unlike last time however, it is entirely because I didn't feel like it was important to organize them.

–Andrew P. Barr
Feb. 13, 2020

SUBJECT:
STRANG'S PIZZA MONSTER

DATE: November 14, 1983

LOCATION: Flimpt, Ontario

Nobody is sure when it first showed up but everyone thought it was just a weird sculpture. The fact the owners of Strang's Pizza and Wings displayed it so prominently in the dining room never really bothered the customers.

Until the night it moved.

SUBJECT:
WALDO AND EARL

DATE: 1970 – 1988

LOCATION: Canada

Throughout the 1970s people in various small towns across Canada claim to have encountered a pair of creatures known as "Waldo and Earl." Their stories typically follow a pattern: Waldo and Earl would wander into town befriend someone in need of help, they help them and then leave. Although the creatures did not appear to know how to speak they are credited with solving various crimes, breaking up spy rings, busting up drug cartels, unionizing workers and in at least one instance, helping someone win a bake off resulting in the winner not losing their home.

SUBJECT:
MECHANOMUMMY

DATE: 1963

LOCATION: Pultman, Ohio

The main clues to a series of crimes, including arson and murder, were traced to the Ancient Artifacts department of the Pultman Museum of Civilization. Many of the witnesses to the crimes described what appeared to be a mummy with three glowing eyes. In actual fact the perpetrator was some kind of robot.

A robot mummy designed for crime.

To this day it has never been apprehended.

SUBJECT:
THE MILLER'S GREEN SASQUATCH

DATE: 1833

LOCATION: Miller's Green, Vermont

Through out 1833 people living in the small mining town of Miller's Green saw a large bipedal creature who would occasionally come into town. Legend had it that if you followed the creature it would lead you to treasure.

One of the strangest things about the legend is that while people claim following the creature leads to treasure there is no story about anyone actually attempting to do this.

SUBJECT:
THE RED BEAST

DATE: 1999

LOCATION: Helstrom, Maine

There are rumours that in 1999 a group of teenagers found a strange box in the basement of an abandoned mansion. When the box was opened an army of mummies attacked the town. At some point after the authorities failed to turn the tide people claimed the town was saved by a woman in a strange costume armed with what appeared to be some kind of laser gun.

Some people claim the woman was either a witch or the descendant of a witch that had owned the abandoned mansion.

SUBJECT:
THE GREAT SCHULP

DATE: October 31, 2000

LOCATION: Kingsbow, Massachusetts

Since the 1800s the predominant religion in Kingsbow was the Order of Nine-Pointed Star. People who lived near Kingsbow tended to shun the town because of this religion. Not much is known about the Order or their beliefs because of how secretive the group was.

In late 2000 a series of murders in and around Kingsbow drew national attention. At the end of October a raid on the town by several law agencies resulted not just in the death of almost the entire town but also the majority of the government agents involved. To this day the town has been quarantined.

SUBJECT:
THE FINGER TAKER

DATE: September 12, 1973

LOCATION: Columbo, Nevada

Aubry Tillson (12) claims that a small red creature came out of hole in the ground and attacked her, biting off several of her fingers and then running back into the hole. Strangely while she lost seven fingers there was no sign of trauma. It was as if she was born without those fingers. There have been reports of other people in Columbo encountering the creature. Most of them escaped without being injured.

SUBJECT:
SMILEY

DATE: 1821 – 2019

LOCATION: Corral, Texas

There are stories of a strange creature running around in the wilderness just north of Corral, Texas.

In 1833, Jebidiah Fitzsimmons, a famous outlaw at the time, is said to have been killed by Smiley when he escaped from the local jail. The history books say he was killed by wolves.

Recently people have reported seeing it running along the high-way.

SUBJECT:
SPHYNKS

DATE: March 2, 1953

LOCATION: Porkpie, Kansas

Shortly after a meteor landed in the forest near Porkpie, Kansas people reported seeing strange blobs of flesh moving around after dark. Catherine Flores (44) said that she approached one she found in her backyard, the creature asked her a series of questions. After answering the questions the creature pointed a tentacle toward the sky and then crawled away. The next morning a lump of a strange metal was found on the steps at her back door. Scientists have not been able to determine what kind of metal the lump is nor have they been able to translate the symbols that appear on it during certain phases of the moon.

SUBJECT:
THE NEIGHBOURHOOD WATCHER

DATE: 1982

LOCATION: Bennett, Michigan

In 1982 people in Bennett, Michigan reported seeing something wandering the streets at night in areas that had high crime rates. Some people claimed the creature was there to defend people from something bad happening to them. Others say the thing was there just for the free entertainment. Either way violent crime in those areas increased by 150% over the course of the year. Strangely, from 1983 to 2017 there was zero crime reported in Bennett.

In 2018 reports of the Watcher have begun again.

SUBJECT:
MAJOR TOM BOWIE

DATE: June 23, 1966

LOCATION: Dayton, Nevada

In May 1965 the Oberon XII mission to Venus went missing. This was NASA's first attempt to land a person on that planet since 1956. Earth lost contact with the Oberon four days after it was launched. It was assumed that all four astronauts were lost.

On June 23, the capsule crashed near the city of Dayton. Investigators found the bodies of three of the astronauts. At the same time a series of murders occurred in Dayton. All the victims were bludgeoned to death with a crowbar and seemed to have been exposed to a high level of radiation. Police had tracked the killer to the local power plant but no report of what they found there has been released to the public. The body of the missing astronaut has not been found.

SUBJECT:
GEOFF

DATE: Dec. 25, 1984

LOCATION: Culver City, North Carolina

Timmy Jordon (5) maintains his "imaginary friend," Geoff wasn't happy with the gifts his parents had given him that year for Christmas and took them to the "Peppermint Mine" to teach them the meaning of Christmas. Kevin (25) and Caroline Jordon (24) were last seen on Dec. 24. Jane Jordon (53) says that Timmy didn't have an imaginary friend until earlier that year when Timmy had run away from home and was found in a pit in the woods behind the local College.

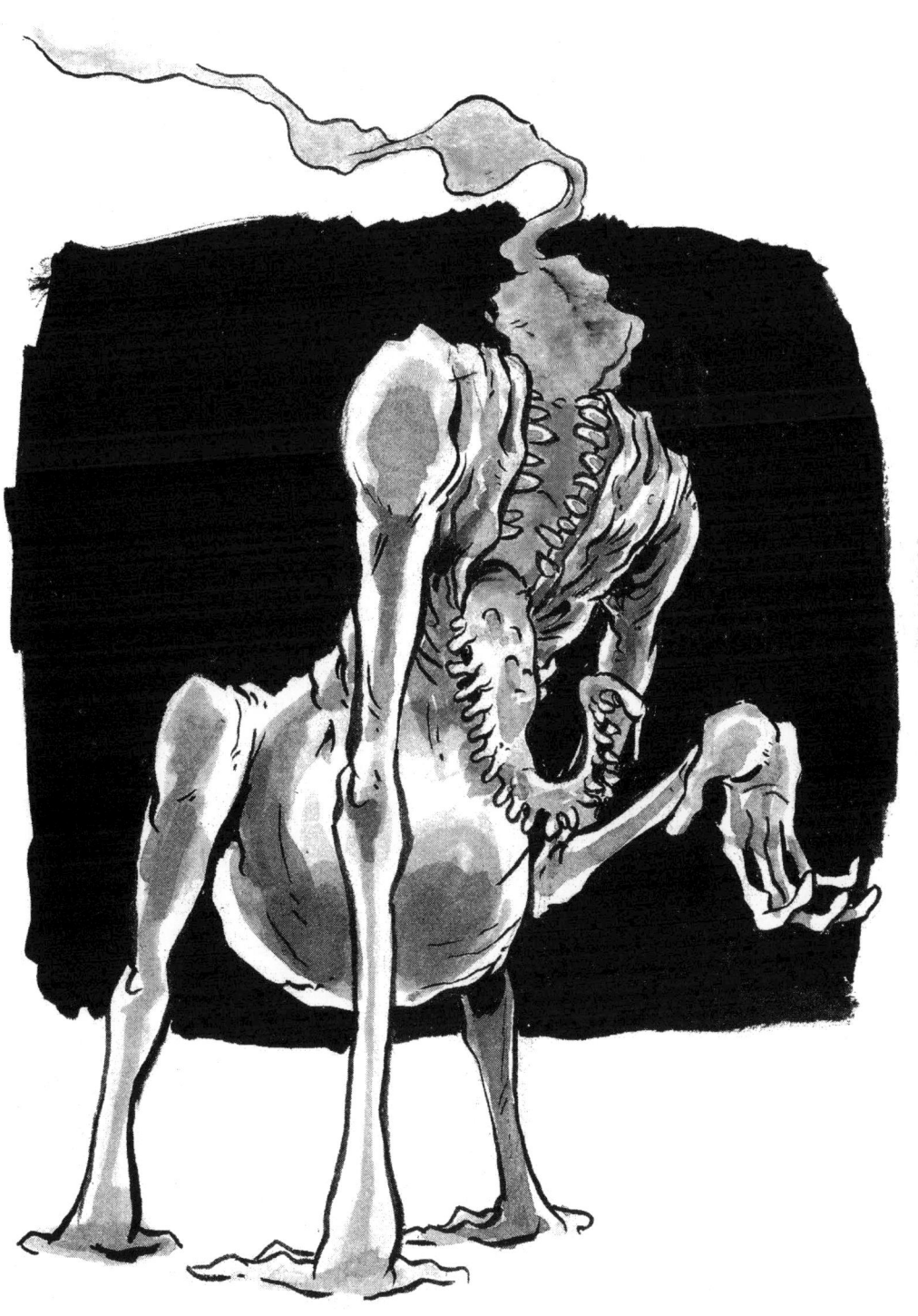

SUBJECT:
CHUCK

DATE: 1988 – 1999

LOCATION: Franklin, Manitoba

There are rumours that the strange phosphorescent fluid found in the abandoned cereal factory comes from a creature nicknamed "Chuck." They say that the fluid enables people to see the future. There are also rumours that "Chuck" was a former employee who the cereal company had tested a new flavour additive on.

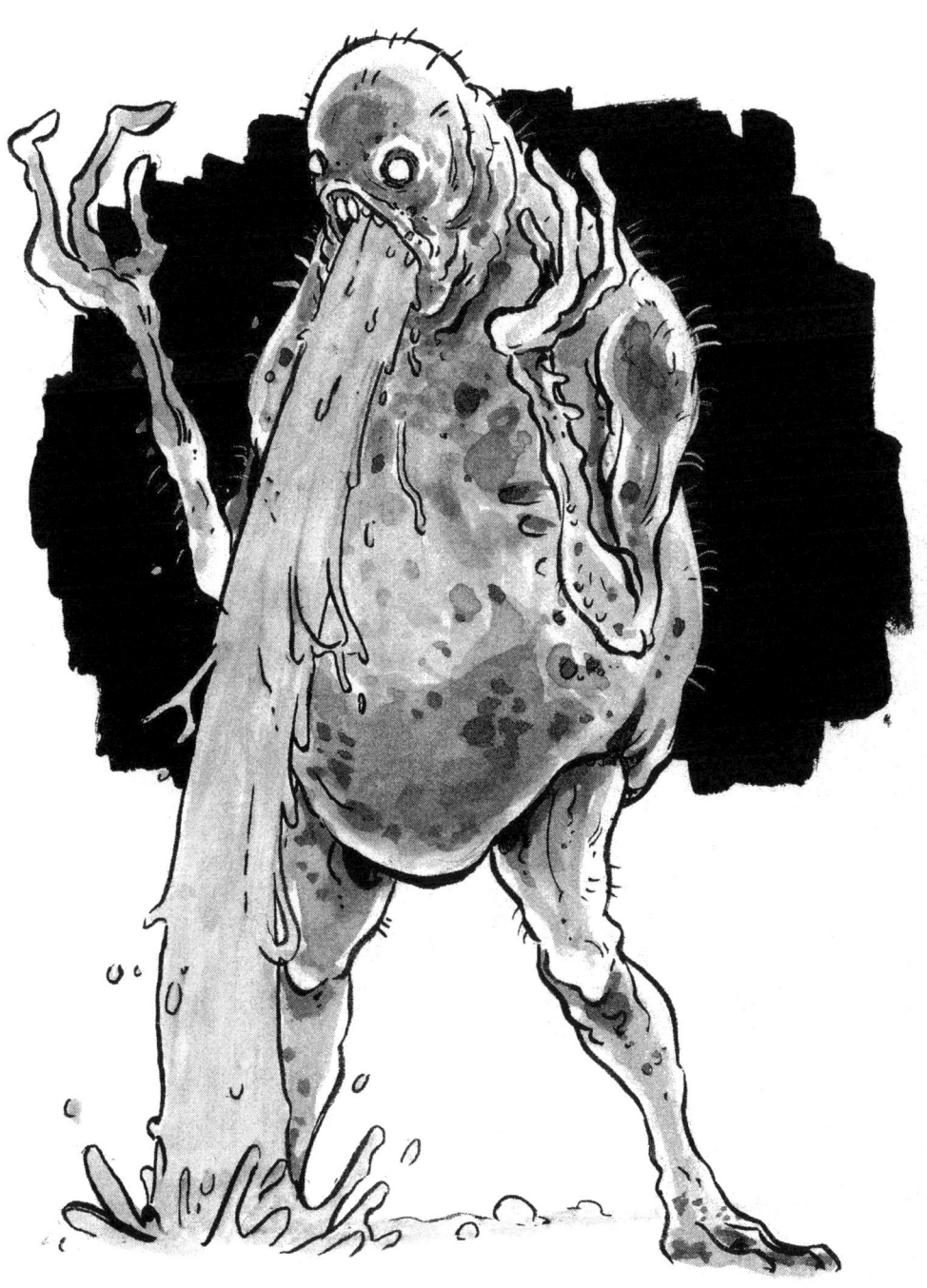

SUBJECT:
BOB

DATE: July 2, 1978

LOCATION: Carry, Saskatchewan

Nicole Trillium (28) gave birth at Stanwick Hospital. Her baby, Bob, has been blamed for the death of the staff at the hospital. The hunt for Baby Bob lasted for three days. The Trillium family claim that Bob was not dangerous, he was just scared. Nicole and Franklin (33) have filed lawsuits against the city claiming the authorities did not need to kill their child and have reached out to other families whose children displayed similar birth defects. They refuse to disclose the names of those families.

SUBJECT:
SLANGASTER

DATE: Unknown – Present

LOCATION: Maryland

A long limbed creature with three glowing eyes and a long, prehensile tongue has been seen through out the state of Maryland. People who have seen the Slangaster say that it smells distinctly of cloves and is very skittish, running away if it senses you saw it. In 1986 the Wellend family claimed that one of them ran across the highway causing them to run off the road. Ironically they were heading a local roadside attraction that claimed to have a mummified Slangaster on display.

SUBJECT:
THE GLORP

DATE: May 5, 1959

LOCATION: Santa Roma, California

Fred (66) a local recluse was absorbed by an amorphous glob of slime that he found in the center of a meteorite that landed near his shack in the hills just outside Santa Roma. The remains of Fred were transfered to an unknown location.

SUBJECT:
THE SHWOOP

DATE: 1953

LOCATION: Freemont, Oregon

During the centennial celebrations in Freemont a large winged creature attacked the town square killing 20 people and carrying off Susan Curry (12). Nobody in town admits any of that happened and say The Shwoop is just a local legend made up to improve tourism.

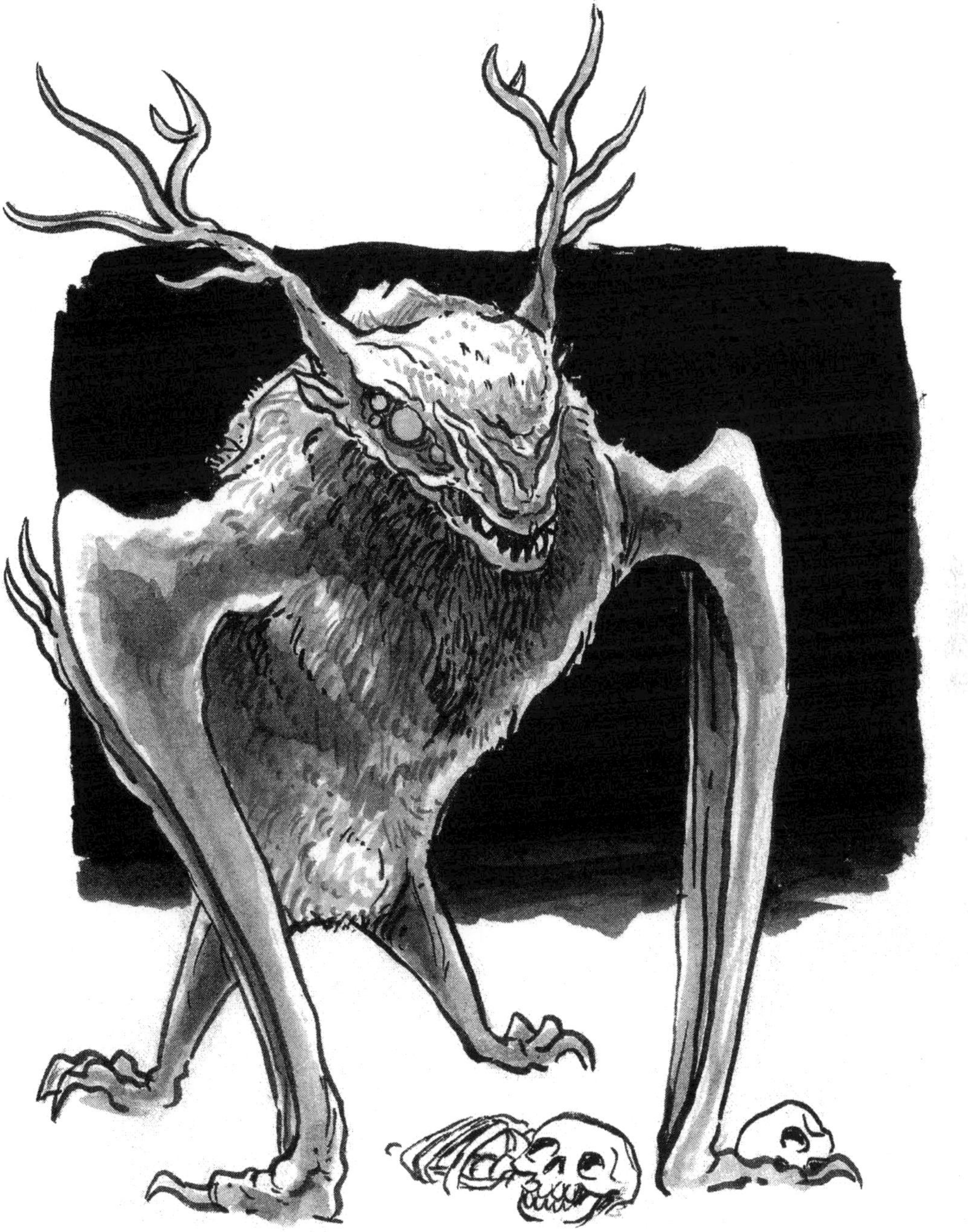

SUBJECT:
KING GOOG

DATE: 1933

LOCATION: Somewhere in the Pacific Ocean

While attempting to fly across the Pacific Ocean, George "Georgie" Georgeson's (31) plane developed engine trouble. He crashed on an uncharted island. He claims that on the island he was rescued and taken care of by a tribe of people who worshipped a giant horned creature they called King Goog. While recovering on the island, Georgeson says that he encountered a whole host of other strange and unusual creatures but none as magnificent as King Goog. Eventually the islanders used their radio to contact a passing freighter and George got off the island. While George shows signs of healed injuries nobody believed his story. He spent the rest of his life searching for the island.

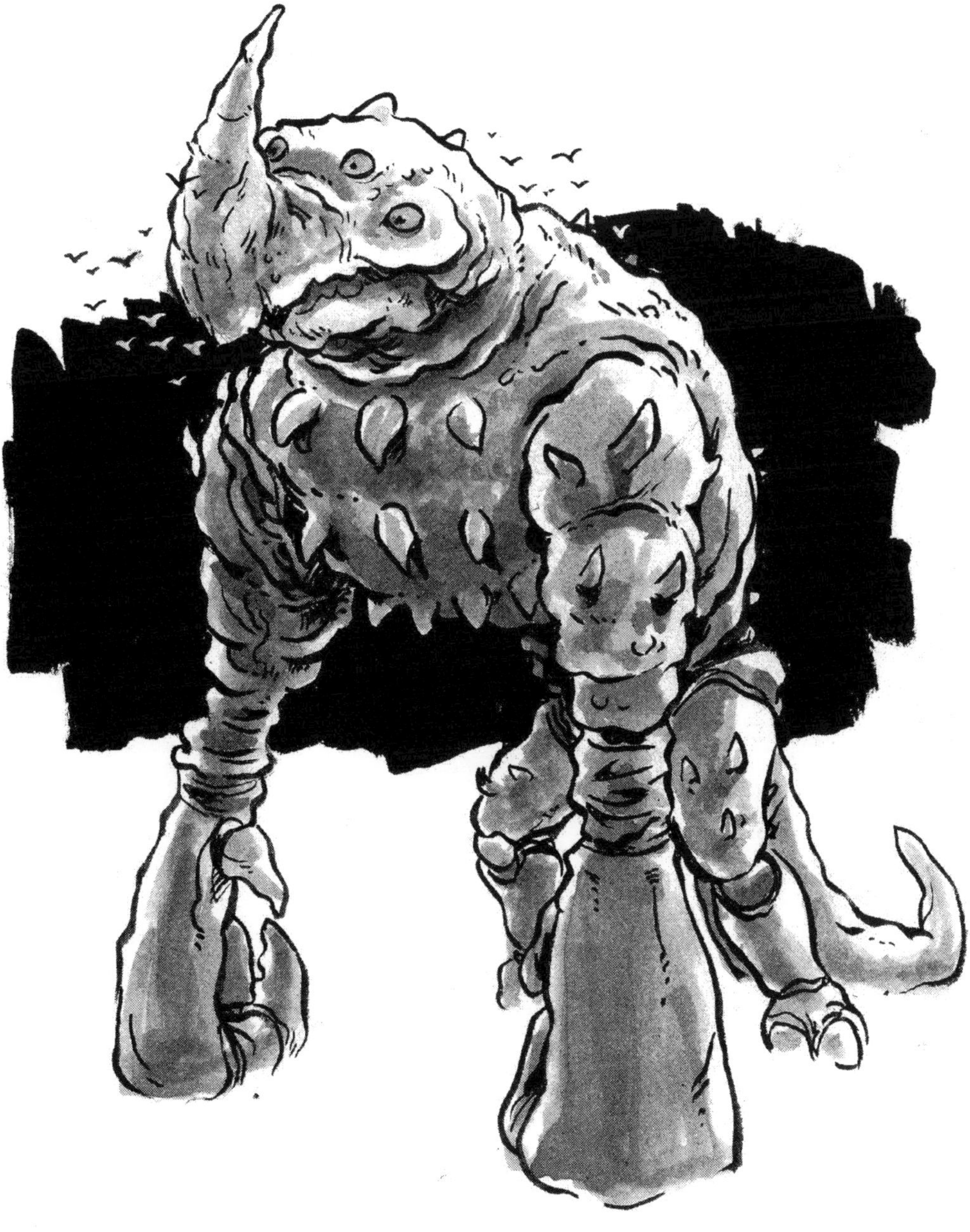

SUBJECT:
FUNGOID MUTATION

DATE: 1955

LOCATION: Sherman, North West Territories

Not many people realize that G. Philo Esterscott's novel **CRY OF THE FUNGOID,** is based on true events that happened at a military base in northern Canada.

On March 20, a top secret project to develop a new rocket engine backfired. It's rumoured that the engine opened a hole into another dimension releasing an alien fungus that infected the people working on the engine. The military was forced to burn the base to the ground.

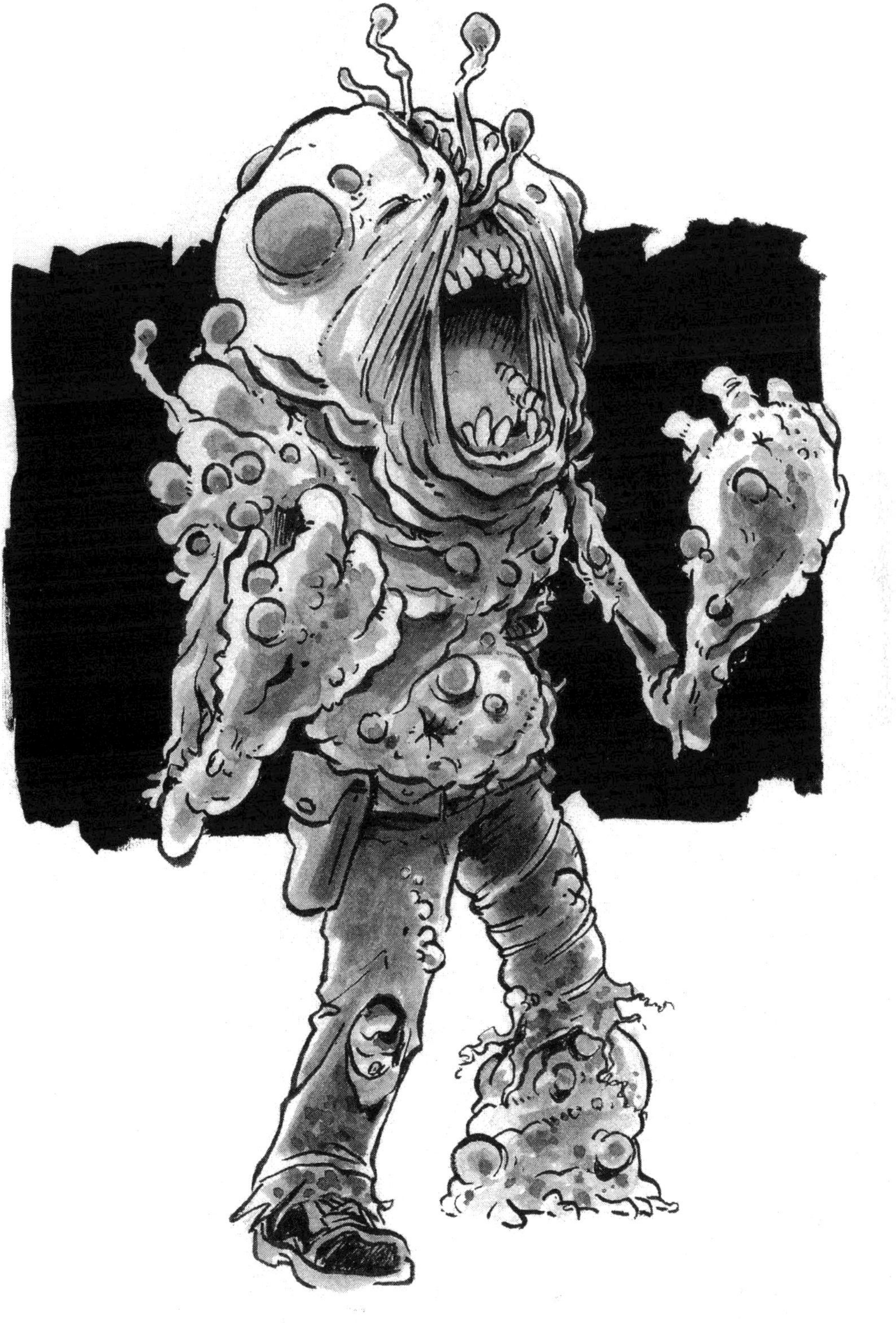

SUBJECT:
THE VOICE OF G'BKHULL

DATE: UNKNOWN

LOCATION: Some where in Egypt

The Voice of G'bkhull is linked to G'bkhull the Devourer. People who have encountered it have been known to experience visions of the future and an obsession with eating bones. While there are people who worship The Voice, they do not considered it a god.

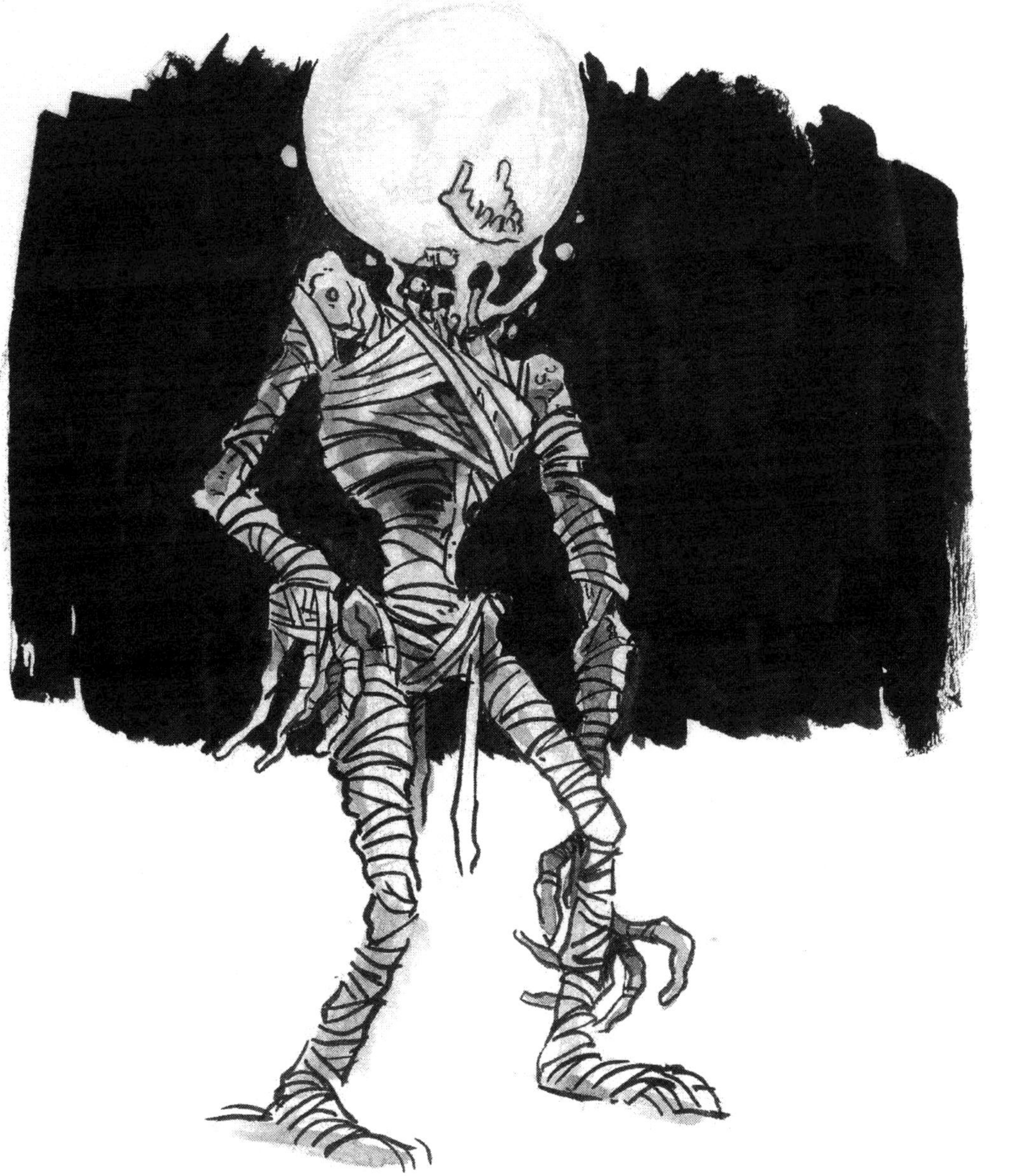

SUBJECT:
G'BKHULL THE DEVOURER

DATE: Unknown

LOCATION: Unknown

The return of G'bkhull the Devourer is supposed to be heralded by the entity known as The Voice of G'bkhull. It was written in the Notchordamnatchoz that G'bkhull was banished to the fifth, sixth and seventh dimensions at some point in the unknown past.

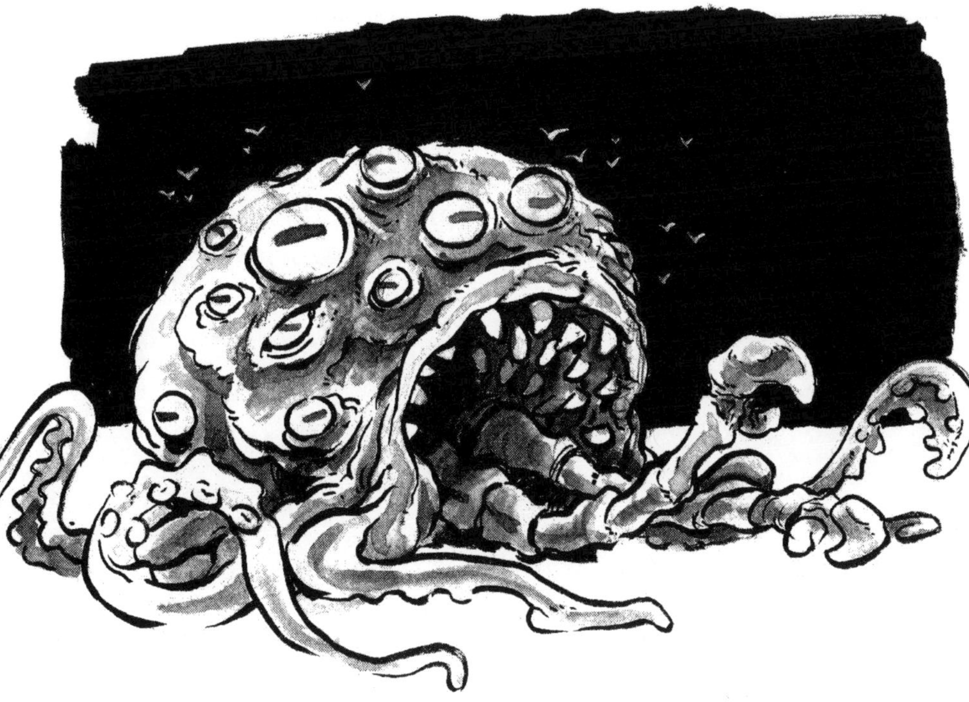

SUBJECT:
BLIK THE SCRABBLER

DATE: Unknown

LOCATION: Unknown

Blik the Scabbler is written about in the Notchordamnatchoz. It is said that Blik can be persuaded to transport a person between dimensions. Many people believe that all pyramids around the world are actually temples dedicated to Blik and if certain rituals are performed with in them you can teleport between them. This would explain why Blik the Scrabbler appears in myths of every culture in the world.

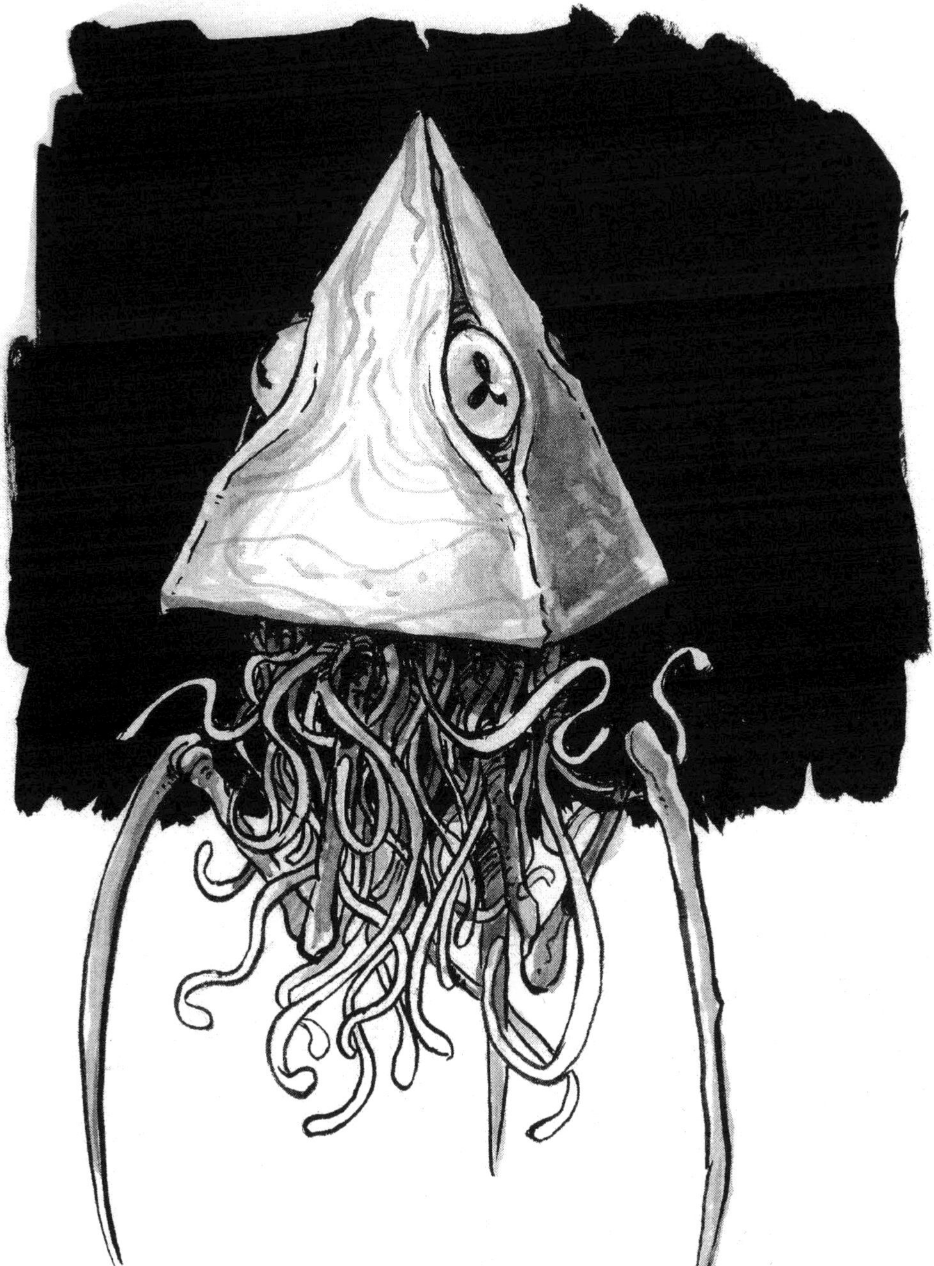

SUBJECT:
ROGER SMYTHESON

DATE: March 6, 1999

LOCATION: Swaming, Montana

Roger Smytheson (35) was a little too curious about the strange canister with a biohazard label he found in the basement of the house he was renovating. Unfortunately for him the canister was not empty. It is believed the canister belonged Dr. Erebus Simonson who owned the house in the 1930s before he moved to Canada in 1962. Roger Smytheson was killed by police after a rampage that took the lives of 15 people.

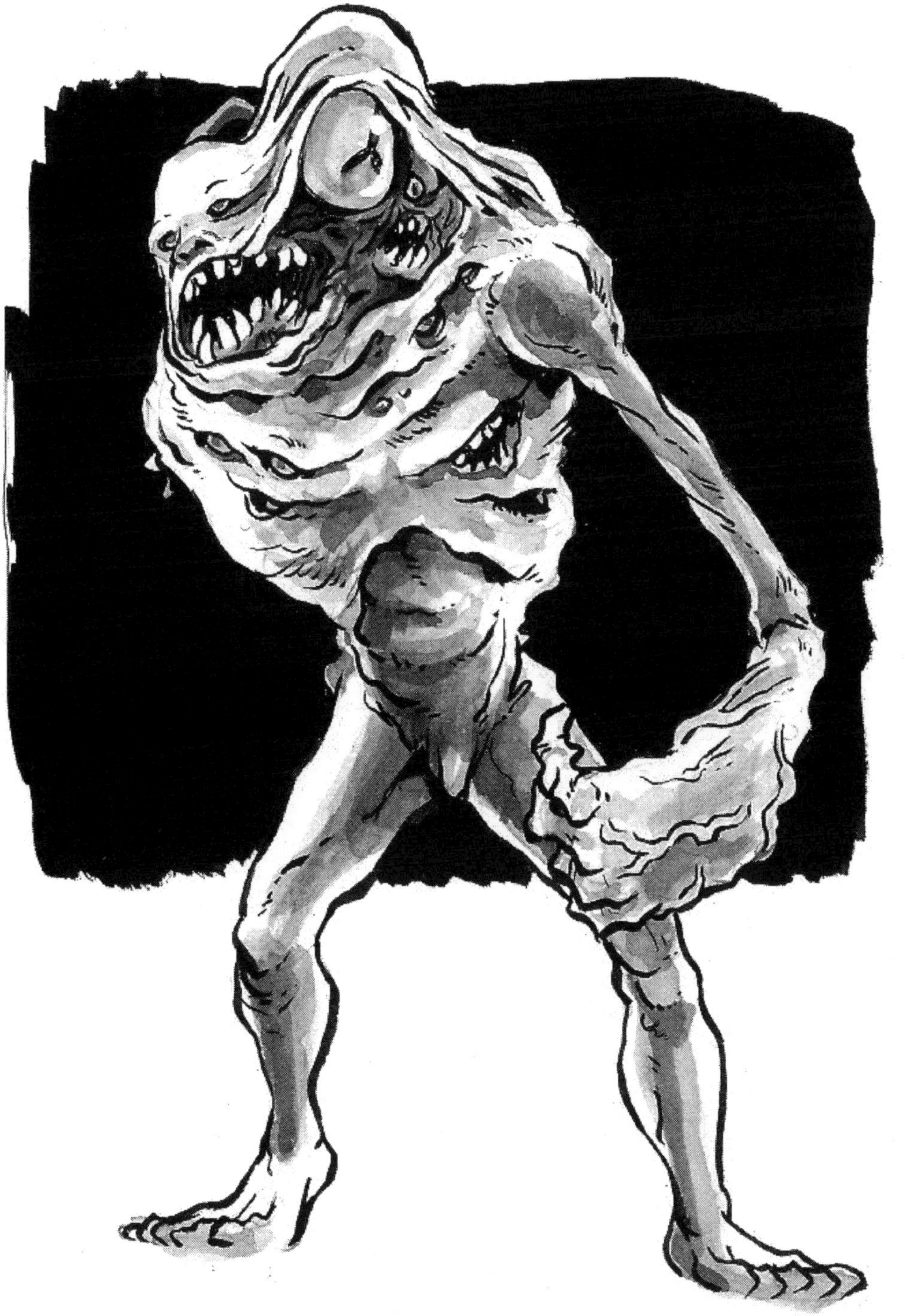

SUBJECT:
THE BALLOON MAN

DATE: May 6, 1978

LOCATION: Trenton, New Jersey

Timmy Cussler (10) was found wandering along the highway 16. When asked what he was doing there he would only respond, "The Balloon Man didn't like mommy and daddy." When asked where he lived he would only say, "The Balloon Man didn't like my house." Timmy's parents were never located, he was eventually released to his grandparents and now lives in Craven, New Jersey where he manages a grocery store.

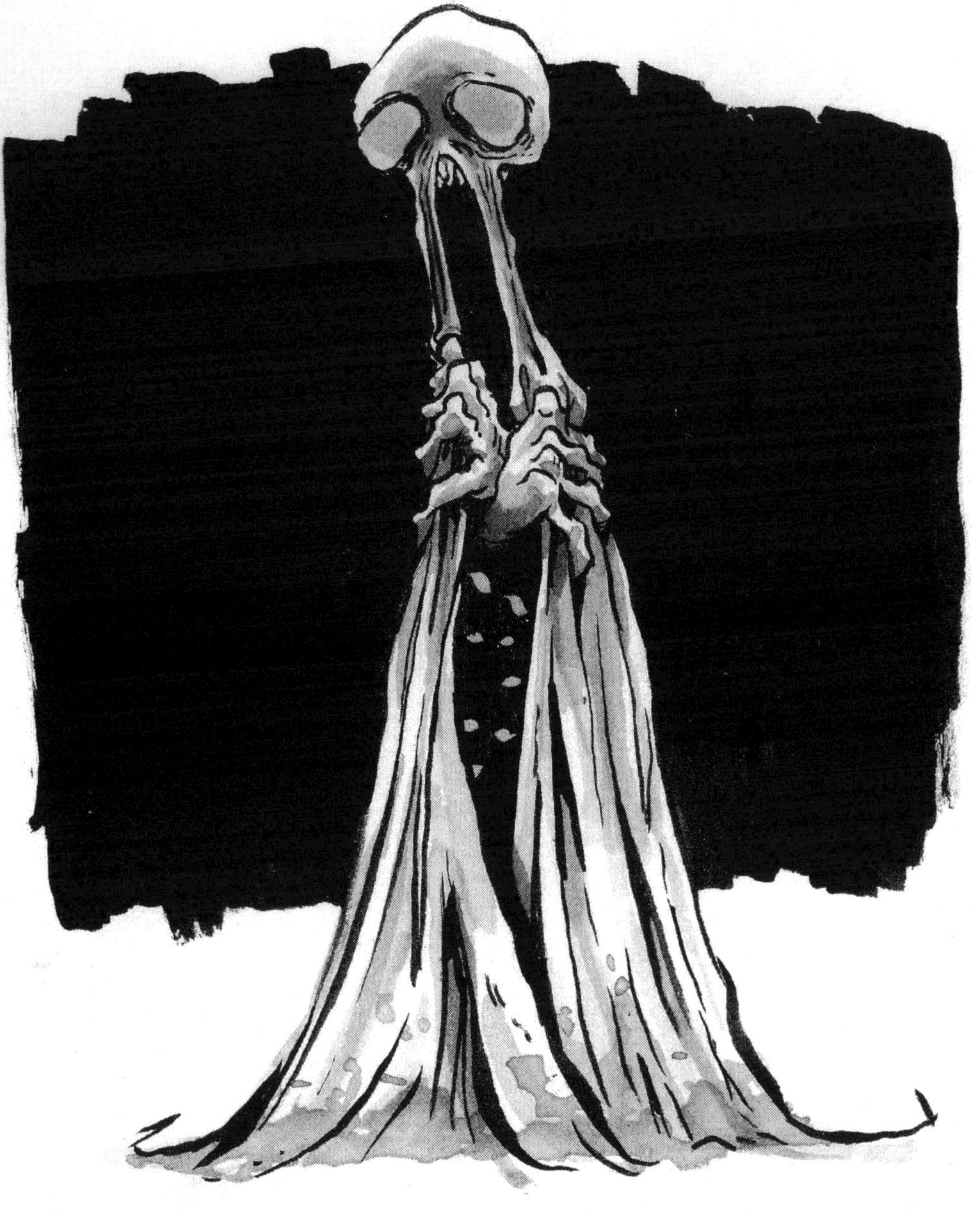

SUBJECT:
THE GLEN FALLS CRAWLER

DATE: 2011 – Present

LOCATION: Glen Falls, Minnesota

Since August 12, 2011, the residents of Glen Falls have been complaining of a horrible sound. They say the sound, which has been described as similar to a shovel dragged across asphalt, starts at random times through out the day and lasts for up to three hours. Some residents have claimed to have seen a strange creature during the times the sound is being heard. They also claim that when the creature is sighted they've suffered bleeding from various orifices and any battery powered electronic device they have loses power.

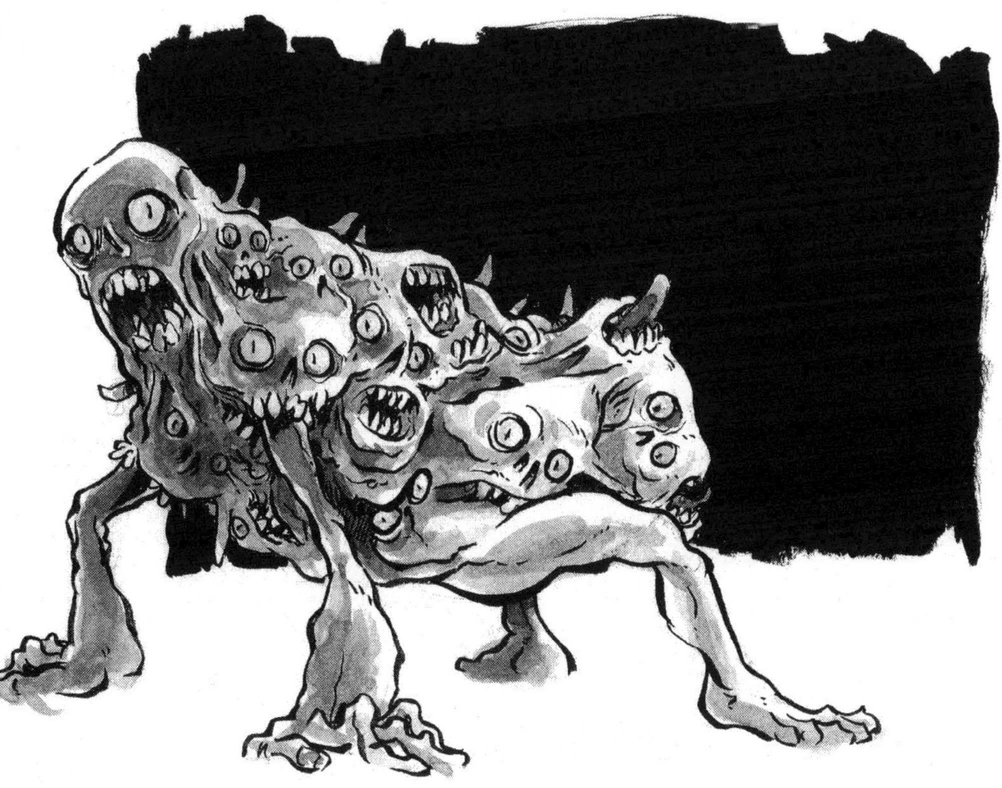

SUBJECT:
BRUCIE

DATE: May 13, 2014

LOCATION: Lake Huron, Ontario

At 21:30hrs, four technicians at the Bruce Nuclear Power Plant report a cascading power failure. At 21:41 those same technicians report seeing something moving in the hallway near the reactor on the security monitors. Nine minutes later security teams report all clear in the hallways. The technicians act as if they have no idea what the security team is responding to and pass out.

Shortly after 22:00hrs the plant returns to normal operations and the technicians revive and return to work behaving as if nothing has happened and the all claim to have no knowledge of anything that happened. When listening to audio recordings of their reports regarding the creature in the hallway, all four technicians lose consciousness.

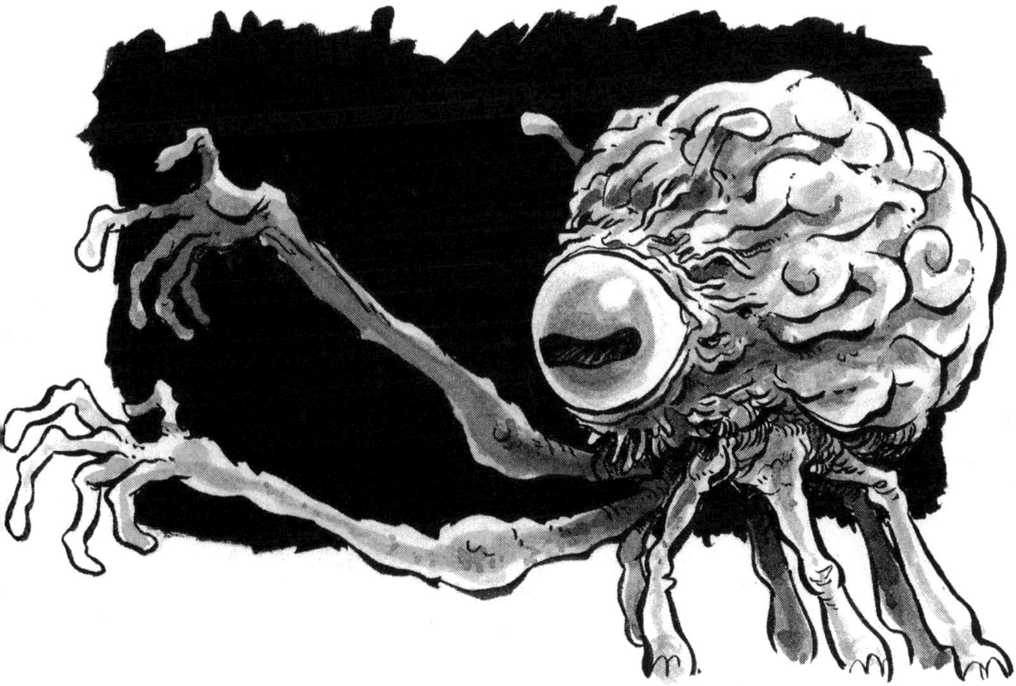

SUBJECT:
THE LEAF BAG THING

DATE: October 30, 1984

LOCATION: Franklin, New Brunswick

Richard Jennings (16), was playing hide and seek with some friends around an abandoned house deep in the woods near his home. During the game he heard a strange whistle he thought was one of this friends doing a terrible job of hiding. When he got closer he saw something he described as looking lie an "eight foot tall, overstuffed leaf bag balanced on baby legs." The Creature chased Jennings out of the woods. His friends did not see the creature and followed the panicked boy out of the woods. The following night, while taking the trash to the curb, Richard heard the same whistling, he retreated to his home and refused to go outside after sundown for the next three months. He claims to have heard the whistling sound every night near his window during that time period. Animal Control reports a rise in missing pet calls during that same month in the same area.

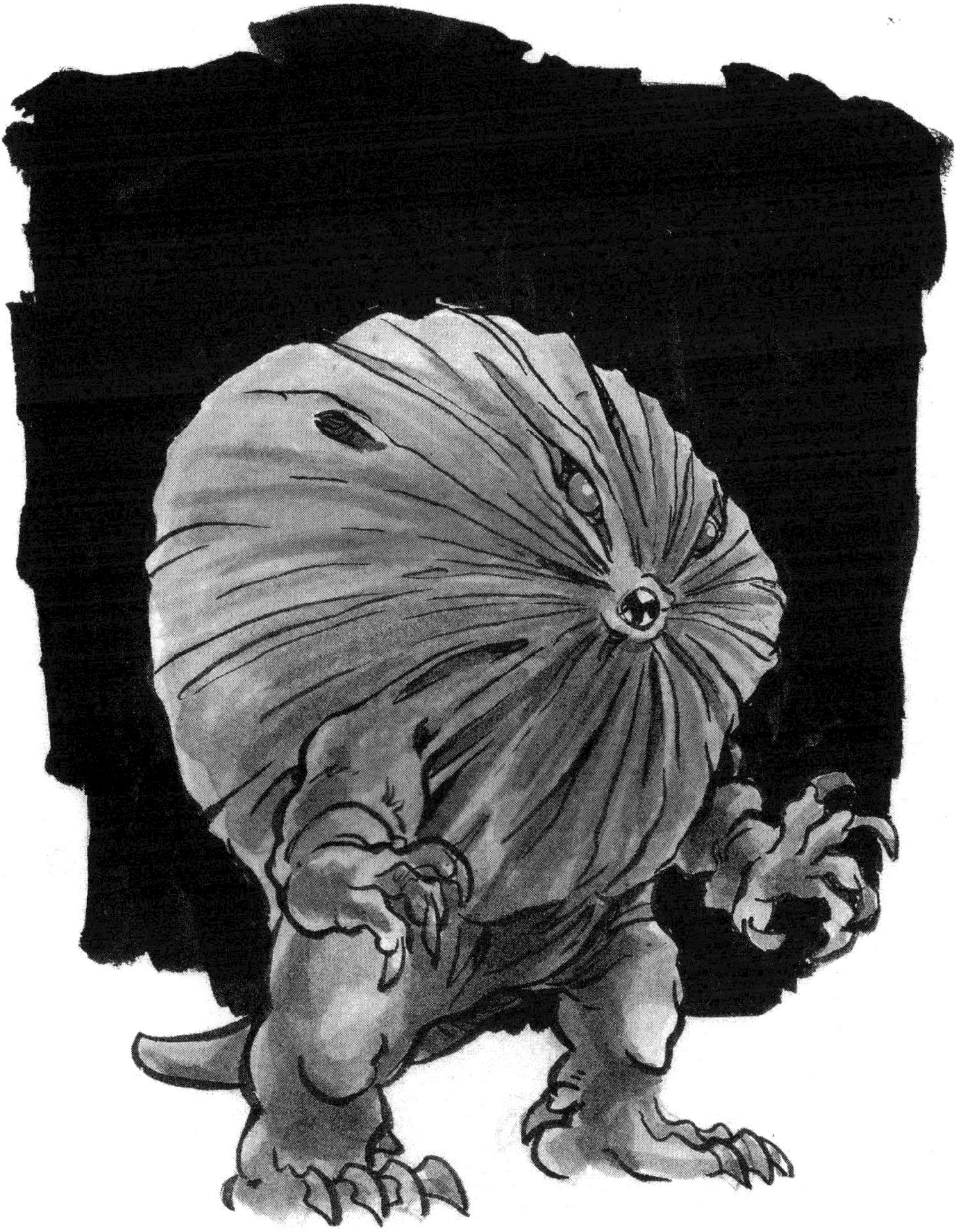

SUBJECT:
NIAGARA FALLS WALKER

DATE: 1930 – present

LOCATION: Niagara Falls, New York

On July 7, 2018, a group of tourists spot something moving near the base of the falls, partially obscured by the mist. The tourists insist it was walking on four legs, not swimming. This marks the fourth sighting of the Walker since 1930. Some people blame the creature for the sinking of the original "Misty Mister" tour boat and the reason the boat tours no longer get as close to the falls as they did in the 1950s.

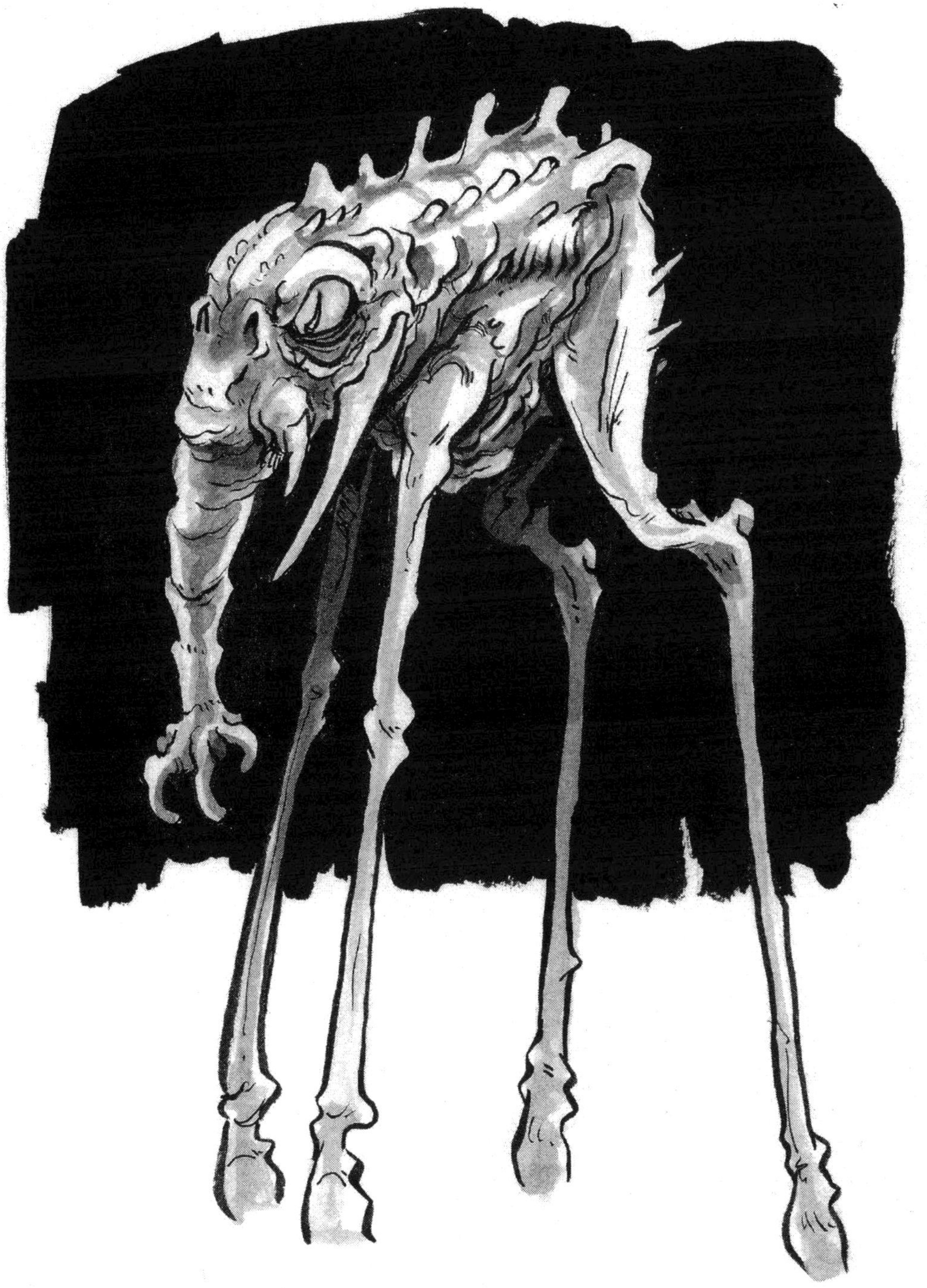

SUBJECT:
BLACKHEATH BANSHEE

DATE: 1943 –Present

LOCATION: Blackheath, Ontario

Blackheath, Ontario has been haunted by a strange creature they refer to as the "Blackheath Banshee" since 1943. Nobody is sure where it came from or where it goes but every new moon it can be seen prowling the streets. Everyone who has seen it has experienced bouts of sleep paralysis that last the entire lunar cycle.

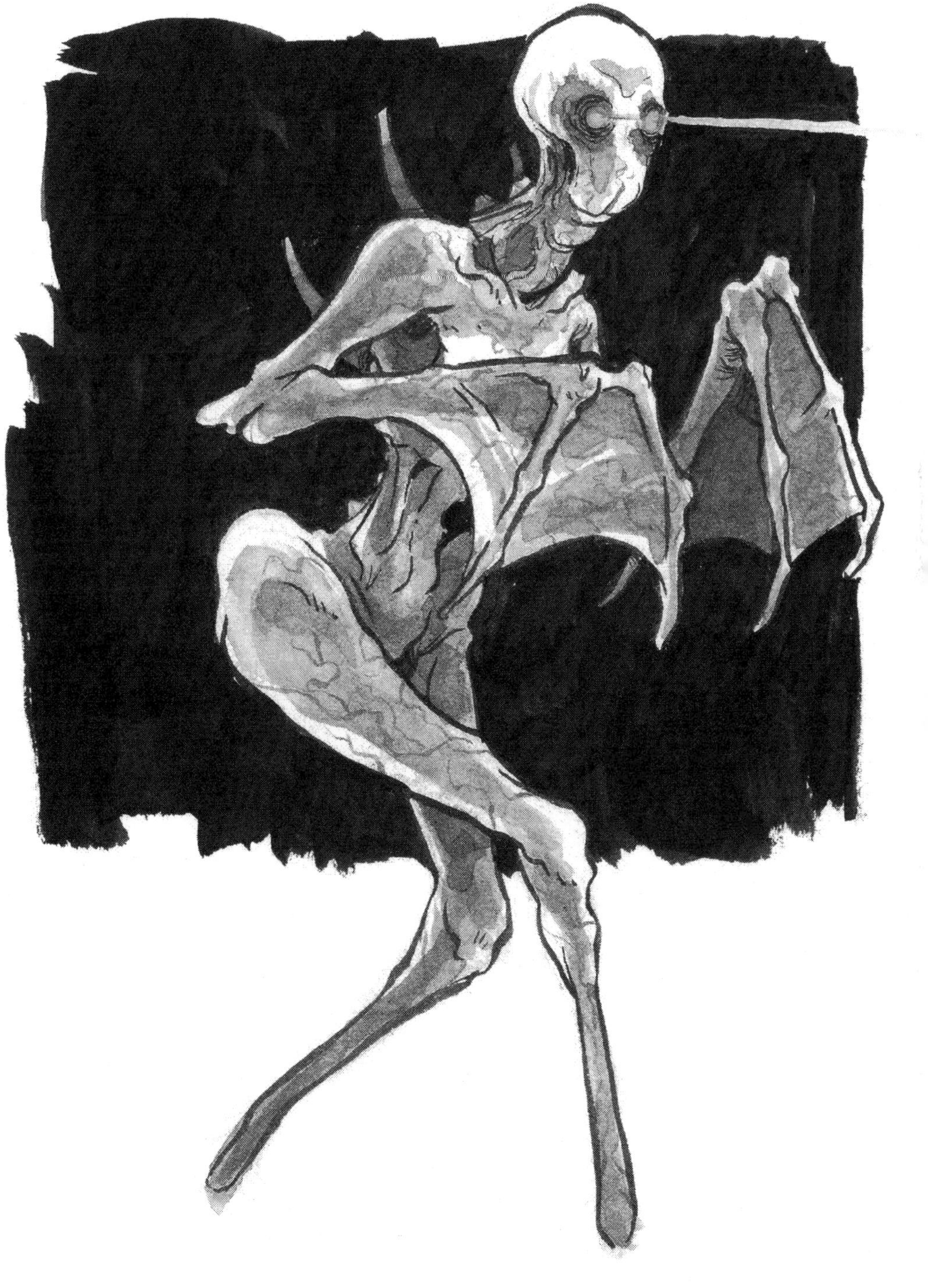

SUBJECT:
ROUTE 66 DEMON

DATE: 1976

LOCATION: California

A 24 car pileup on route 66 kills 5. The drivers at the front of the pileup claim they lost control of their vehicles when a strange creature ran onto the highway.

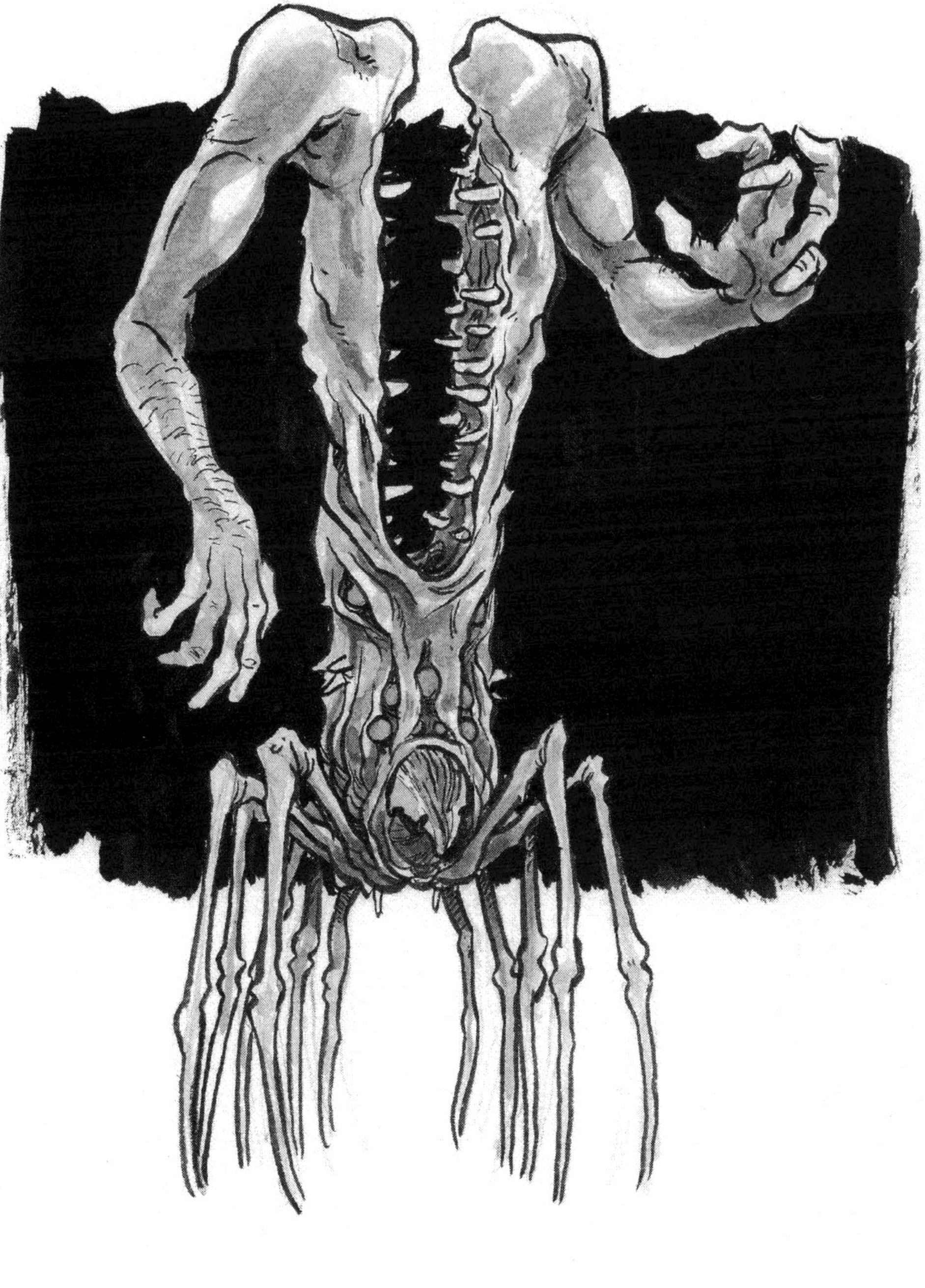

SUBJECT:
BILLY PUS SPINE

DATE: 1955 – Present

LOCATION: World wide

The Story goes: On the night of a half moon if you face south pointing with your left arm straight out in front of you and say his name five times while turning 45 degrees to your left each time you say his name, Billy Pus Spine will appear and tell you how you will die. Although some scholars say this is an incorrect translation of the original legend. They contend the correct translation is if you follow the ritual Billy Pus Spine will appear and kill you.

It turns out both translations are correct.

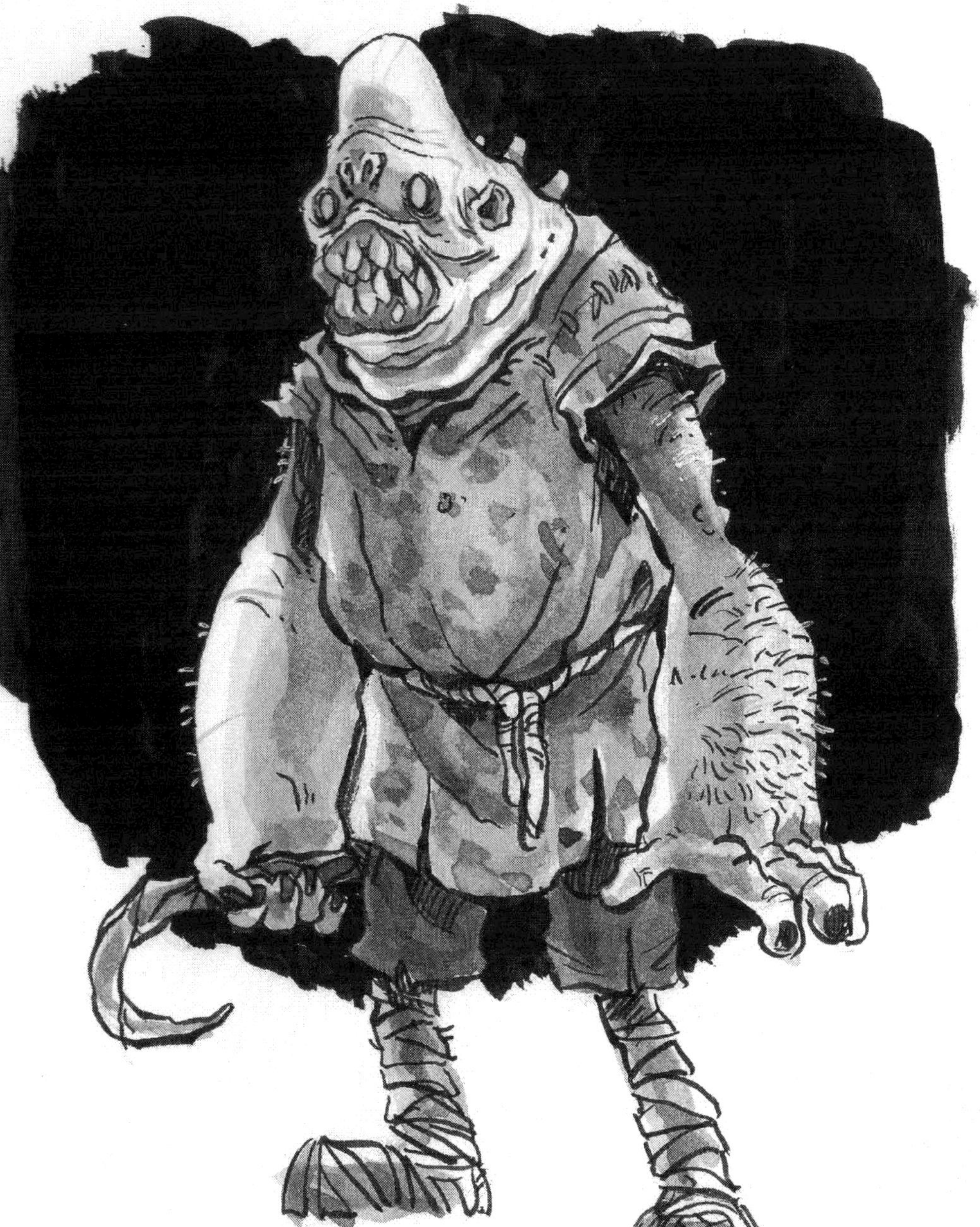

SUBJECT:
THE FACE

DATE: 1960 – Present

LOCATION: Manhattan, New York

There is an area beneath the American Museum of Natural History in Manhattan that staff refuse to enter alone. At some point in the 1960s a box was delivered to the museum. The researcher who received it brought it to one of the labs to study the contents. Three days later the rest of the staff realized they hadn't herd anything from them and went to the lab to see what he was doing. When they opened the door they found the box and its contents, a strange mask, but no sign of the researcher other than a note which read, simply: "The Face." Eventually the box and the mask were moved to a storage area. Since that day people who have been in that area have claimed to have heard the some of people walking around in bare feet and have seen a strange shadow moving around. Some people say they hear what sounds like someone whispering in Pig Latin, but they swear it is not actually Pig Latin unless those rules are being applied to some other language.

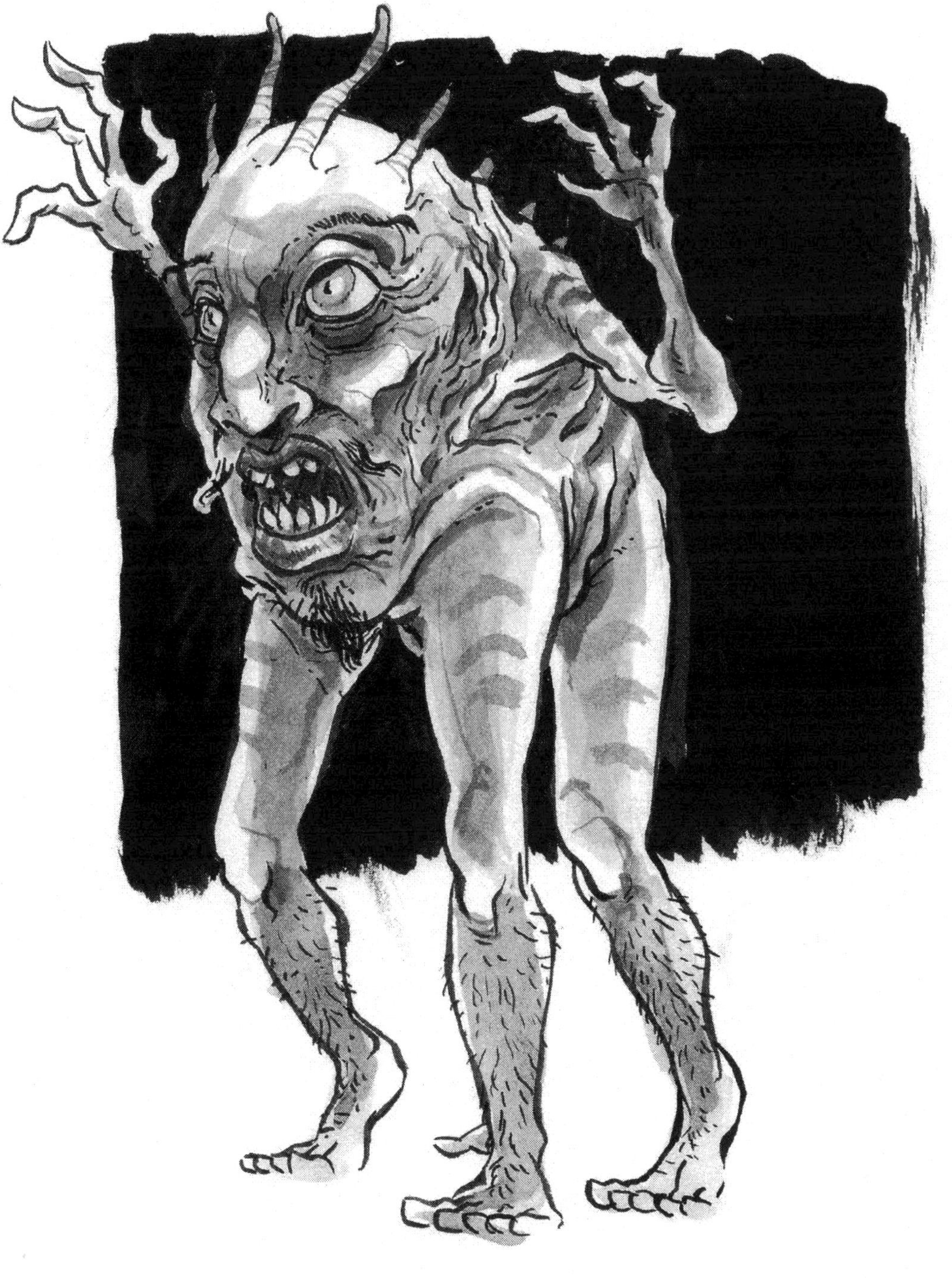

SUBJECT:
Fanscomb Freak

DATE: October 3, 1980 — Present

LOCATION: Salem, Kentucky

People have claimed to have seen something entering and leaving the "Fansombe" tomb in St. Stevens' Cemetery. While the tomb is one of the oldest tombs in the oldest cemetery in Salem, there are no records of who is buried there.

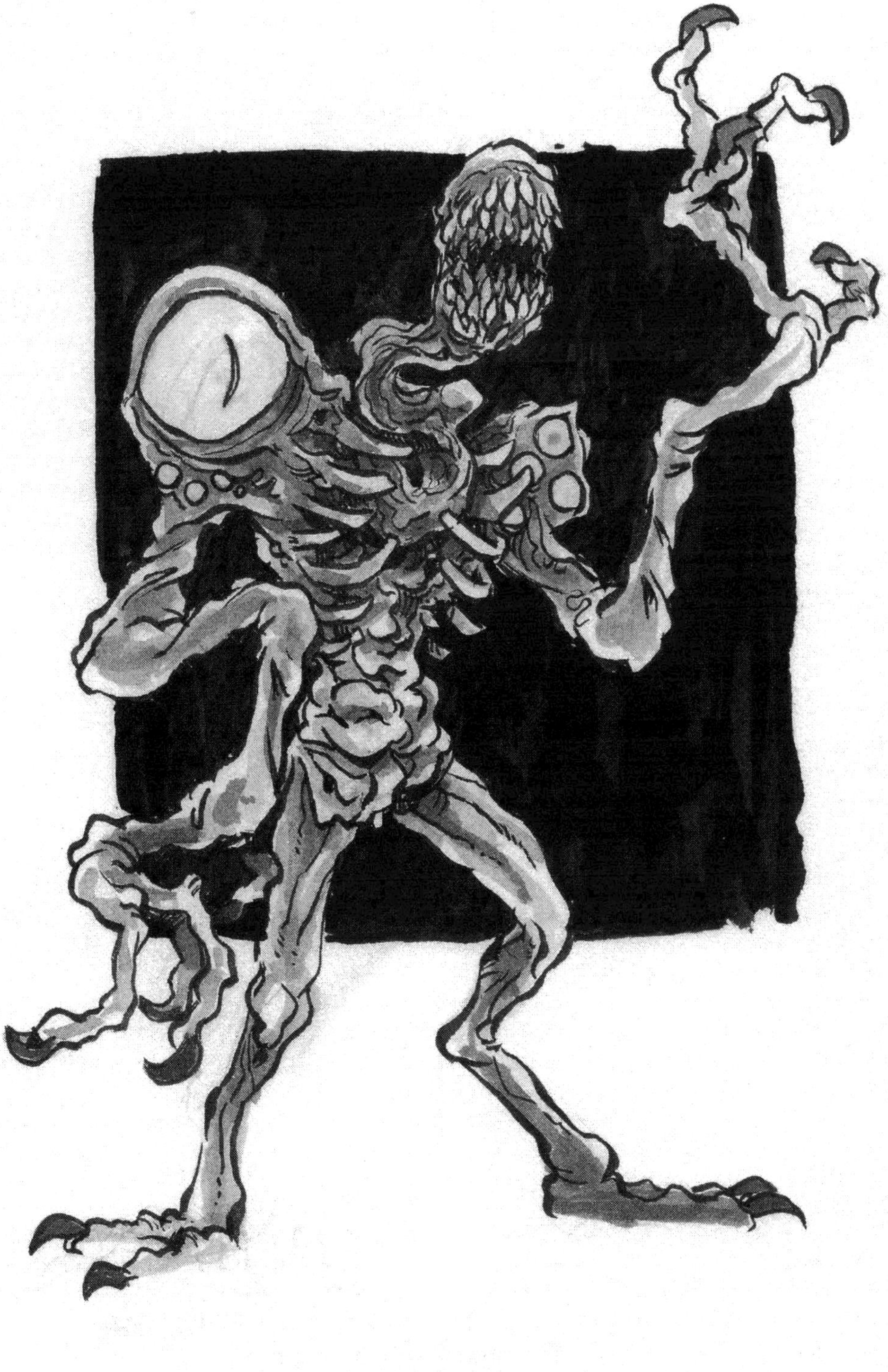

SUBJECT:
SUBWAY STEVE

DATE: 2000 – present

LOCATION: Toronto, Ontario

Right in the heart of Downtown Toronto near Saint Andrew Subway station people claim to have seen something in the subway tunnel. Usually it is spotted when a train is stuck between Saint Andrew and Union due to the frequent power failures or fires on the tracks. The TTC continues to deny theses reports but can't offer explanations as to why that section of track is closed for maintenance more frequently than any other part of the system.

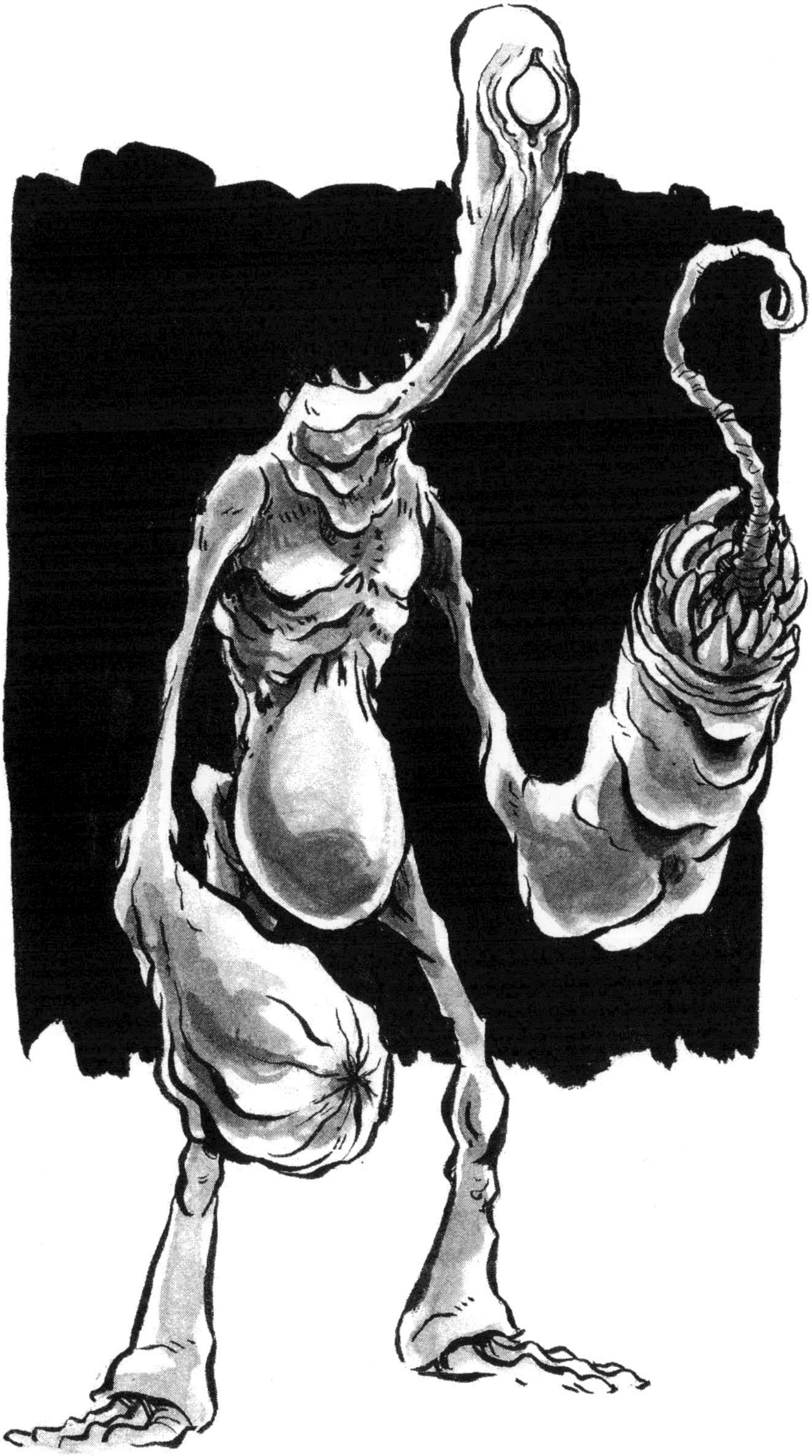

SUBJECT:
PUSLINCH JELLYFISH

DATE: August 1, 2017

LOCATION: Puslinch, Colorado

The Montgrief family was enjoying their annual camping trip / family reunion in Puslinch, Colorado when they heard a low pitched hum coming from the center of the lake. They saw something approaching but dismissed it as a drone they saw some other campers playing with earlier in the day. As the object got closer they noticed the hum changed pitch and almost sounded like singing. The all began to feel an intense sense of Déja Vu.

And that's when the nosebleeds started.

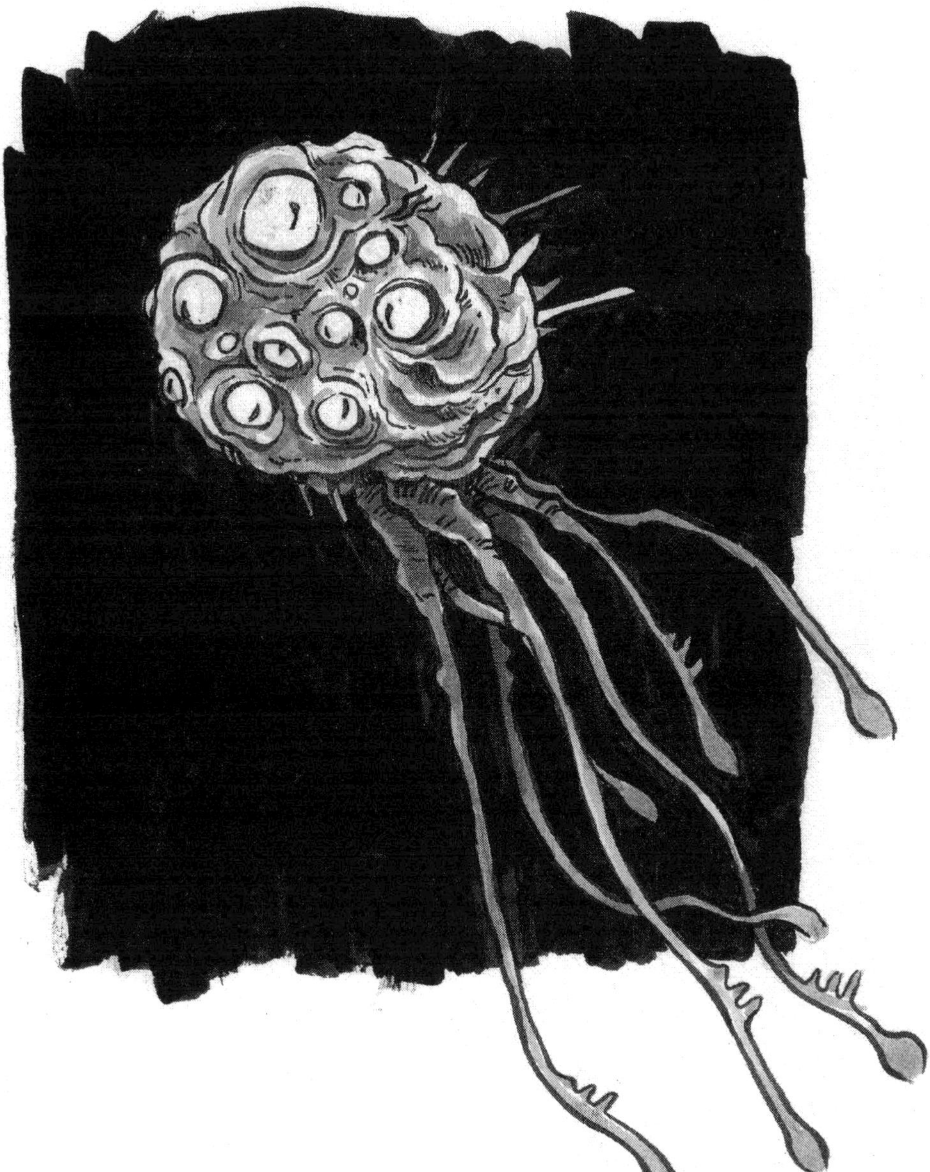

| **SUBJECT:**
| # SURPRISE

DATE: 2002

LOCATION: Winnipeg, Manitoba

They found the crate in the basement of The Manitoba Museum in 2002. There was no paperwork explaining where it came from. When it was opened they found a single sheet of paper with a series of strange hieroglyphs. In 2010 a researcher finally translated the paper. The hieroglyphs translated as "Surprise!"

The researcher hasn't been seen since.

A strange shape has been seen on security cameras around the museum since that day.

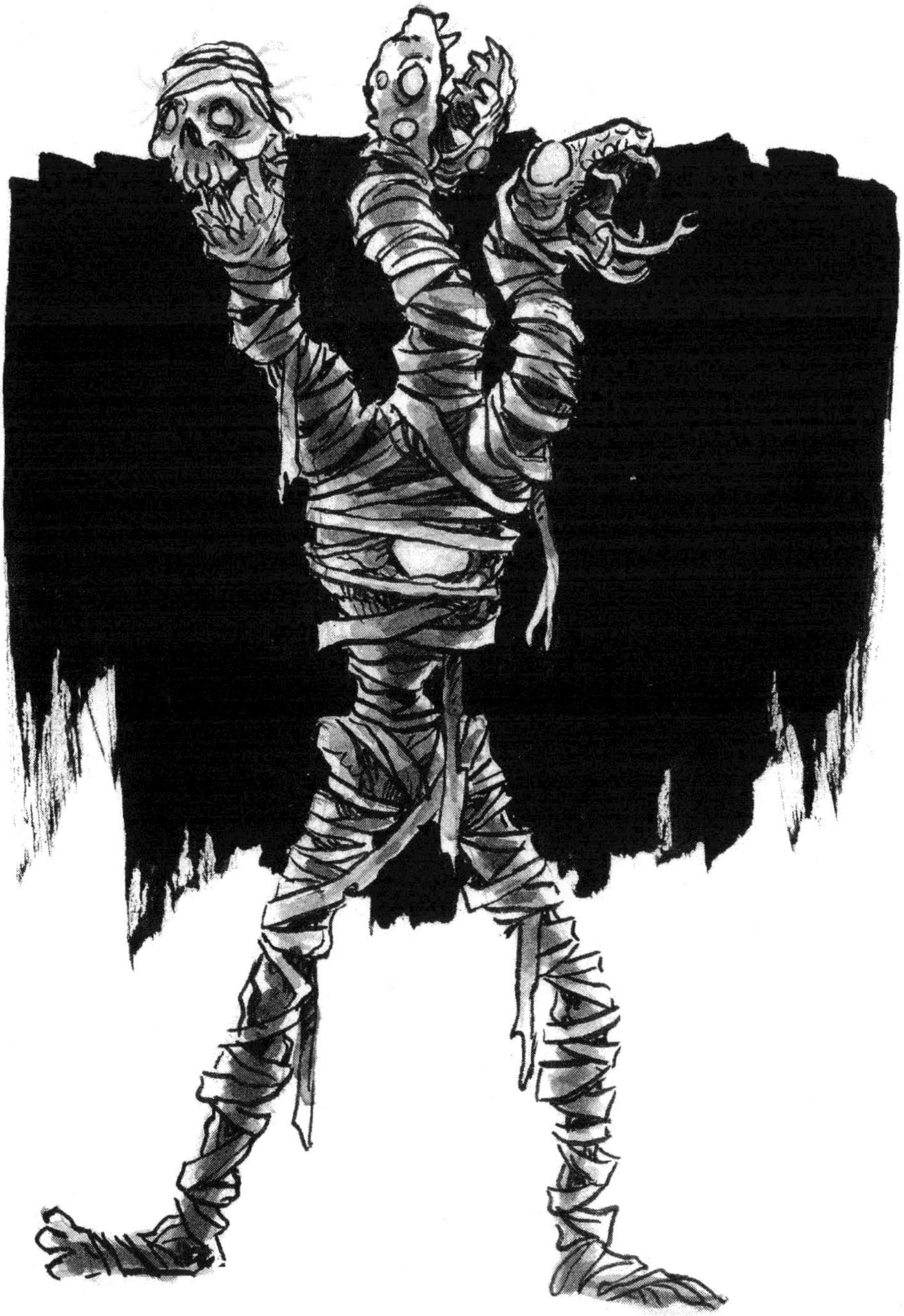

SUBJECT:
GUTS

DATE: August 2, 2018

LOCATION: Short Valley, Washington

While completing his rounds at the recently shut down Short Valley Hospital, Security guard Chuck Stephenson (58) heard shuffling footsteps coming from behind a door that was previously sealed with biohazard tape and marked "do not enter." Stephenson, having not seen the warning tape, opened the door to chase the intruder away.

He was found the next day at a bar in the neighbouring town of Gladhaven.

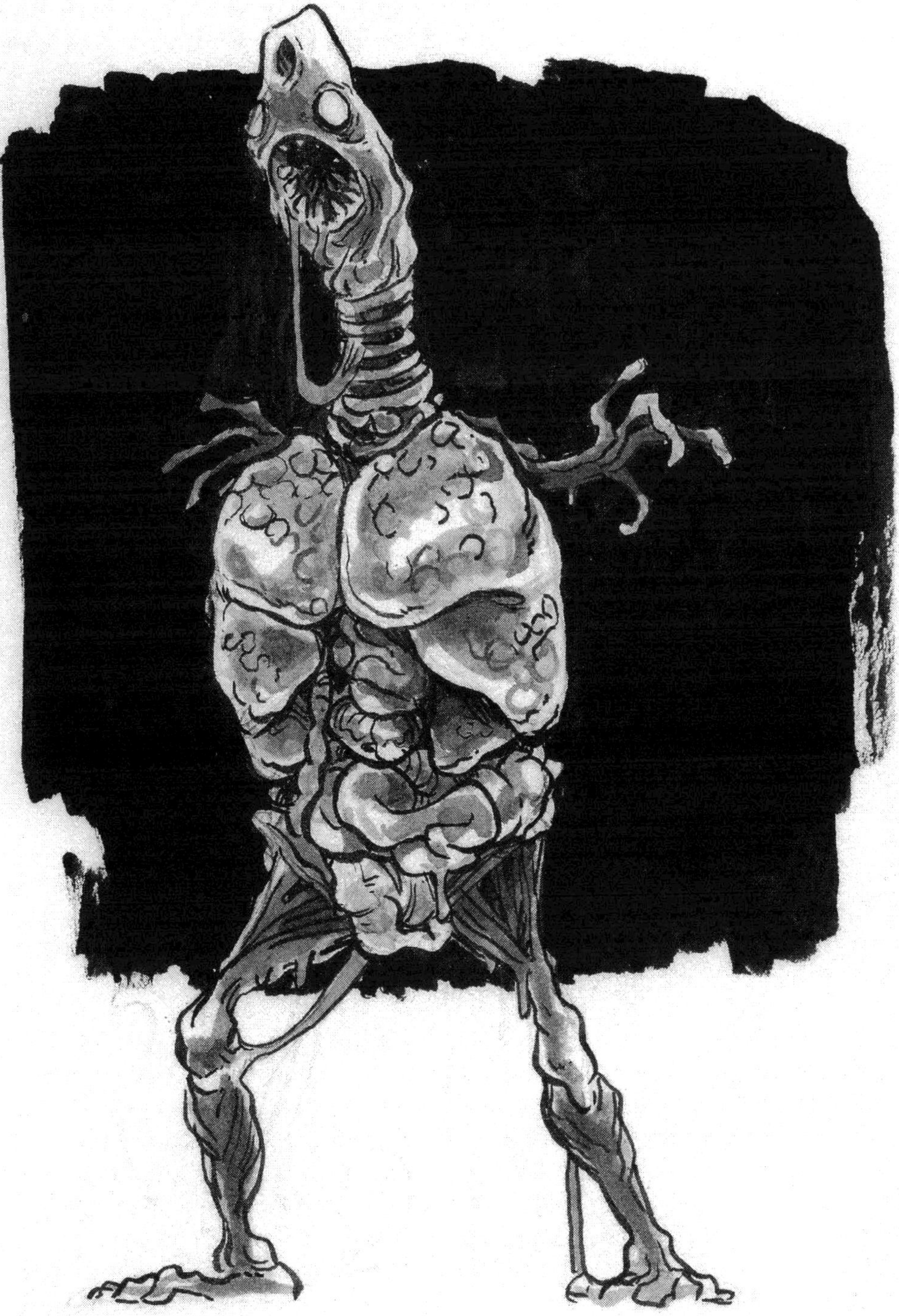

SUBJECT:
THE WHITCHURCH FIEND

DATE: 1974 – Present

LOCATION: Whitchurch, Oregon

Since a fire destroyed a small stone church off Intestate 305 near Whitchurch people have reported seeing something walking around near the ruins whenever it rains. Nobody remembers the name of the church nor what denomination it belonged to, just that it was there on the hill and that at some point it burned down.

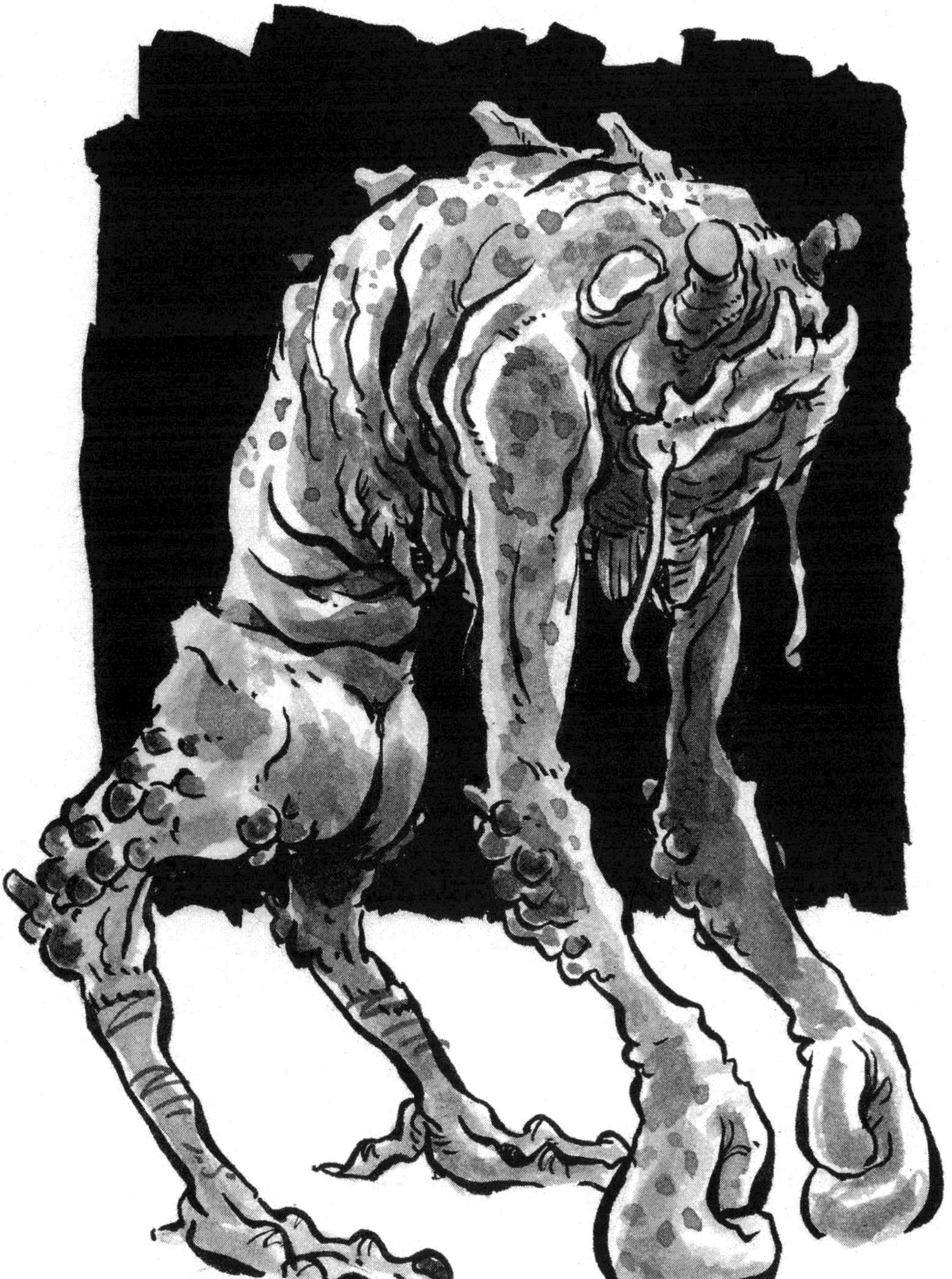

SUBJECT:
NANTOK SPIDER

DATE: May 13, 1985

LOCATION: Nantok, Michigan

On May 12, 1985 a mine collapsed in Nantok. The following day the town was over run by a swarm of large spider-like creatures that seemed drawn to certain colours. Many of the town's residents say that the creatures could control peoples minds by inserting a long, almost jelly like tentacle into their victims mouths and then riding around on their face like "some kind of hideous gas-mask."

Strangely there were no lasting effects of the infestation.

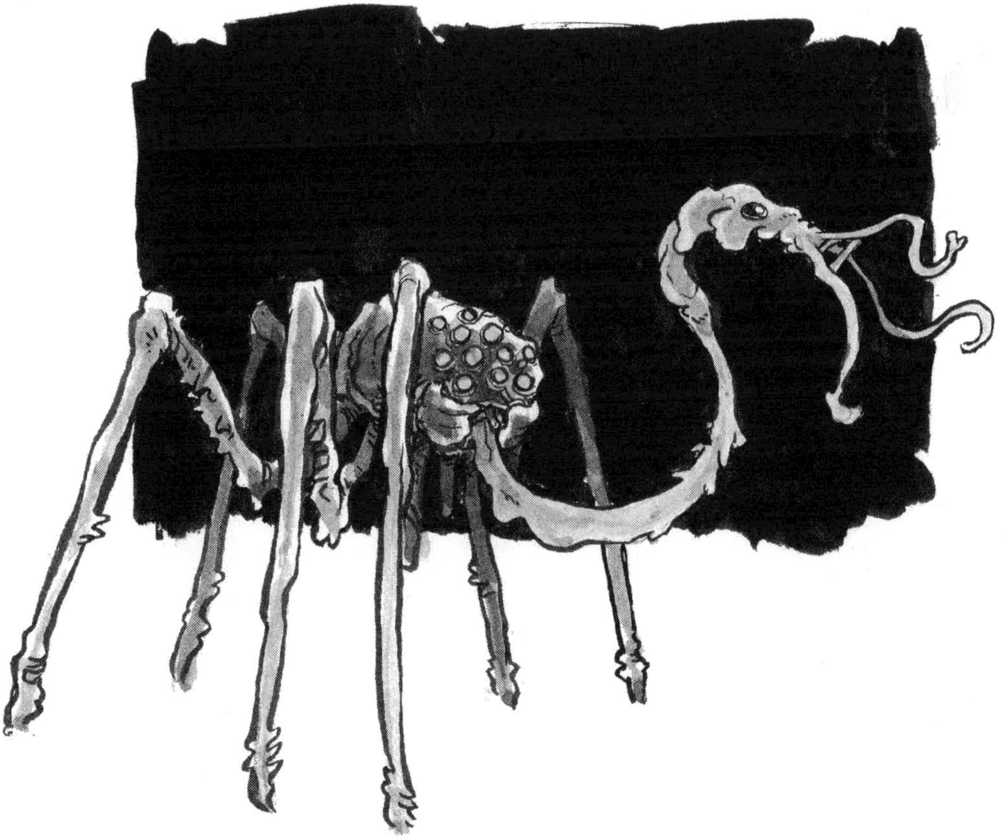

SUBJECT:
THE AXE MAN

DATE: Sept. 23 – 25, 1983

LOCATION: New Orleans, Louisiana

After moving into their new home, the Francland family realized the home had a basement. The basement was full of strange books and paintings. Knowing it is highly unusual for a home in New Orleans to have a basement, they did some research and discovered the home was originally owned by a famed painter, Leopold Argless. Argless was killed in 1883 by a group of people who claimed he was in league with the devil. The Franclands also discovered that there was no basement on the original blueprints for the home.
On Sept. 26 1983, the entire Francland family was found murdered with an axe.

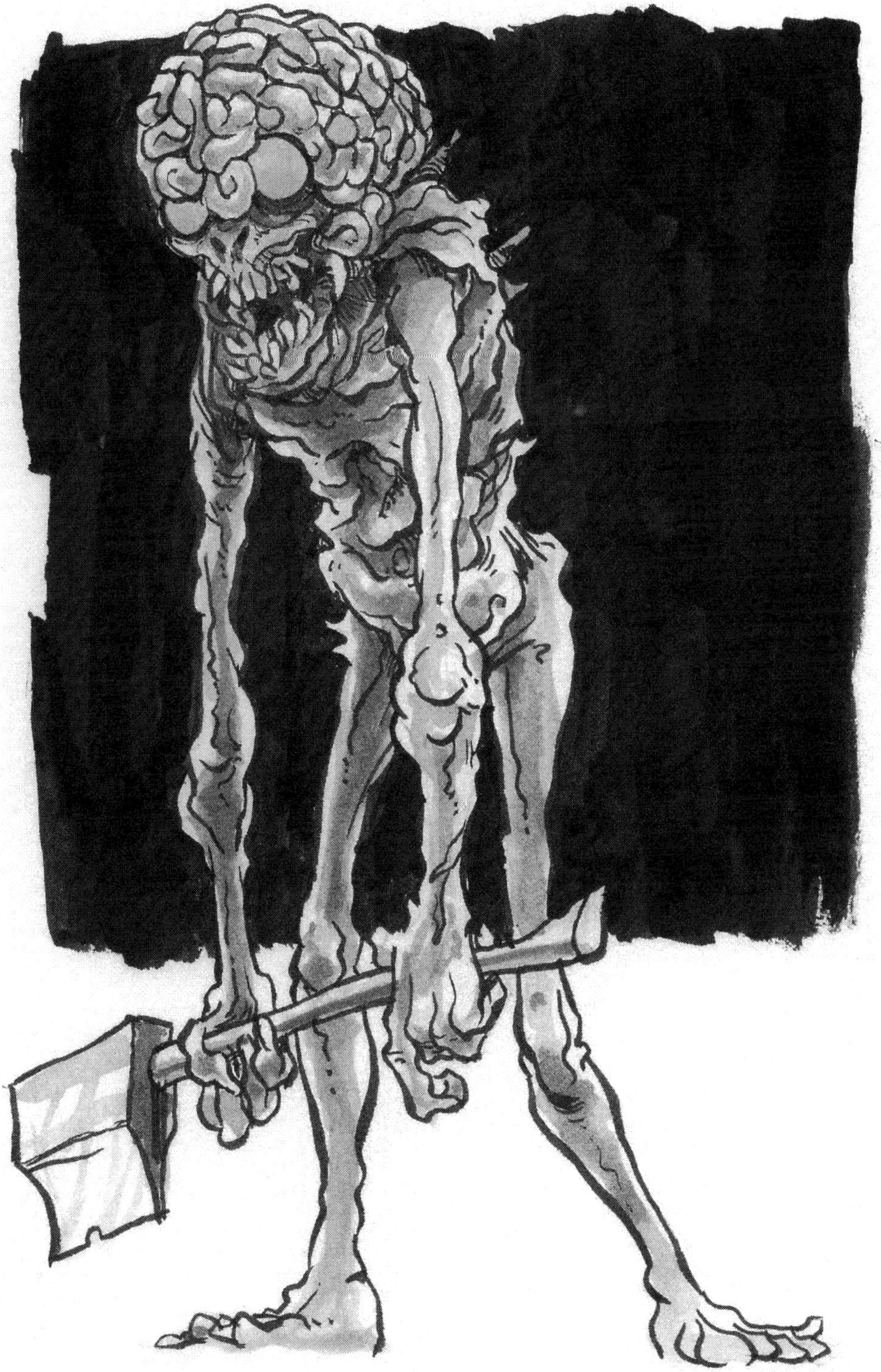

SUBJECT:
THE GIGGLER

DATE: November 6, 1983

LOCATION: Moncton, New Hampshire

Sam Doleman (12) is charged with arson for burning down the Stang Paints warehouse. He says it was the only way to make 'The Giggler' go away. Reports of children talking about 'The Giggler' have increased since that day.

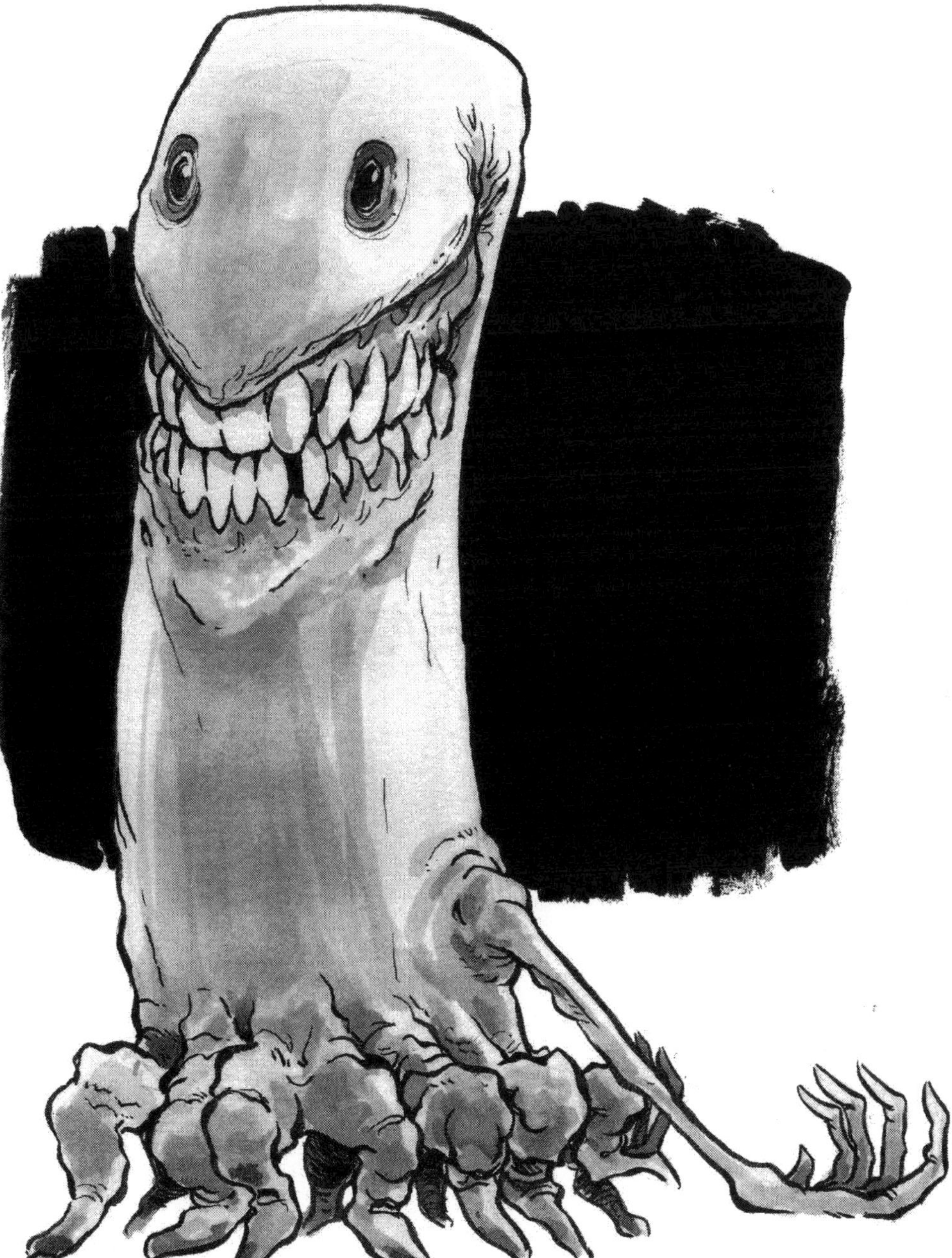

SUBJECT:
EAGLESTONE SAUCER MAN

DATE: 1982

LOCATION: Eaglestone, British Columbia

In 1982, Cliff Jimson claimed that a flying saucer chased him into the woods near Eaglestone, British Columbia. He took refuge in a dilapidated cabin which was laid siege to by the pilot of the craft. Eventually the creature left, leaving behind a piece of paper with some unintelligible symbols and a weird crystal orb. Cliff told this story to a local police officer who had pulled him over for having a malfunctioning brake light.

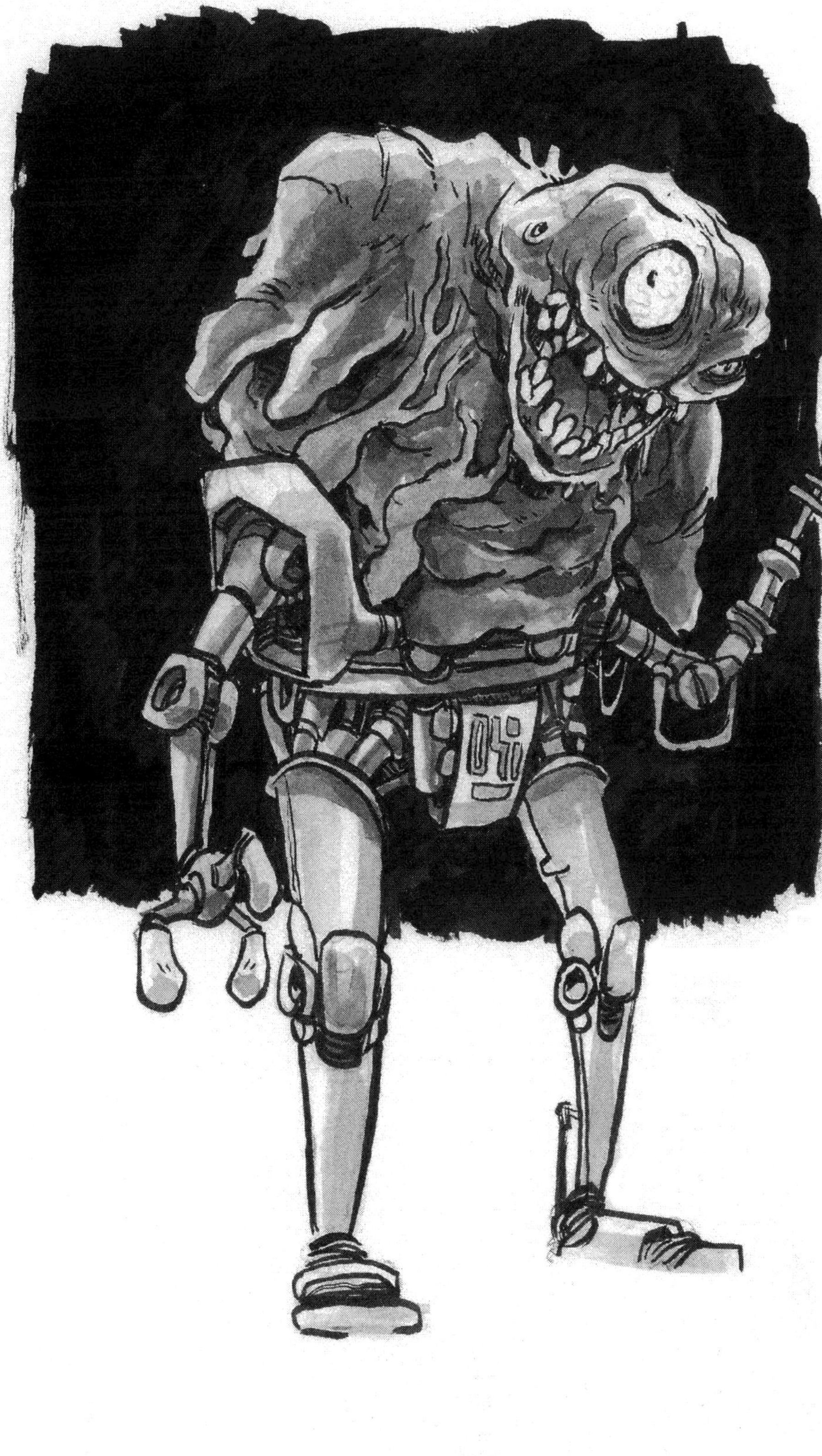

SUBJECT:
THE LIAR

DATE: Unknown

LOCATION: Eastern North America

Be careful when you walk by certain cemeteries after 3am during the month of October. If you hear a voice don't answer it. It's also best to try to ignore what it says.

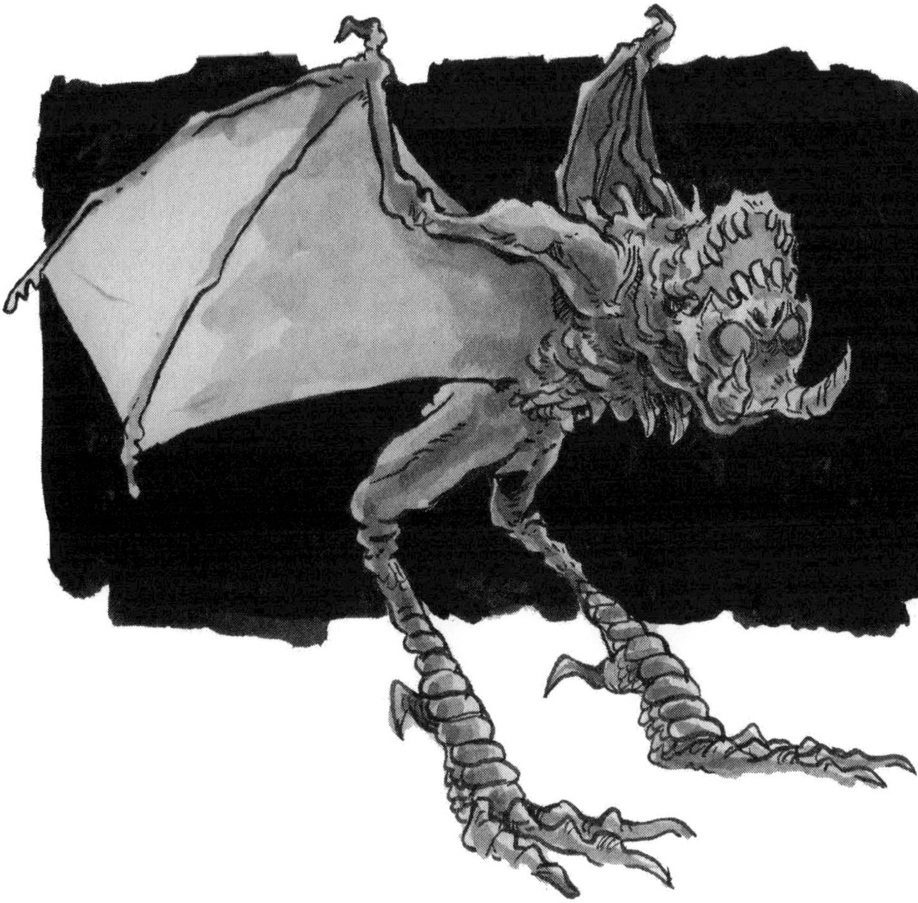

SUBJECT:
THE ONE-EYED KING

DATE: 1892 – Present

LOCATION: Scrantch, Quebec

The Fillsolm family brought the castle over, brick by brick from "oh, you know, Europe?" in 1892. Strangely while it seems nobody has ever lived in the castle there are stories that was not always the case and the Fillsolm's owe their longevity to the thing that lives there...

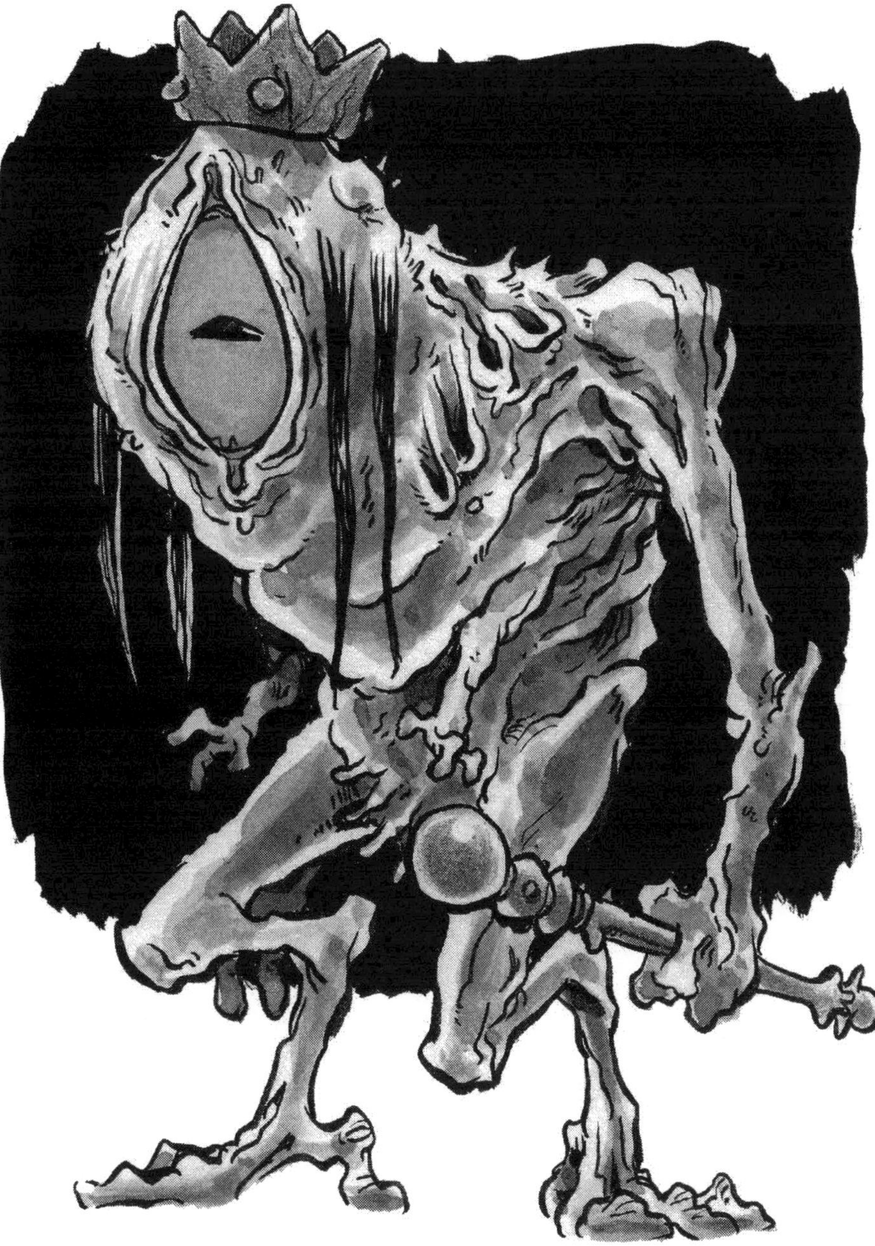

SUBJECT:
THE BASEMENT MAN

DATE: November 18, 2018

LOCATION: Pumikan, Ontario

Martin O'Keefe (11) was admitted for psychological observation. Martin claims to have been told "hideous secrets" about the nature of reality by "the man in the basement." He claims he found a door in the basement of an abandoned house on Filmore Rd. People who have searched the house could find no evidence of the door, however a large part of the back yard of the house had recently been swallowed by a sinkhole.

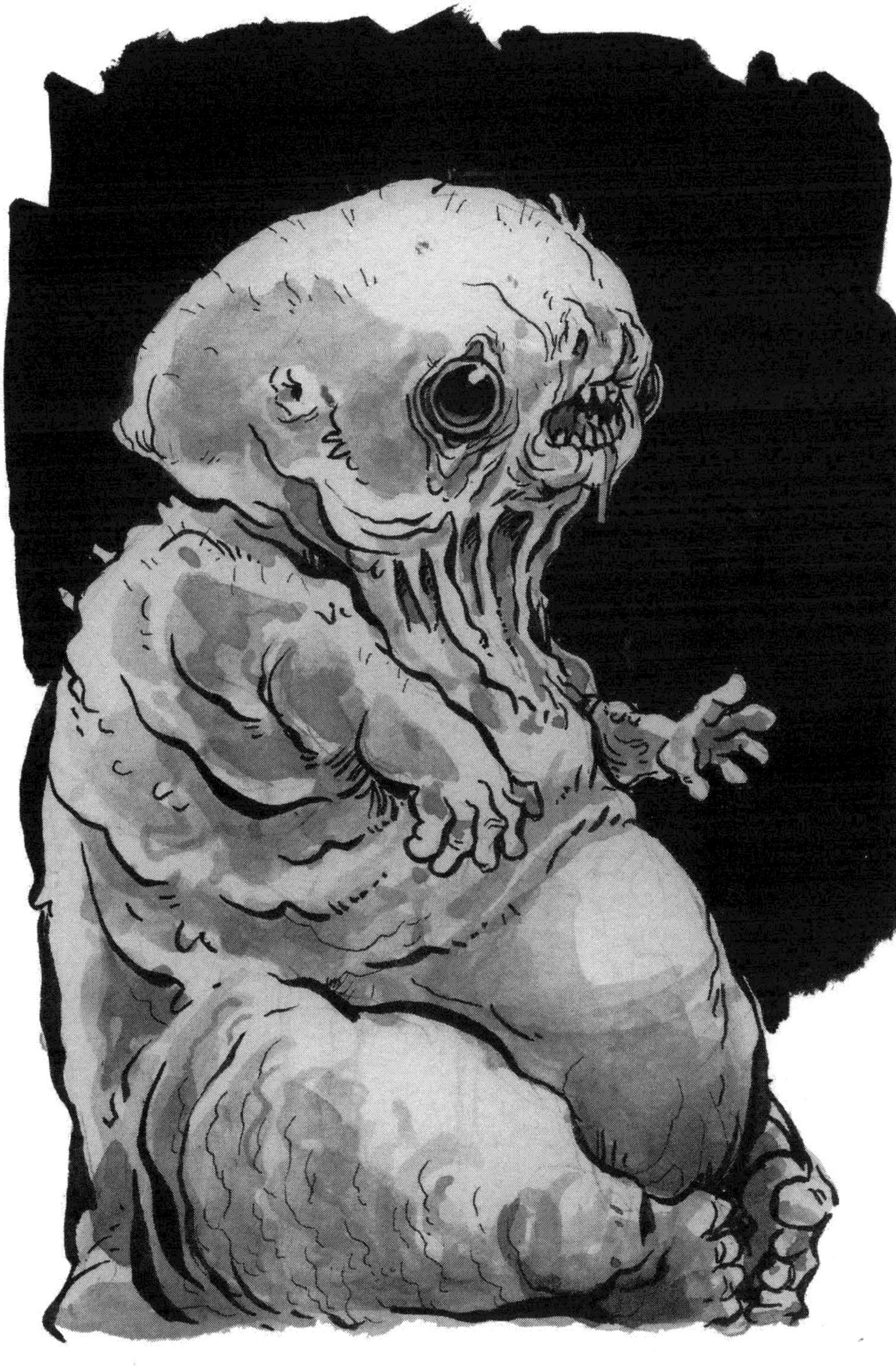

SUBJECT:
GINGERBREAD DEER

DATE: 1340 – Present

LOCATION: World Wide

As it gets closer to Christmas time you may hear the sound of hooves on rooftops and smell gingerbread when none is around. Be as quite as possible, one of harbingers of K'rzcreengal may be near.

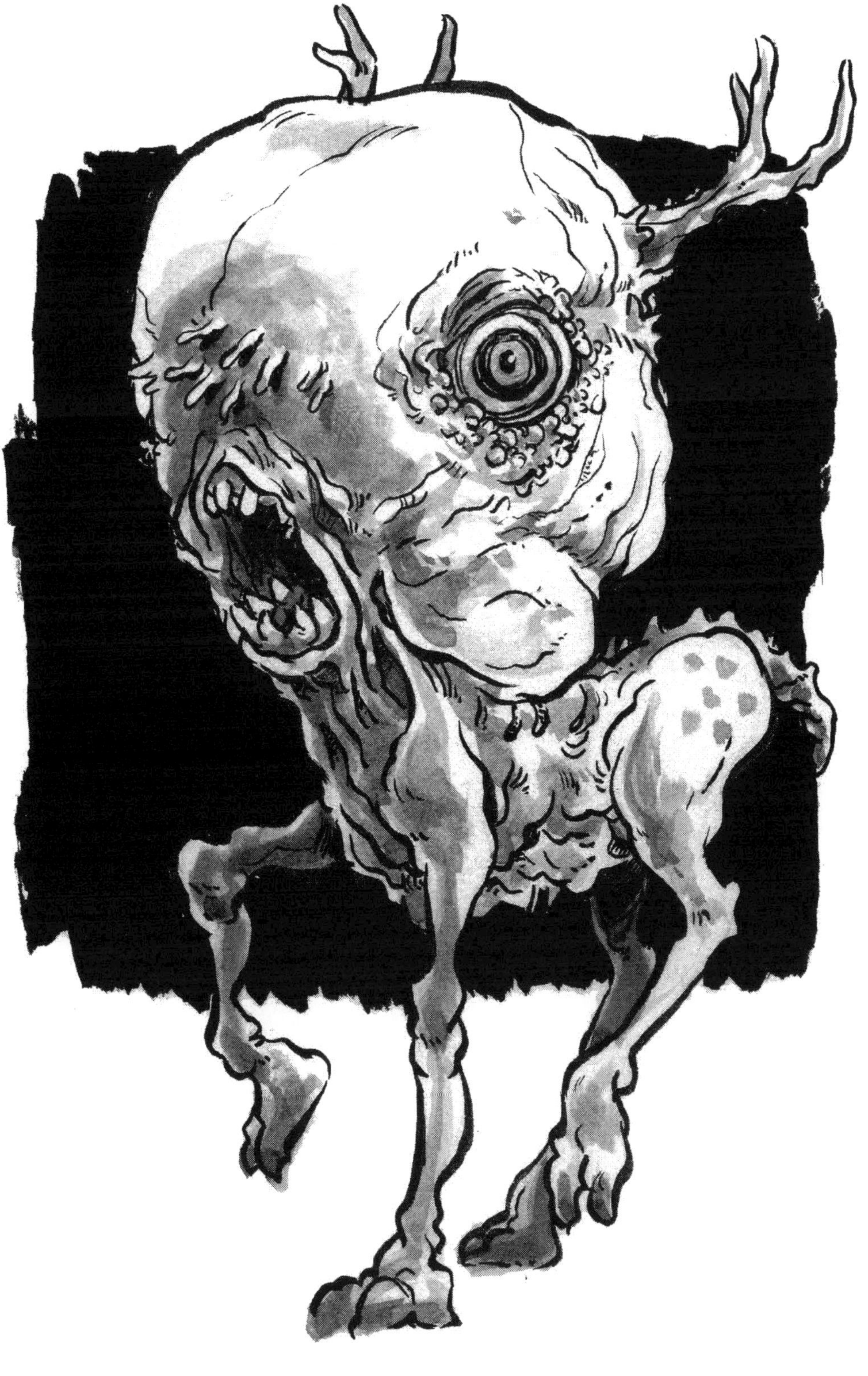

> **SUBJECT:**
> # THE SOURCE OF ROWELL

DATE: Dec. 24, 1997

LOCATION: Ronson, Vermont

During their family reunion The Rowell family discovers a bricked up chimney in the main house at the old family farm. Since that day they refuse to celebrate Christmas or Halloween. A large number of the family members have also asked their doctors to test their DNA.

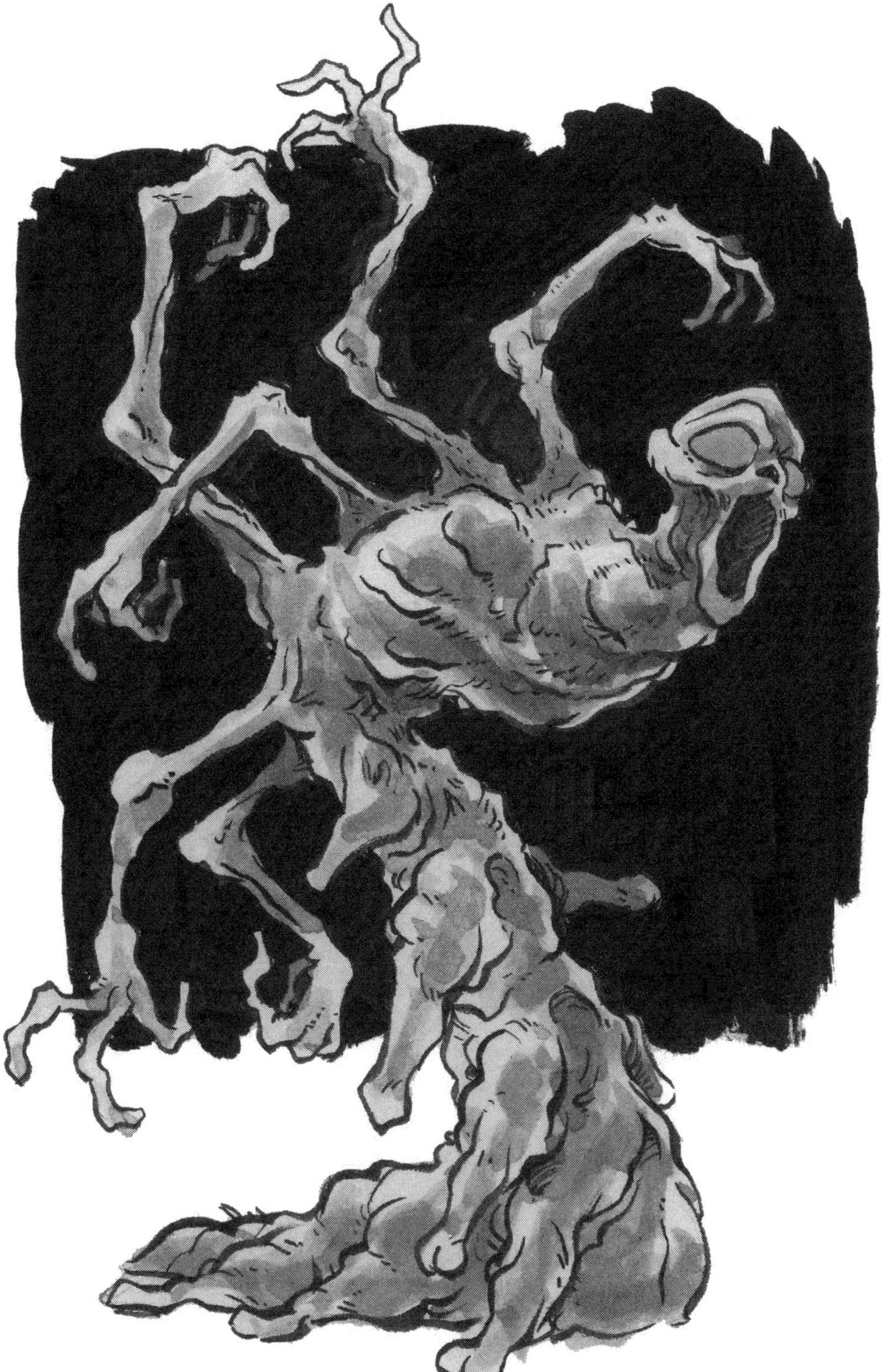

SUBJECT:
THE MATHEMATICIAN

DATE: 1930 - Present

LOCATION: Toronto, Ontario

They say there's a room at the ROM that can be accessed through the east stairwell which houses certain artifacts. Some people claim that the room is haunted. They are wrong. However there is something that wanders among the artifacts. People who claim to have encountered the being have been found in a trance state writing what appears to be very complicated mathematical formulae. They claim to not understand the math.

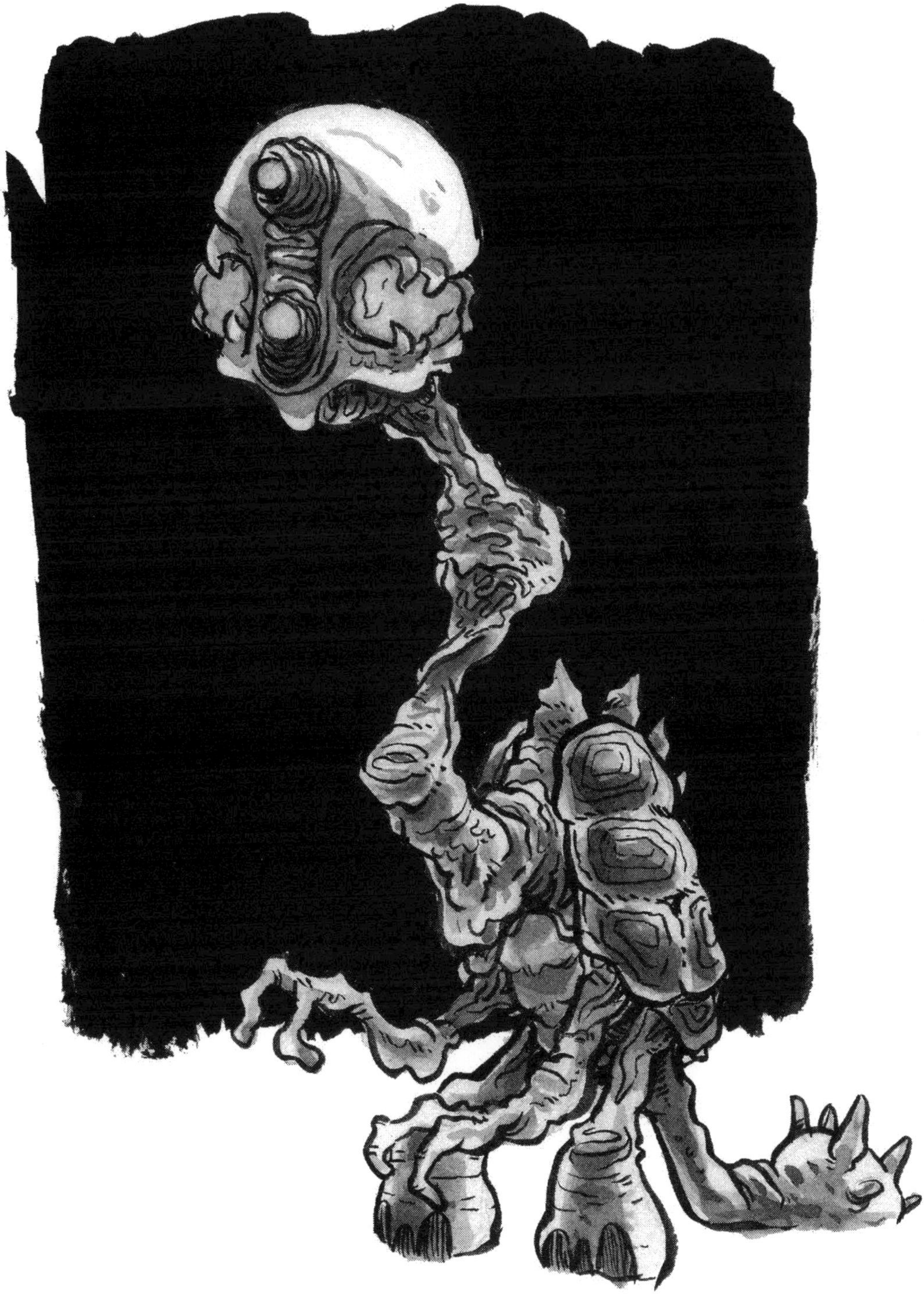

SUBJECT:
ROSWELL RODS

DATE: 1994– Present

LOCATION: Roswell, New Mexico

Jose Escamilla discovered the rods on March 19, 1994 while attempting to film a UFO.

Sure people want you to think they're just moths or something caught in flight by a camera with a slow shutter, but if that's true explain this drawing.

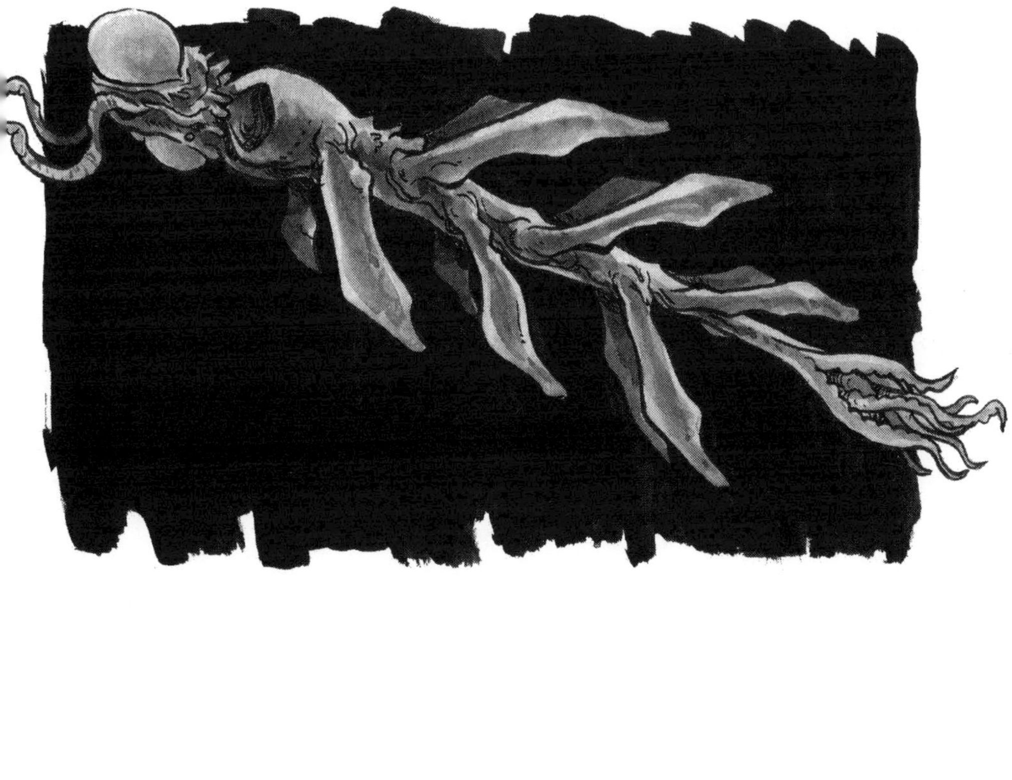

SUBJECT:
BATSQUATCH

DATE: 1980 – Present

LOCATION: Skamania, Washington

Batsquatch! Weird that they call it a Batsquatch since it's got a wolf/fox kind of snout, primate body, and bird feet. It's also got blue fur and pink skin and can somehow affect car engines. Similar to the Ahool and the Orang Bati of Southeast Asia.

First seen after the eruption of Mount St. Helens.

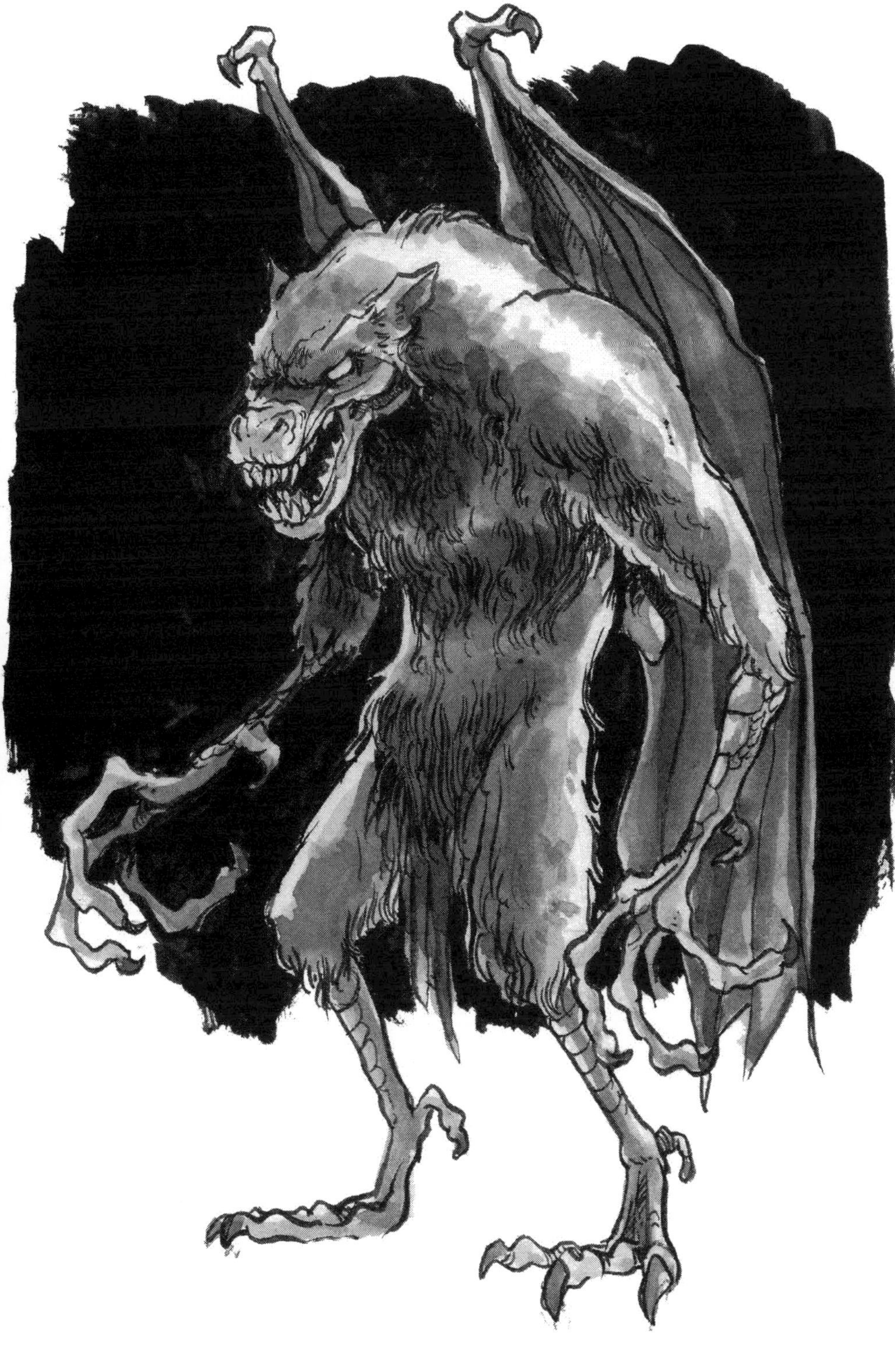

SUBJECT:
PHANTOM OF SLATE STREET

DATE: 1911 — Present

LOCATION: Owl Falls, Ontario

In Owl Falls, Ontario, people tell stories about what they call The Phantom of Slate Street. Supposedly since 1911 there have been sightings of a strange creature wandering through the remains of a house that was owned by a woman who claimed to be a medium. People who have been near the house claim to have strange prophetic dreams for weeks after.

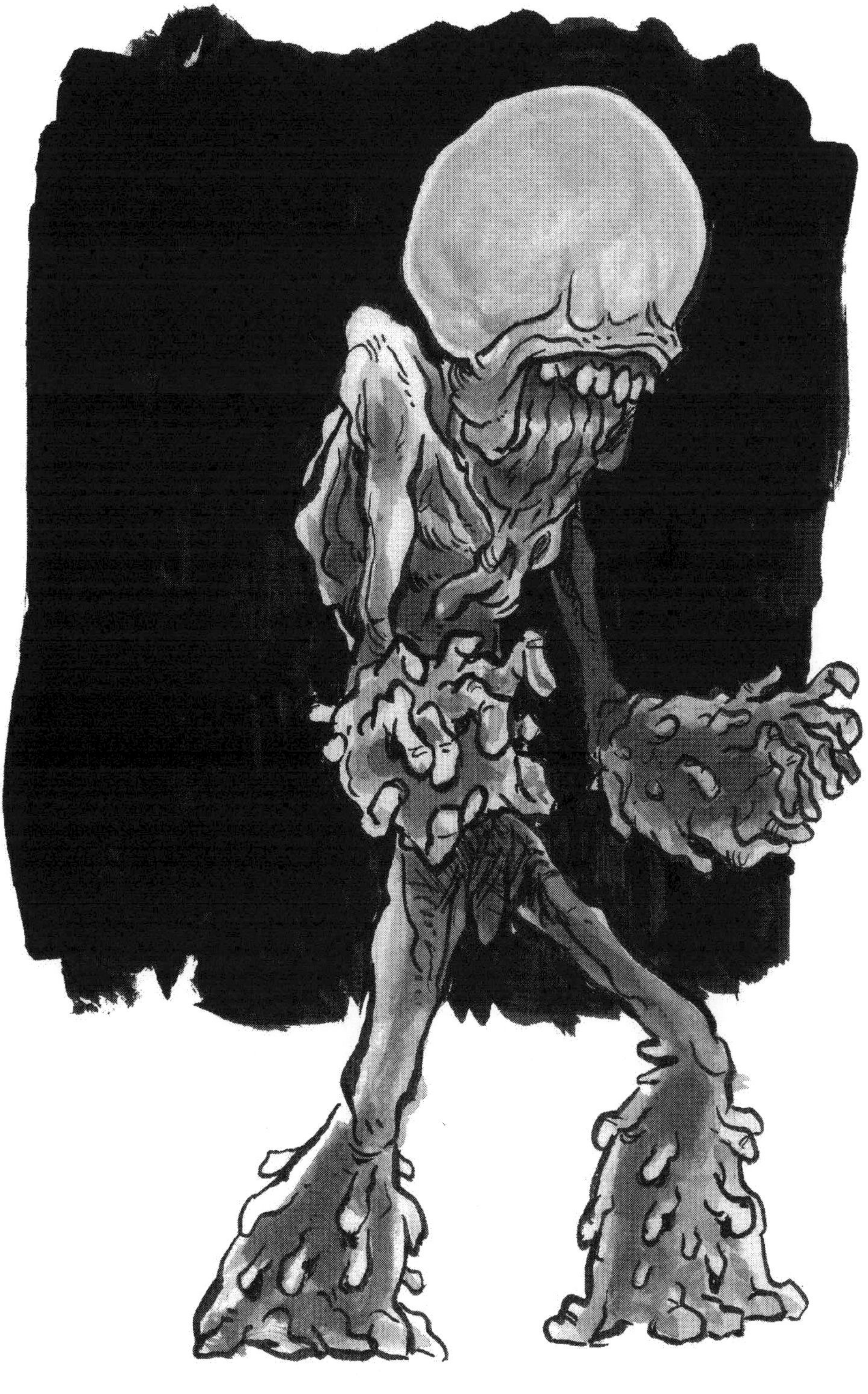

SUBJECT:
THE CLIFT GOBLIN

DATE: December 1984

LOCATION: Flamptville, Alberta

Georgina Clift (79) claims to been attacked every night by a strange creature since her neighbour's oak tree fell over during a storm revealing what appeared to be a tomb in his backyard.

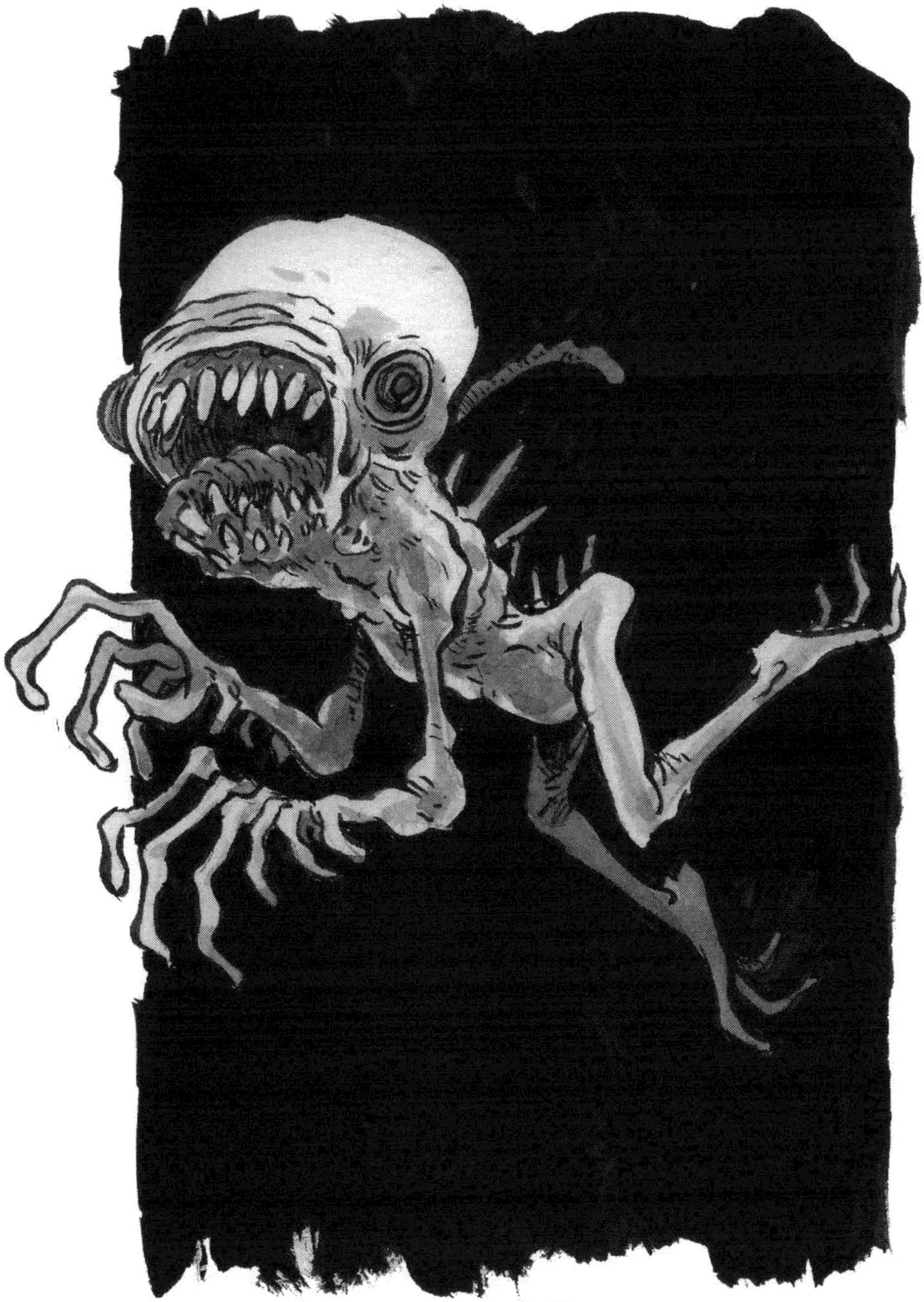

SUBJECT:
"THREE-EYED JERK"

DATE: October 1972

LOCATION: Russel, Texas

After a night at the Grill 'n Gas, Carl "Ace" Muncie, (21) claims he got in a fight with a 12 foot tall "Three-eye jerk with a knife." Police could find no other evidence of what happened to Muncie that could explain his injuries.

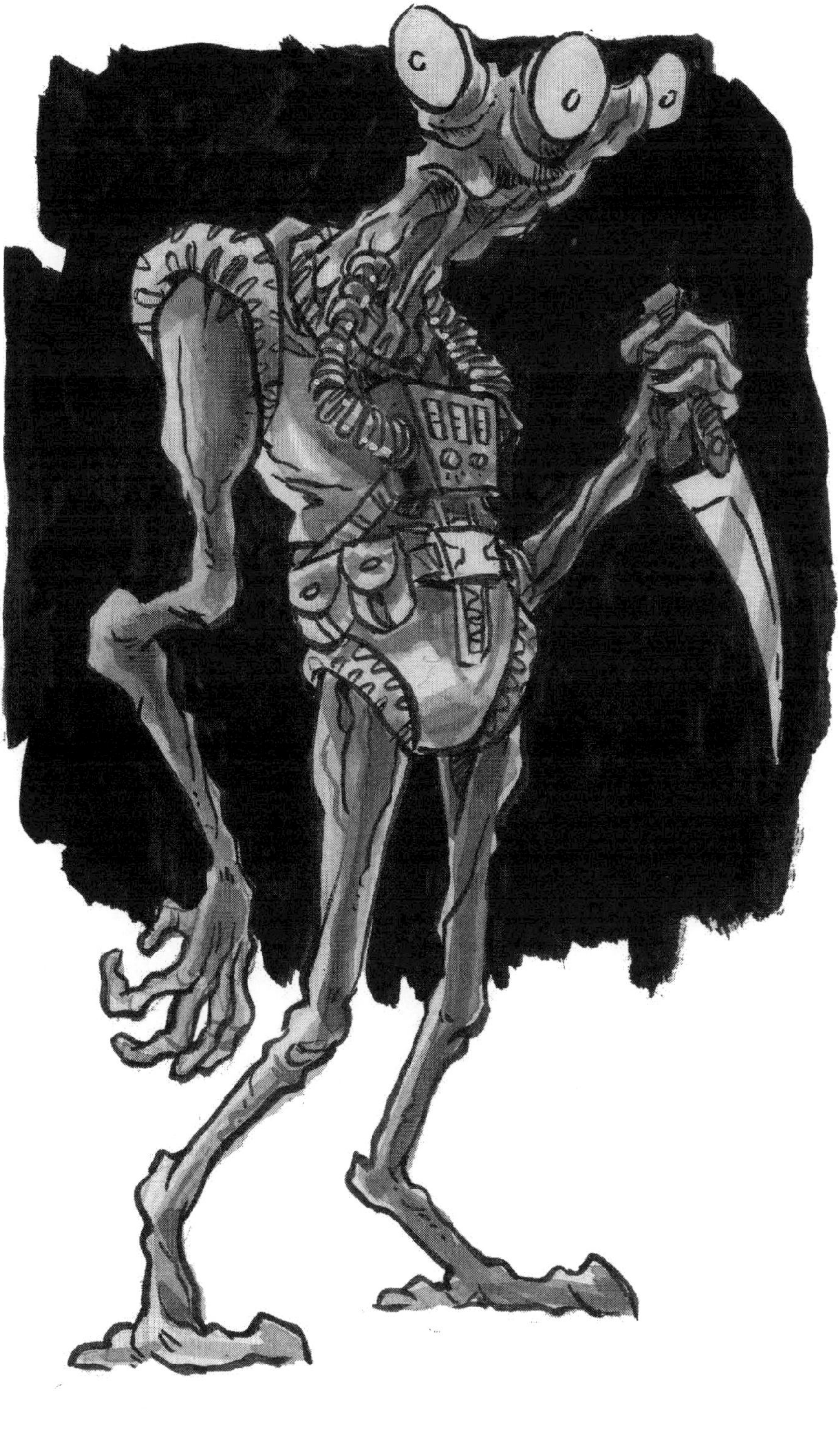

SUBJECT:
WEIRD GOBBLER

DATE: June 12, 1988

LOCATION: Wichita, Kansas

Benjamin Quint (55) heard a strange clicking noise coming from his backyard. When he went to investigate it he was knocked to the ground by a large bird like creature, breaking his left wrist. Other than Quint's injury no evidence of the bird could be found.

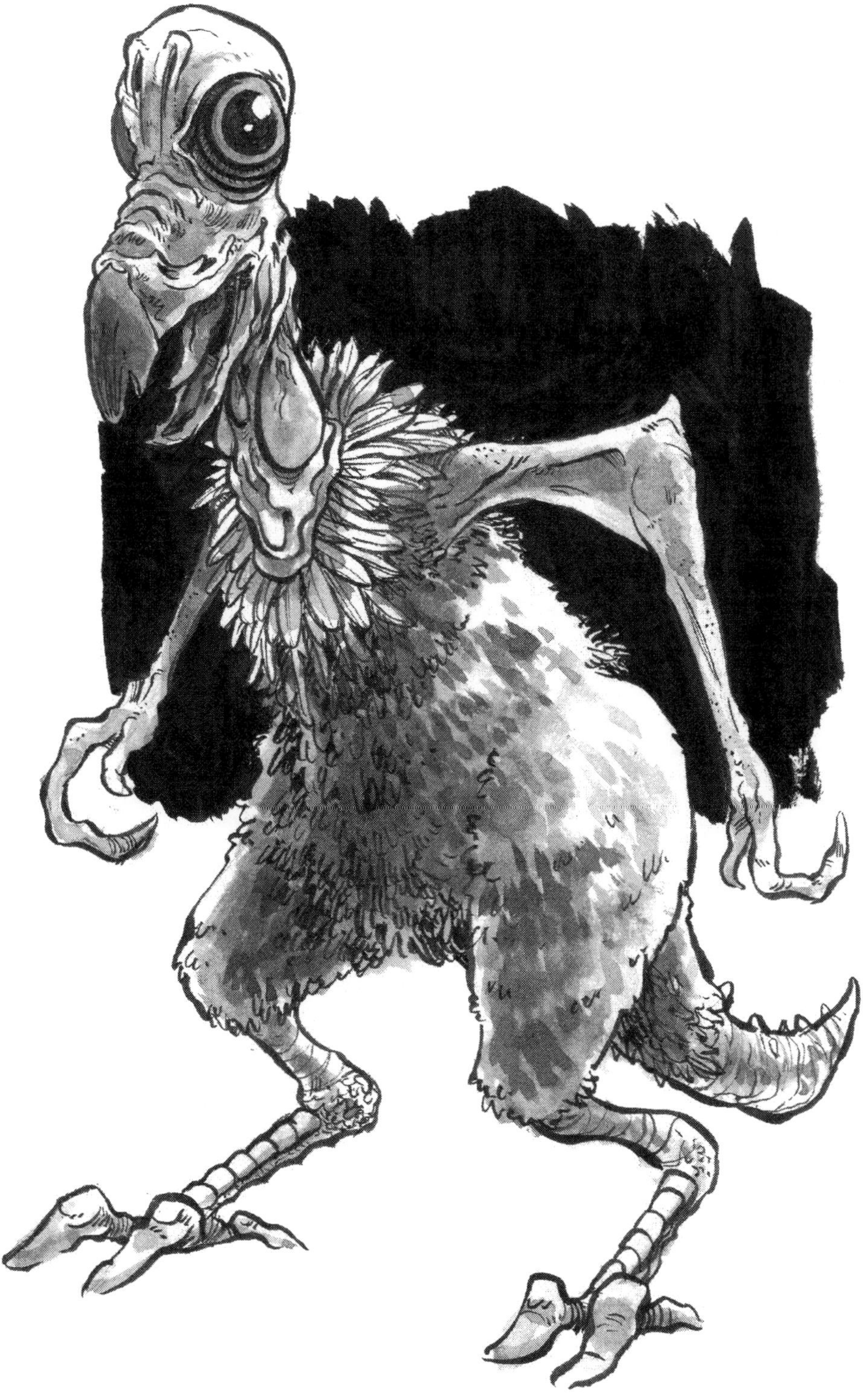

> **SUBJECT:**
> # THE NIGHT SLOG

DATE: February 6, 1954

LOCATION: Stelbrook, Manatoba

During the annual community hockey championship in Stelbrook, Man. something ran out of the woods and across the outdoor rink interrupting the game. Witnesses maintain it was not a moose. There had been no sightings of the creature before or since.

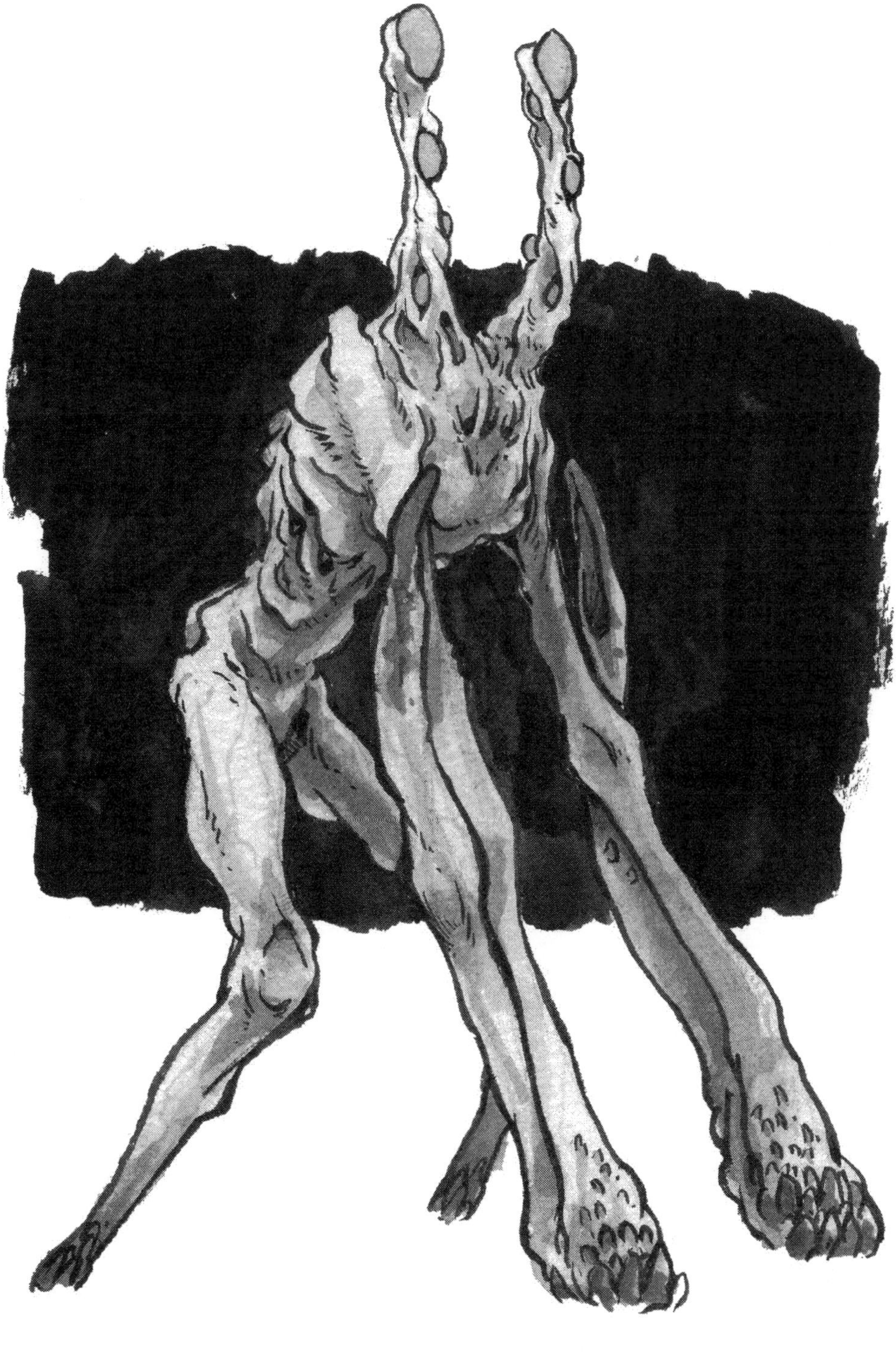

SUBJECT:
SHIRLEY STRONHAM

DATE: 2012 – Present

LOCATION: Simone, Ontario

There are reports that a strange figure has been seen near the burned out remains of the old Ritz Dance Hall. Some people claim it's the ghost of Shirley Stronham. Shirley Stronham (36) denies these claims since she's still alive.

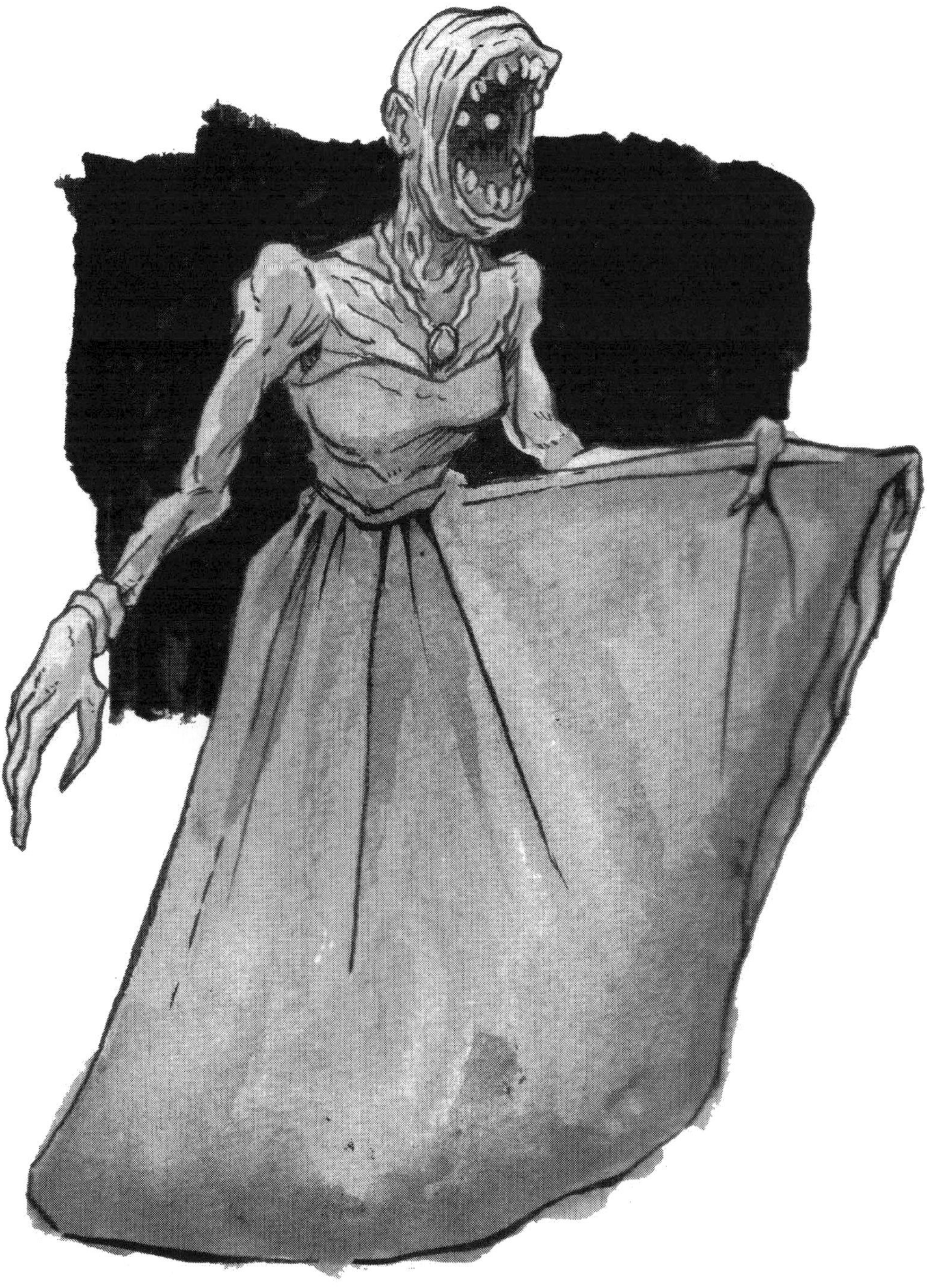

SUBJECT:
THE SCRAMBLER

DATE: August – December, 1966

LOCATION: Plymouth, Saskatchewan

"There was a flashing around the corner, like light reflecting off something metal. Then the sound of naked feet slapping against the sidewalk. It's Shape was vaguely human but with too many arms and not enough heads..."
- The Scrambler, G. Philo Esterscott

Most people are unaware that G. Philo Esterscott's first novel was based on the true story of events that happened in Plymouth, Saskatchewan in 1966. All the witnesses to the murders gave police the exact same description of what they saw, and yet nobody was ever apprehended for the murders. It is considered one of the worst killing sprees in Saskatchewan history.

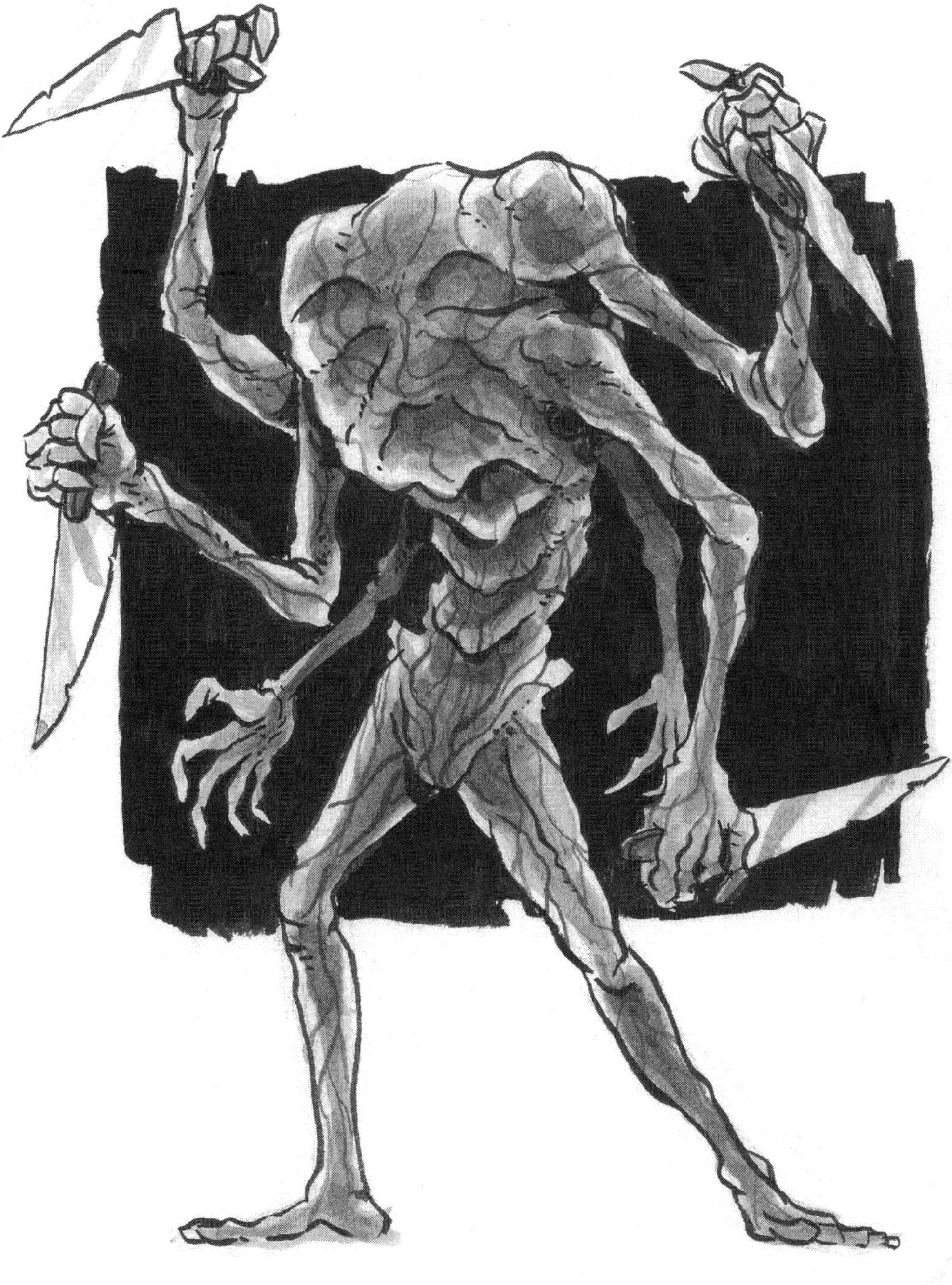

SUBJECT:
SPECIMEN – R

DATE: 1973 – Present

LOCATION: Birmingham, Manitoba

Another creature most of you probably know from the film adaption of G. Philo Esterscott's novel "The Night the Moon Screamed," but did you know this creature has actually be seen many times near the old Sherman Refinery in Birmingham, Manitoba?
Does this mean the likes of Mrs. Flense or The Face Snatcher are real? Archduke Esterscott assures me that they might be and to leave him alone and get back to documenting these creatures for the Field Guide.

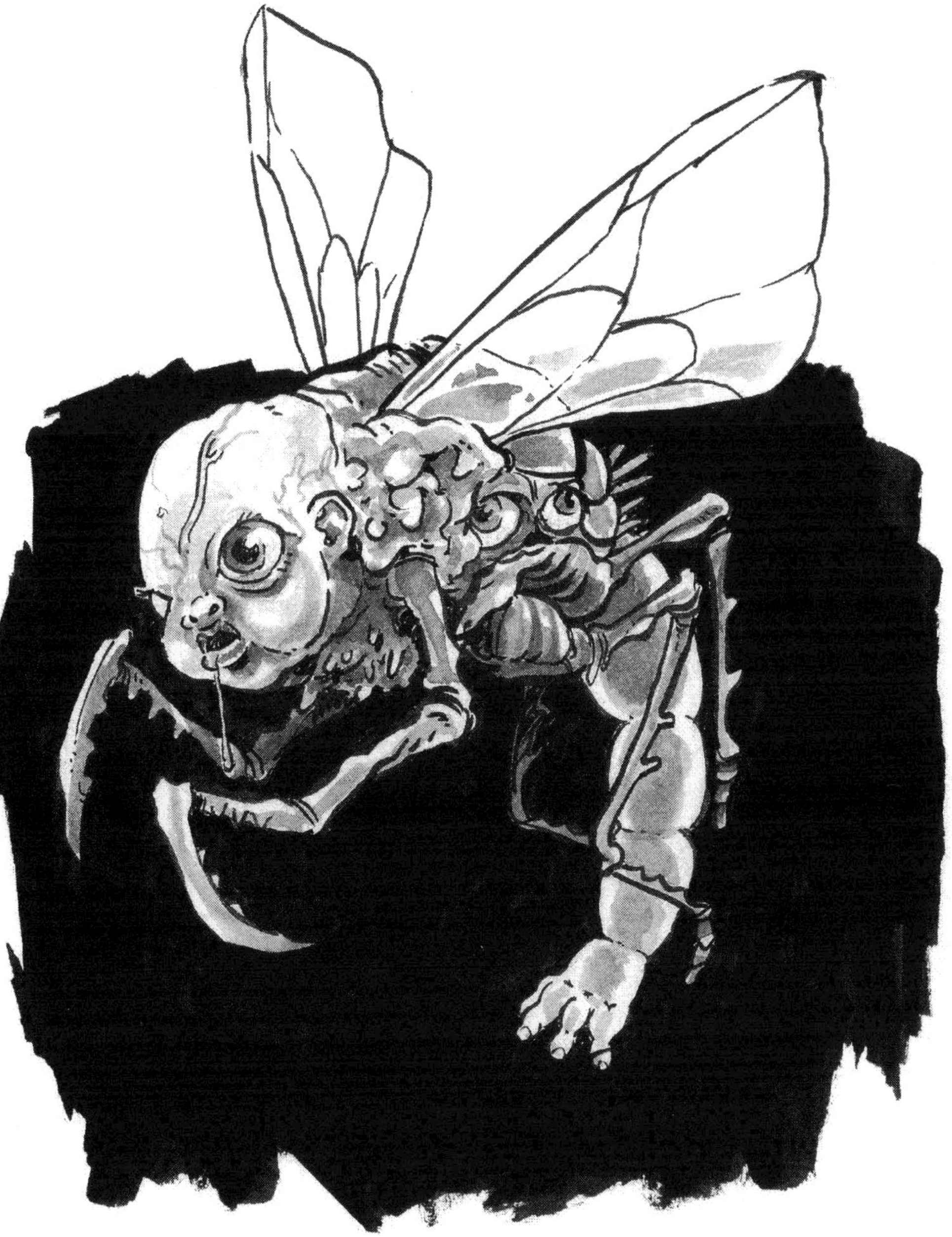

SUBJECT:
SWEETIE

DATE: July 1, 1966

LOCATION: Cramhole, Yukon

People have claimed to have seen a strange creature moving in and out of the caves near Sweet Water Gorge in Cramhole. Witnesses say that when they've seen it the have an overwhelming sense of calm, as if all is right with the world but exactly 45 minutes later they suffer a short bout of amnesia.

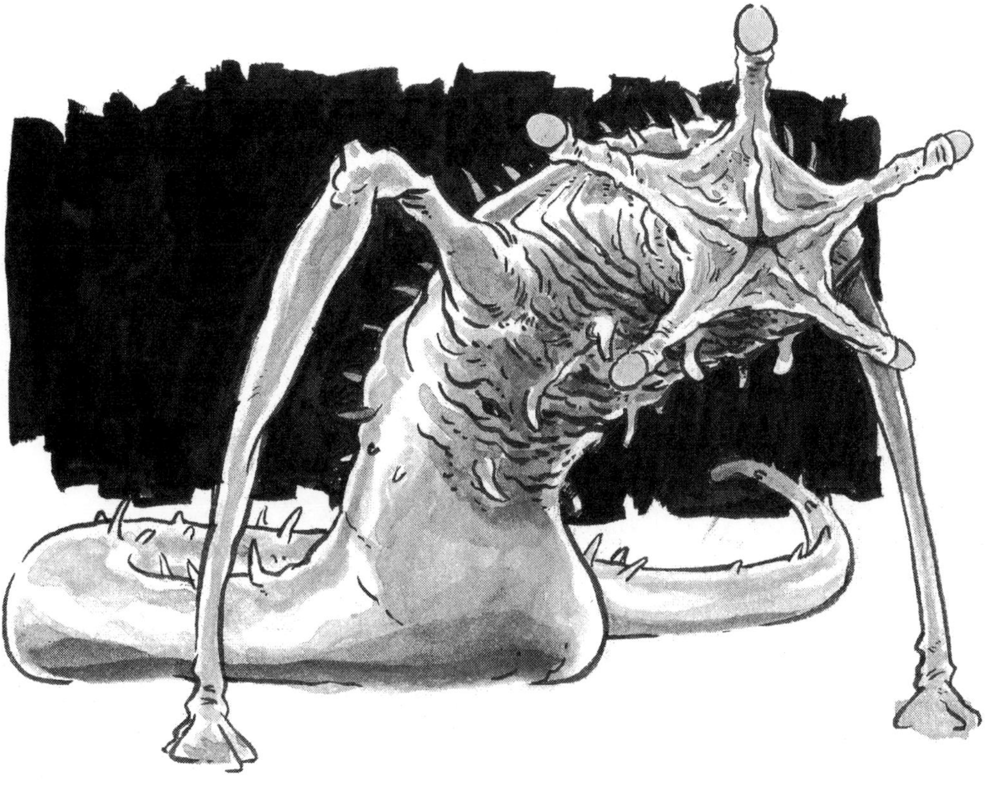

SUBJECT:
THE NIGHT STALKER

DATE: 2016 – Present

LOCATION: Sanctuary, New Mexico

Something has been eating Carl Hamilton's (66) cattle. For the last 4 years a large bipedal lizard has been seen on Mr. Hamilton's property. He says it's about six feet tall and has no eyes. Some of the other ranchers nearby claim there is at least four of them and for some reason they are only interested in Carl's cows.

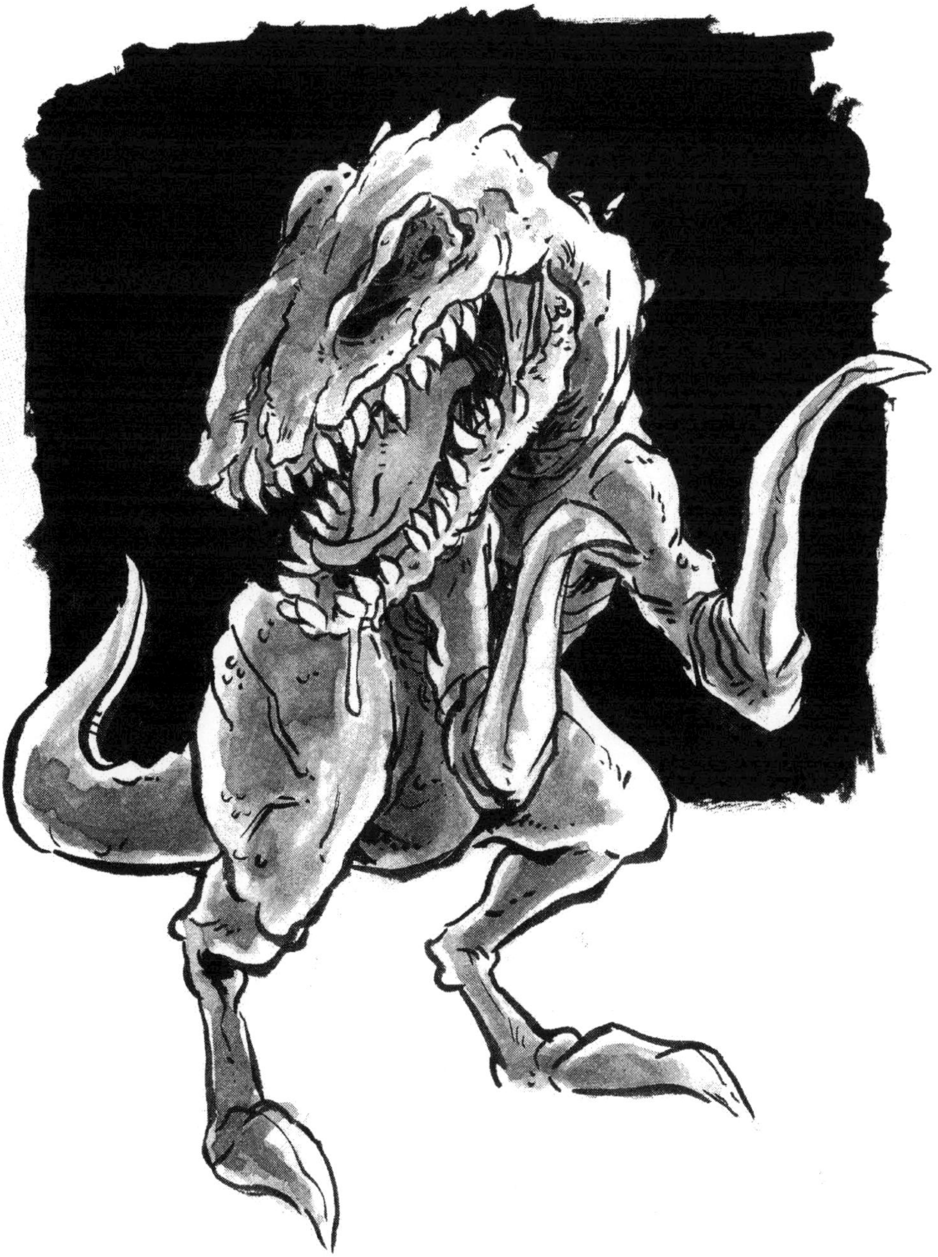

SUBJECT:
GH'THUTIC, THE UNNAMEABLE

DATE: 1880 – Present

LOCATION: Eglinton, Ontario

It is believed that Gh'thutic may have been the entity that corrupted the monks at **The Temple of the Blind Eye.** Other than that It has been connected with a variety of esoteric orders through out the world. Due to climate change and the shrinking of the arctic ice shelf a 100 meter gold statue of Gh'thutic was found in 2019. Nobody has heard from that expedition since the discovery.

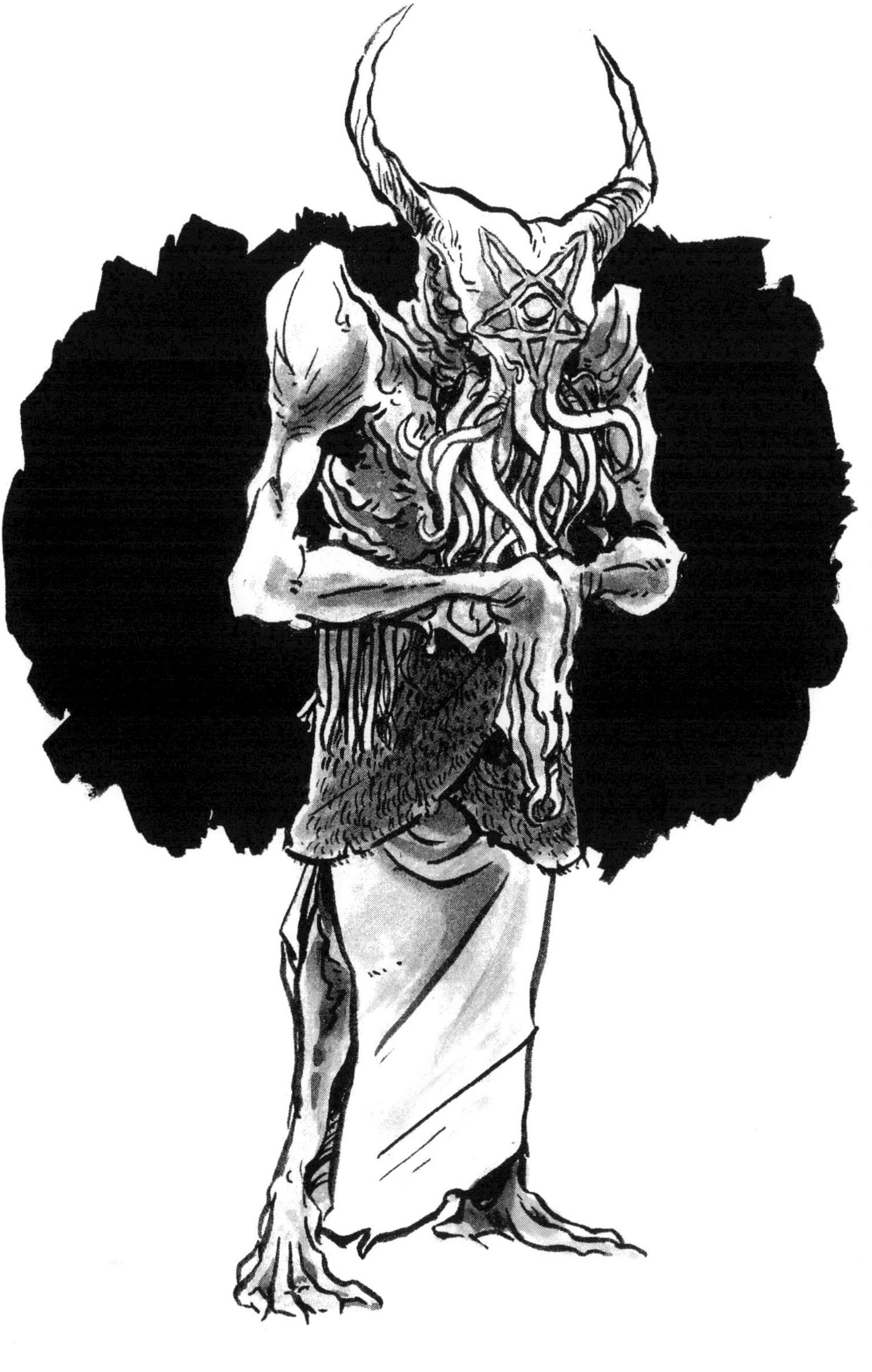

SUBJECT:
STRANGE CRAB

DATE: Dec 22, 2018

LOCATION: Elfont, Newfoundland

A small fishing vessel was found floating off the coast of Elfont with nobody aboard. Reports say the last entry in the log book said, "It said we were friends." Since that day people say you can hear voices coming from the ocean and occasionally see ghostly faces in the waves.

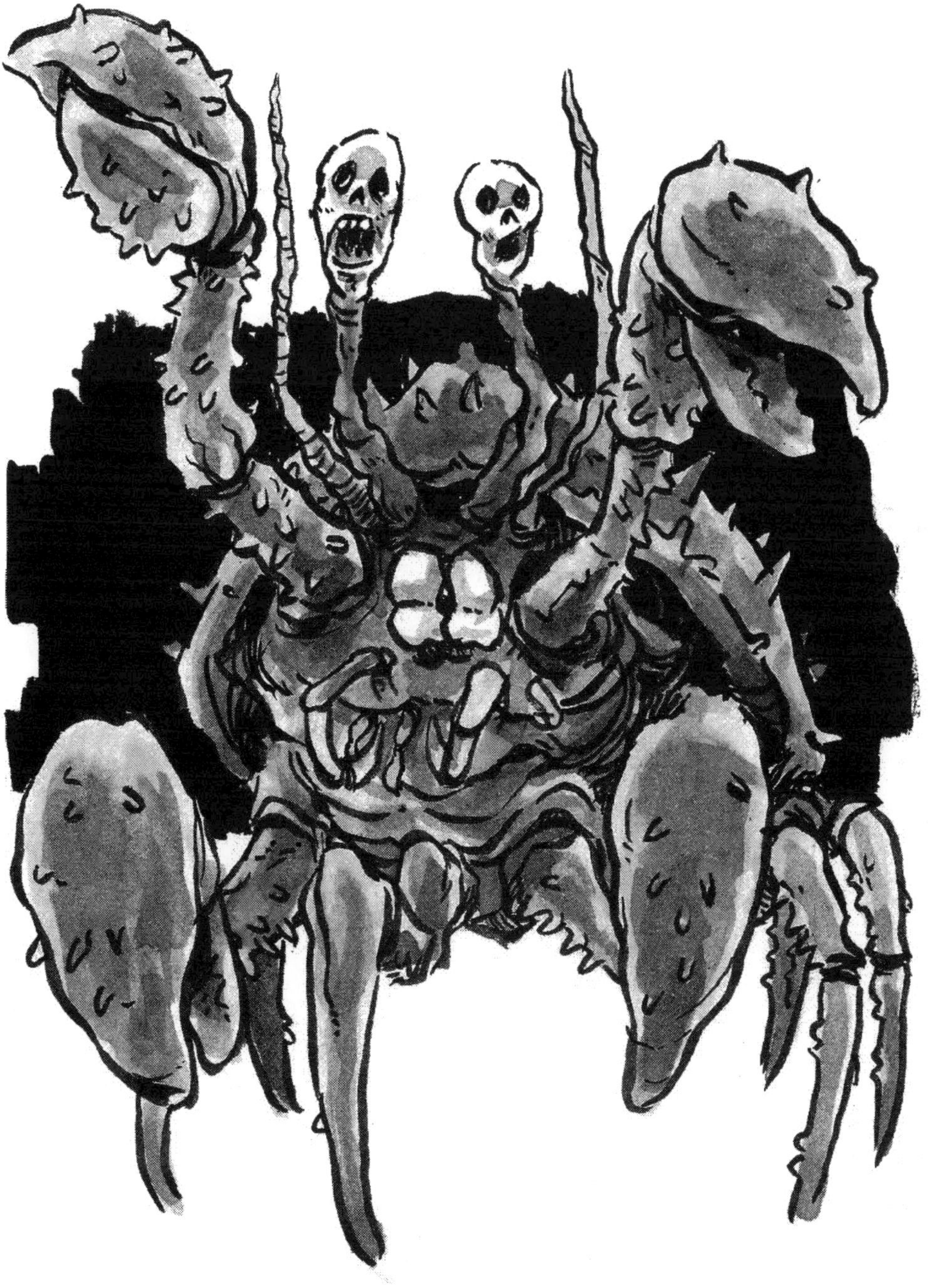

SUBJECT:
ASTRO-DEVIL

DATE: 1974 – Present

LOCATION: Cape Canaveral, Florida

People say that they've seen clumps of what look like five legged mushrooms moving around some of the off limits buildings at the Kennedy Space Center. Many say that they've occasionally seen military personnel with flame throwers near those buildings as well. The government, of course, denies these claims.

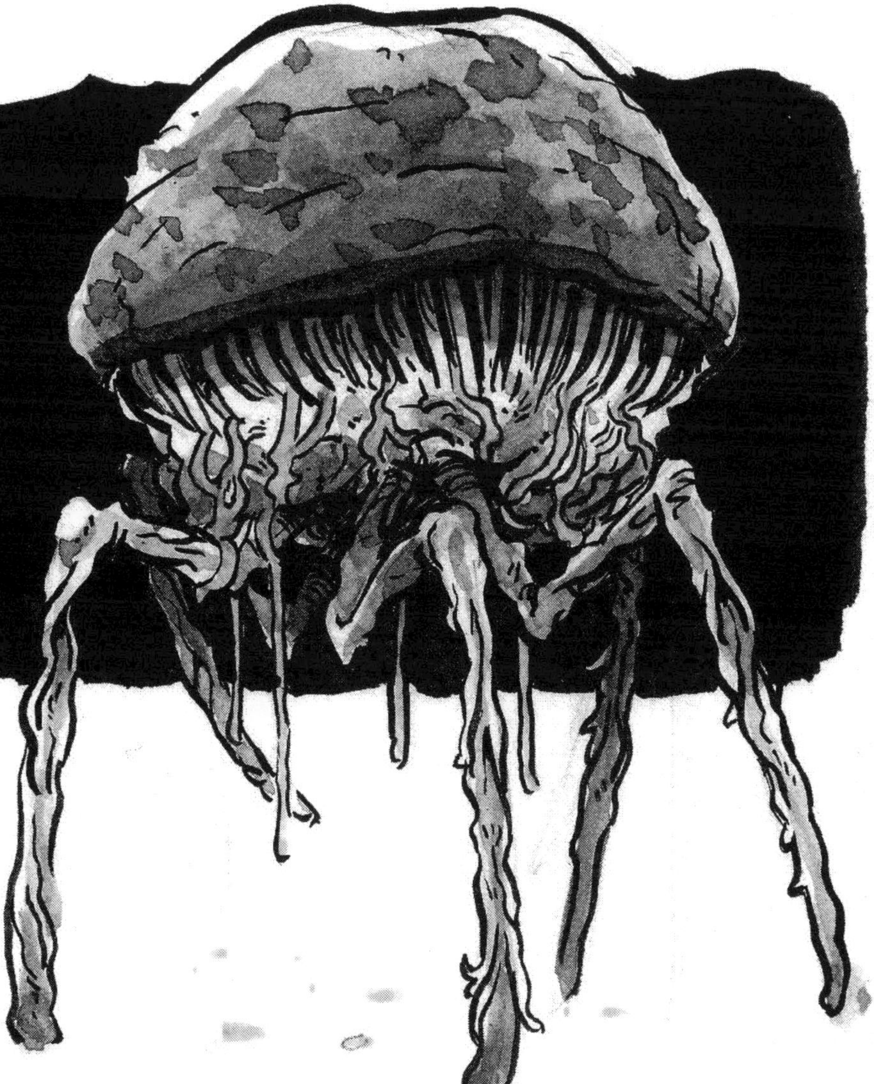

SUBJECT:
OFFSPRING OF SKROG, THE SHAMBLING BLIGHT

DATE: Unknown

LOCATION: Sherman, Tennessee

For 20 years, Karen Hogarth (55) has been institutionalized at the Shambrock Asylum. She maintains that the vagrant whose body was found in her basement was not human but a host vehicle one of the offspring of Skrog, The Shambling Blight. She claims she and her husband were contacted by Skrog through her Samsung phone to find a suitable host.
The body in the basement was found to be missing all of its internal organs and skeleton. Aaron Hogarth (56) is still missing.

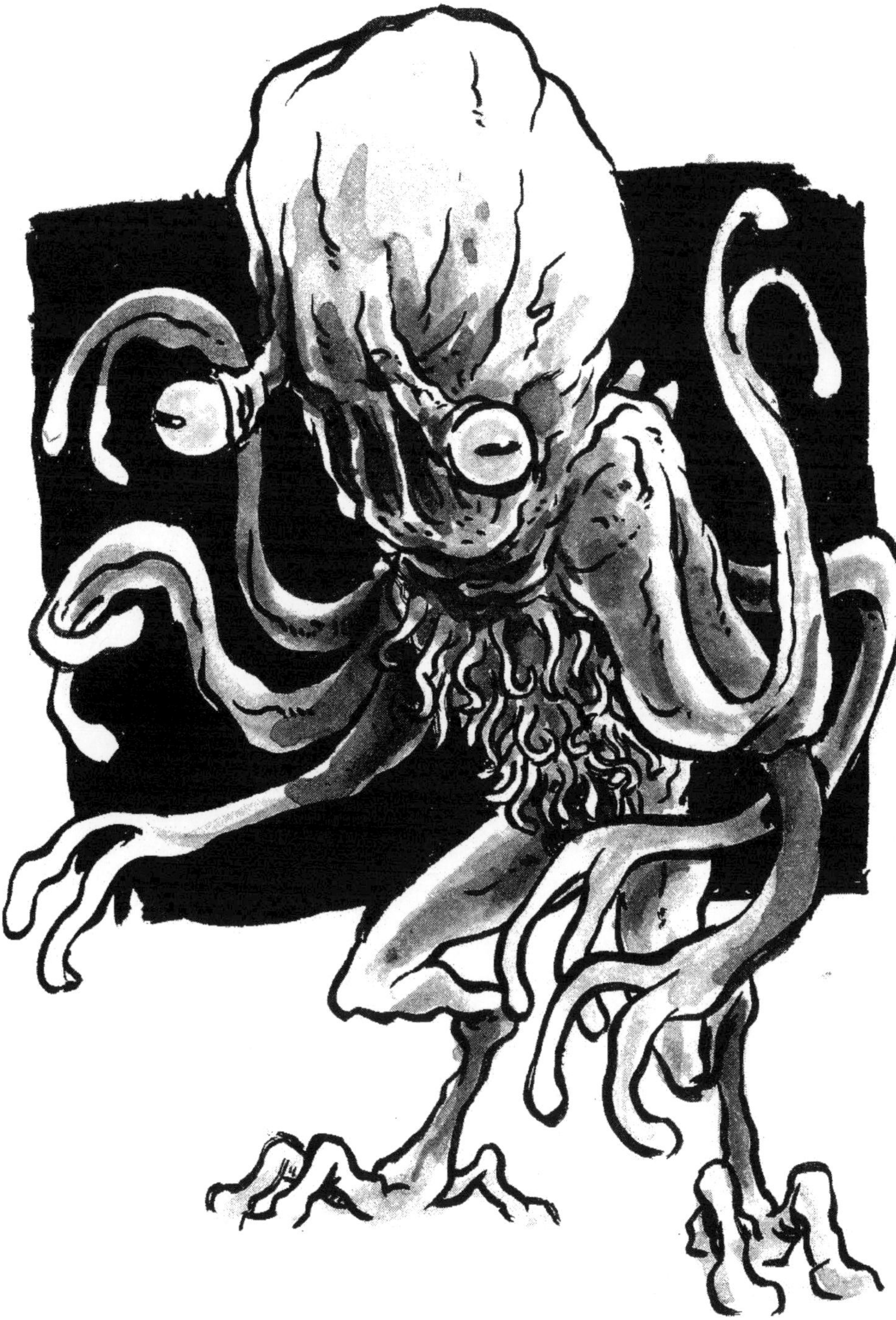

SUBJECT:
THE GREY EMPEROR

DATE: 1988

LOCATION: Paris, Washington

There are rumours that a cult who believed in a being known as The Grey Emperor was responsible for the fire that destroyed 150 acres of woodland and two thirds of downtown Paris. The cult had been passing out literature extolling the virtues of The Grey Emperor and how a life under his control would benefit the town shortly before the fire. Oddly no member of the cult, alive or dead, could be located after the fire was extinguished.

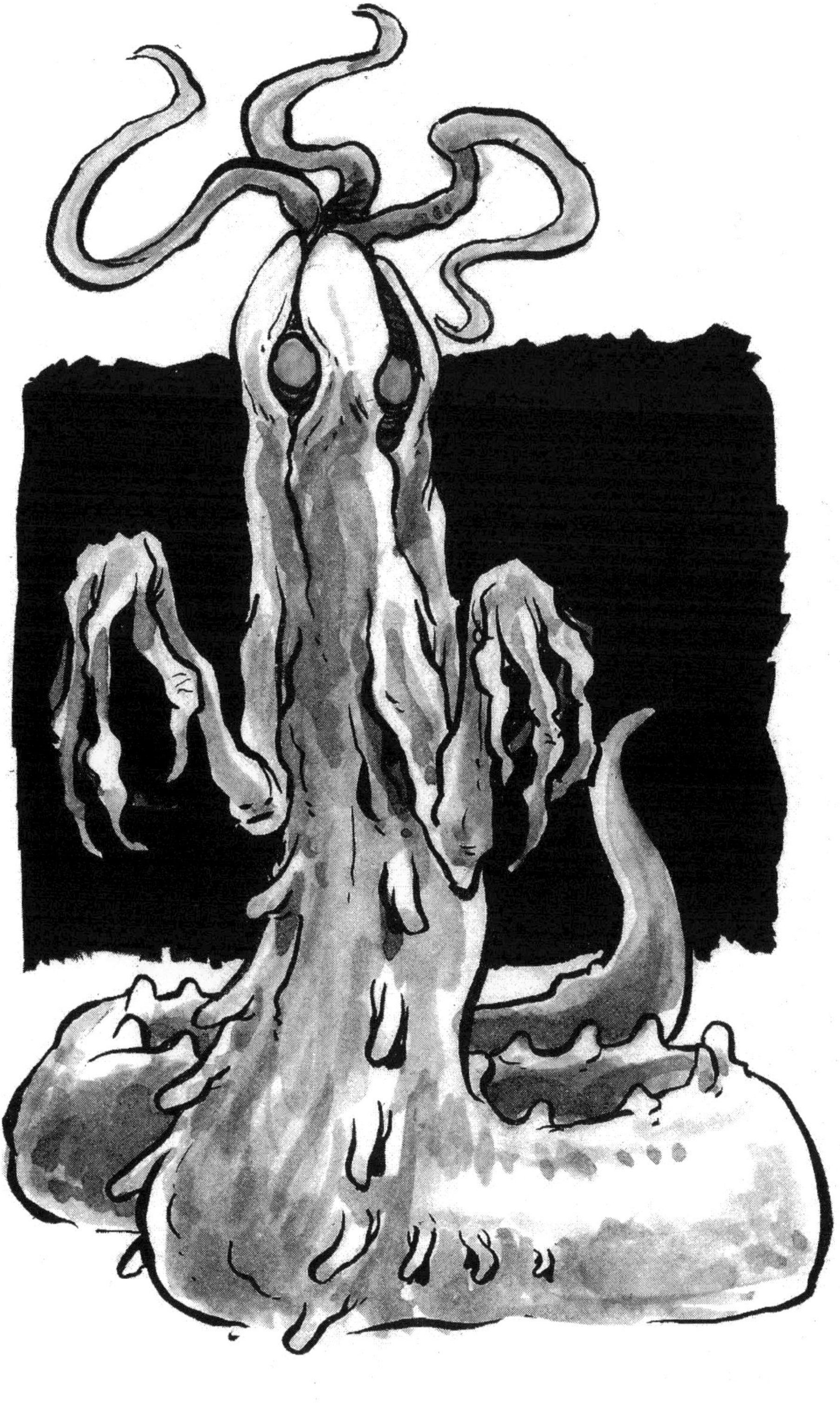

SUBJECT:
UNKNOWN

DATE: August 13, 1983

LOCATION: Stones Throw, Vermont

Survivors of the Camp Konkachew massacre claim that Susy Quinn (18) was not responsible for the deaths. It was, in fact, a large winged creature that lived in a cave on the outskirts of the property. If anyone human was to blame, it was Johnny Hanson (19) who refused to listen to Ol' Dave (44) a local hermit who told them not to knock down any of the standing stones near Grinning Cave.

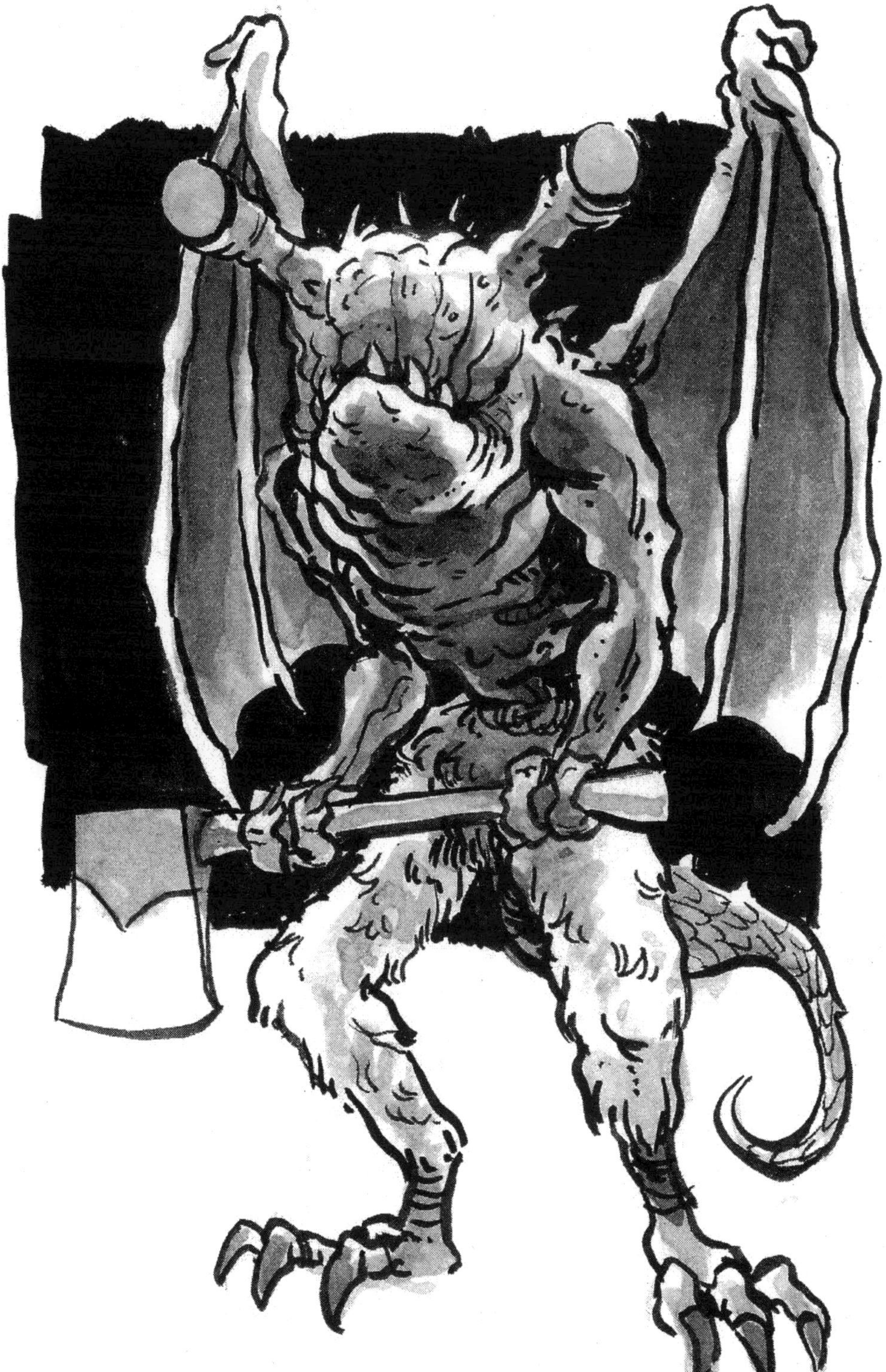

SUBJECT:
SAMPLE PARASITE / SKULL CRAB

DATE: July 4, 1973

LOCATION: Sample, Rhode Island

The entire population of Sample was infected by a parasite that came from a tainted batch of crab meat. Scientists still have no idea where the parasite originally came from. The first symptom of infection is a slight headache, quickly followed by all the flesh on the victim's head falling off and claws springing from their eye sockets. The parasite is then free to move around wearing the skull of it's victim.

The entire process takes about thirty to sixty seconds, depending on if there is anyone around to see it.

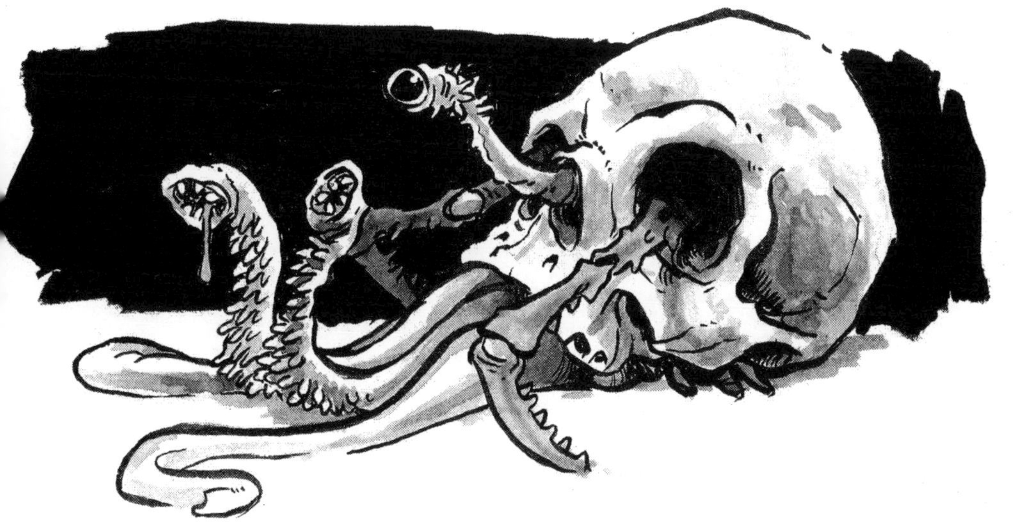

SUBJECT:
PHANTASMOTRON

DATE: February 13, 2000

LOCATION: [REDACTED], California

After the disastrous results of his original experiment to power a robot with ghosts, Dr. [REDACTED]'s son Lawrence moved his operations to an abandoned hotel in [REDACTED], California hoping to prove his father's theory was correct.

The experiment's results were the same. Lawrence was among the 12 bodies found at the hotel. The Phantasmotron is still missing.

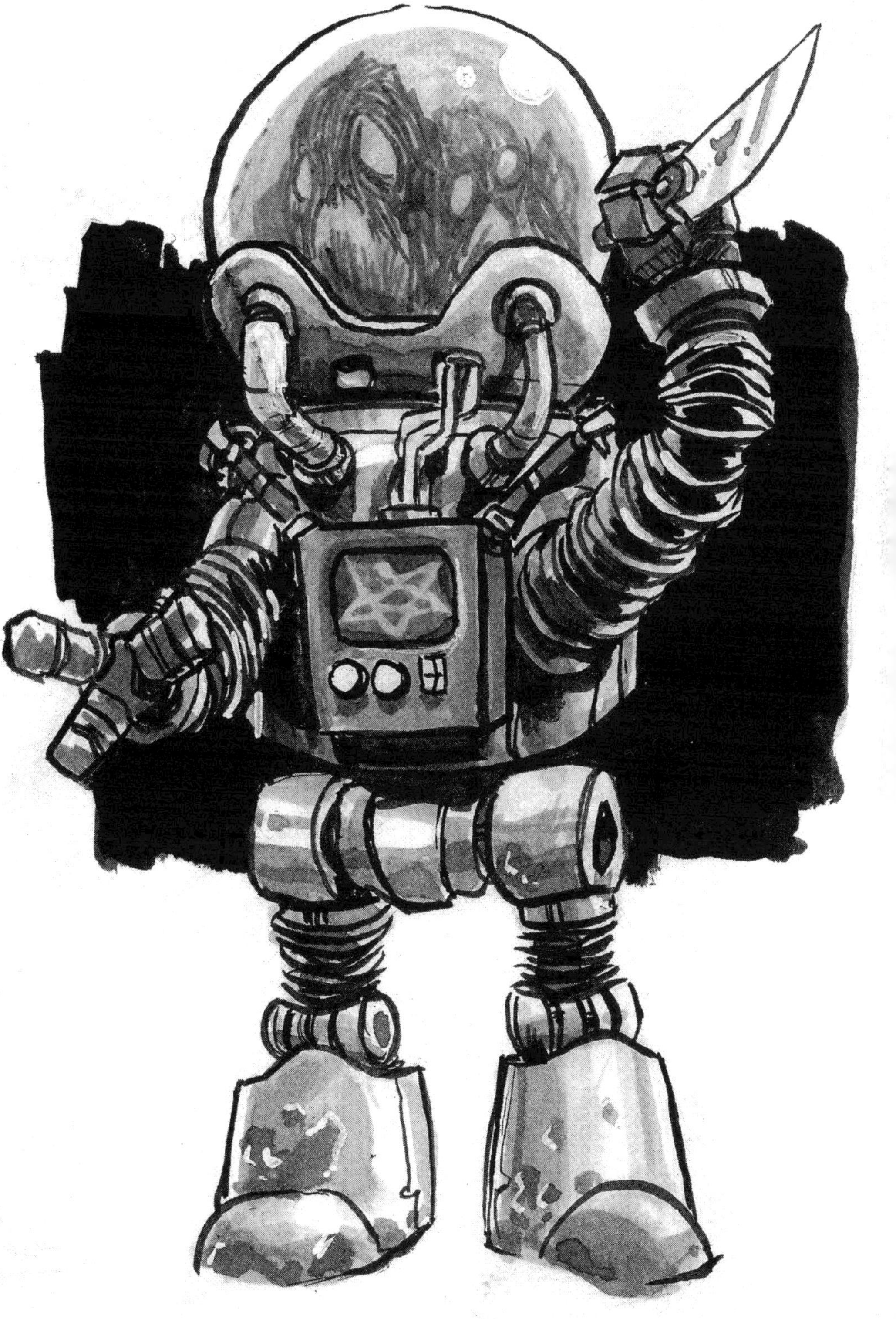

SUBJECT:
THE PALE FIGURE WITH GOLD EYES

DATE: 1932 – Present

LOCATION: Wold wide

It's been seen around places that have suffered flooding. Sightings are usually followed by a rash of disappearances. People. Animals. Small personal items...

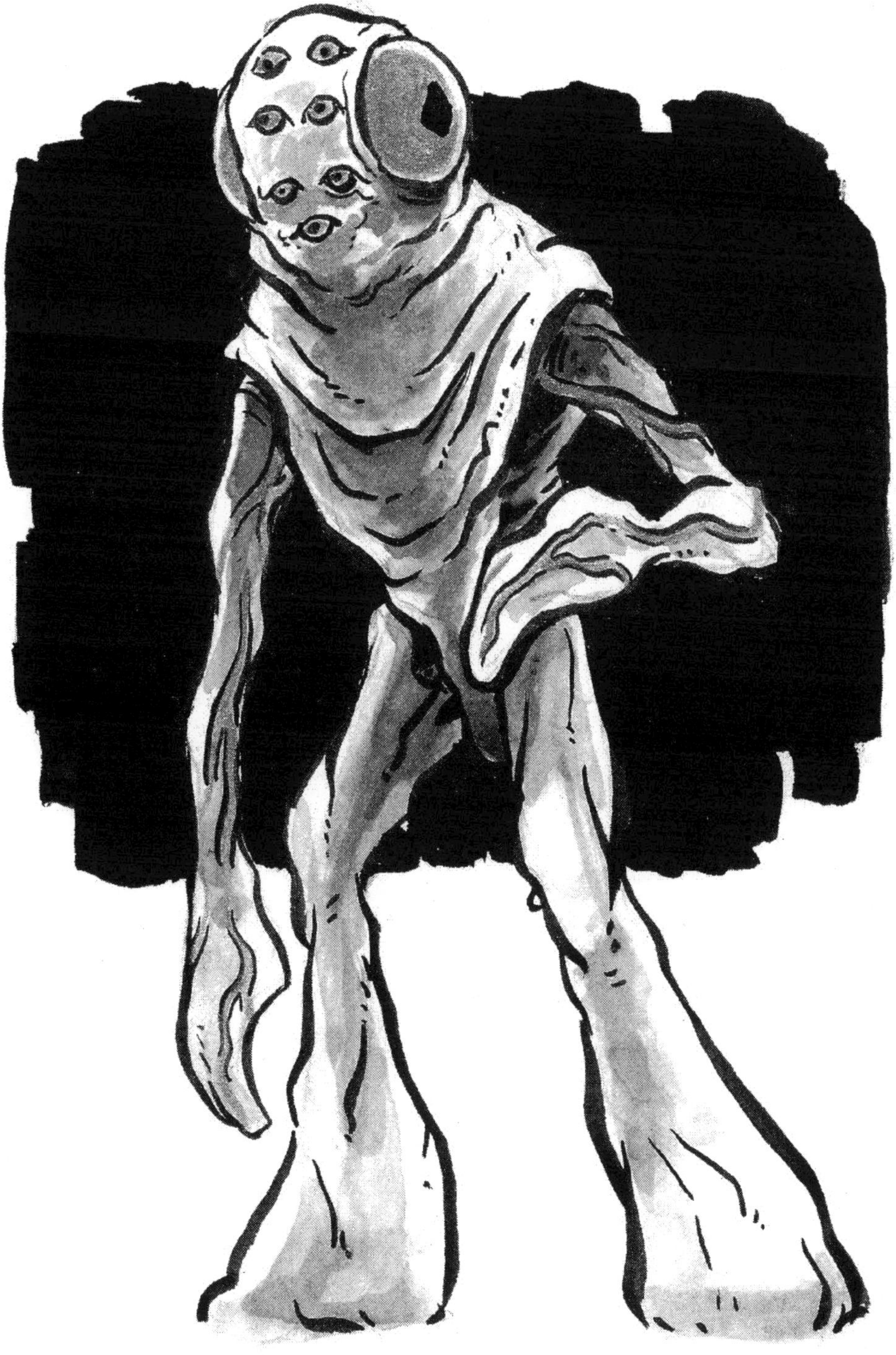

SUBJECT:
SANDHILL SENTINEL

DATE: June 5, 1932

LOCATION: Slump, Pennsylvania

Residents of Slump, claim that on June 5, 1932 something came down from the sky and stood on the top of Sandhill Sentinel. Some of them believe that it is the father of the child Joy Hersfelst gave birth to on August 5. This is all the information anyone has been able to get from the residents. The Hersfelst family refuse to comment on the situation.

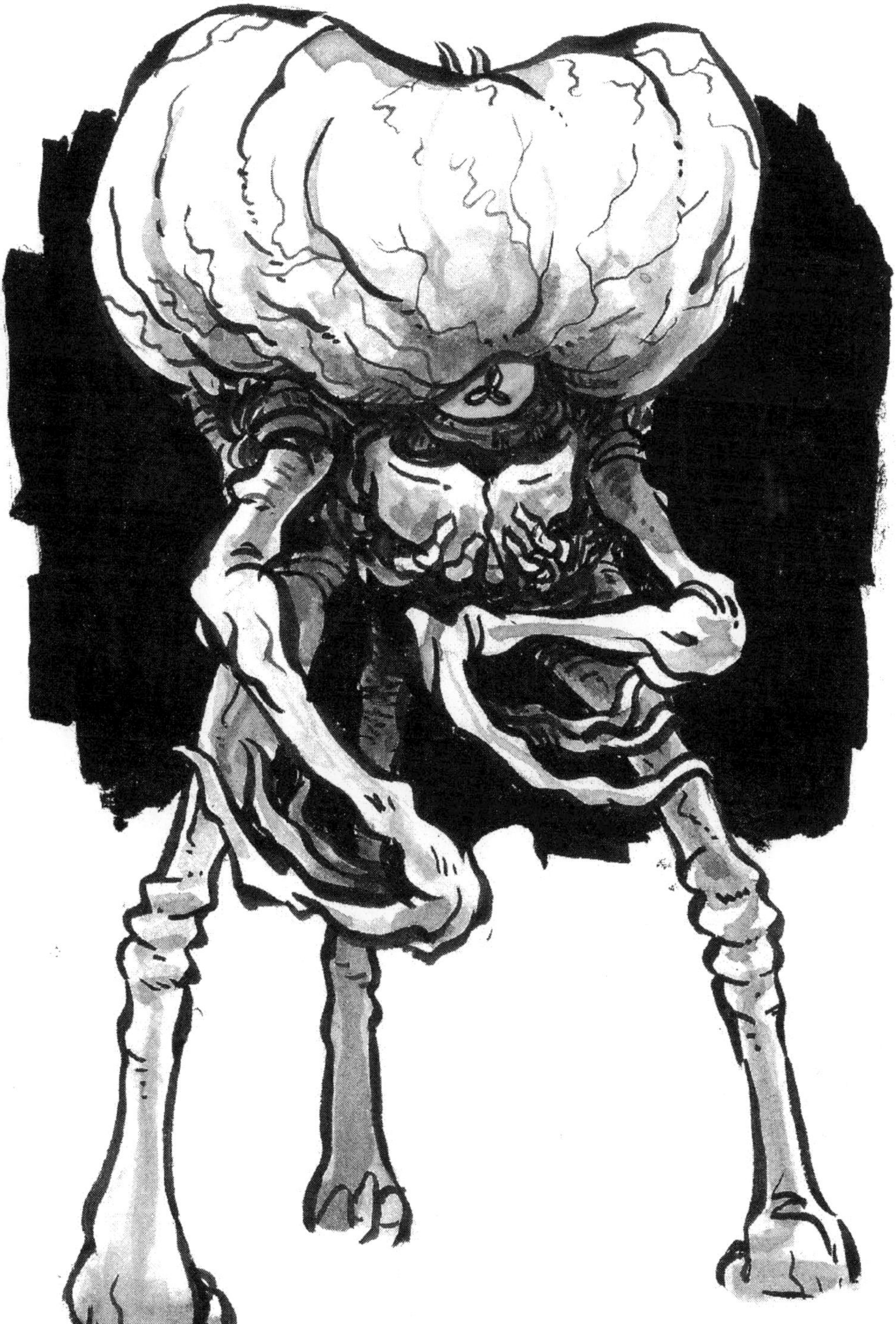

> **SUBJECT:**
> # MUCK MAN

DATE: April 4, 1962

LOCATION: Aarontown, Manitoba

Errol Conway (4) says that a Muck Man came out of the sewer and took his older brother and their dog. John Conway (12) is still missing.

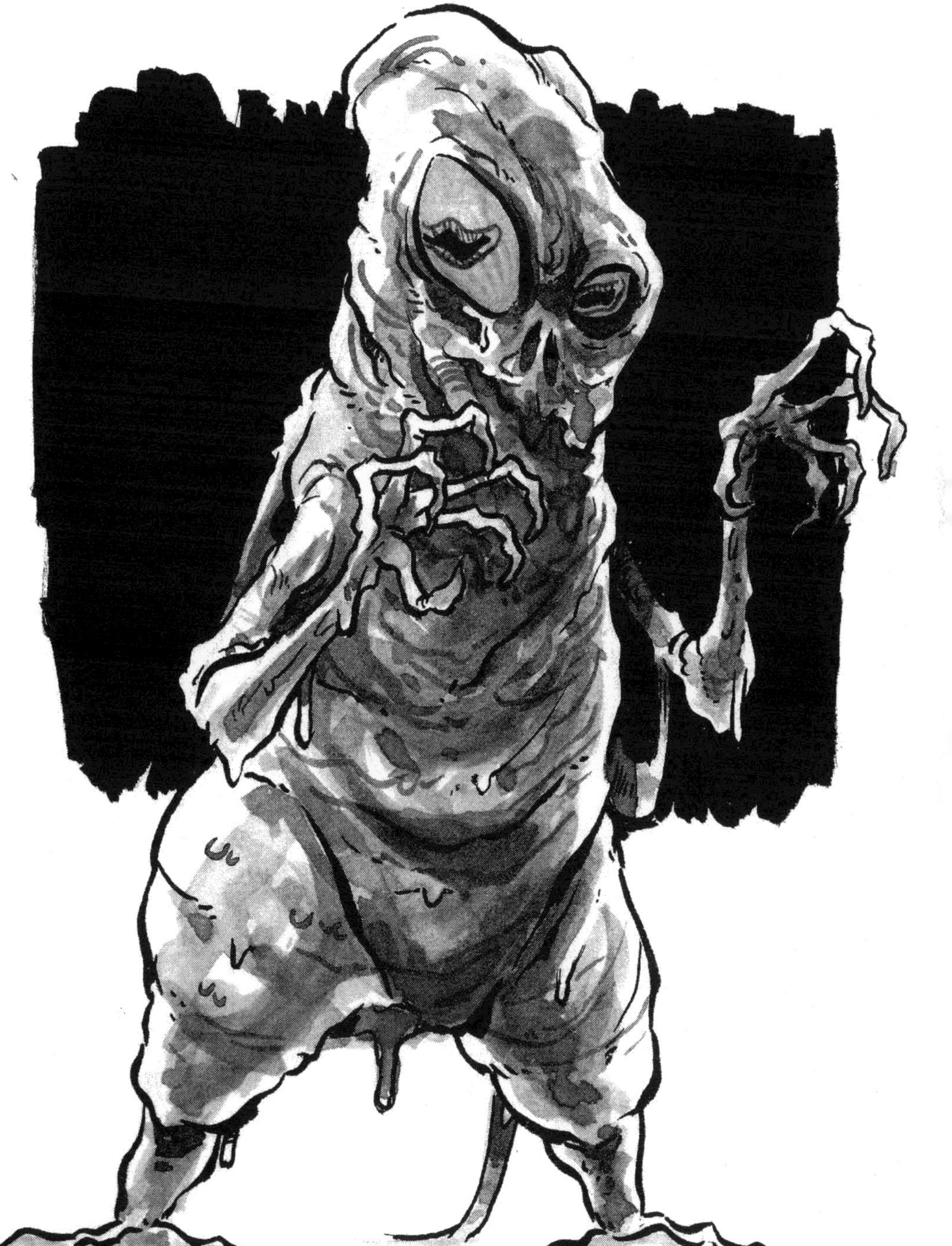

SUBJECT:
GHOST OF WHITLEY UNIVERSITY

DATE: Mid-2000

LOCATION: Whitley, Ontario

As part of a hazing ritual a group of fraternity and sorority pledges spend the night in the closed parapsychology and advanced robotics building. Authorities say the resulting carnage was in no way connected to events in Jan. 1999 that originally lead to the closure of the building.

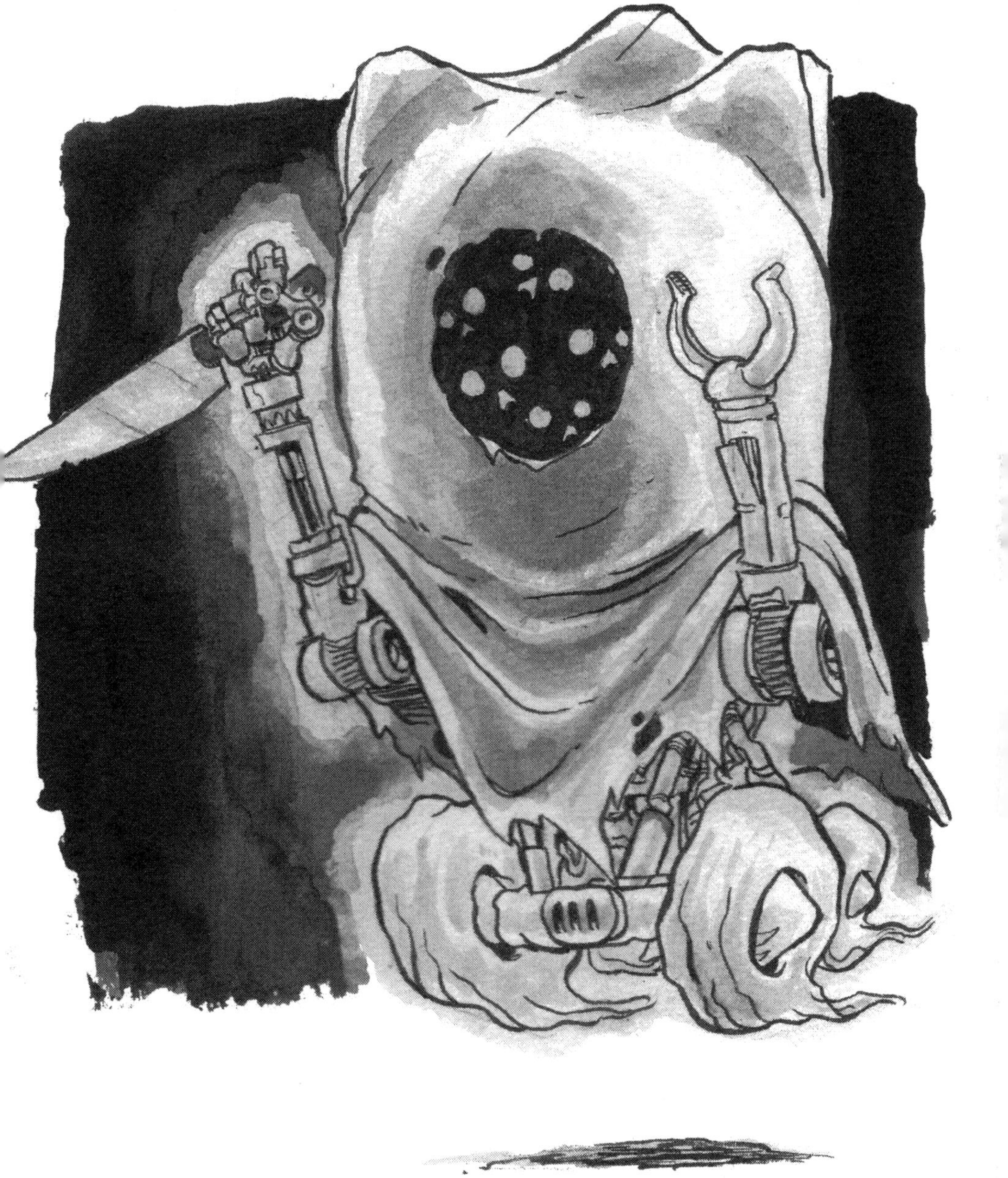

SUBJECT:
THE BEAST OF TWELFTH STREET

DATE: March 16, 1973

LOCATION: New York, New York

After the storm damaged the main building at Special Chemicals they said there was no risk of contamination, that the leak was contained. But something was affected, and it's not very happy.

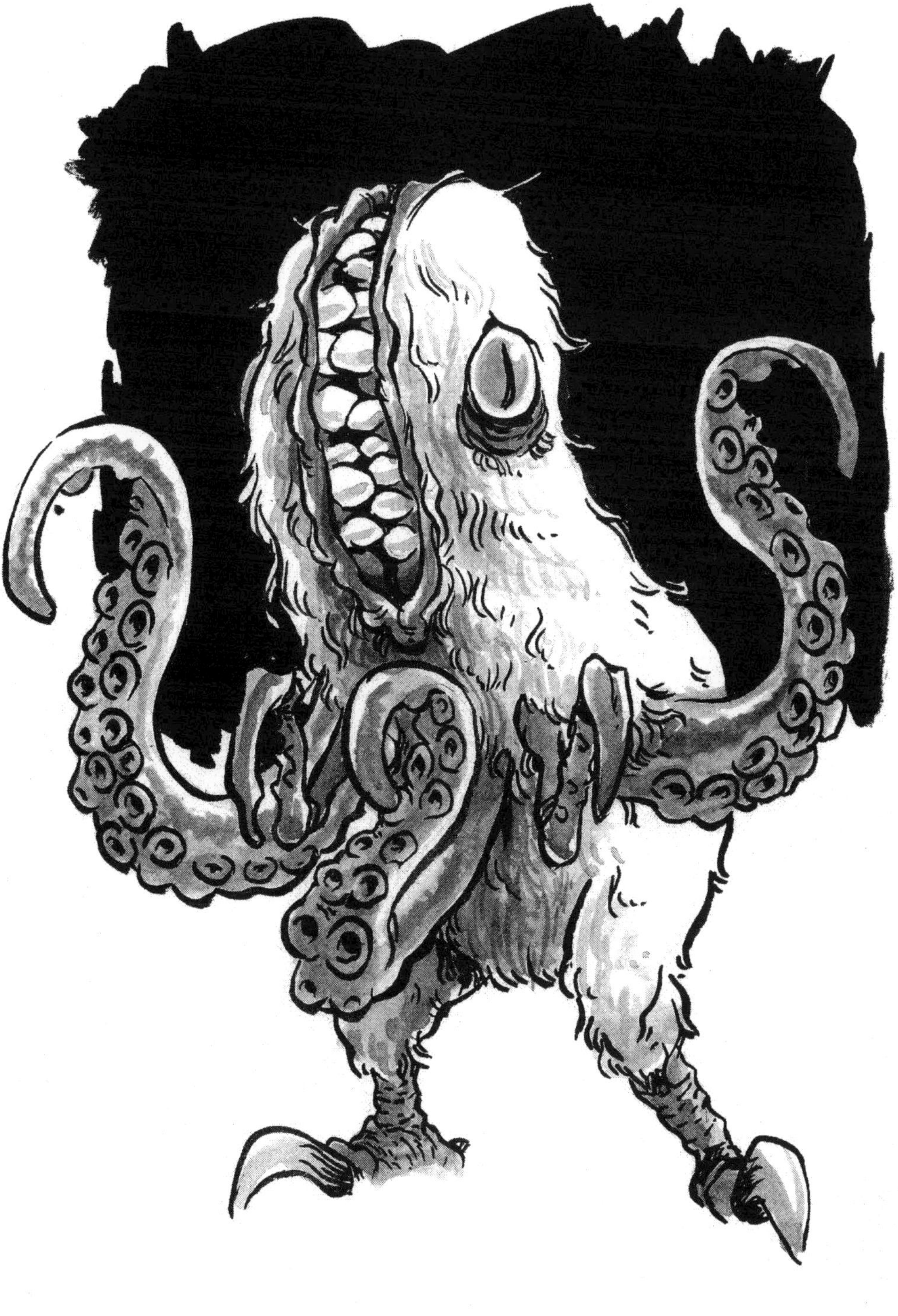

SUBJECT:
OL' SICKLEFOOT

DATE: 1832 – Present

LOCATION: Lake Sleed, Minnesota

It can be found in the woods near Lake Sleed, Minnesota. They say spotting it is good luck, which is strange since everyone who claims to have seen it has died due to wasting away within days of having claimed to have seen it.

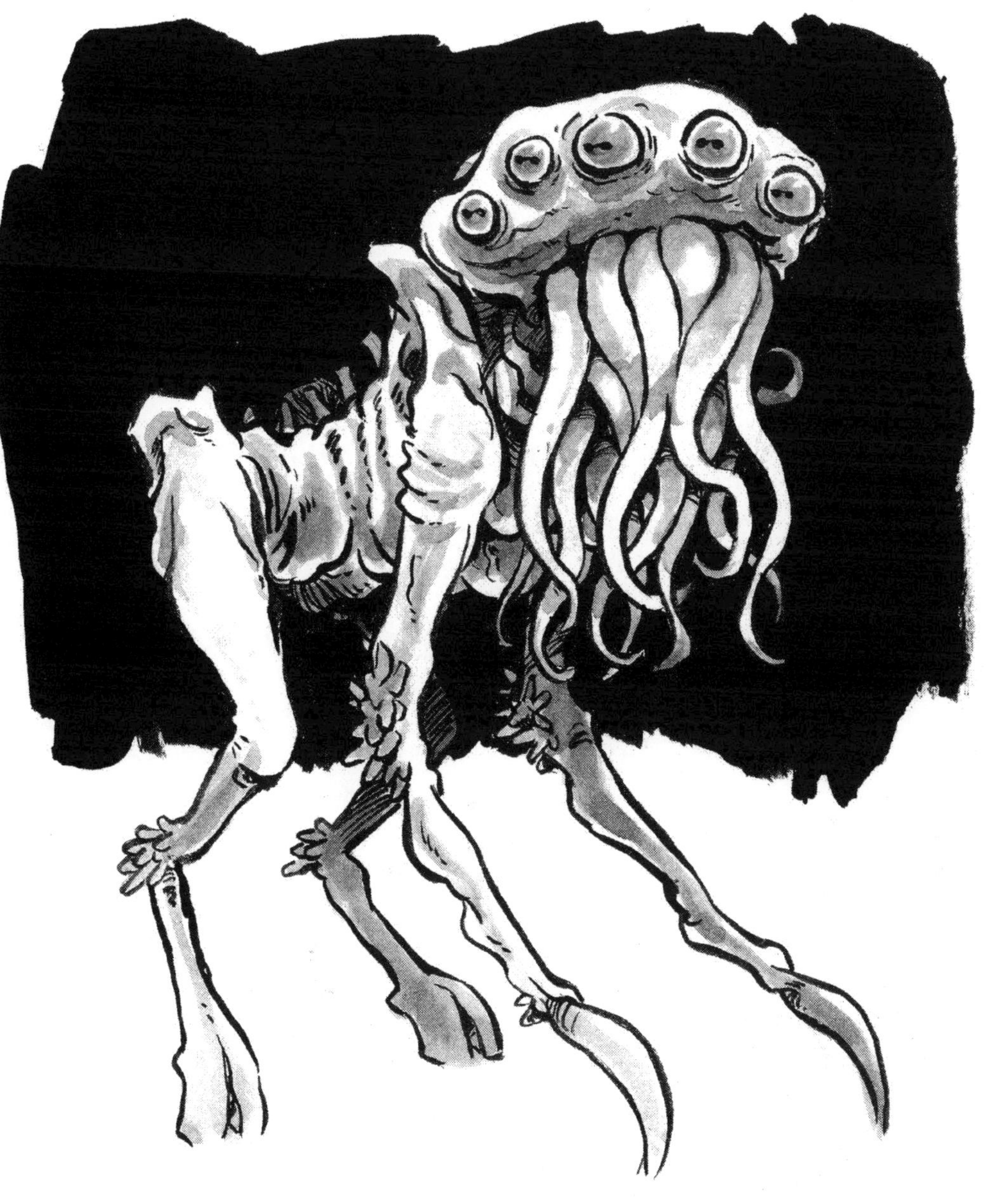

> **SUBJECT:**
> # THE SCREECH

DATE: 2019

LOCATION: Grant, Manitoba

There's an abandoned office block just off highway 15. Urban explorers who have entered it say that it's unnerving, there are no 90 degree angles anywhere in the building and all the signage is backward. Some people say you can see a figure lurking around on the 7th floor but nobody ever gets close enough to be sure it isn't just a trick of the light.

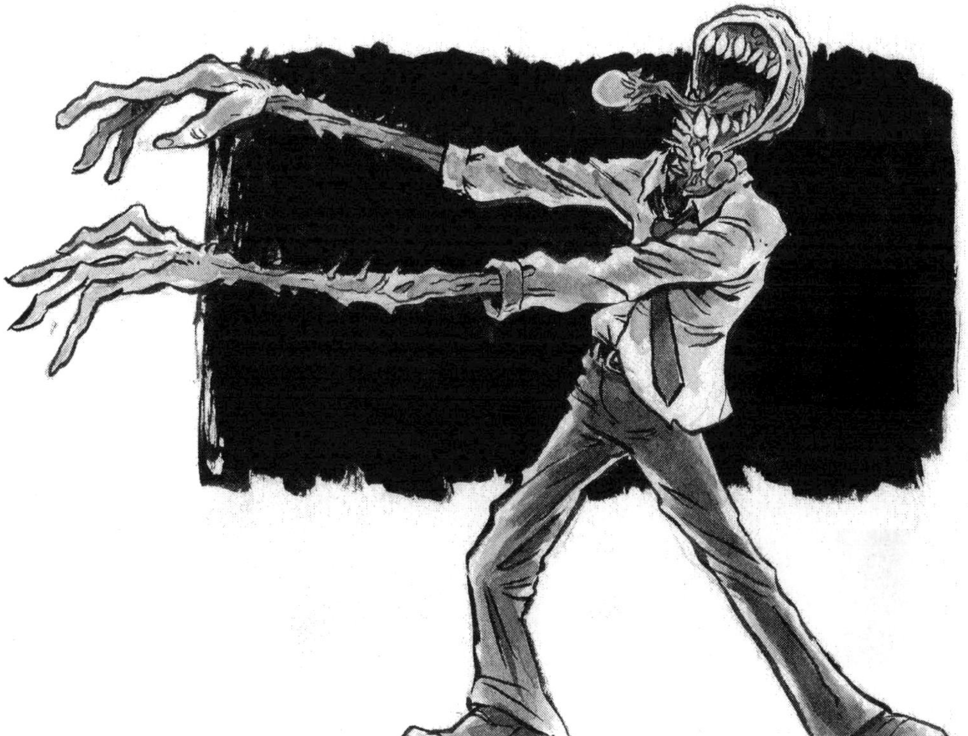

SUBJECT:
SKELETON GUY IN A ROBE

DATE: 1970s – 1990

LOCATION: Europe

Throughout the 1970s and into the 1980s a series of break-ins at museums and electronics stores baffled authorities, all attributed to a "weird skeleton guy in a robe." To this day nobody is sure what if anything was stolen in the break-ins or who the robed person was. Was it all a hoax?

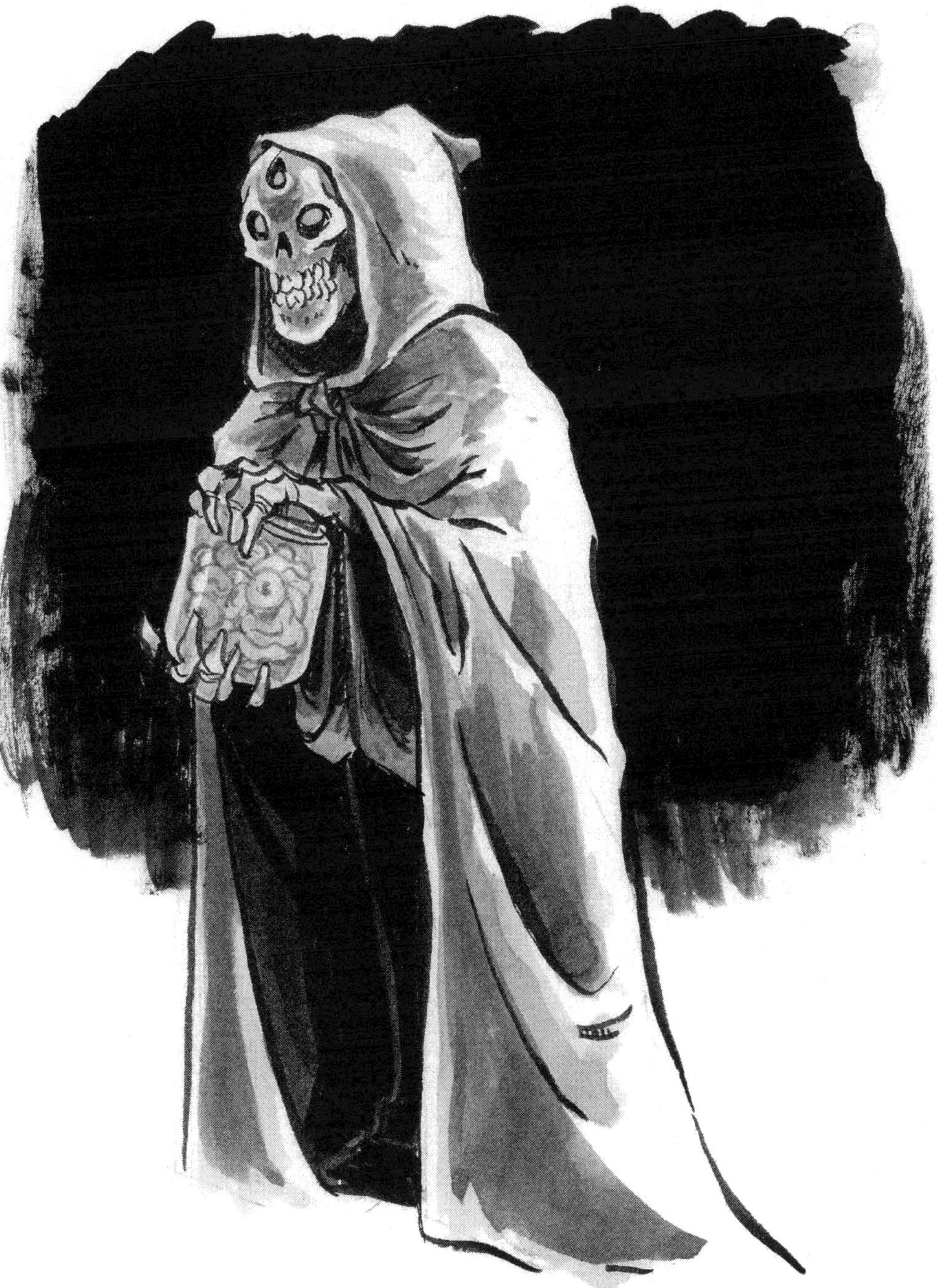

SUBJECT:
SLUG FACED MUGGER

DATE: April 29, 1988

LOCATION: Chunt, Kansas

Mike Robert George (38) was found suffering multiple stab wounds. He claimed he heard a voice ask for change, when he said he had none he was stabbed. He claimed he only got a brief glimpse of his assailant when it rummaged through his clothes taking his wallet, keys and anything else he had in his pockets.

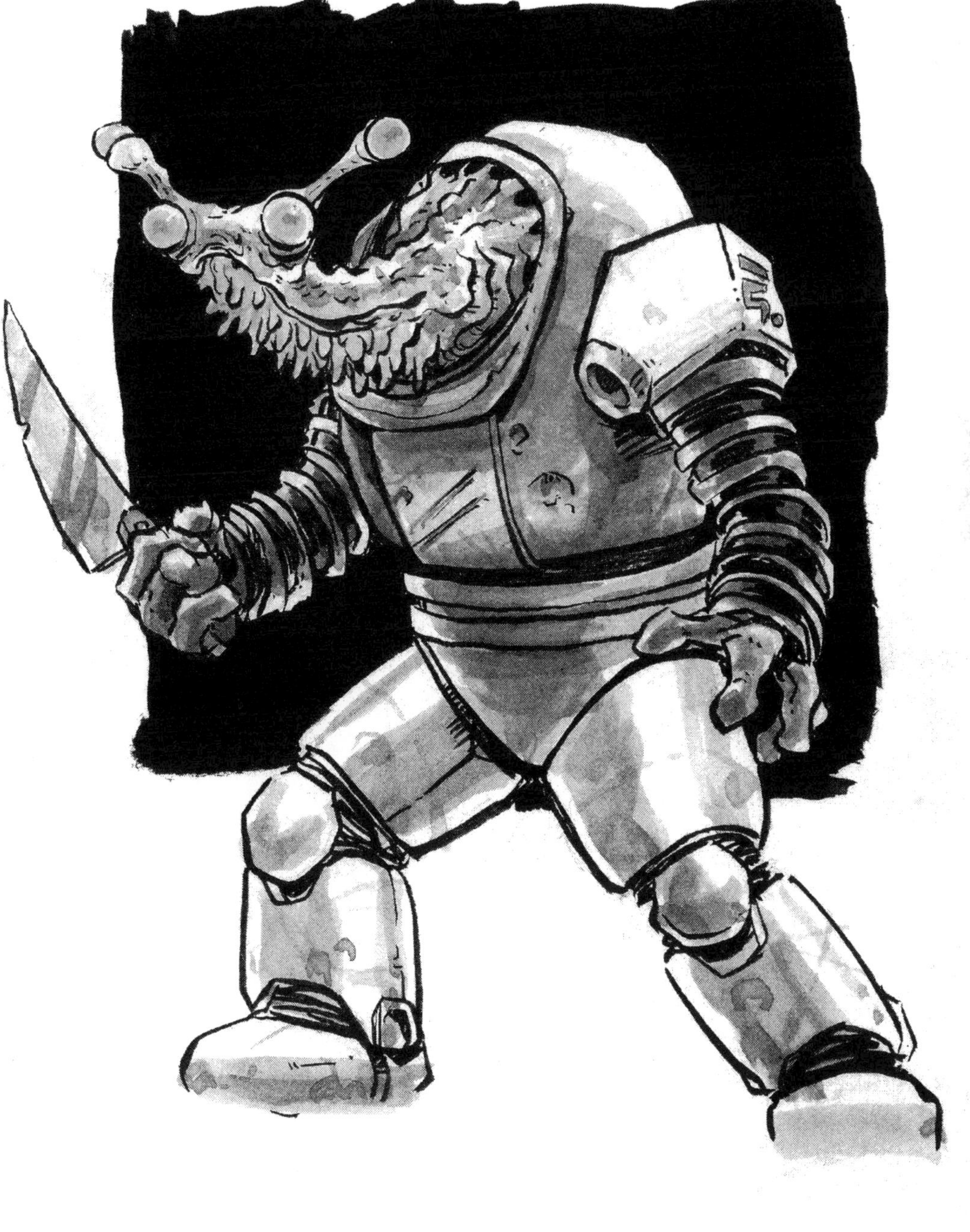

SUBJECT:
WORMFACE

DATE: 1643 — Present

LOCATION: Lake Superior

Seen in and around Lake Superior since 1643. People claim that it guards a treasure, unfortunately everyone who has seen it find themselves 50 to 100 km from where they first see it with no memory of how they got there or what they did.

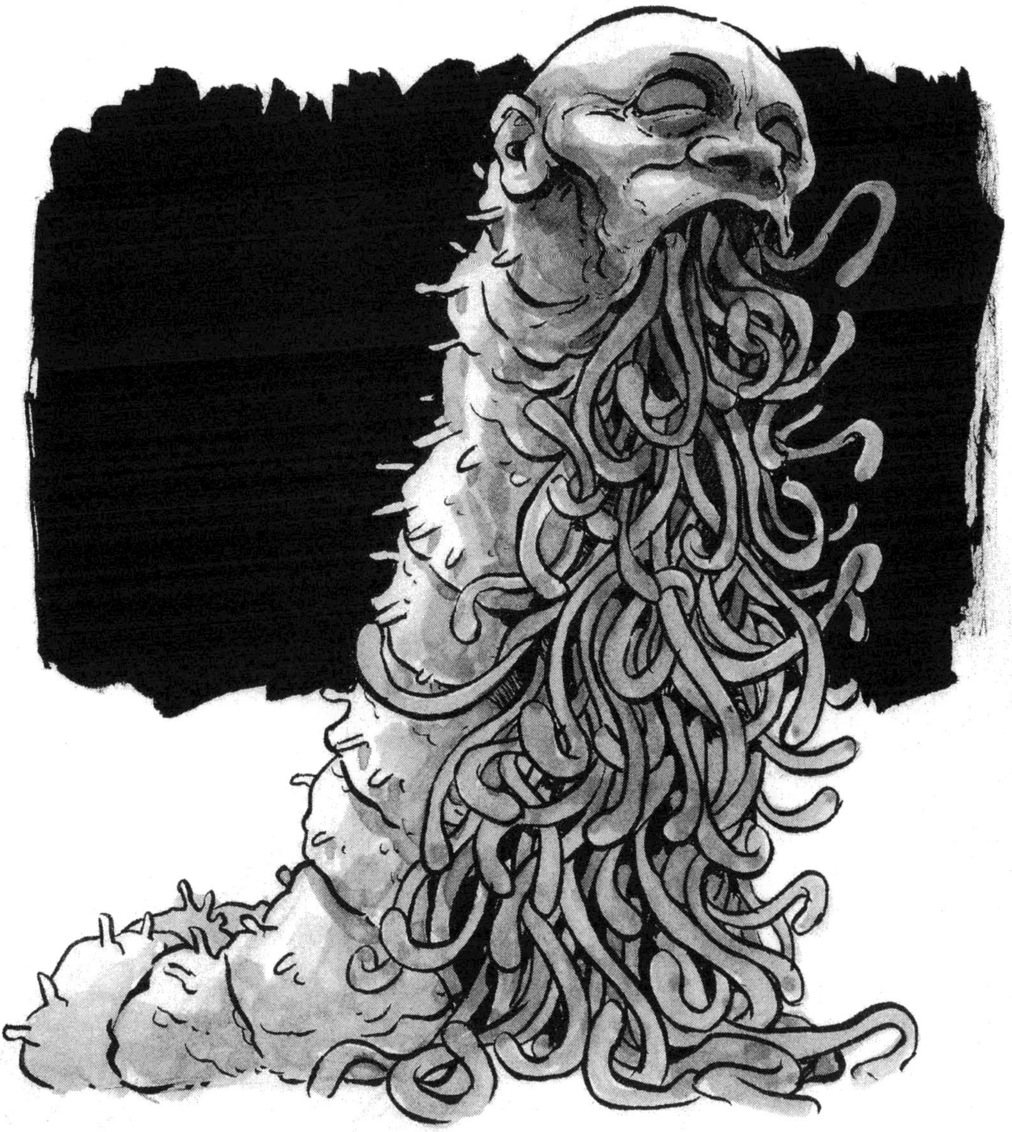

SUBJECT:
MUSH-HEAD JOE

DATE: June 8, 1958

LOCATION: Mt. Sugar, Pennsylvania

Kimberly "Kimmy" Daughtry (16) survives crashing her car into a tree suffering a broken wrist, the car is damaged beyond repair. Kimberly maintains she saw something "huge like a rhino" run across the road in front of her. She swerved to avoid it losing control of her car. The animal then rammed the car twice and then tore off the rear bumper before turning around and running back the way it had came. No sign of the bumper was found.

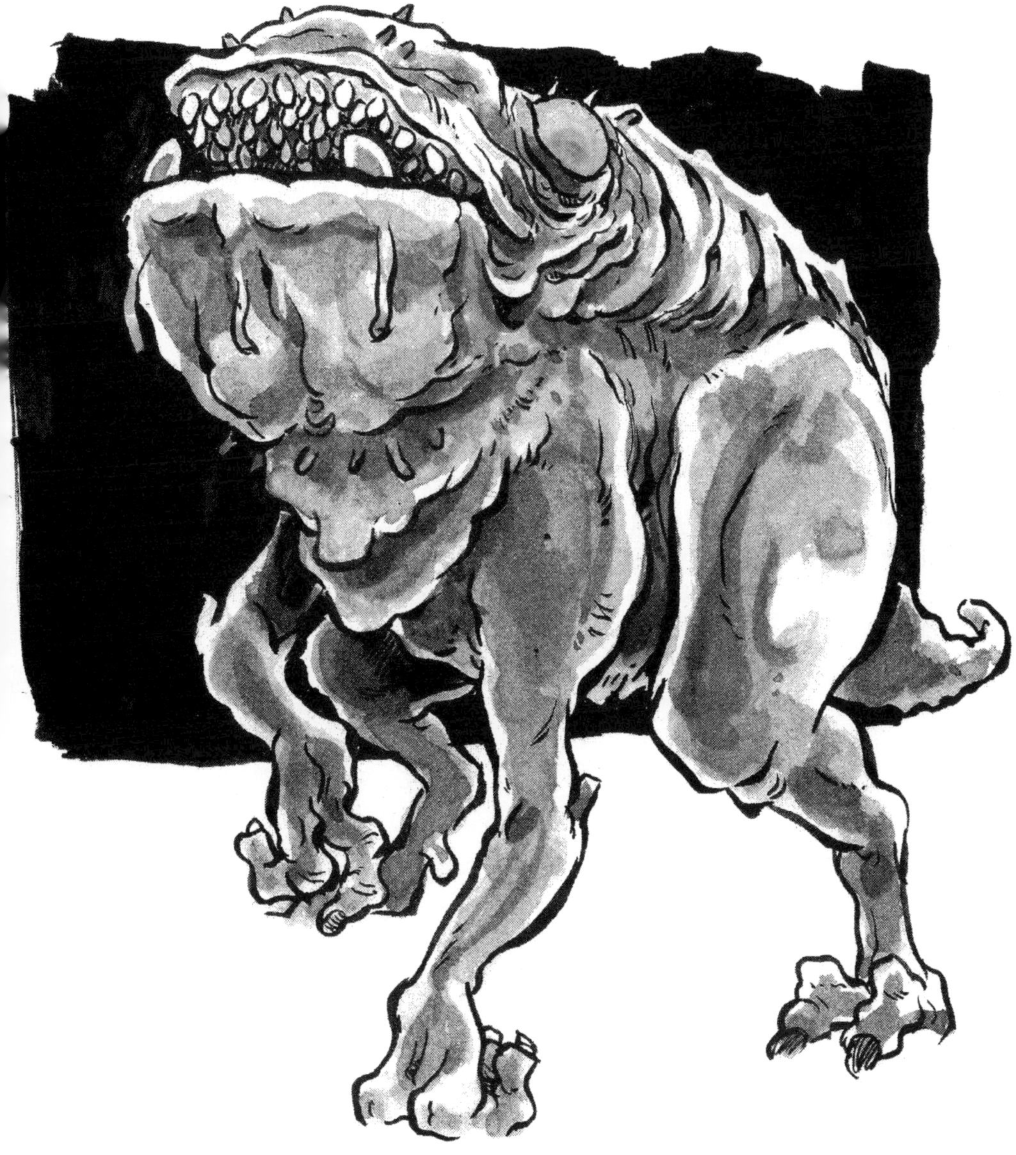

SUBJECT:
WOMANTIS

DATE: 1982

LOCATION: World wide

There have been sightings of a giant insect that appears to be half human. It is said that it only attacks men. Strangely most of its victims appear to have been involved in criminal activity, sometimes as minor as littering.

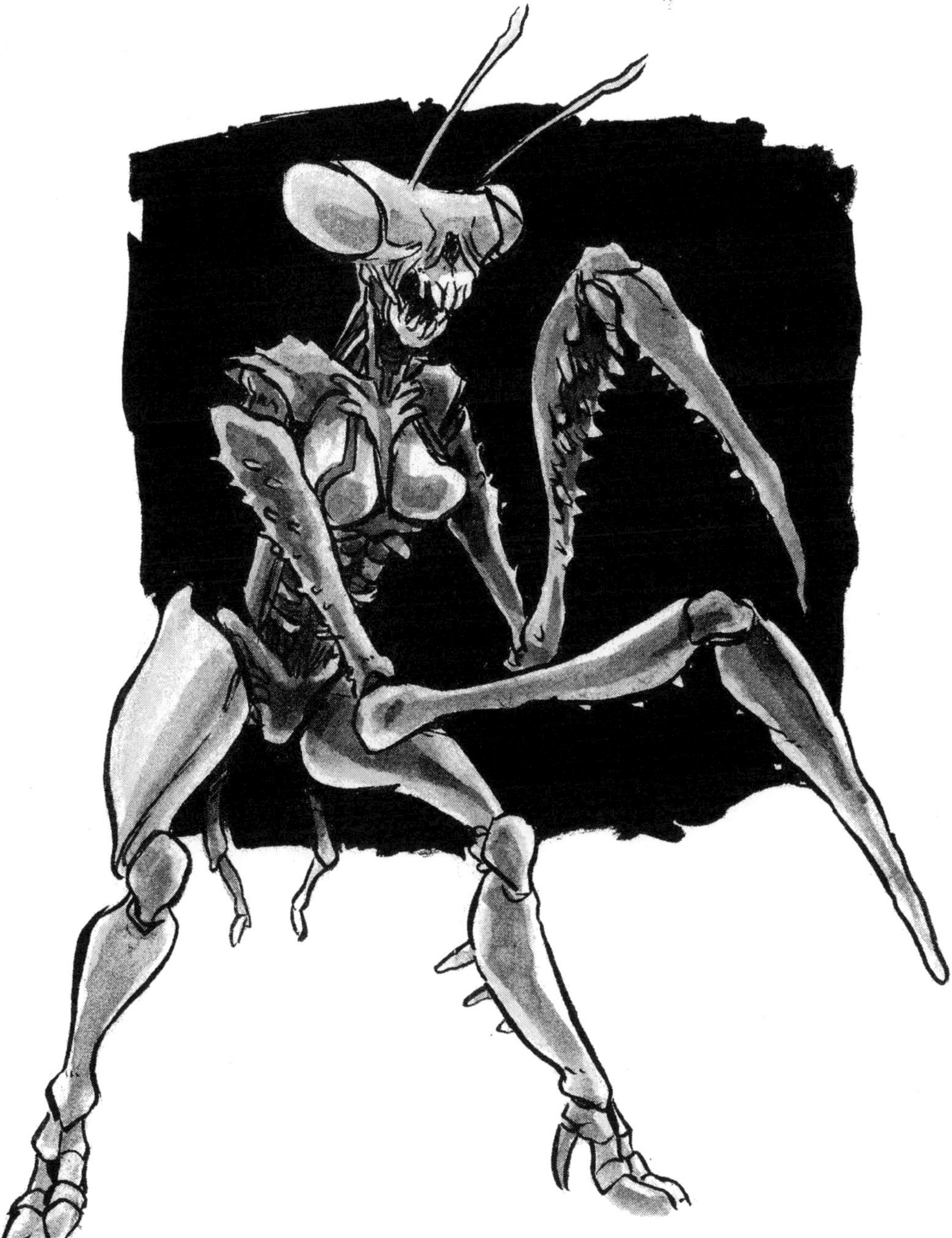

SUBJECT:
HOOK HANDED HORROR OF HAUNTED HILL

DATE: 1900 – Present

LOCATION: New York State and Ontario

They call it "The Hook Handed Horror of Haunted Hill." I spotted it on the weekend wandering around the woods in Niagara region. It seemed shy and ran deeper into the woods so I quickly lost sight of it. Not sure if it really deserves the "horror" part of its nickname, but it is pretty big, maybe 8', and really ugly.

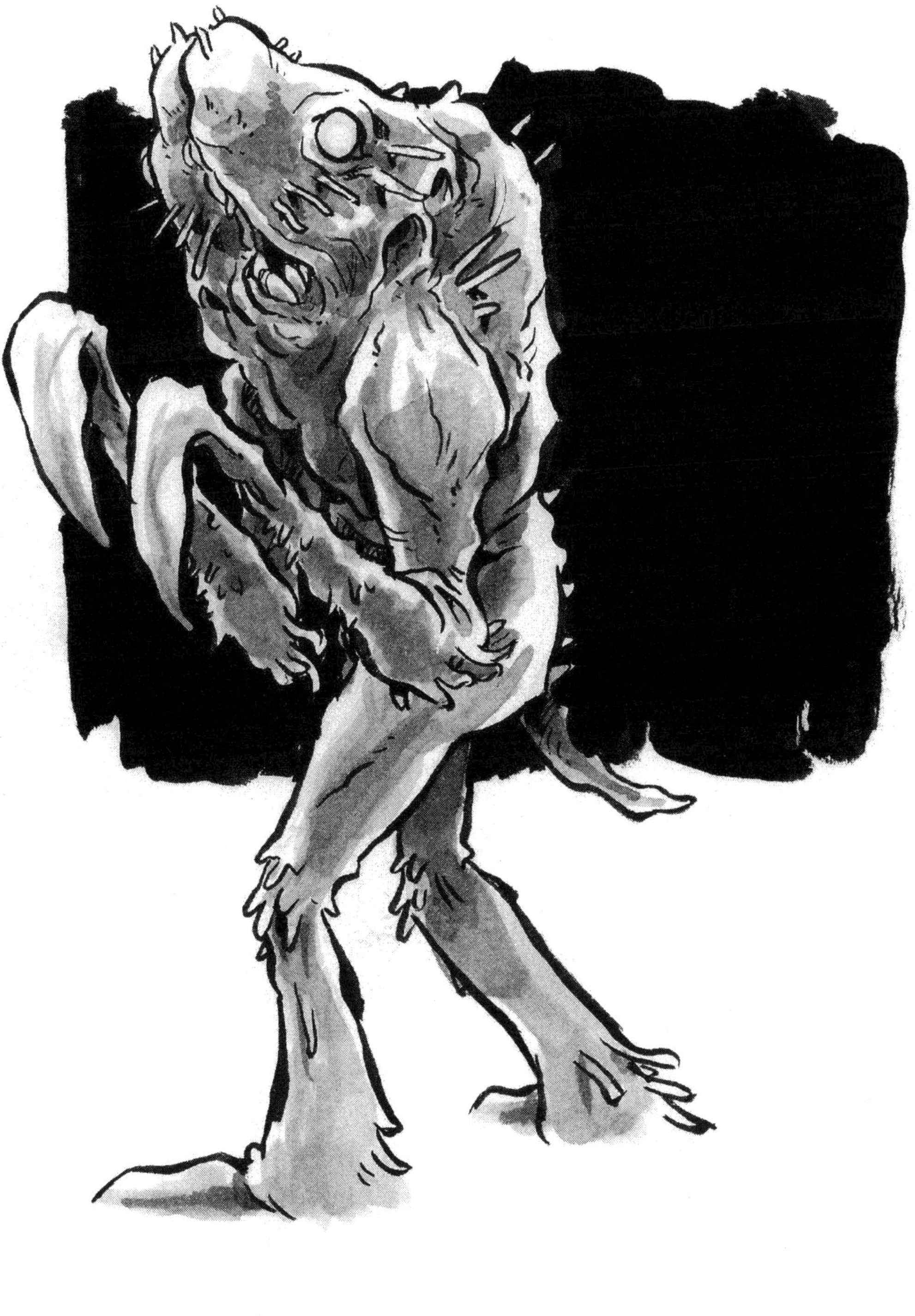

SUBJECT:
UNKNOWN

DATE: June 8, 2018

LOCATION: Kingsville, Alberta

June 8, 2018 12:30am. Kingsville fire department responds to a call for a house on fire at 175 Pictman Lane. When they arrive they hear shots fired from inside. A voice from inside, assumed to be Professor Argyle, a history teacher at the local high school and owner of the property, demands the Fire department leave the area and "mind your own business." Two volunteer fire fighters are than wounded by gunfire as they approach the building. More shouting and gun fire from inside the building is heard as the fire intensifies. Police arrive and are also fired upon and told to leave. A stand off ensues as the building, now fully engulfed in flames, continues to burn. 1:15 am, three individuals escape the burning building, they are taken into custody by the police and appear to be suffering from minor burns and other injuries and one individual has a broken arm. By 2am the house has been completely destroyed by the fire. During the subsequent investigation the remains of ten bodies are found through out the house. There are reports an eleventh body was found in the basement. Some people claim that the remains were not human.

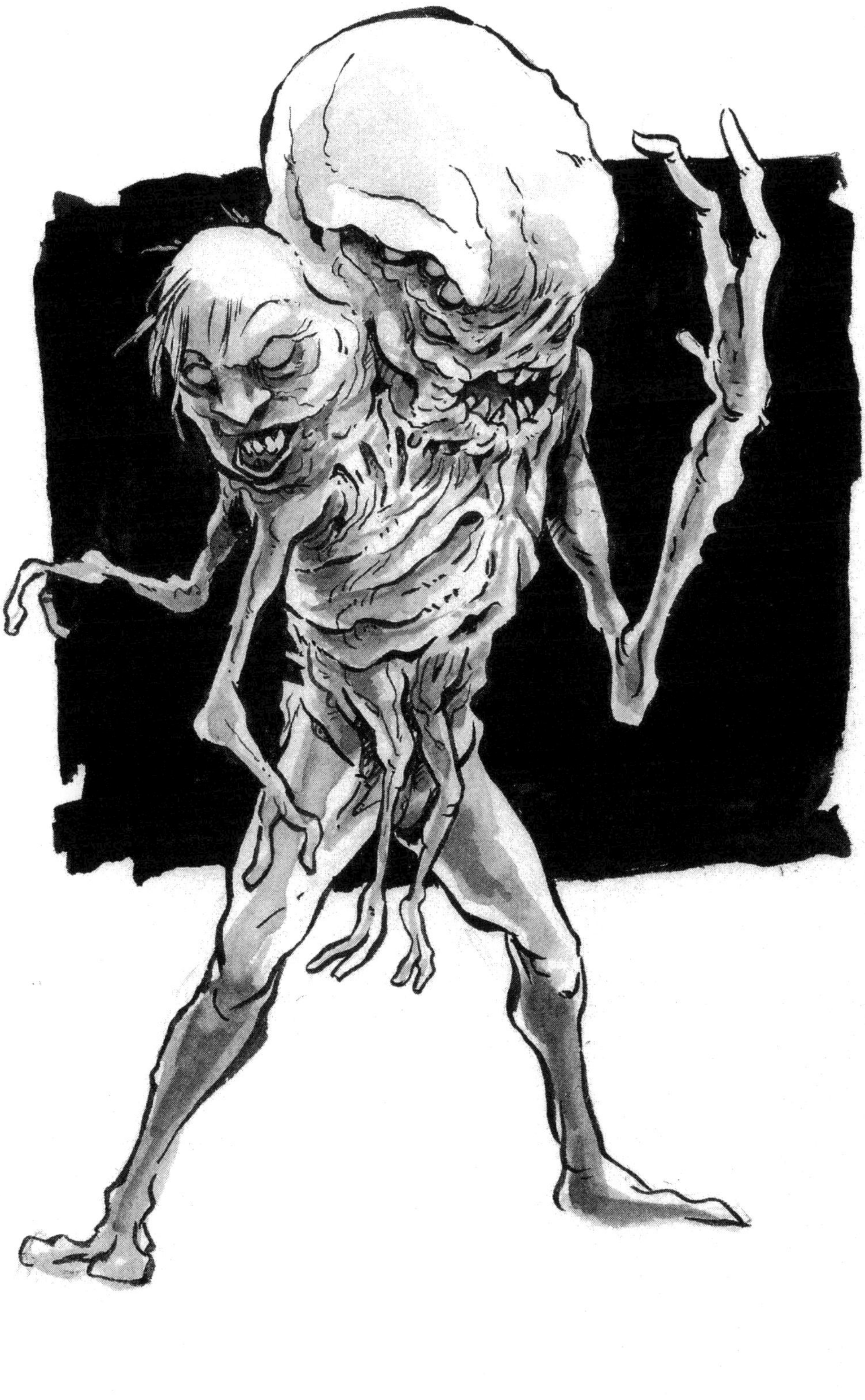

SUBJECT:
OGDEN WEREWOLF

DATE: 1946

LOCATION: Summerville, Oregon

During the summer of 1946, Graham Ogden reported something attacking the livestock on his farm. In September of that year Graham was committed to an asylum and the attacks on the livestock stopped. Was this a coincidence?

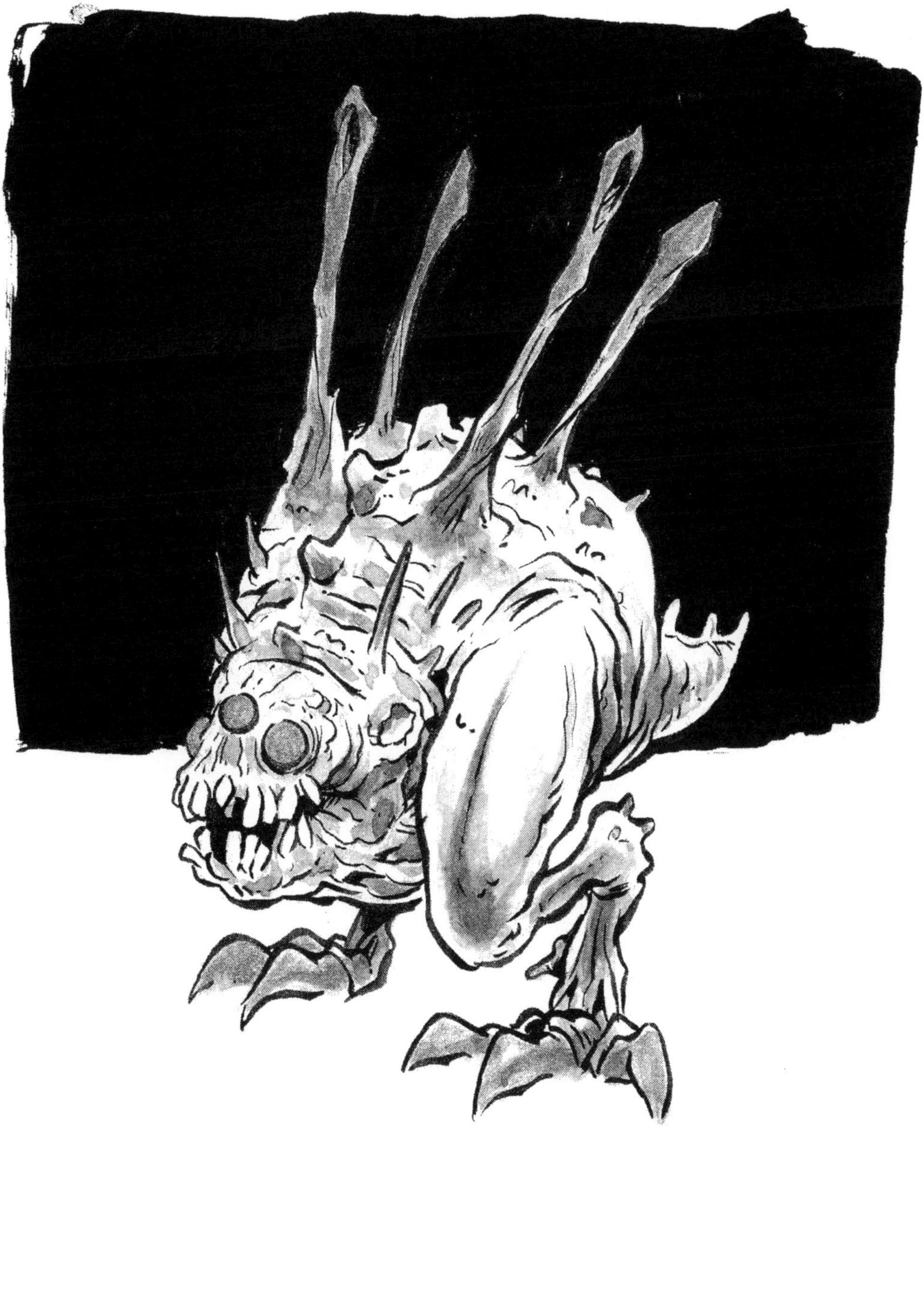

SUBJECT:
FOREST VALLEY LAKE MONSTER

DATE: June 13, 1974

LOCATION: Greenhill, New Hampshire

June 1974, police are called Camp Forest Valley counsellor training camp. They arrive to a scene of carnage. The sole survivor claimed they were attacked by something that came from the lake.

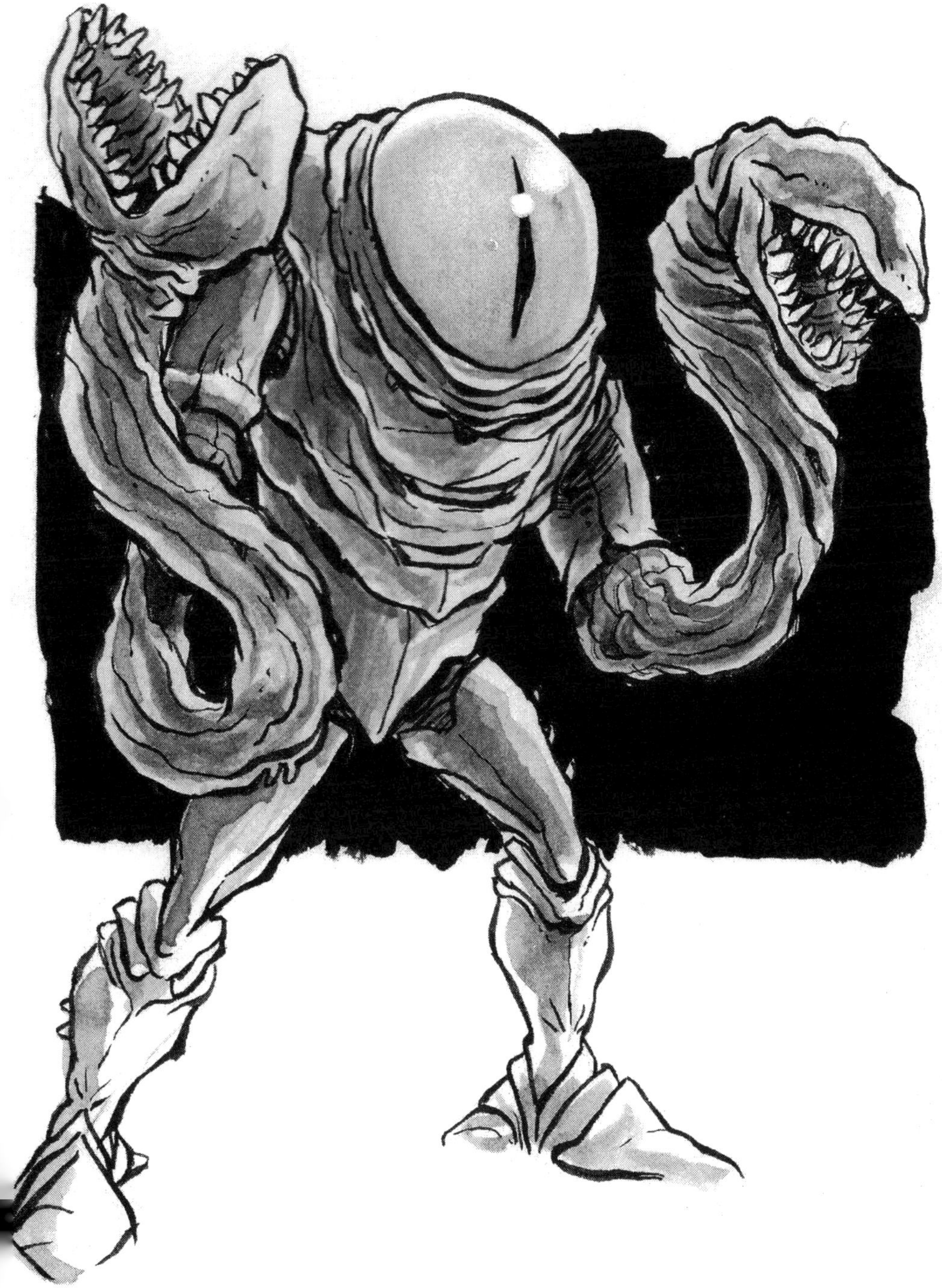

SUBJECT:
YOSEMITE SHAMBLER

DATE: May 12, 1989

LOCATION: Yosemite National Park, California

May 12, 1989 the Nelson Family disappears while on vacation in Yosemite National Park. In 2006, a group of hikers find the rusted remains of the family's station wagon, a video camera is found inside the car. After analyzing the tape fellow monsterologist Trevor Henderson discovered a sequence that appears to show a strange not quite human shape caught in the vehicles headlights he made the image public on his social media feed. The Nelson family is still missing. Mr. Henderson has a series of images from strange video cassettes on his feed, I'd suggest you check it out.

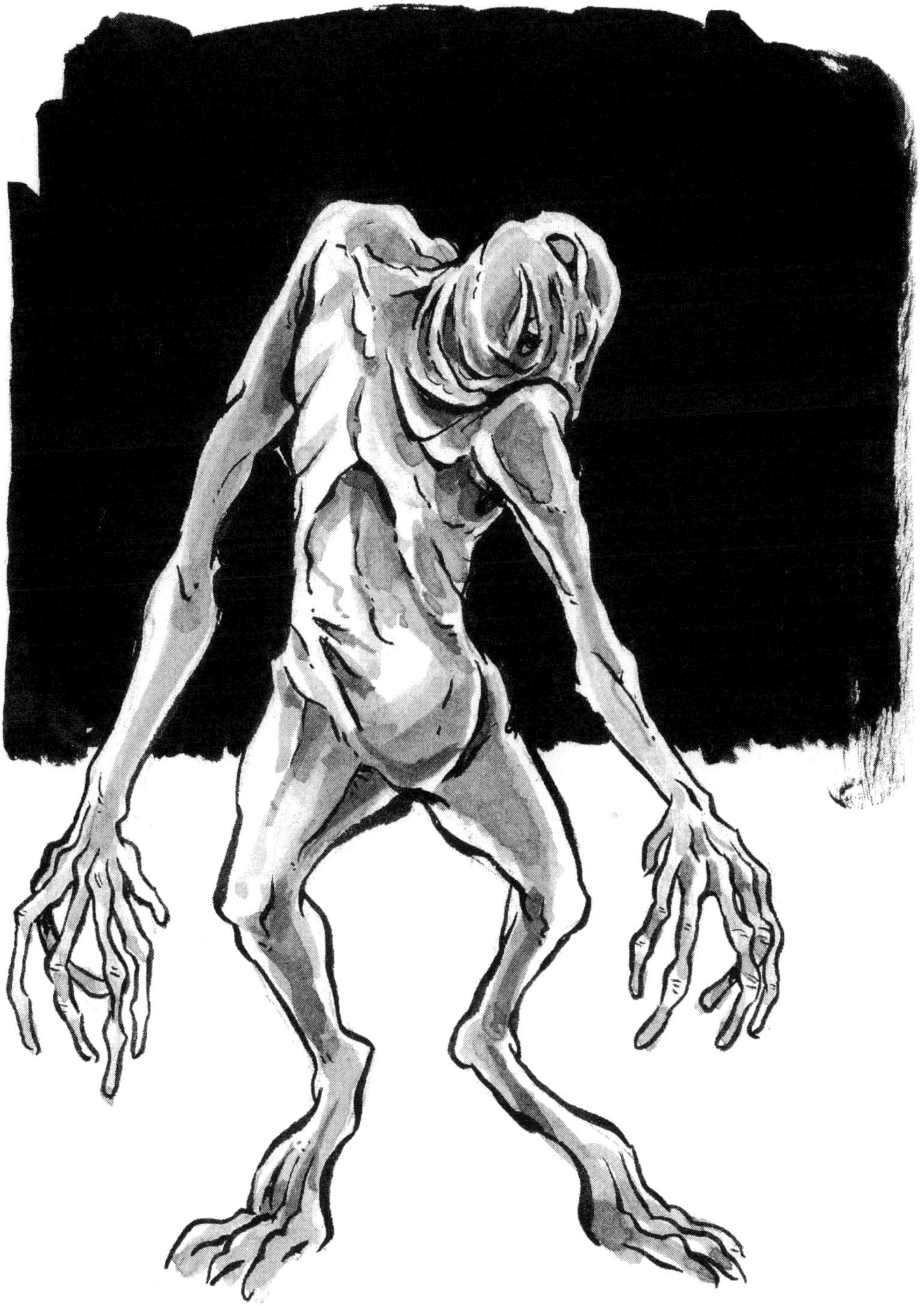

SUBJECT:
CHESTER

DATE: March 3, 1963 — Present

LOCATION: Whilchester, New Jersey

People claim to have seen something moving around in the tunnels under the abandoned North Whilchester Veteran's Hospital. Nobody knows why the hospital was abandoned, but it's been the focus of rumours and legends since it's construction in 1896. The most consistent rumours focus on the evening of March 3rd, 1963 when a meteor landed in Stephen's lake and the residents of the surrounding area were mysteriously rendered unconscious. Those residents were taken to NWVH for treatment. They say the meteor was also taken to that hospital for study

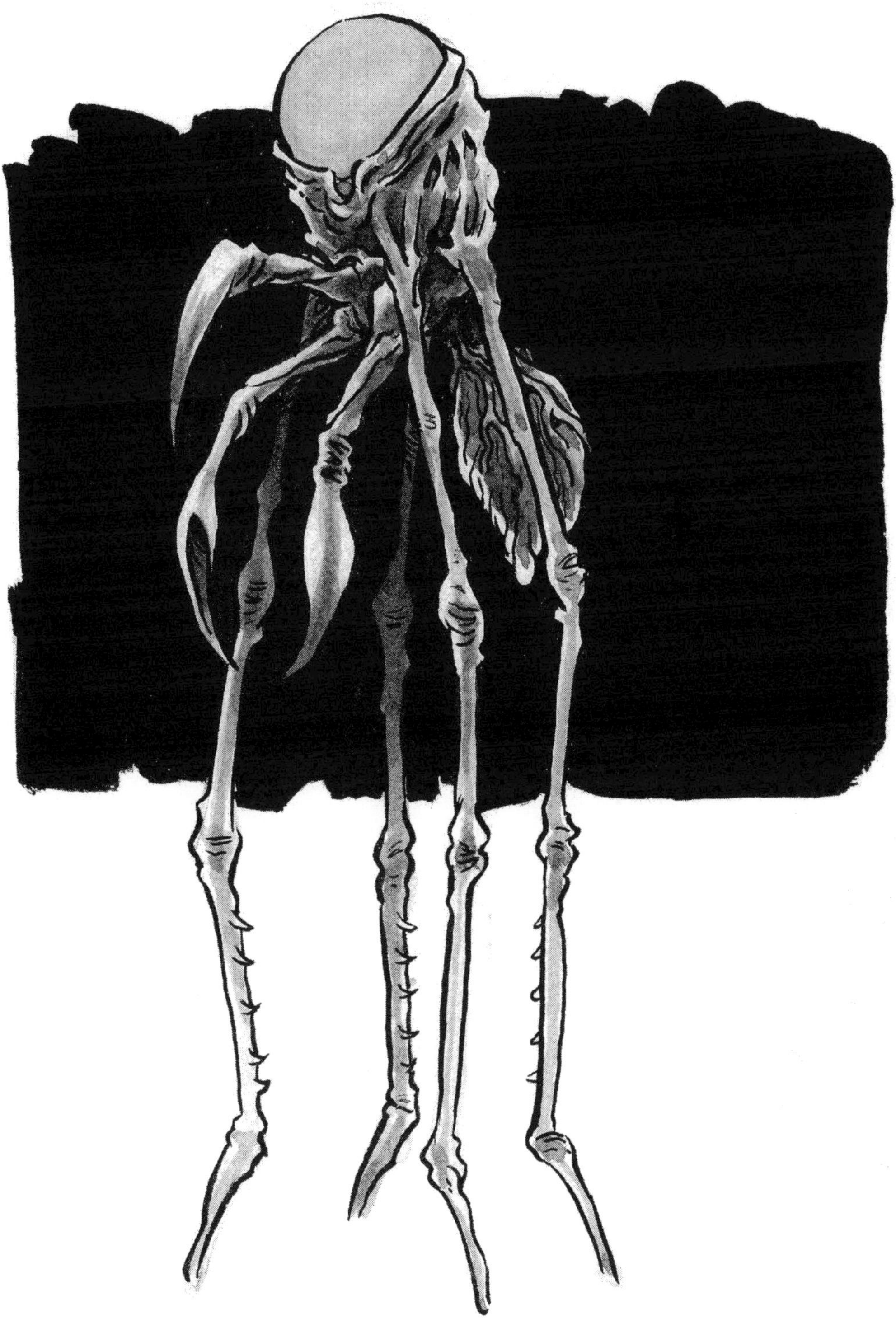

SUBJECT:
MILLER'S LAWN INVADER

DATE: October 31, 1939

LOCATION: Miller's Lawn, Ontario

The residents of Miller's Lawn, Ontario are thrown into a panic when the local radio station interrupts its regular broadcast to present a story that claims the station is under siege by horrific monsters. The broadcast ends when the station goes off the air at 11:30 that night. When the station doesn't come back the following morning, people go to investigate. They find the broadcast antenna destroyed and the staff of the station missing. While there is no official report as to what happened, many believe there was a government cover-up. Popular opinion is that it was just another "War of the Worlds hoax."

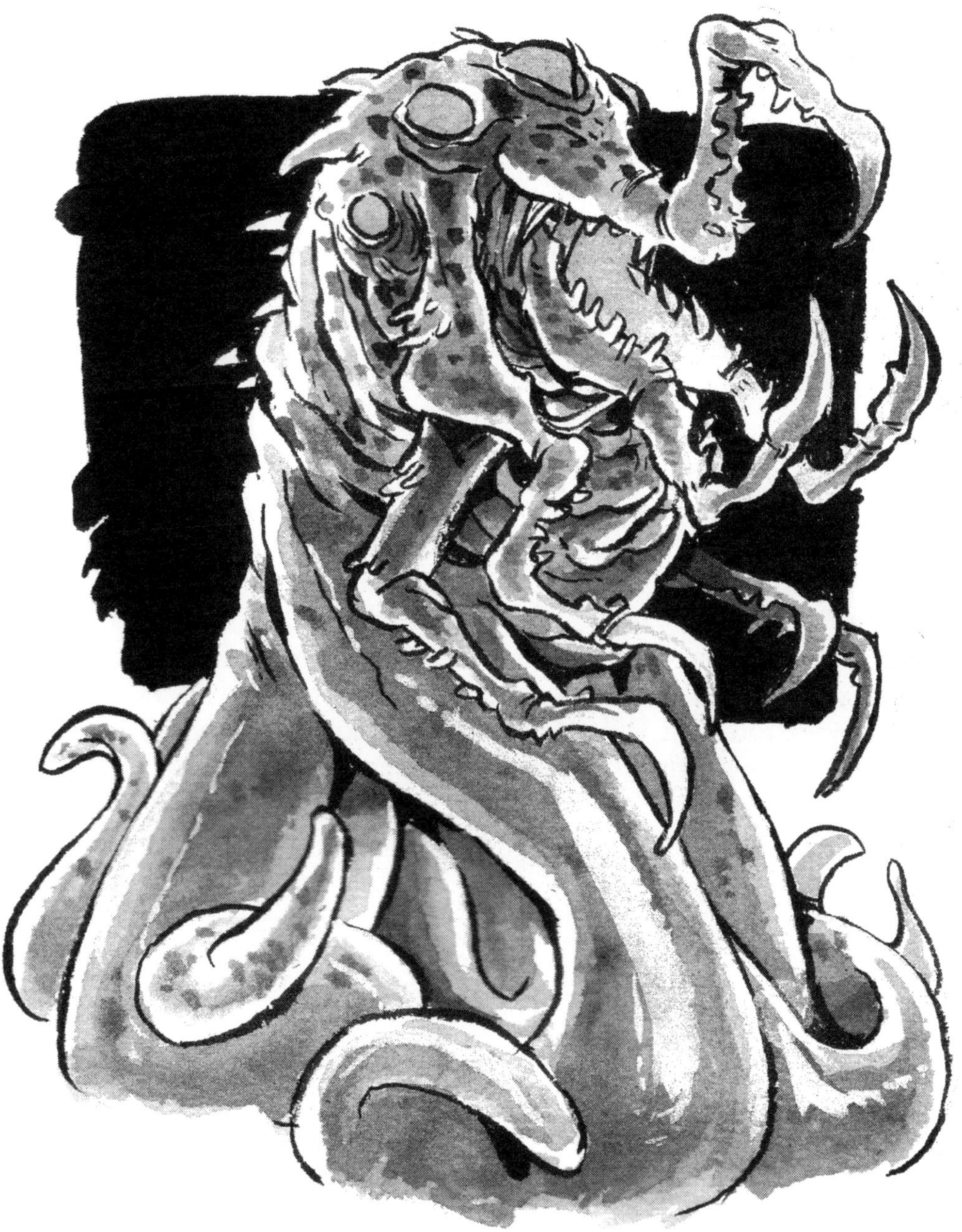

SUBJECT:
THE RAINMAN

DATE: June 23, 2018

LOCATION: Toronto, Ontario

During a sudden unexpected and intense thunderstorm people reported seeing a figure walking east on College street in Toronto, Ont. A few people claimed that when the figure looked at them they had strange hallucinations or visions, but they refused to elaborate on what these visions were. Many of these people have since sought psychological help to deal with intense manias and phobias they had no signs of before that day. Strangely, meteorologists insist no such rainstorm occurred at that time. People on neighbouring streets at the time also agree they did not experience any adverse weather

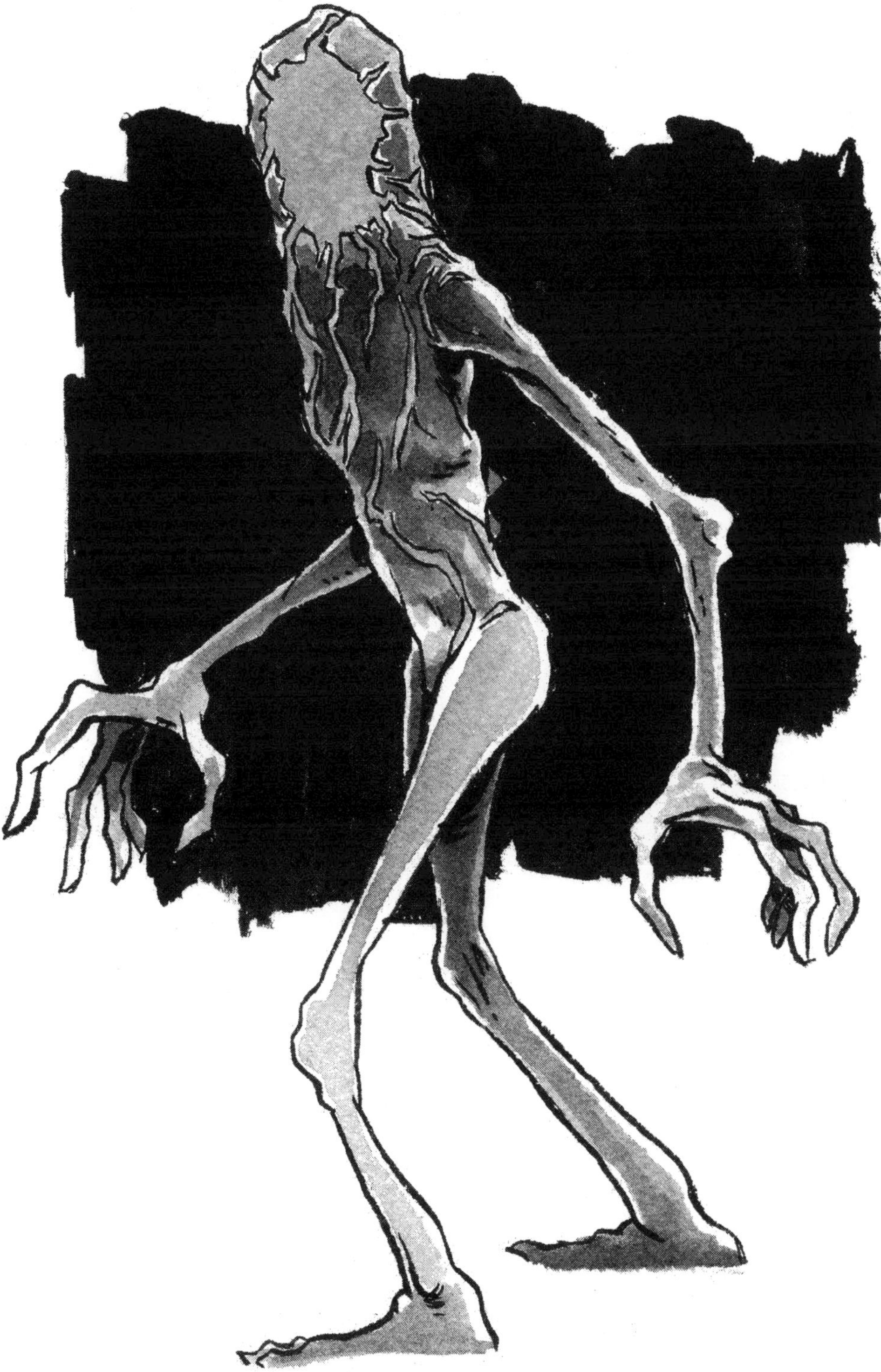

SUBJECT:
PINE VALLEY STALKER

DATE: 1792 – Present

LOCATION: Oakpines, Nebraska

They say something big lives out in Sherman Woods. Something that doesn't like visitors. Something that's intelligent. Most people think it's just a bear, those people are wrong.

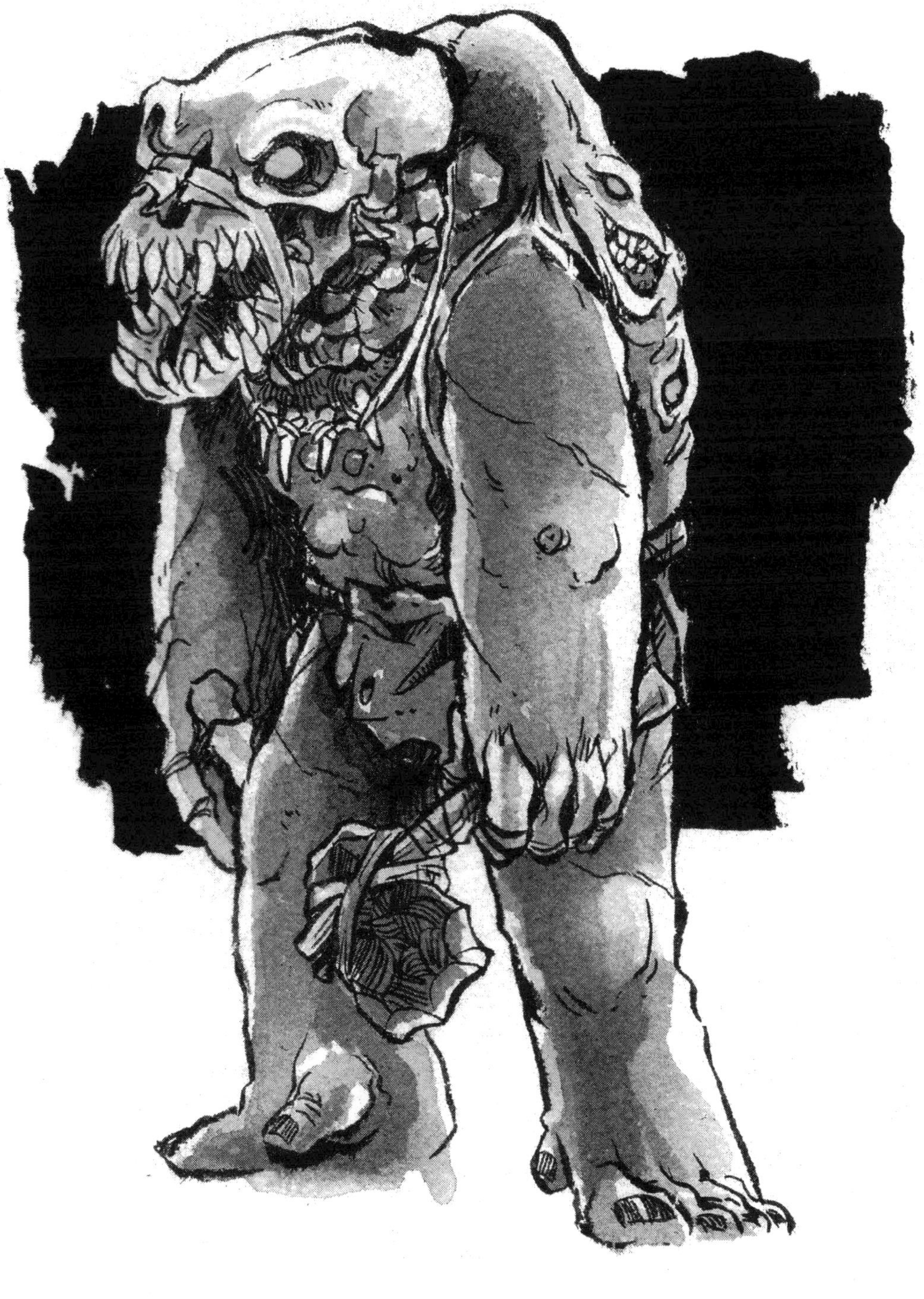

SUBJECT:
Glome the Belligerent

DATE: July 23, 1987

LOCATION: Heaven, Vermont

On July 23, 1987, while camping in Prescott Forest, Patrick Deacon (45) says he was harassed by a demon who claimed camping was illegal in that section of the woods. When he refused to leave the demon branded him with the mark of p'Laquin. Since nobody knows what that is, his family and friends assume Patrick just got drunk and cut his forehead after falling down while he was camping.

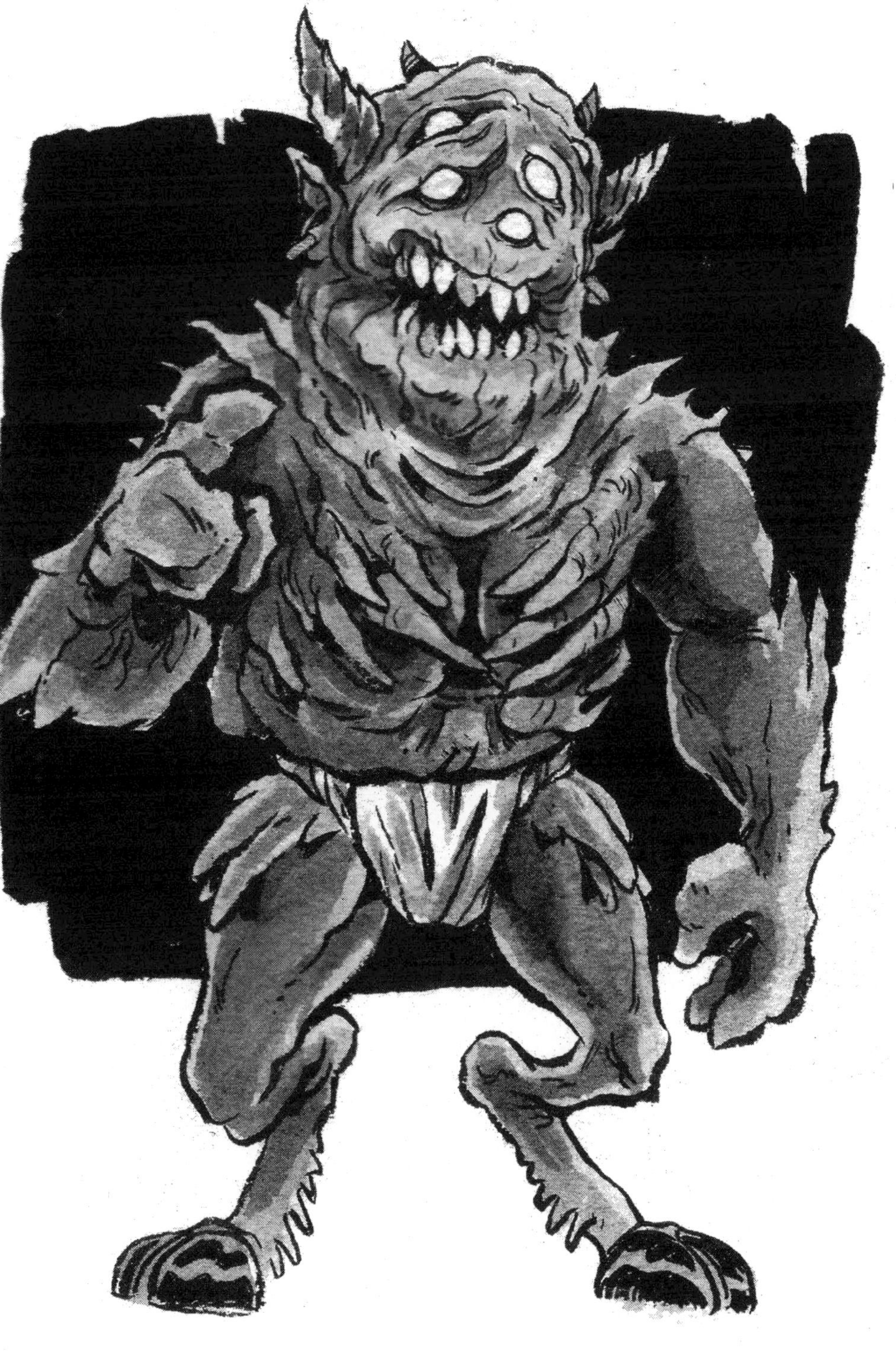

SUBJECT:
[REDACTED]

DATE: Unknown — Present

LOCATION: Niagara Falls, Ontario

They say if you stand near the base of Niagara Falls and call its name eight times, [redacted] will appear and do your bidding for 8 days, 8 hours, 8 minutes, 8 seconds. If a task you assign it takes more than that amount of time [redacted] will absorb you. If it finishes everything you tell it to do before the end of the time limit, [redacted] will absorb you.

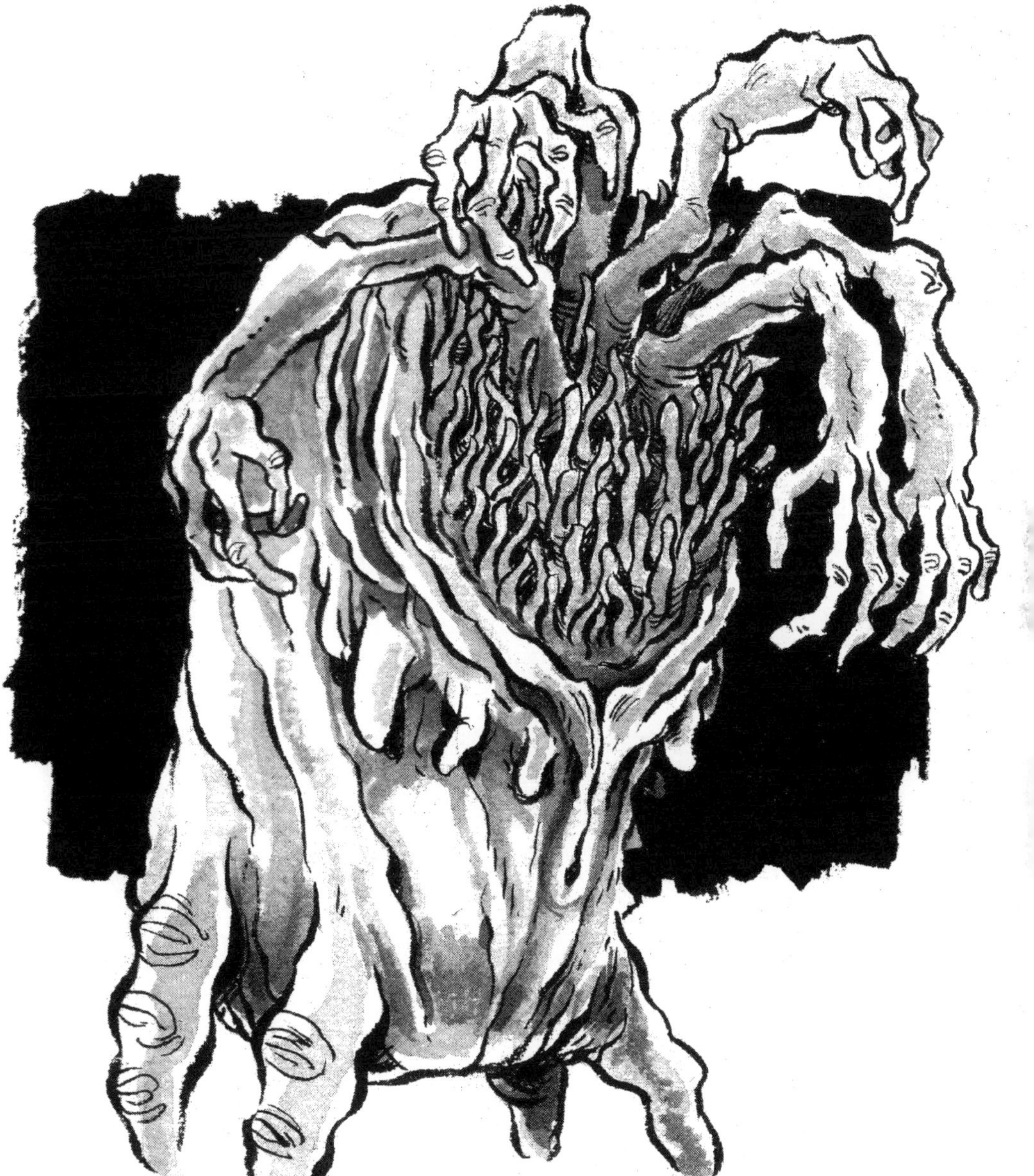

SUBJECT:
THE FRANKLIN BAY MERMAID

DATE: 2019

LOCATION: Savepoint, Maine

People say they've seen something around the lighthouse near Franklin Bay. Caretaker Jimpson denies there's anything to see.

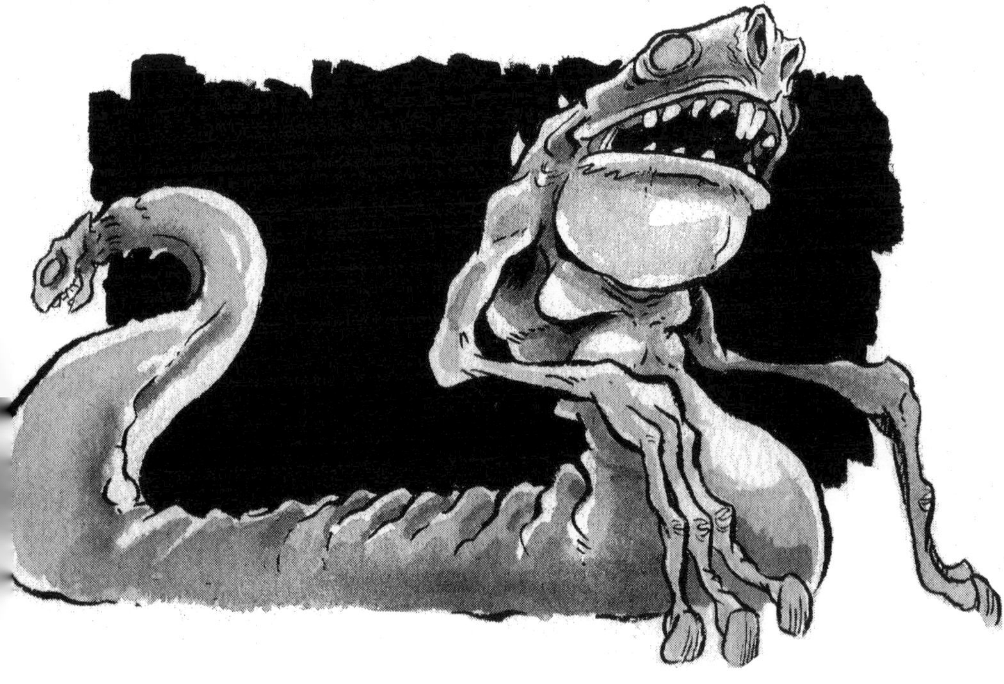

SUBJECT:
RICKTON RICK

DATE: 2012 — Present

LOCATION: Rickton, Maine

In the town of Rickton people have been seeing what they have believed to be a homeless person wandering the streets, picking through trash, things of that nature. They all say the person seems lost but tends to run away if anyone gets too close.

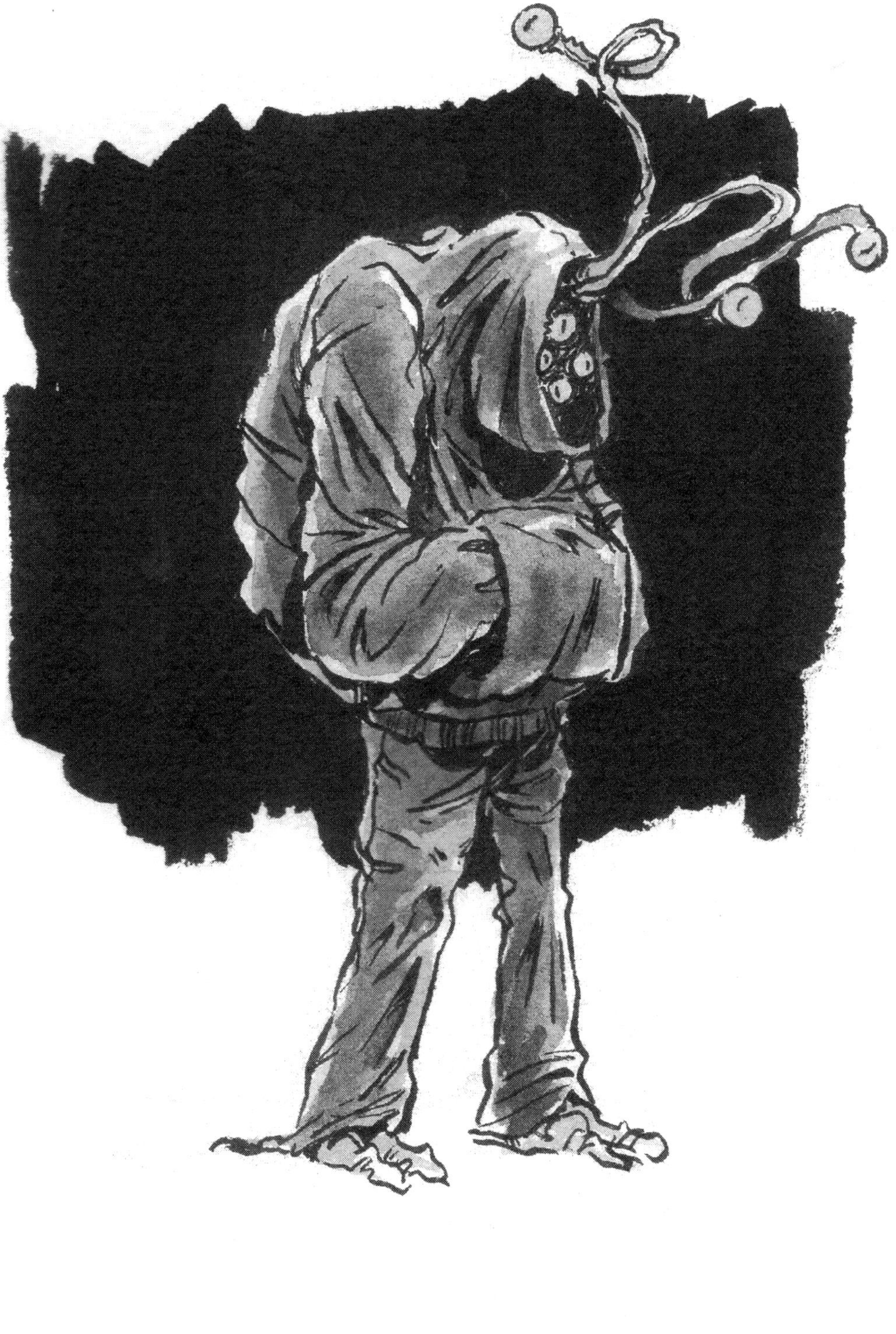

SUBJECT:
THE SUNDWICH TERROR

DATE: June 6, 2018

LOCATION: Sundwich, Massachusetts

On June 6, 2018 Thom D'amore (66) was in a single car accident on RR 145 near Sundwich. He claims that he had swerved to avoid hitting "this big weird thing" that was standing in the middle of the road. He maintains that this "thing" approached his car after he had hit a telephone pole and seemed to be making sure he was OK. Officials claim Mr. D'amore was drunk at the time of the accident, his wife claims this is impossible since Mr. D'amore has "never had even a sip of alcohol" as long as she has known him.

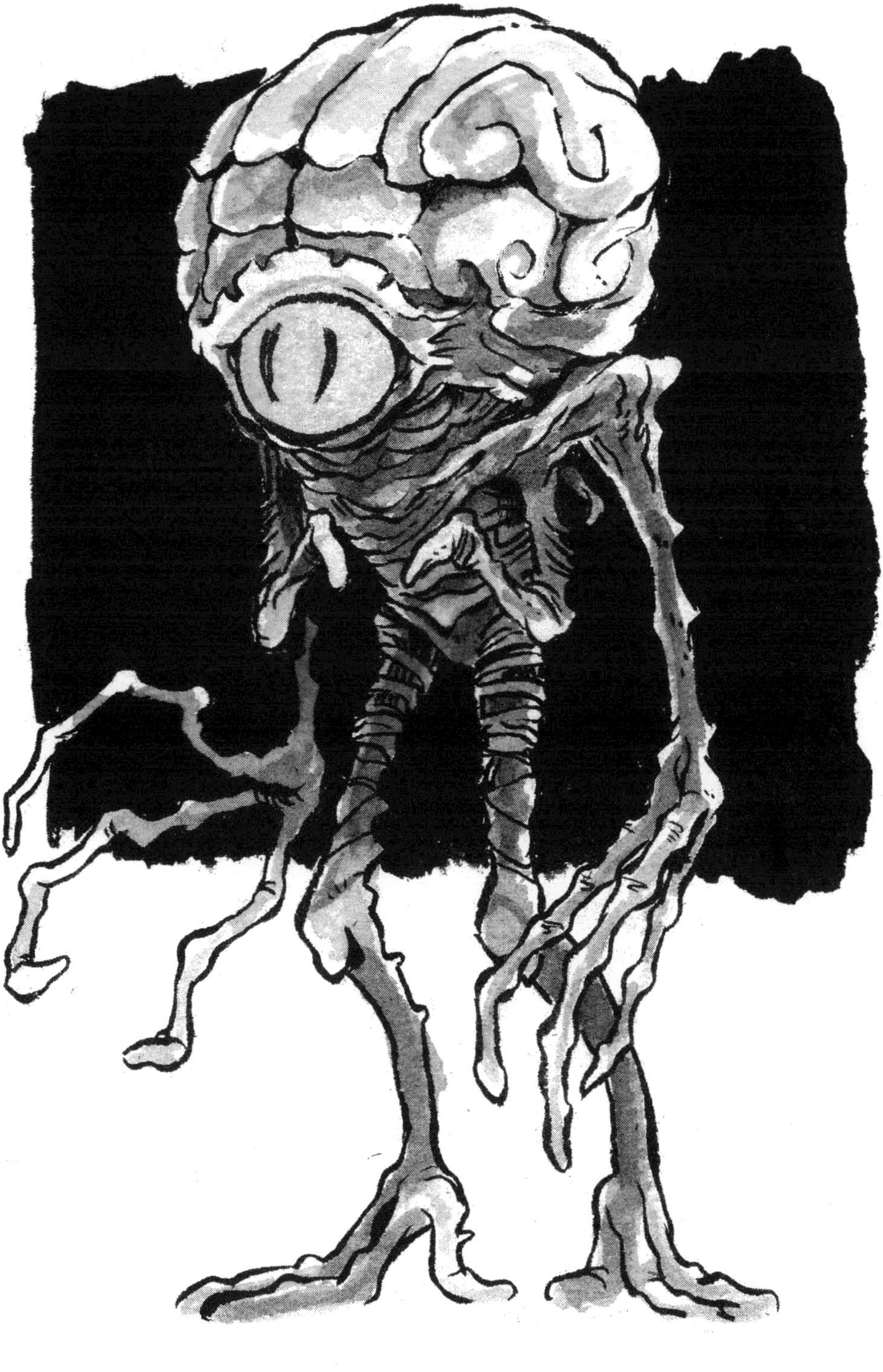

SUBJECT:
THE OAKVILLE MERMAN

DATE: June 22, 2018

LOCATION: Oakville, Ontario

Something washed ashore near Walker Street Promenade in Oakville, shortly after the area was closed to the public..

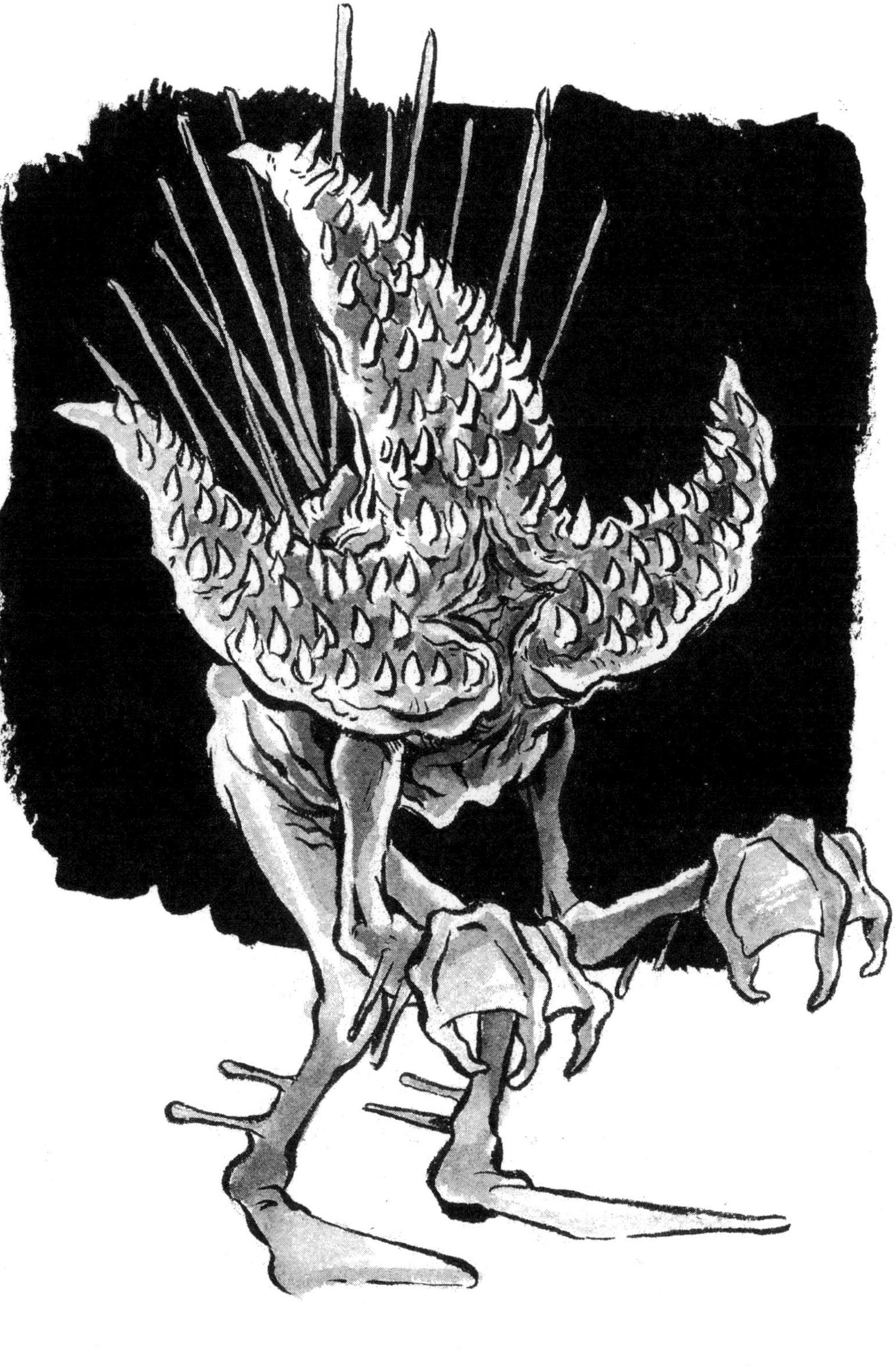

SUBJECT:
THE CRAB WITCH

DATE: 1999 – Present

LOCATION: Franklin Shore, Labrador

Starting in March 1999, the people of Franklin Shore have been reporting sightings of a large crab-like creature with a human face. They say that unlike a crab this thing seems entirely fleshy. Some of the stories say that people have been told where to find lost objects or people by the creature. Others claim that it eats people who spend either too much or not enough time fishing in certain areas.

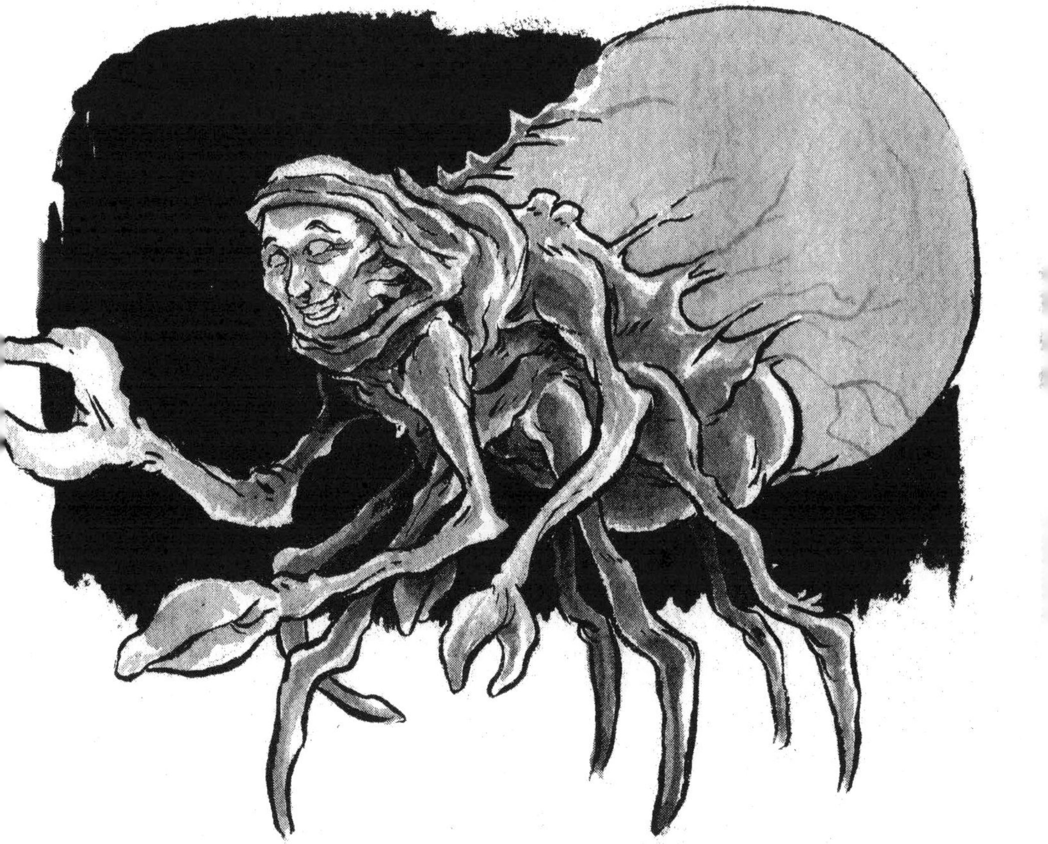

SUBJECT:
HAWTHORN HORROR

DATE: 1952

LOCATION: Hawthorn, Scotland

Angus Abernathy (23) was lost on the Hawthorn moors when he was chased by something. Abernathy says that he was following the path of a falling star when a strange mist rose up around him. While wandering through the mist he saw a pair of bright pink lights moving toward him. After shouting to it thinking it was one of his friends from town, he realized that its shape seemed wrong to be a person. Suddenly the shape ran toward him, making a loud rhythmic clicking sound. Angus has no memory of what happened next.

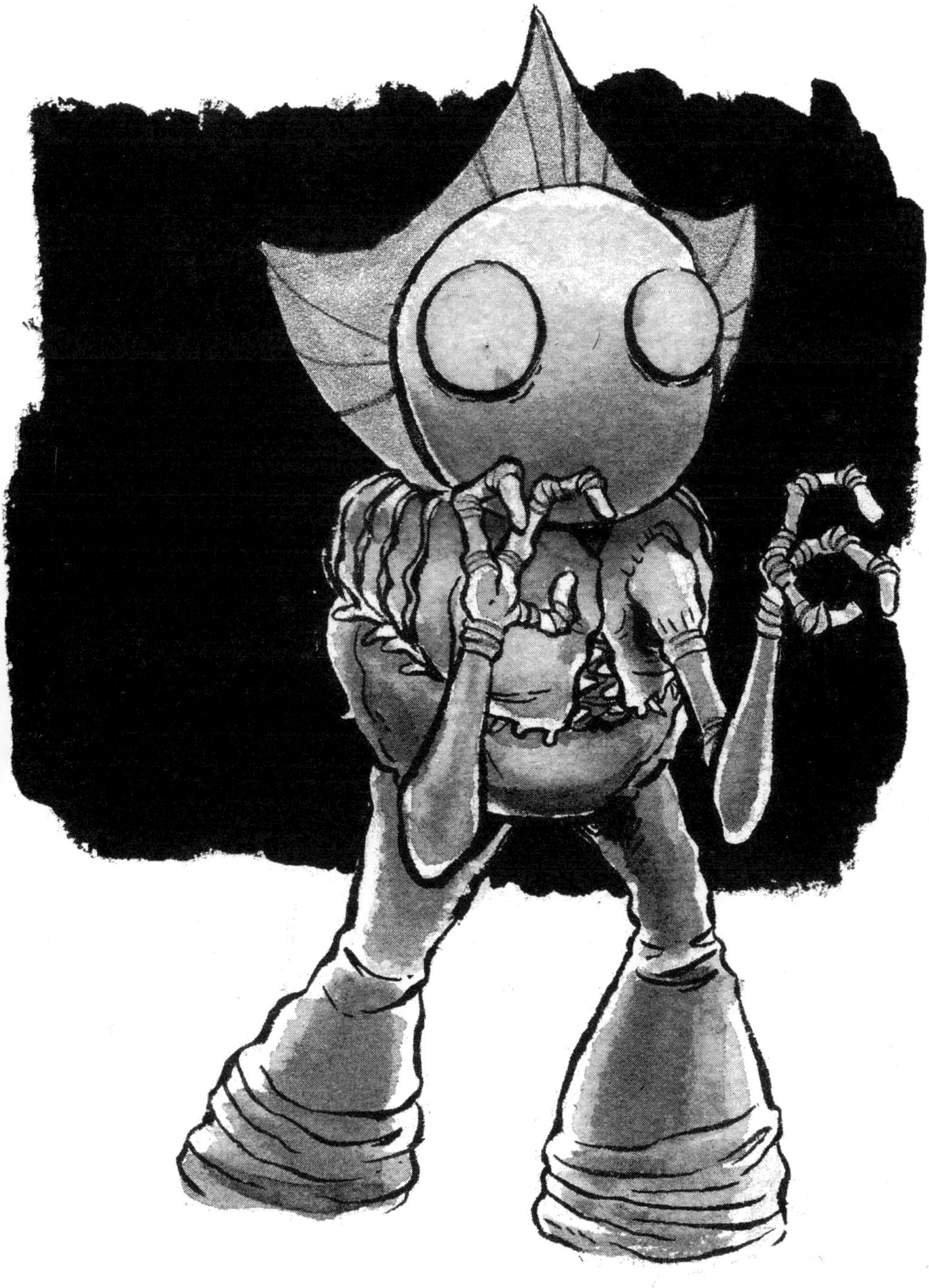

SUBJECT:
GOLD FACED MUMMY

DATE: April 24, 1966 – Present

LOCATION: Gallium, Quebec

Something has been walking the streets of Gallium since their historic society building burned down after being struck by lightning. It seems to be interfering with radio signals. Reports claim that radios in the vicinity of the walker broadcast what sounds like a series of random numbers and letters in Latin. People who have approached within a radius of eight feet of the creature become catatonic until they are outside that range.

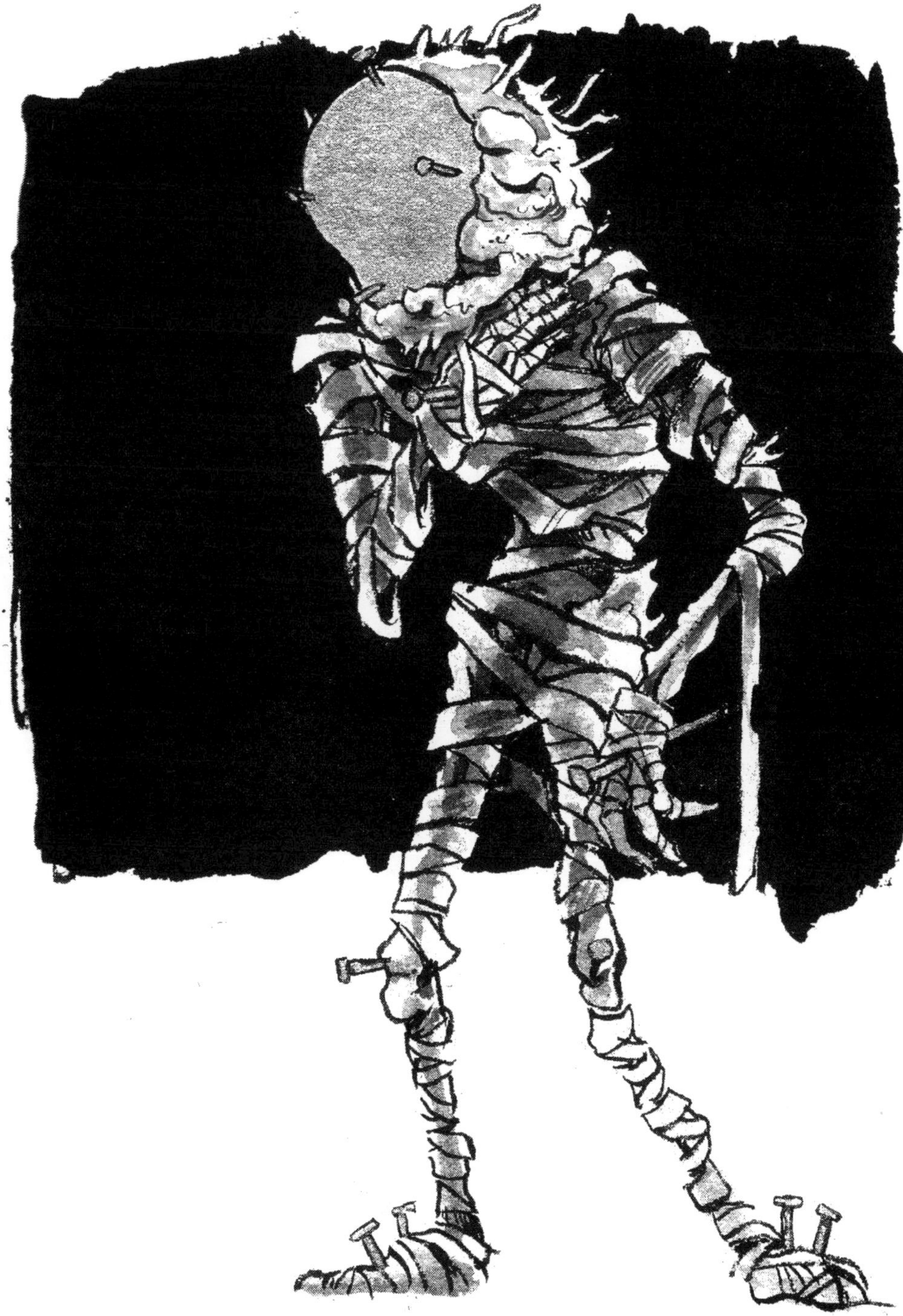

SUBJECT:
MR. FINGERBUTT

DATE: 1890 – Present

LOCATION: Kilgore, New Brunswick

The residents of Kilgore speak in hushed tones of the creature they call Mr. Fingerbutt. The story goes that it lives in a cave near Herron lake and it comes out to feed every three days. It mostly feeds off of road kill or any other dead wildlife it comes across but it's also been known to dig up graves in the local cemetery. Some say that it is the deformed son of the town founder Mr. Herman Kilgore, since the cave is within the property his mansion stood on, but there is no evidence he ever had any children and he was never married. Stories of Mr. Fingerbutt go back to the founding of the town in 1868.

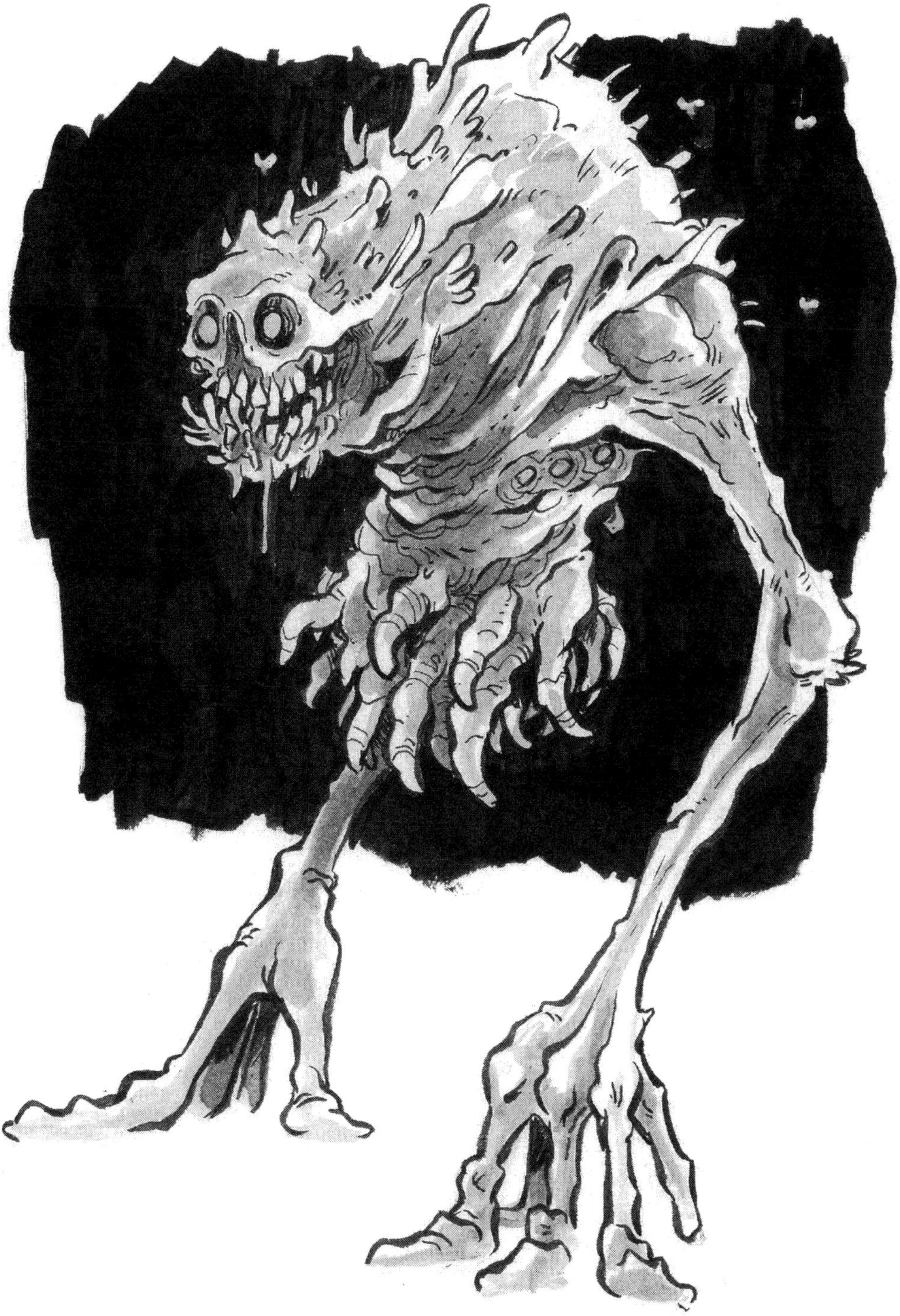

SUBJECT:
THE BURNING FIEND

DATE: 1959 – Present

LOCATION: Constance, Manitoba

There's an abandoned church just off the 401 near Constance, people who have explored the area say it's haunted. 60 years ago the church was investigated by the RCMP following a string of disappearances and rumours of some kind of cult operating out of the church. The investigation found no evidence linking the disappearances to the cult. Three years after the investigation the cult left the area. Some claim the cult member just disappeared one night when a loud explosion was heard in the area, the shock-wave broke windows in Constance and as far away as Franklin! People thought the church had exploded, yet when they went to investigate they found it completely intact. The only thing missing was the cult that had been living there. Since that time the building has been shunned. However, to this day people say that at night you can see lights within the church as if someone carrying a torch was walking around

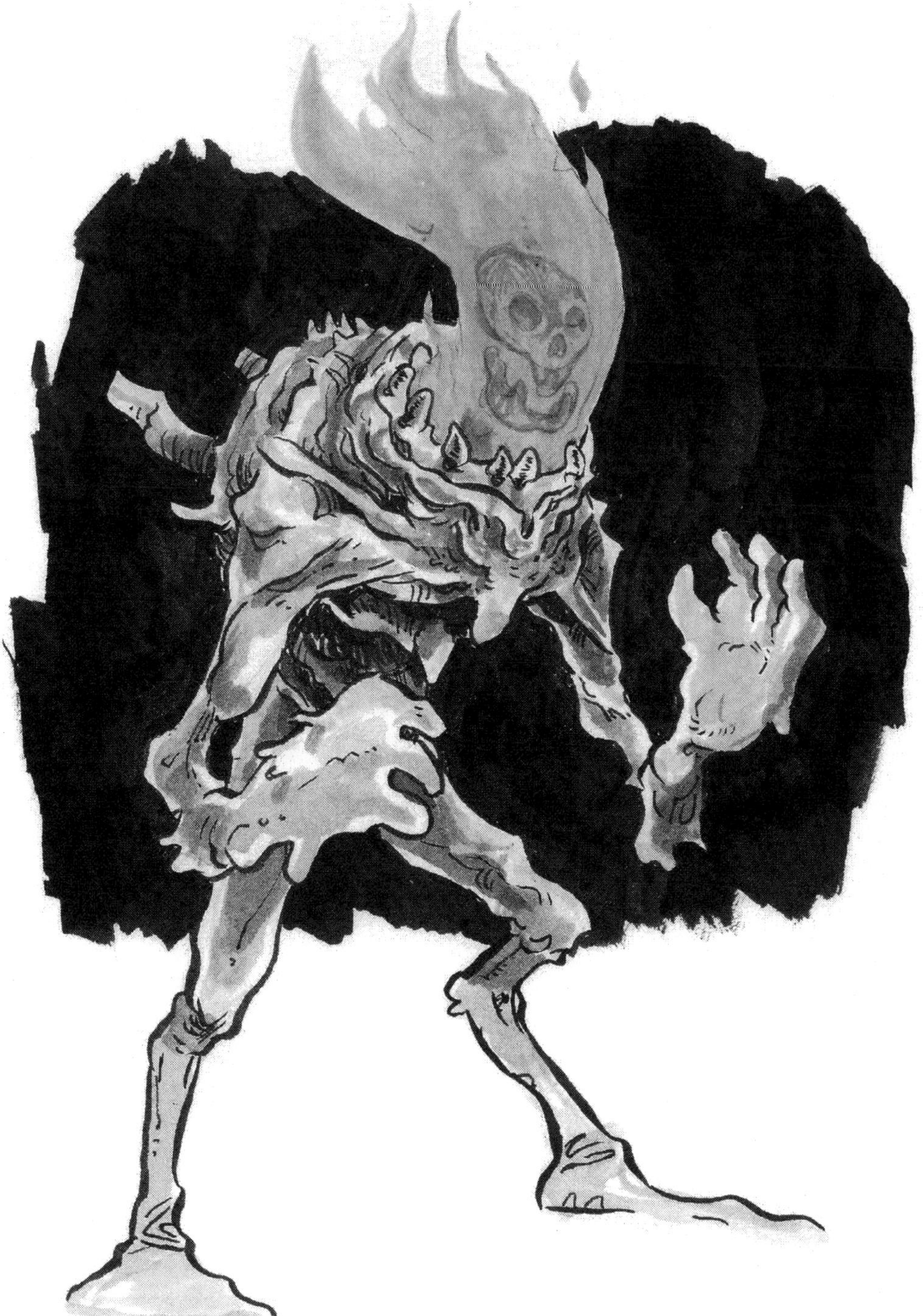

SUBJECT:
GRIMES' FARM INVADERS

DATE: August 1, 2019

LOCATION: London, Ontario

Abraham Grimes (45) and his family enter the local police precinct in London, Ont. claiming their farm was under siege by strange creatures and they had been trapped there for the last 6 days and needed help either capturing or killing these things. They claimed that two of their farm hands and Abraham's father, Cornelius (72), had been killed by the creatures that morning and what remained of the Grimes family had escaped while the creatures were distracted, eating their victims. When the police arrived at the farm they found evidence of what appeared to be a gun fight, spent cartridges, bullet holes through doors and windows, damaged farm equipment, but no sign of the creatures nor the missing farm hands nor Cornelius Grimes nor any of the animal kept on the farm.

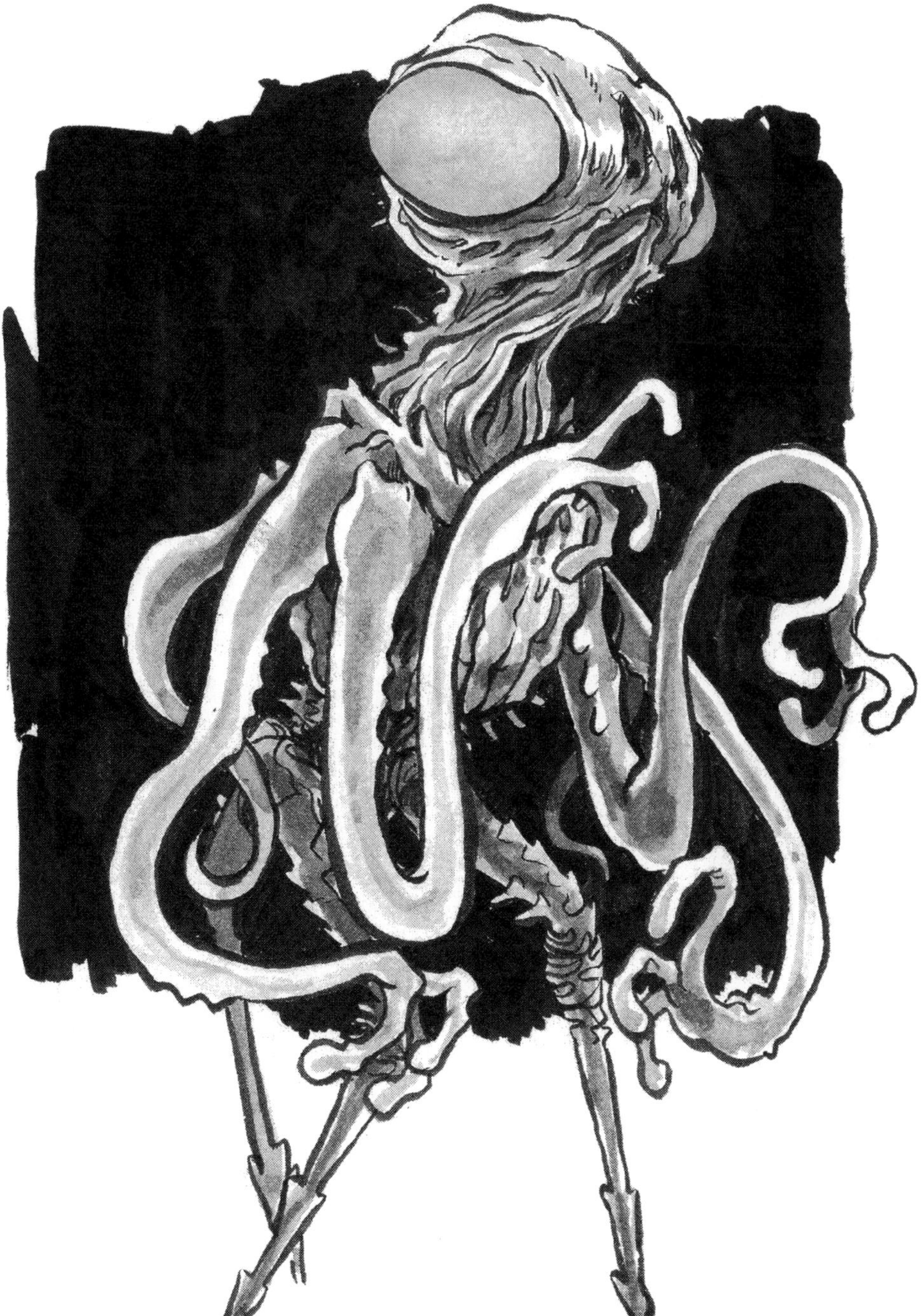

SUBJECT:
LI'L MIKE

DATE: 1898 – Present

LOCATION: Ontario / Quebec

Jeff McGuinn (25) claims while he was out ice fishing near the Quebec/Ontario border he was chased off the lake by "this big, weird yeti thing." Locals named it 'Li'l Mike,' and claim it's not dangerous as long as you don't provoke it. Nobody's sure where it got it's name but people say the first sighting of it was some time around 1898.

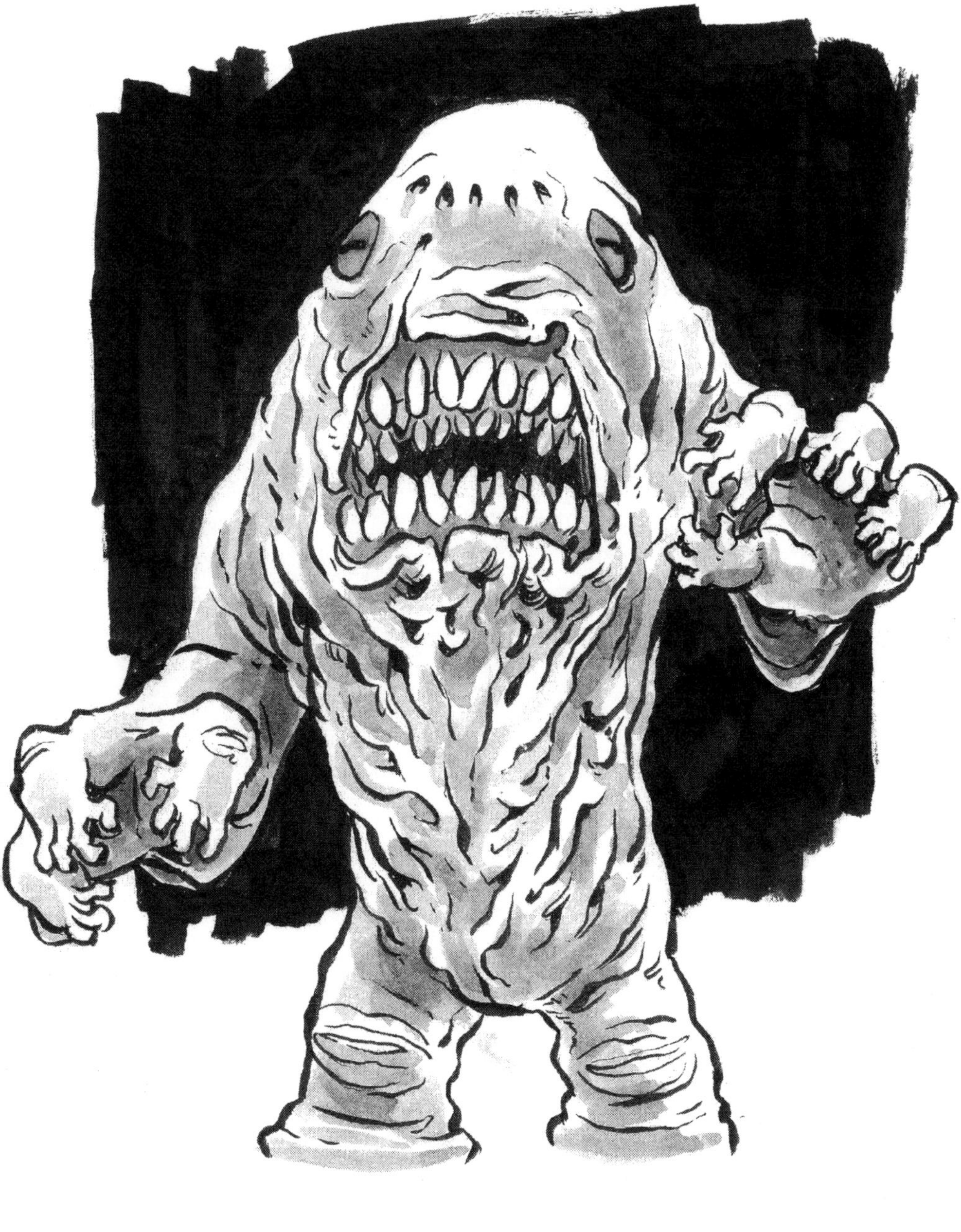

SUBJECT:
SAM'S BUTCHER

DATE: October 11, 1988

LOCATION: Fountaine, Quebec

Police were called in to investigate rumours of something odd going on in the back room at Sam's Butcher Shoppe. While the police will not explain what they found, Sam's Butcher Shoppe was closed permanently after the investigation. Most of the clientele of Sam's have also been placed in quarantine with no explanation given.

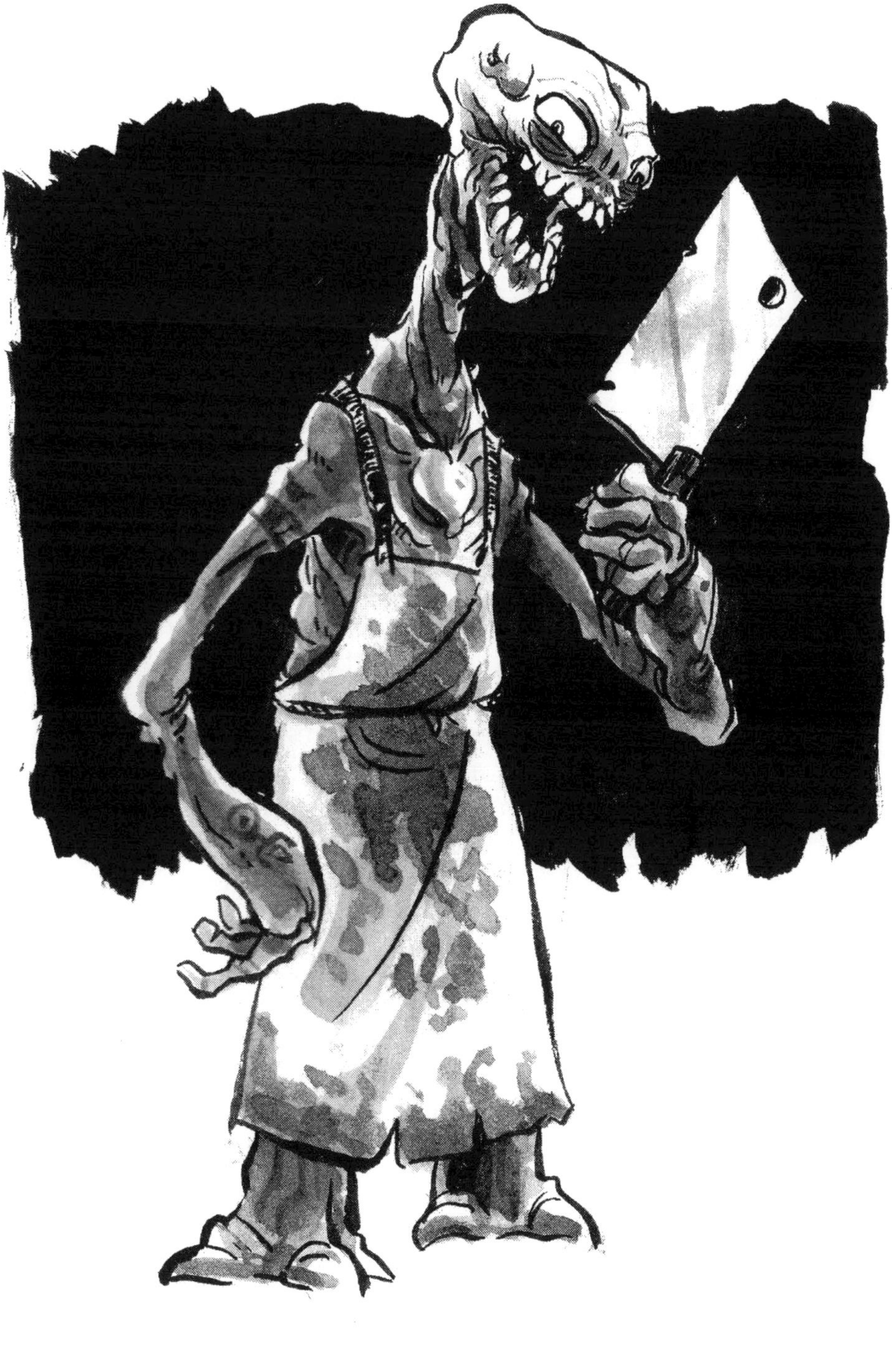

SUBJECT: CARNIVAL CREATURE

DATE: Unknown — Present

LOCATION: Canada

There have been stories throughout Canada that if you go out to places with very little traffic (in or outside major cities) late at night and listen close you might hear a voice calling "Roll up! Roll up and see the greatest show on earth!". People who have followed the voice claim they have come upon a strange carnival set up, and the call seems to be coming from a strange looking man standing in front of a giant gate shaped like a screaming face. They have a hard time describing anything else but they have vague memories that they had a fantastic time riding strange rides, playing weird games and seeing bizarre shows. Most of the people who claim to have experienced this claim to have been marked on the back of their hand with a tattoo that they can only see when the moon is full. Some of them are lying.

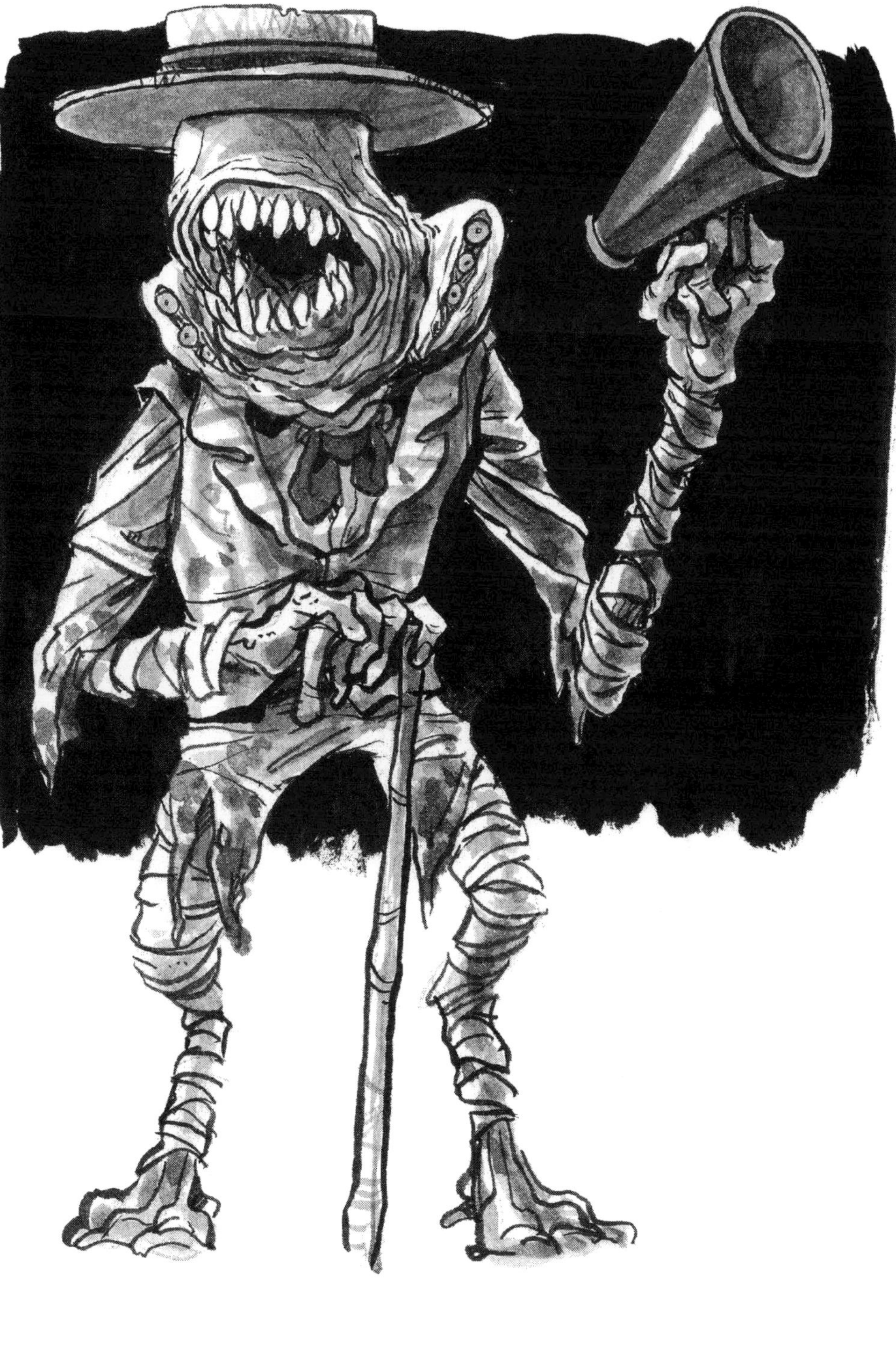

SUBJECT:
EDGAR McCONTRAIL

DATE: 1985

LOCATION: Scrumpton, Oregon

Steve McContrail (13) claims that he had no intention of creating a robot for his high school science project but when his brother Edgar (18) was mysteriously killed by a lion in a public park he had no choice.

Authorities refuse to confirm that the lion belong to a local crime boss or that Edgar may have run afoul of said crime boss.

Either way Krissie Frome (18) says she's just happy to have Edgar back.

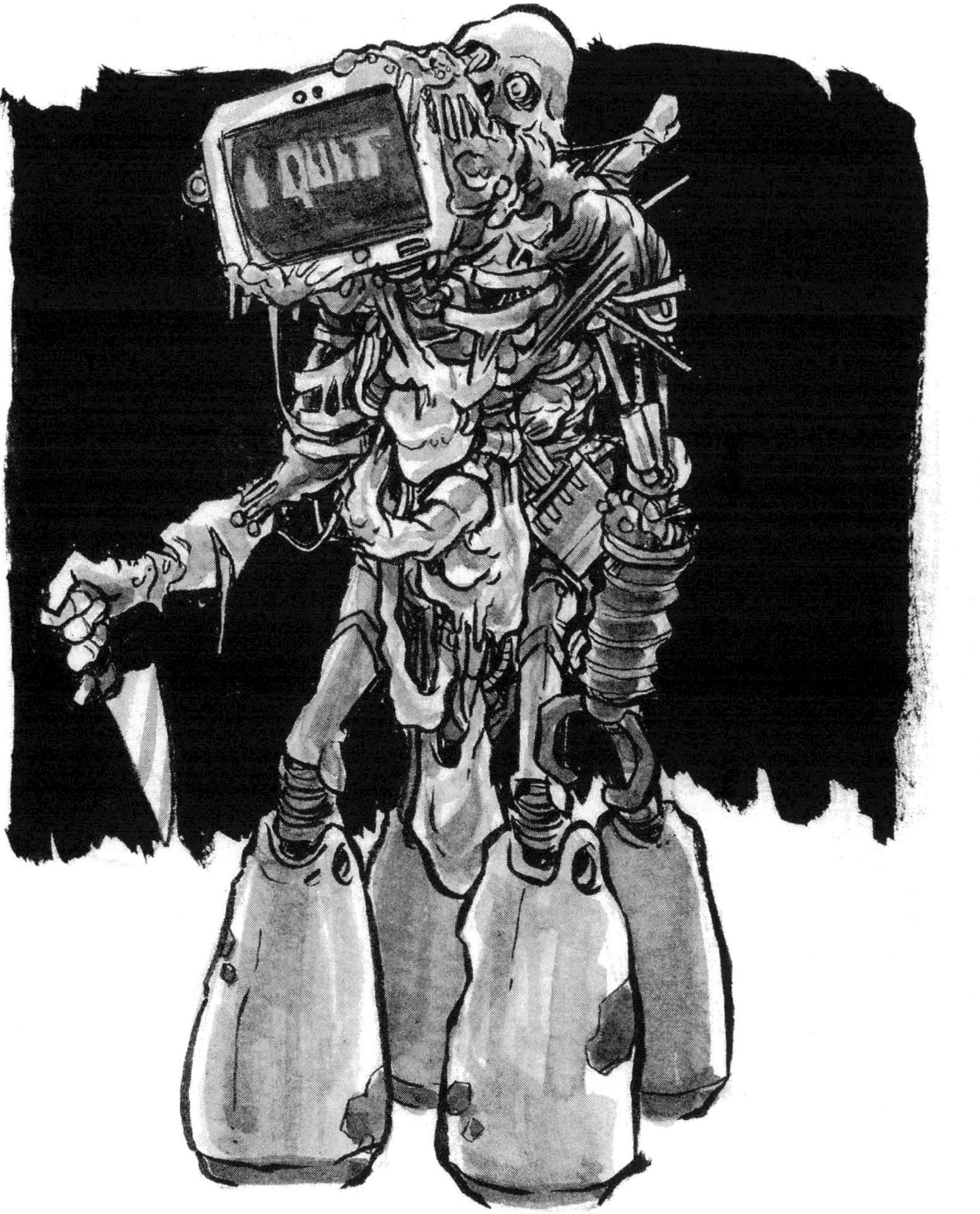

SUBJECT:
THE BURNING HANDED FIEND

DATE: Sept. 7, 1954

LOCATION: Hollywood California

Everyone thought it was just a special effect created for the premiere screening of Anton Felss's latest horror film THE FIEND WITH THE BURNING HAND, until the horrible burned body of Anton Felss was found in the projection booth. To this day nobody has seen the film, some say that the only print of it was destroyed that night in 1954.

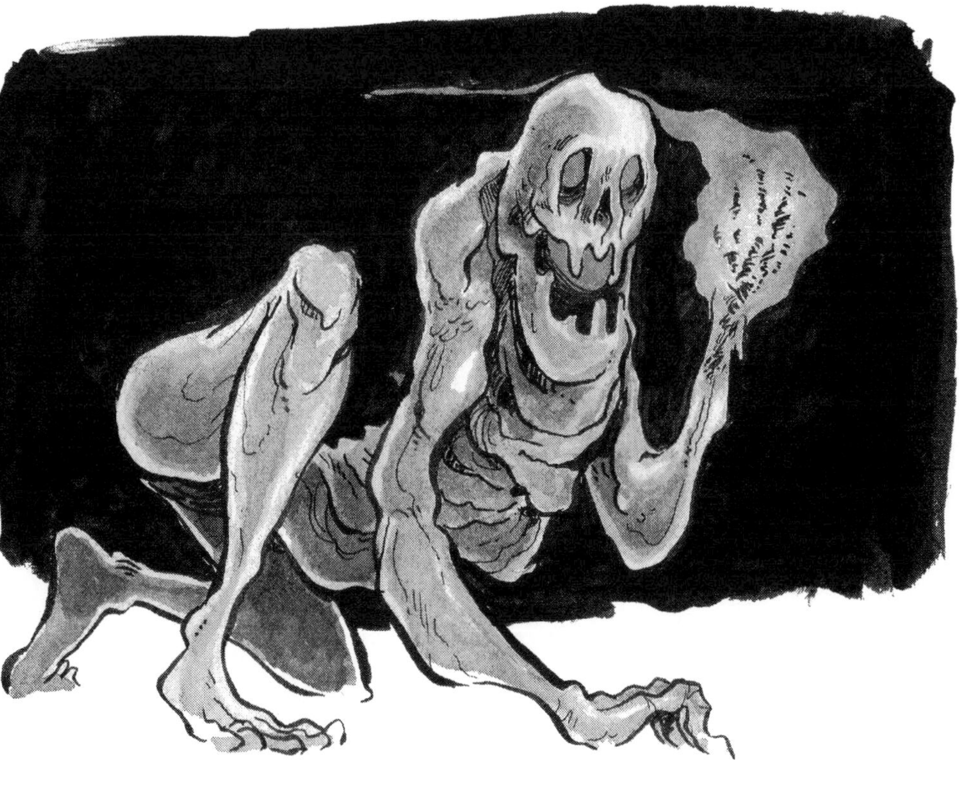

SUBJECT:
SPIKY MIKE

DATE: October 7, 2018

LOCATION: Cavendish, Prince Edward Island

Janice Wilsh (17), saw something shuffle out of the shed in her backyard while she was attempting to sneak back into her bedroom to avoid her parents who did not know she had snuck out to attend a party at Sam Tucker's house. She claimed what she had seen was approximately 90-120cm tall and was walking sideways like a crab. Her parents were awakened by her screams and she was grounded for 4 weeks.

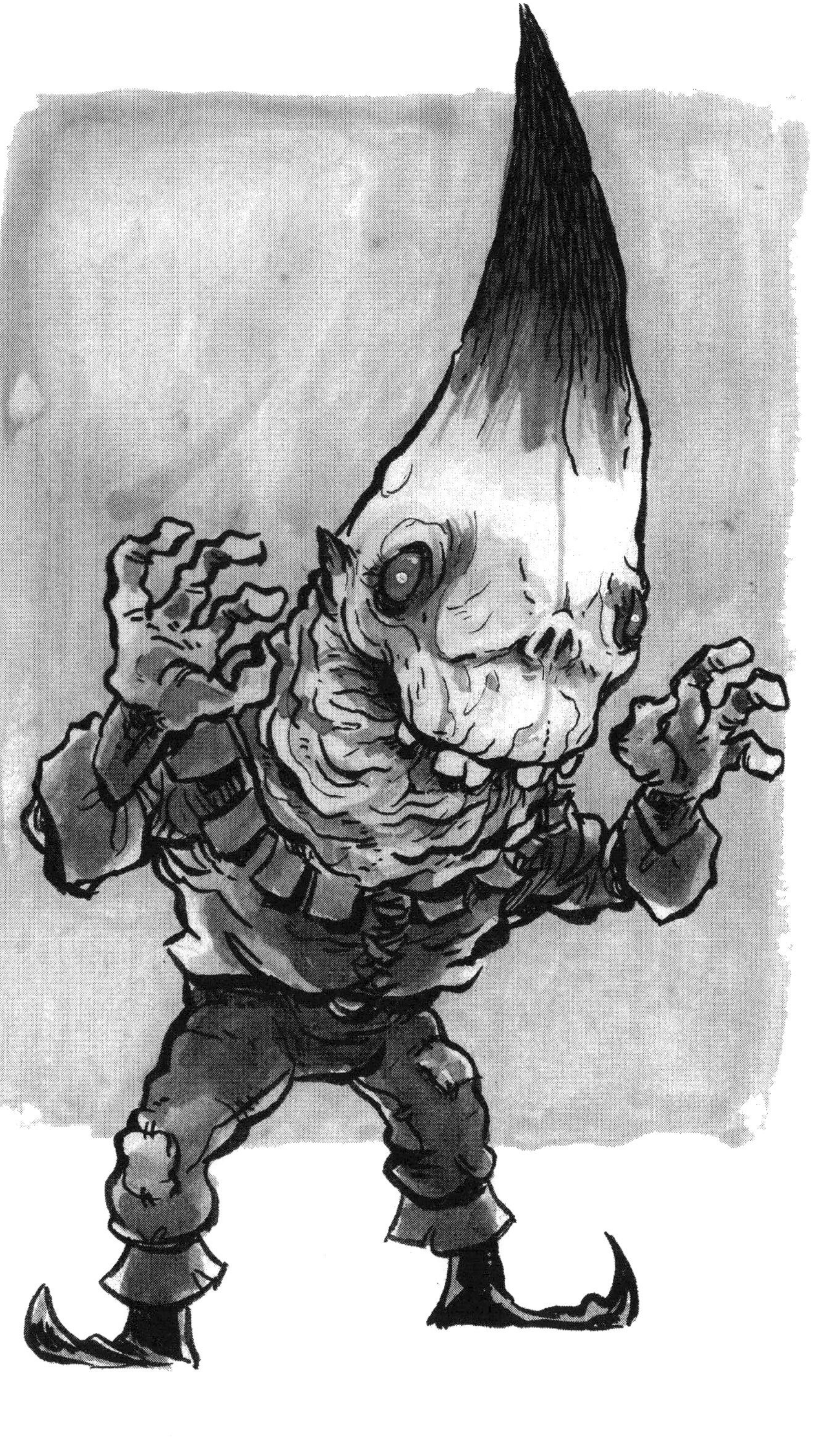

SUBJECT:
THESIFRANE

DATE: April 2018

LOCATION: Chilblame, Alberta

It's rumoured that in 1975 a cult took over the small rural town of Chillblame, Alberta. Not much was known about the cult nor it's reclusive leader. The stories also claim the government sent Police and Military forces into Chillblame in 1984 to deal with the cult resulting in the death of the entire population. It's interesting to note that while there are records of a massive police and military exercise in Ontario at the time, there is no record of the town of Chillblame. In 2018 while hiking in northern Alberta, Jacob Franchmen (23), Cheryl Grotts (22), Susanne Franks (22), Frank Gilman (24) and Montrose Grady (23) came across an abandoned town with a large church in remarkably great shape. Miss Grotts claims they had heard singing in the church so they entered the building. She has no memory of what happened after, nor the location of her friends

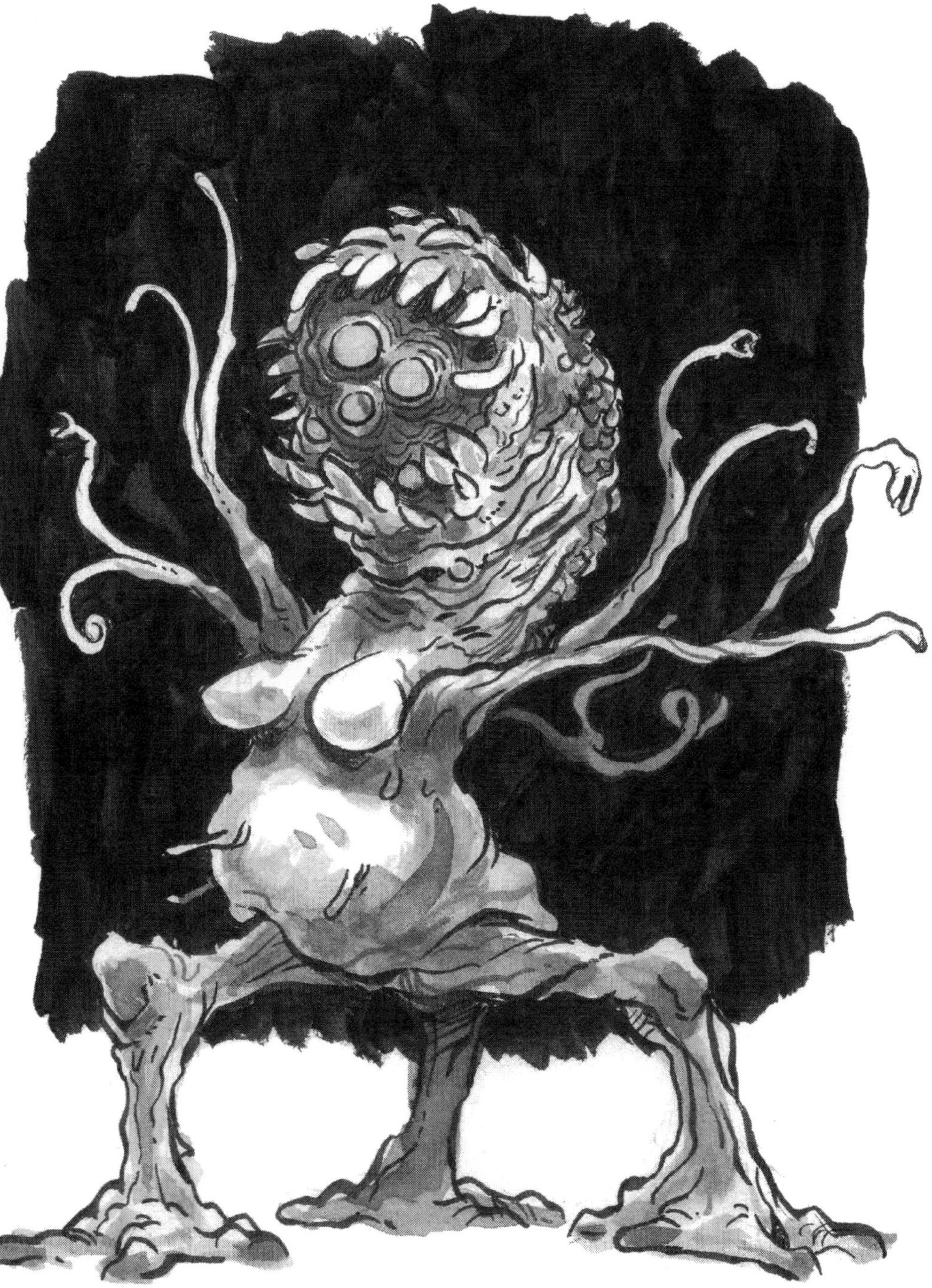

SUBJECT:
CRUMMLIN MOLLUSK

DATE: March 12, 1956

LOCATION: Crummlin, Ontario

On March 12, 1956 what was reported as an earthquake opened up a fissure in the middle of Crummlin, Ontario unleashing a hoard of strange 1.82 meter tall mollusks. A large part of the population were eaten by these creatures before it was discovered they could be destroyed by electricity.

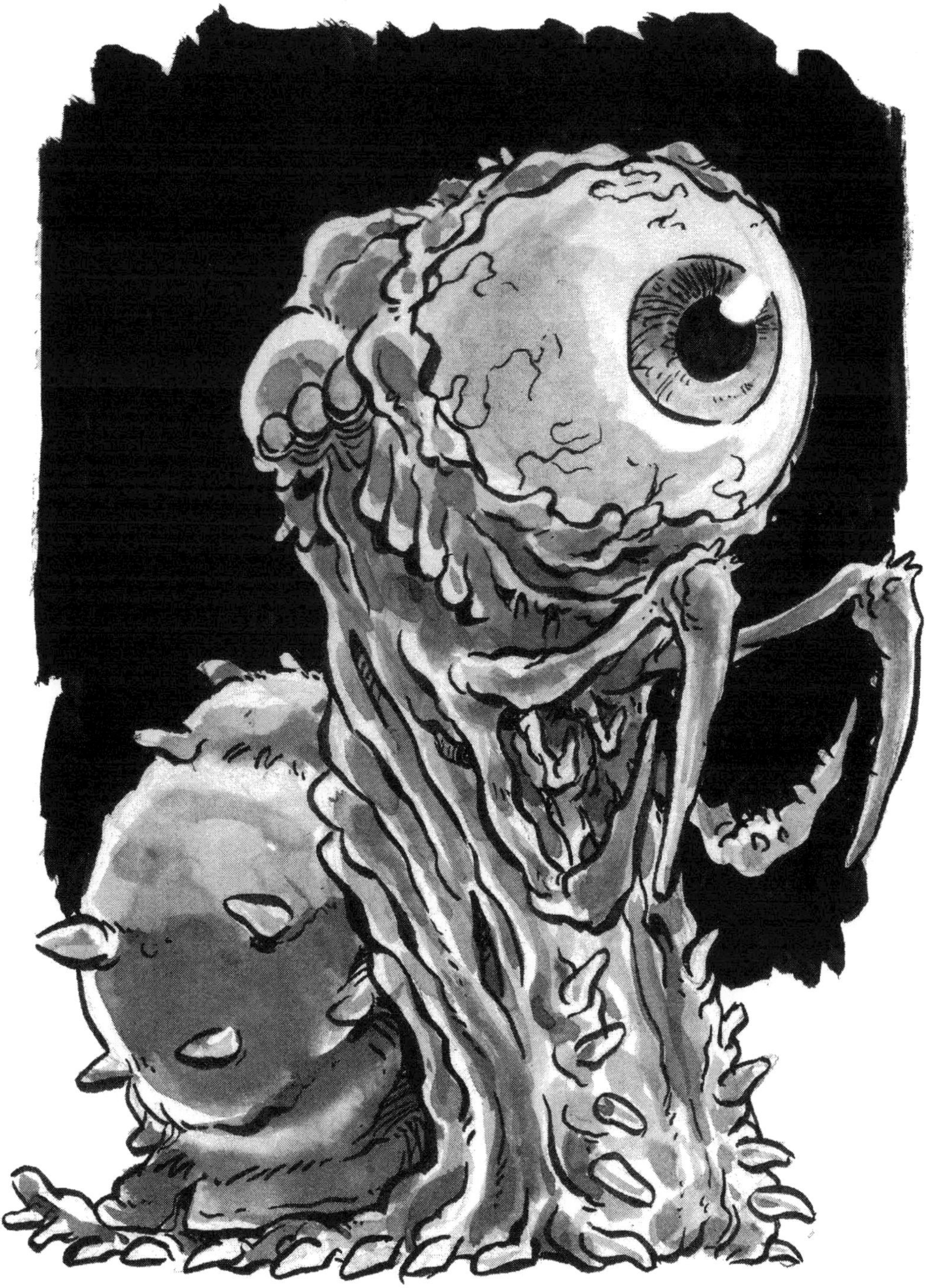

SUBJECT:
CHUPS

DATE: November 1, 1980

LOCATION: Frenchton, Nova Scotia

Peter Gemmer (8), who had been missing since the third of October, returns to his parents home . He claims a creature he called 'Chups' found him when he got lost in the woods and brought him home. Peter claims he was gone for, at most, 4 hours. "Because I'm hungry for dinner, now." It's also interesting that there is no significant forest in the area

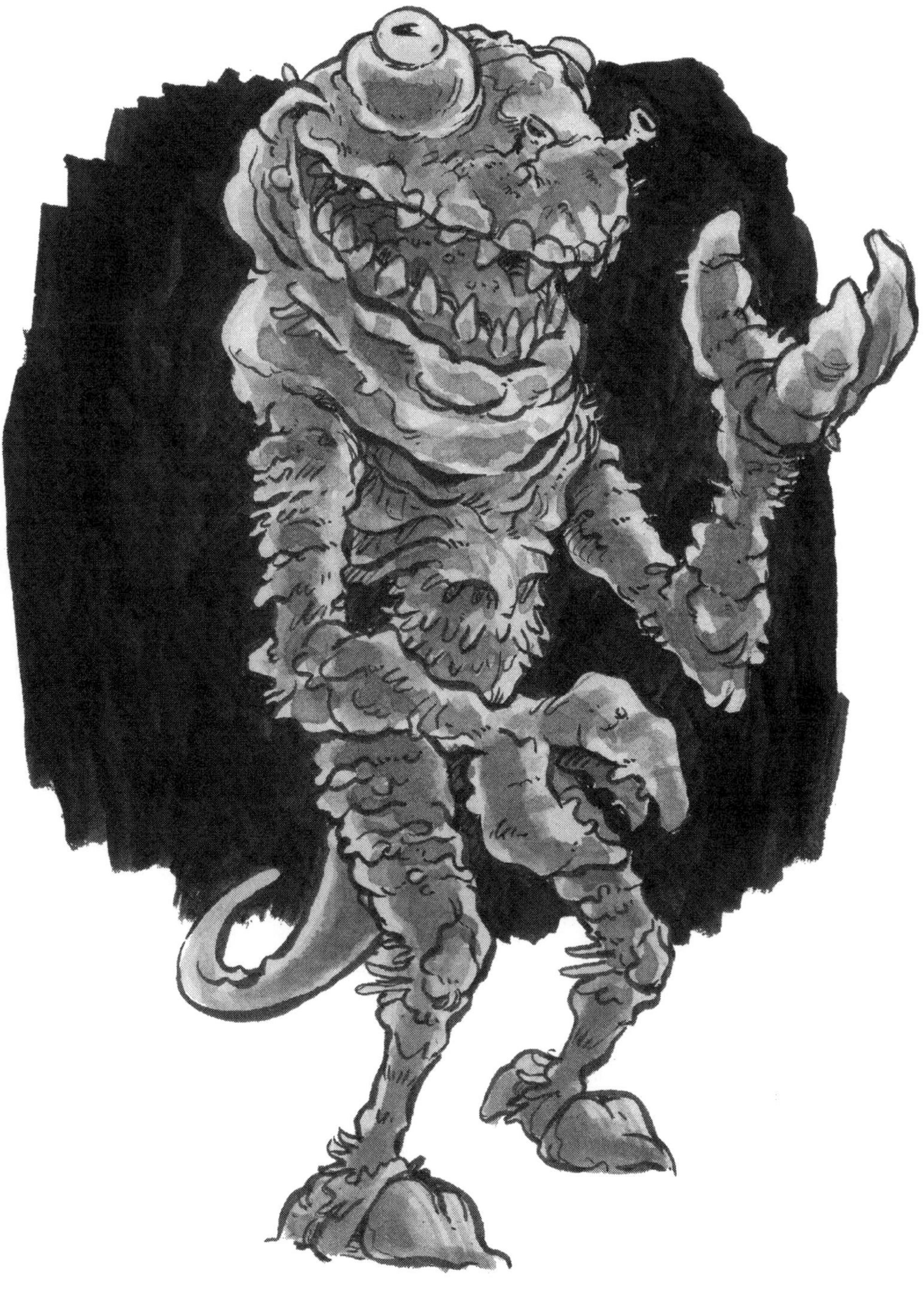

SUBJECT:
INDRID COLD

DATE: November 2, 1966

LOCATION: Parkersburg, West Virginia

Woodrow Derenberger was driving along interstate 77 when he saw what appeared to be a giant "old-fashioned kerosene lamp" shaped vehicle land in the road. A grinning man with a dark tan and his arms folded in what looked like an uncomfortable fashion exited the vehicle and approached Derenberger. The man said his dame was Indrid Cold and just wanted to know more about the human race. After their conversation Cold told Derenberger he'd visit him again and left.

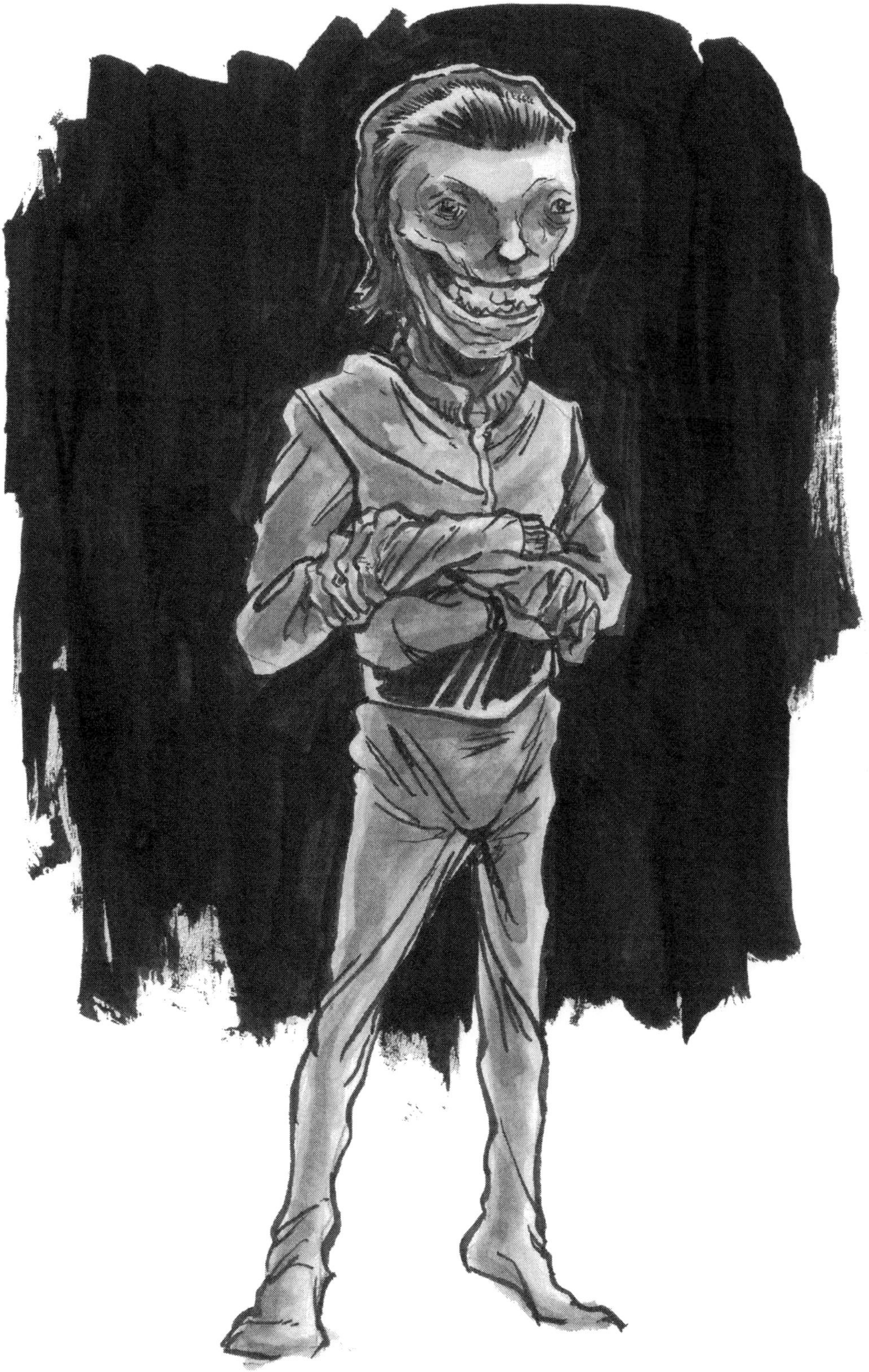

SUBJECT:
LOVELAND FROGMAN

DATE: 1955 — Present

LOCATION: Loveland, Ohio

According to local legend, a man saw three frog like-men with leathery skin, webbed hands and feet at the side of the road. Some stories claim that someone was watching a group of these frogmen having a conversation until one noticed him and raised a wand above it's head that fired a spray of sparks. The observer than ran away.

In 2014 a musical based on the Frogman was written titled, **HOT DAMN! IT'S THE LOVELAND FROG!**

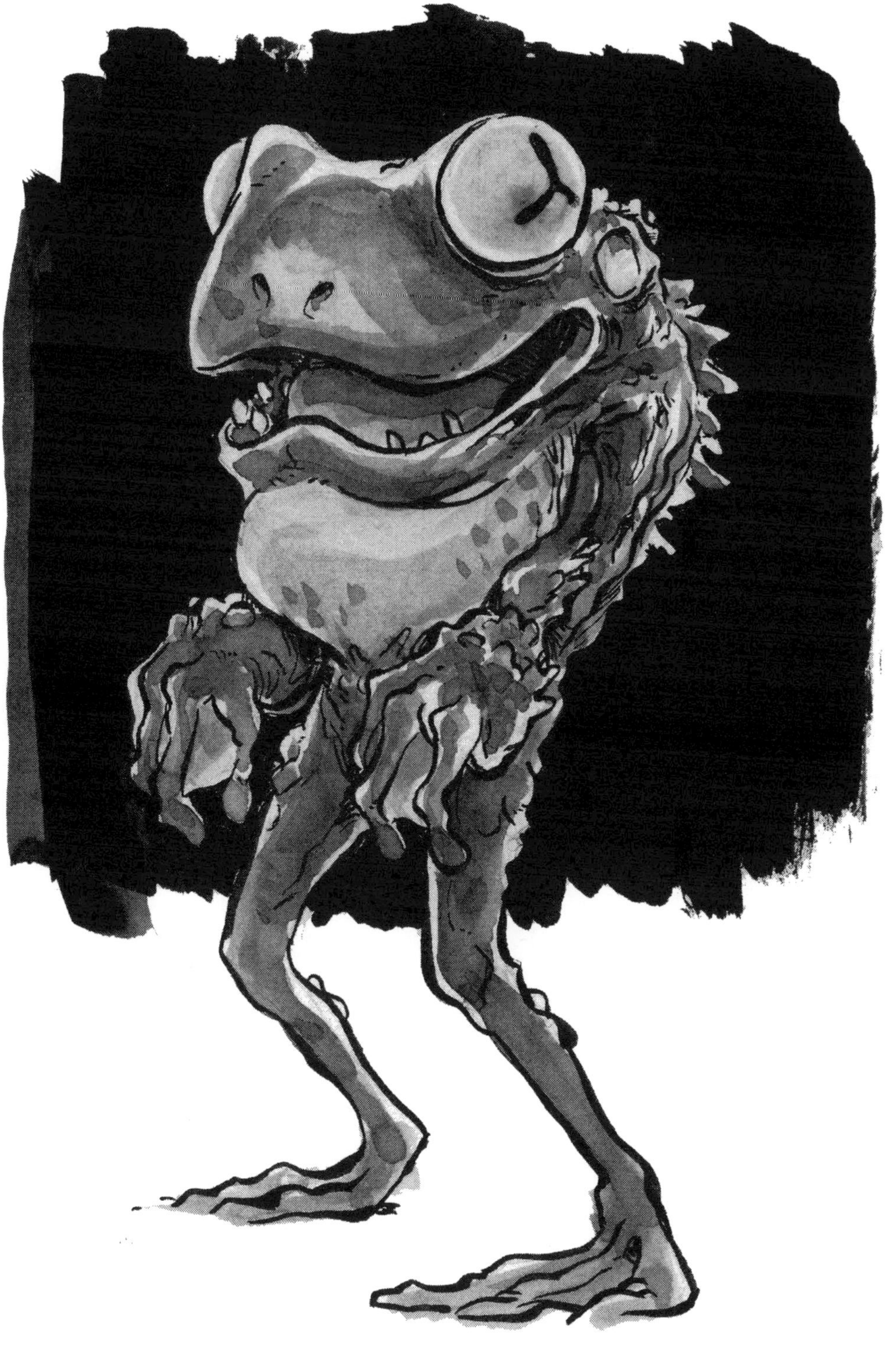

SUBJECT:
JACKALOPE

DATE: Unknown — Present

LOCATION: North America

"A fearsome critter" described as a Jackrabbit with antelope horns. It is said they are able to mimic human speech and are quite violent. Supposedly they are only able to mate during thunder storms and are fond of whiskey.

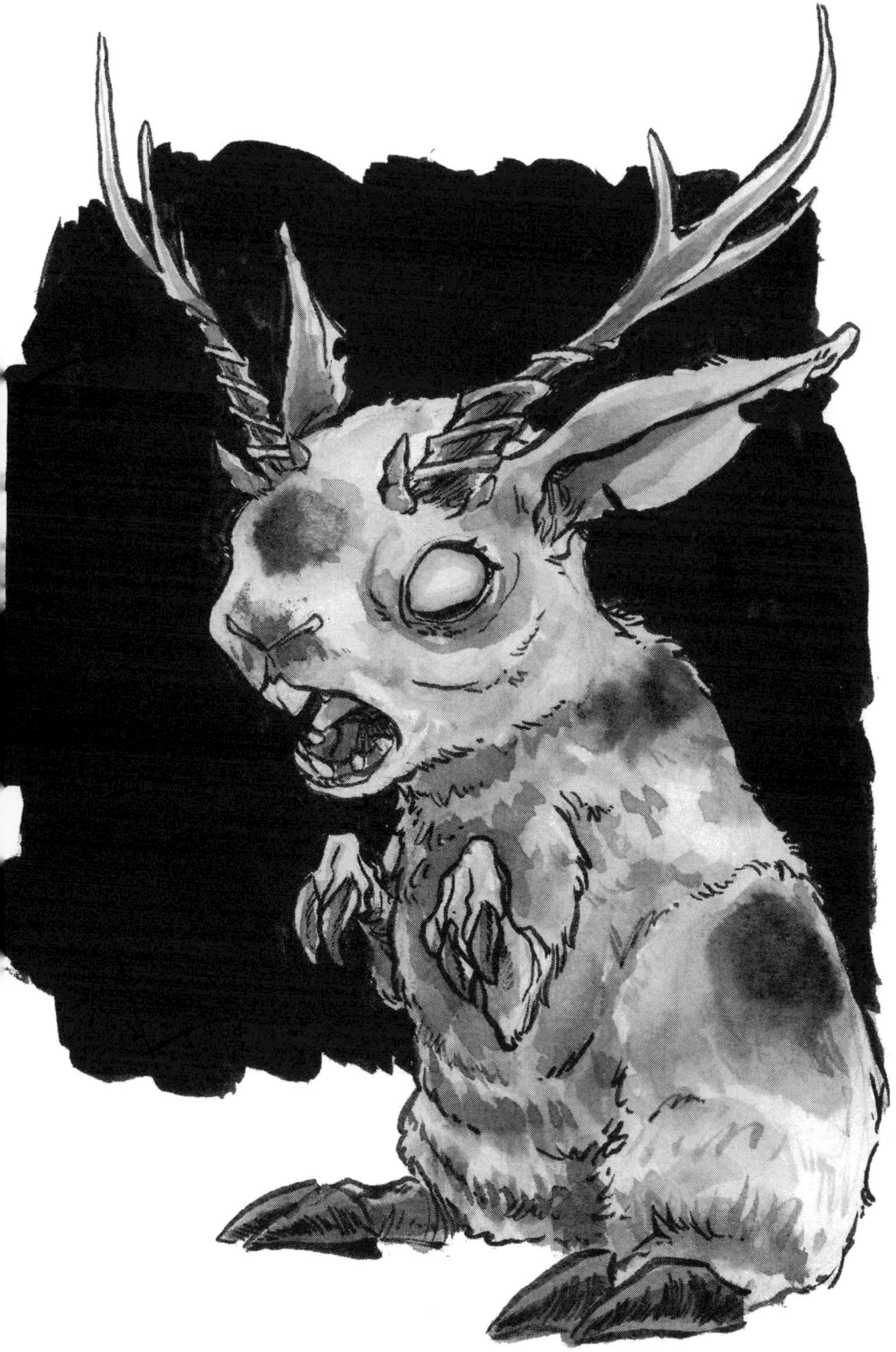

SUBJECT:
THE ALKALI LAKE MONSTER

DATE: Unknown – Present

LOCATION: Walgren, Nebraska

People in Nebraska claim a 12 meter long horned alligator like beast lives at the bottom of what is now known as Walgren Lake.

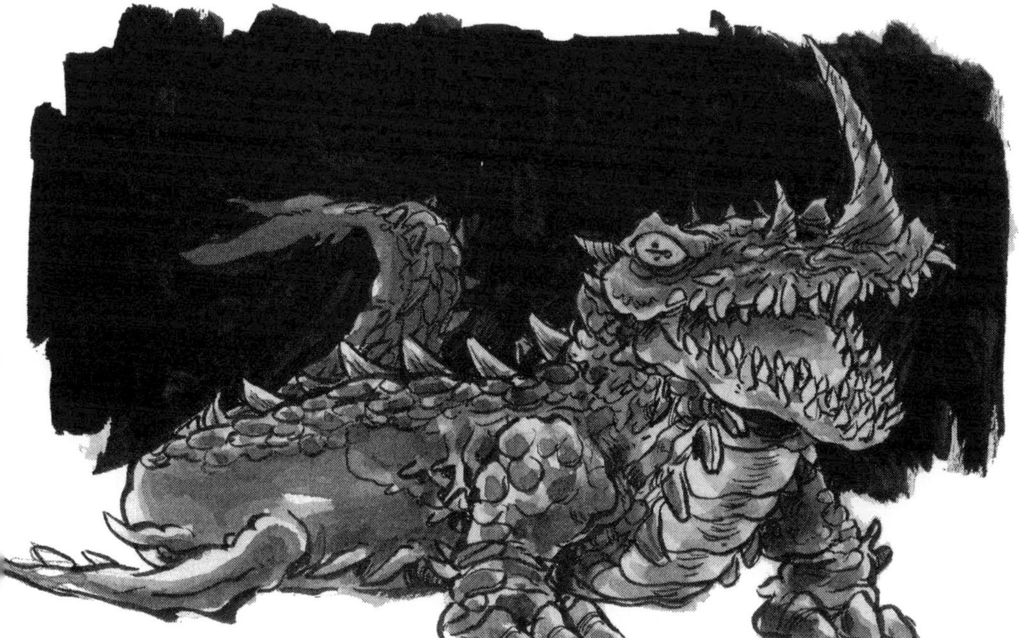

SUBJECT:
KELLY-HOPKINSVILLE GOBLIN

DATE: August 21, 1955

LOCATION: Hopkinsville, Kentucky

After seeing a UFO fly over his farmhouse Elmer Sutton and his family are attacked by 12 to 15 small creatures, cornering them in the house. Sutton and the four other adults in the house spend the next four hours shooting at the creatures.

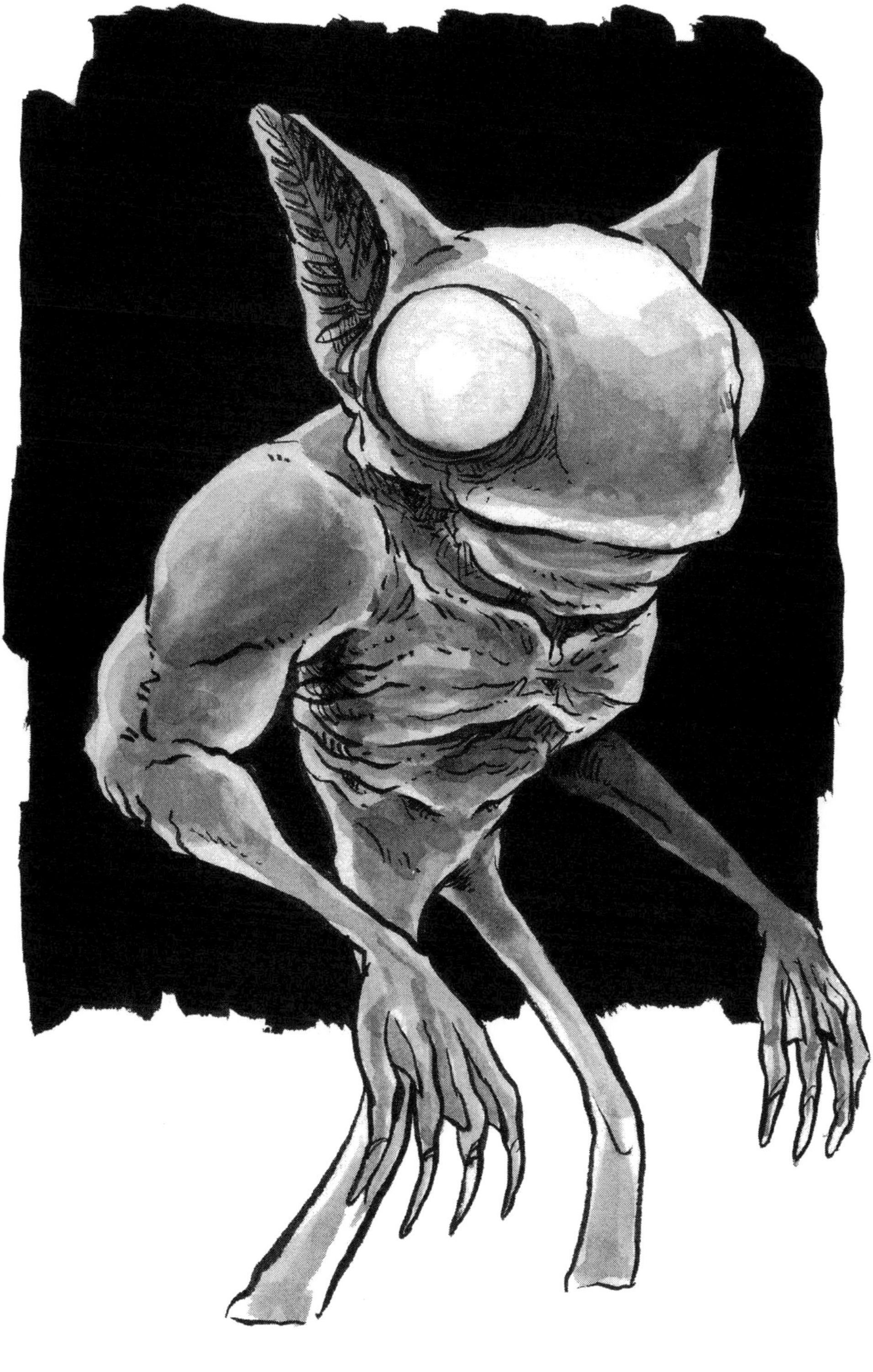

SUBJECT:
THE FLATWOODS MONSTER

DATE: September 12, 1952

LOCATION: Flatwoods, West Virginia

Edward and Fred May and their friend Tommy Hyer tell their mother the say a bright object land in their neighbour's property. The boy's, their mother and a group of other local children and a National Guardsman head to the neighbours property to investigate the object the boys claim to have seen. When they reach the place where the object landed they see a tall figure who hisses at the group and flies toward them. Panicked, the group flees.

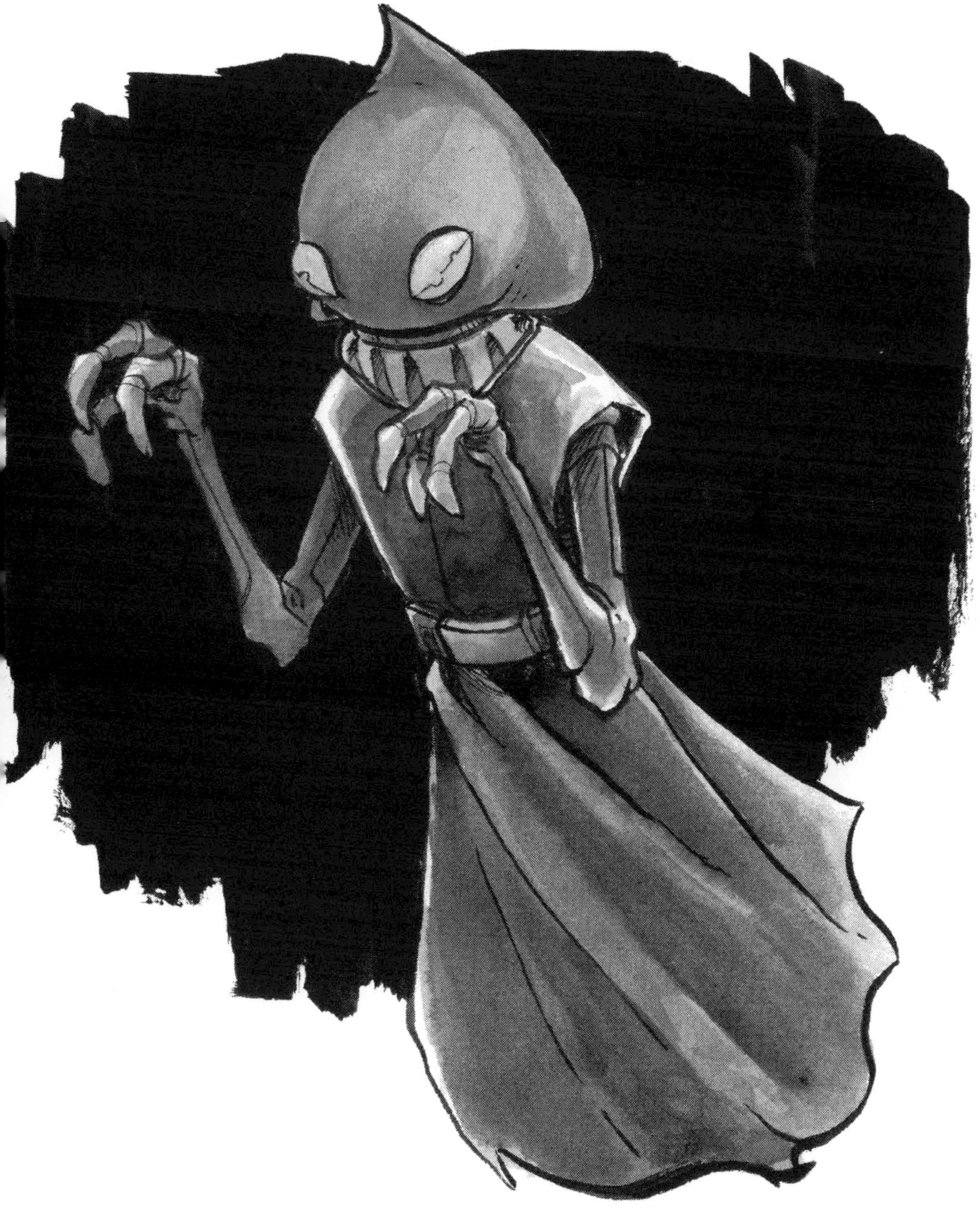

SUBJECT:
MELONHEADS

DATE: Unknown — Present

LOCATION: Michigan, Connecticut and Ohio

Small human-like creatures with large malformed heads are seen in the forests of Michigan, Connecticut and Ohio. While each state has a different story for the origin of these creatures, the one thing they all agree on is that they prey on people who get lost in the woods.

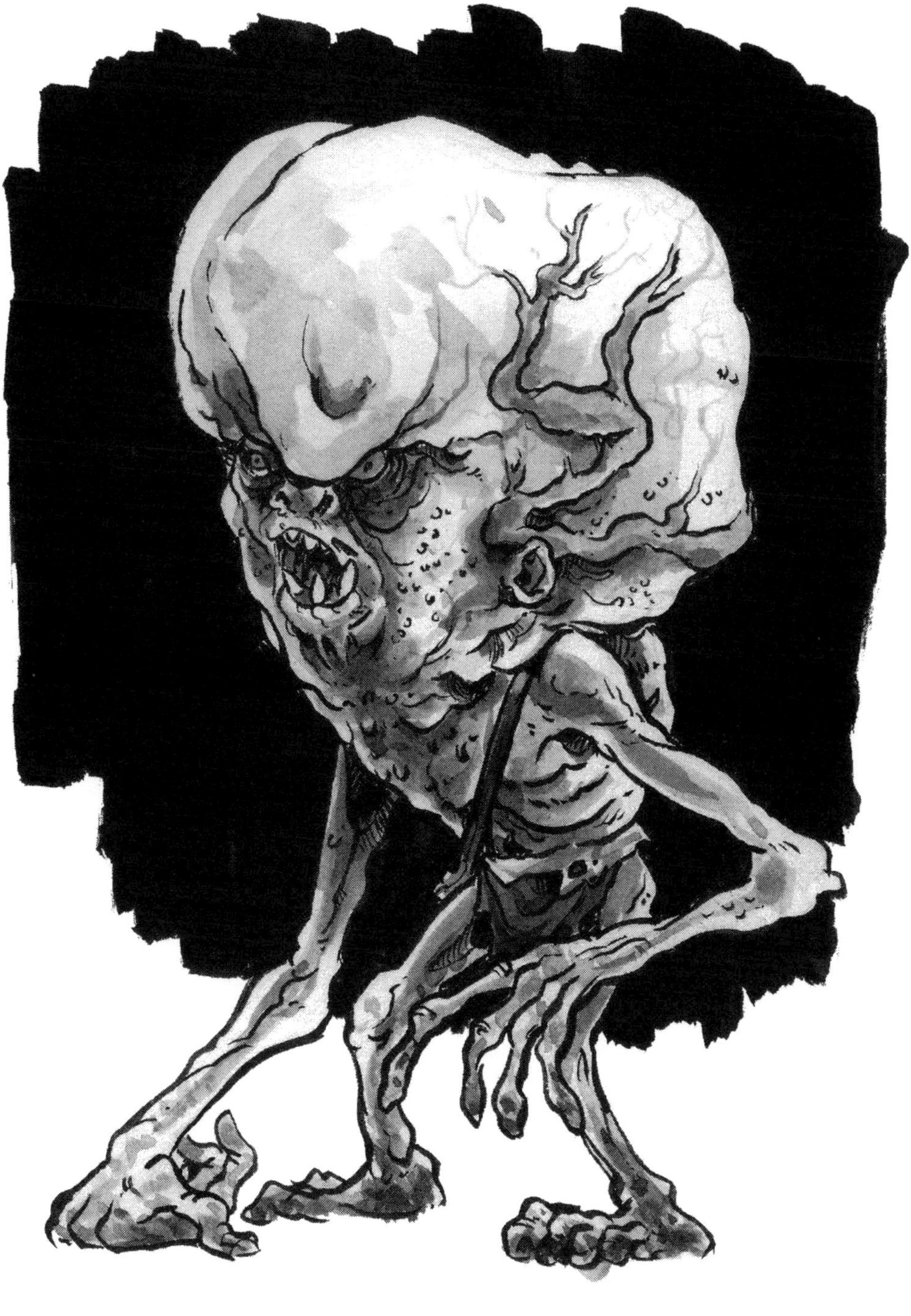

SUBJECT:
NINGEN

DATE: 1960 – Present

LOCATION: Waters around Antarctica

Over the past several years sailors have been reporting sightings of these giant humanoid creatures floating in the icy waters off the coast of Antarctica. Most sightings seem to happen at night. What are they? What do they want? They tend to dive deeper underwater as soon as a ship gets close to one.

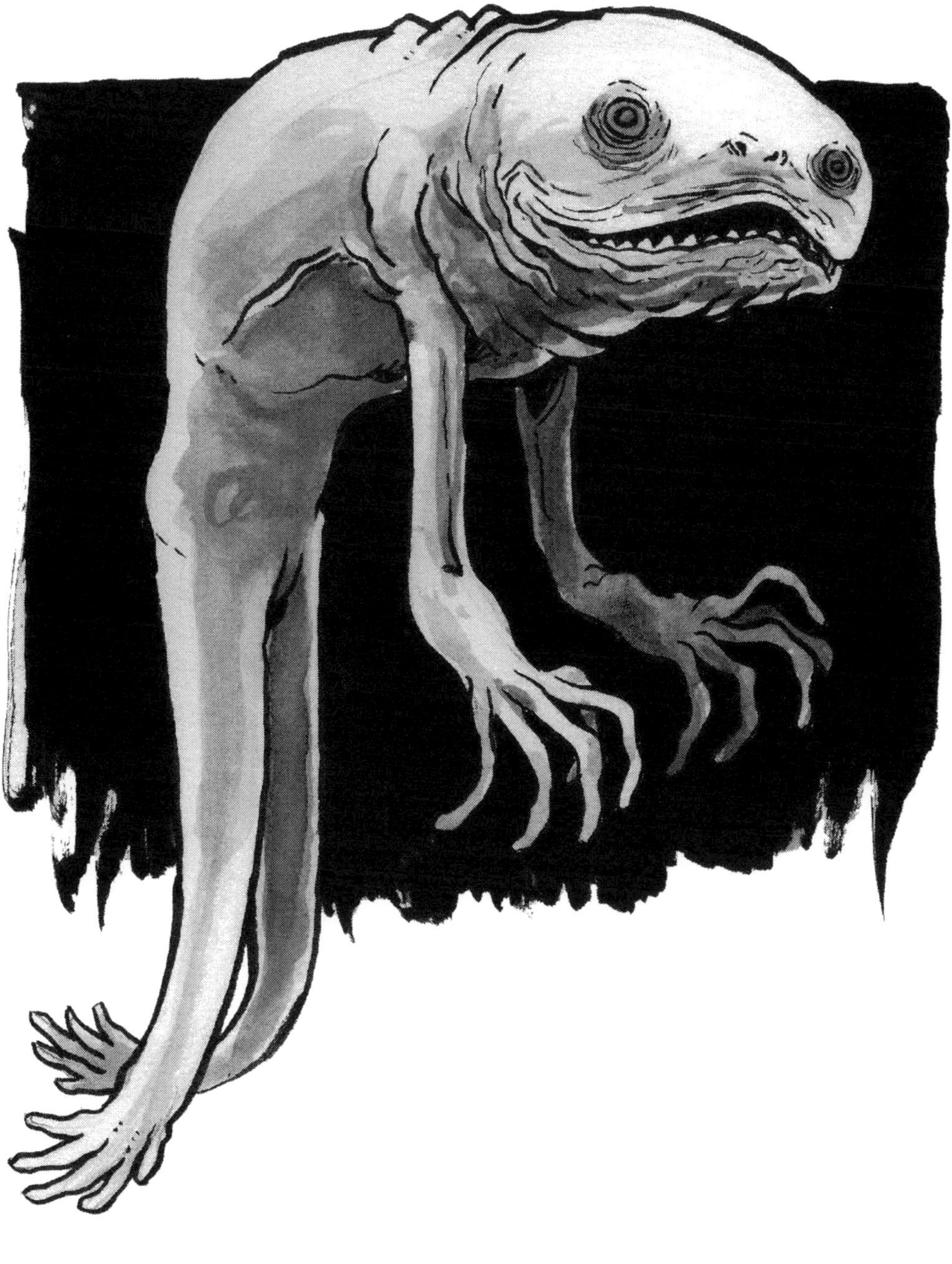

SUBJECT:
HODAG

DATE: 1893- Present

LOCATION: Rhinelander, Wisconsin

A large dangerous creature known to inhabit the forests of Northern Wisconsin. In 1893, Eugene Shepard and a group of local people claim to have killed one using dynamite,

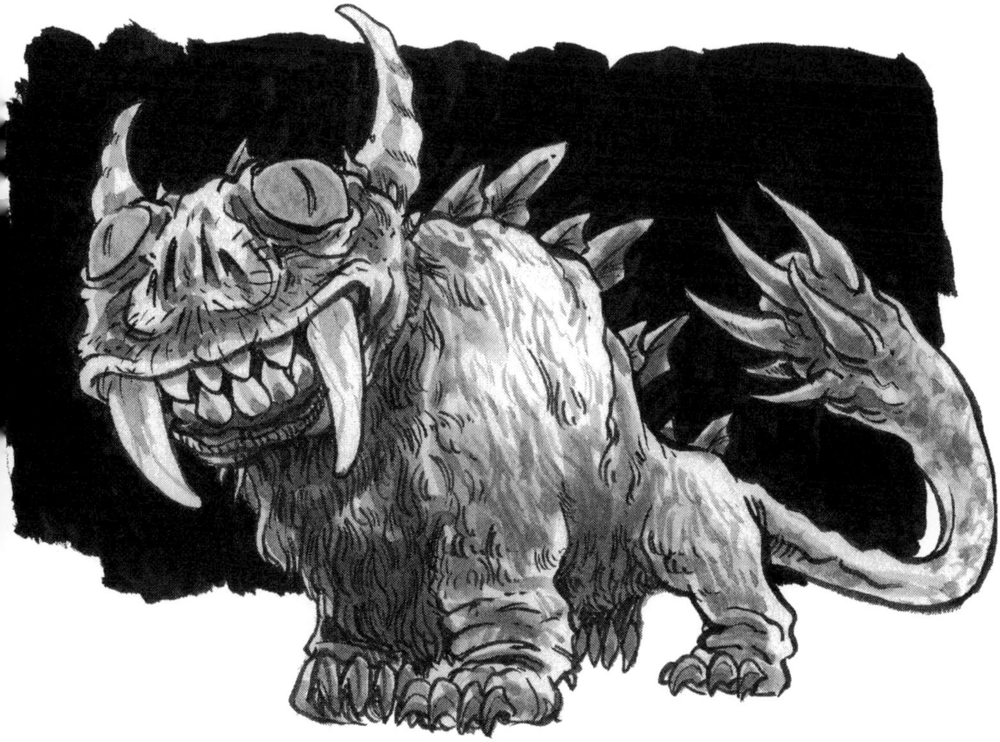

SUBJECT:
CRAWFORDSVILLE MONSTER

DATE: September 5, 1891

LOCATION: Crawfordsville, Indiana

Two ice delivery men see a horrible apparition that fills them with dread hovering above them. Later in the day a Methodist pastor and his wife see the creature float past them. The creature emits a wheezing plaintive sound even though it does not seem to have a mouth. The following evening hundreds of people see the creature as it flies across town. It has never been seen since.

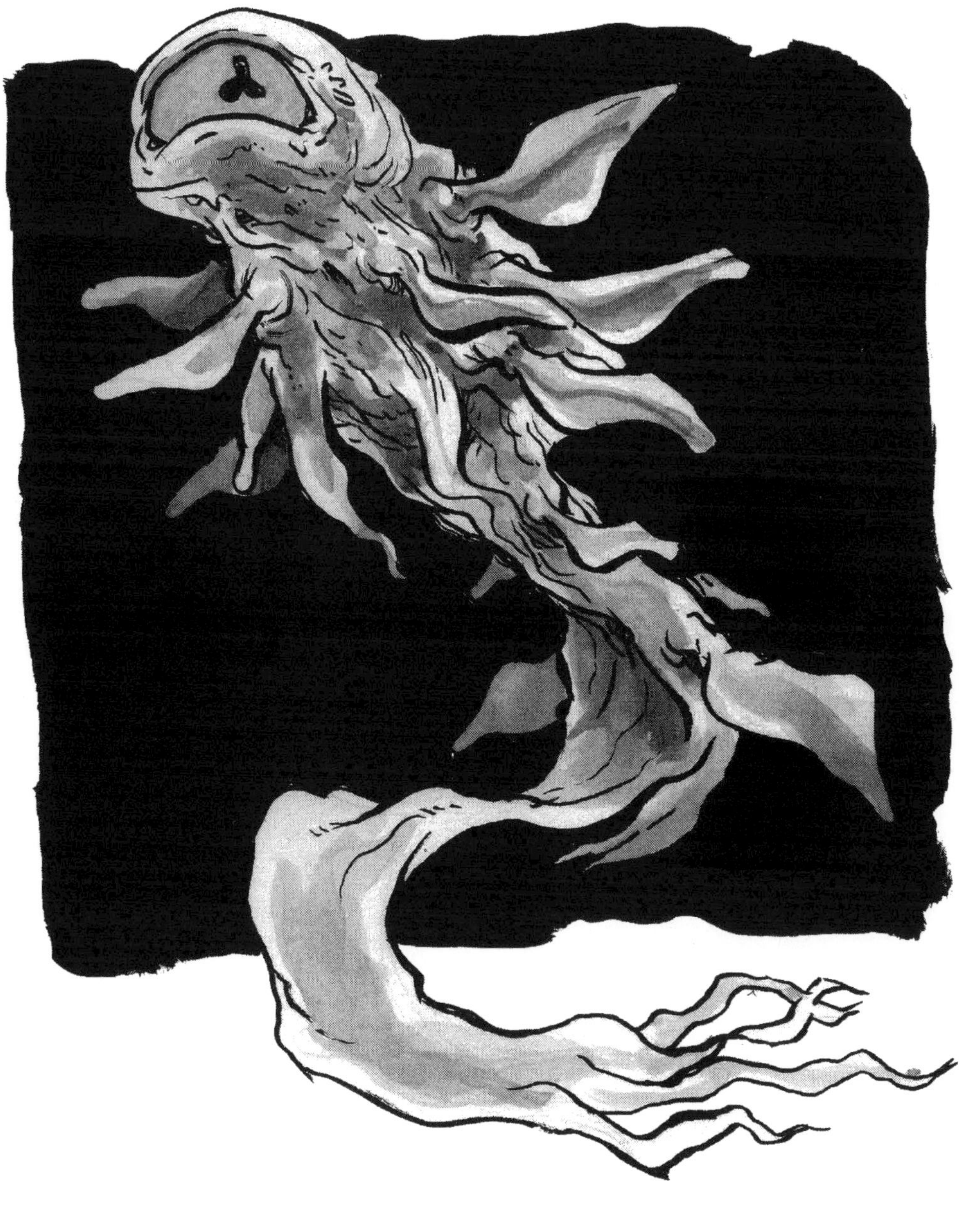

SUBJECT:
OL' YELLOW TOP

DATE: September 1906 – August 1970

LOCATION: Cobalt, Ontario

A Sasquatch like creature with a patch of blond hair on its head was seen by a number of different people over a 64 year period near the mining town of Cobalt, Ontario.

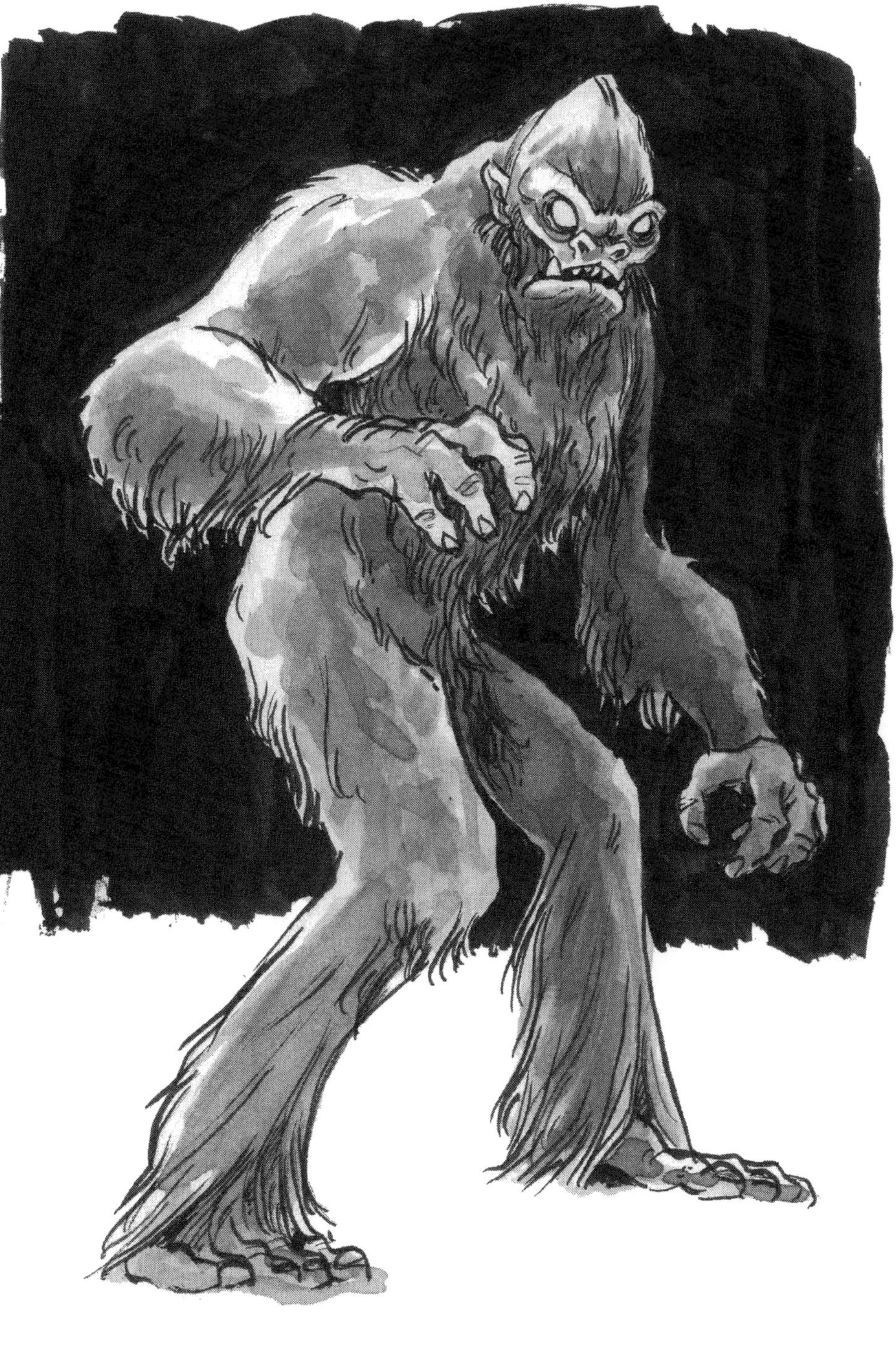

SUBJECT:
THE DOVER DEMON

DATE: April 21, 1977

LOCATION: Dover, Massachusetts

William Bartlett (17) claims that while driving on April 21 he saw a large eyed creature with tendril-like fingers on top of a broken stone wall near Farm St. John Baxter (15) reports seeing the same creature later that evening closer to Miller Hill Road. The following evening Abby Brabham (15) sees the creature on Springdale Ave. When all three sightings are plotted on a map it shows the creature was moving in a straight line for over two miles.

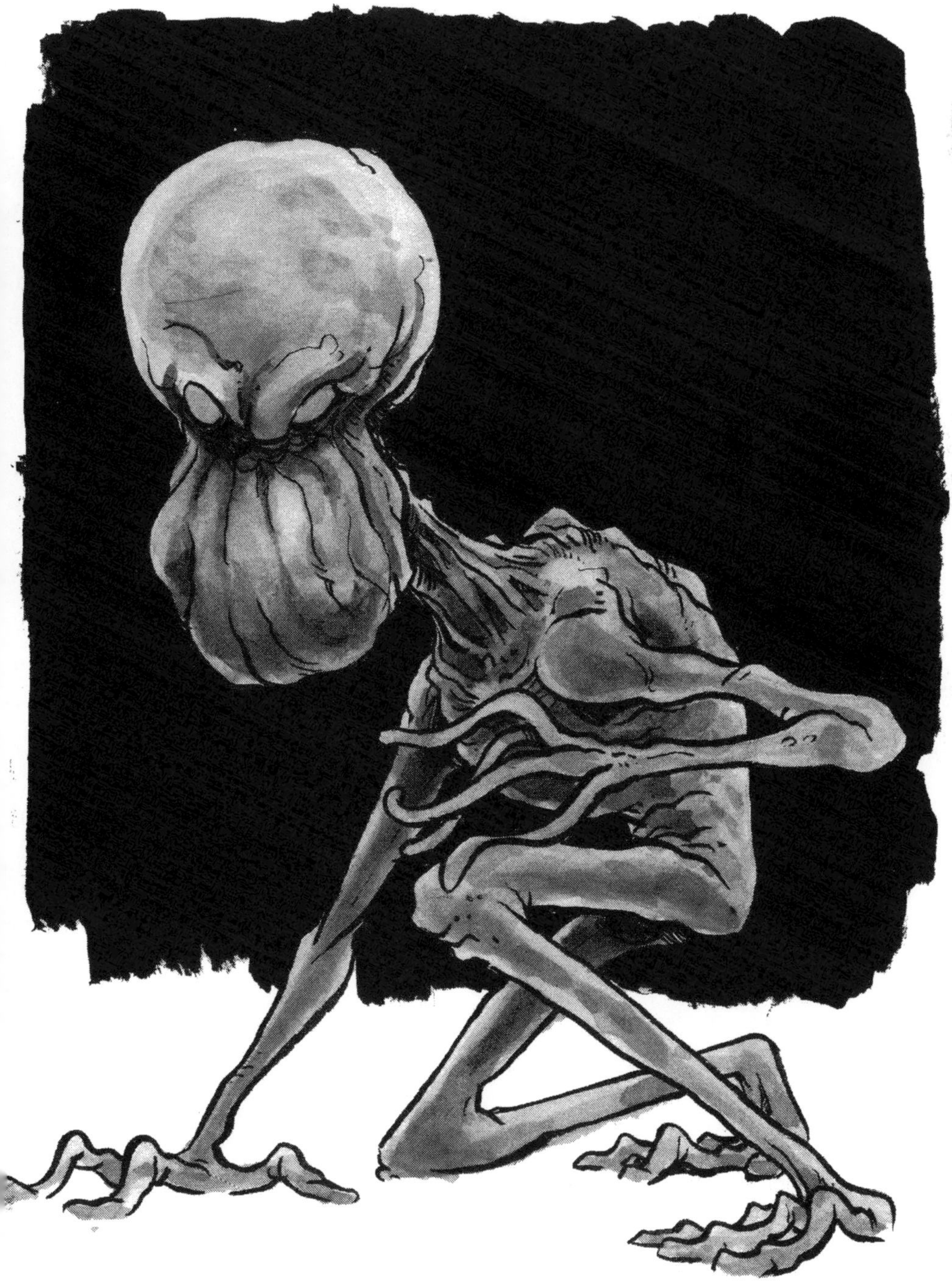

SUBJECT:
THE WHITE MAN

DATE: February 6, 2019

LOCATION: January, Manitoba

The Donalds family is awoken by the sound of someone moving around in their Kitchen. Edgar Donalds (33) claims to have seen "someone" rooting around in the refrigerator, he doesn't remember what happened after he turned on the kitchen light. The next day many items were found missing from the kitchen and Edgar seemed to be suffering from a sunburn.

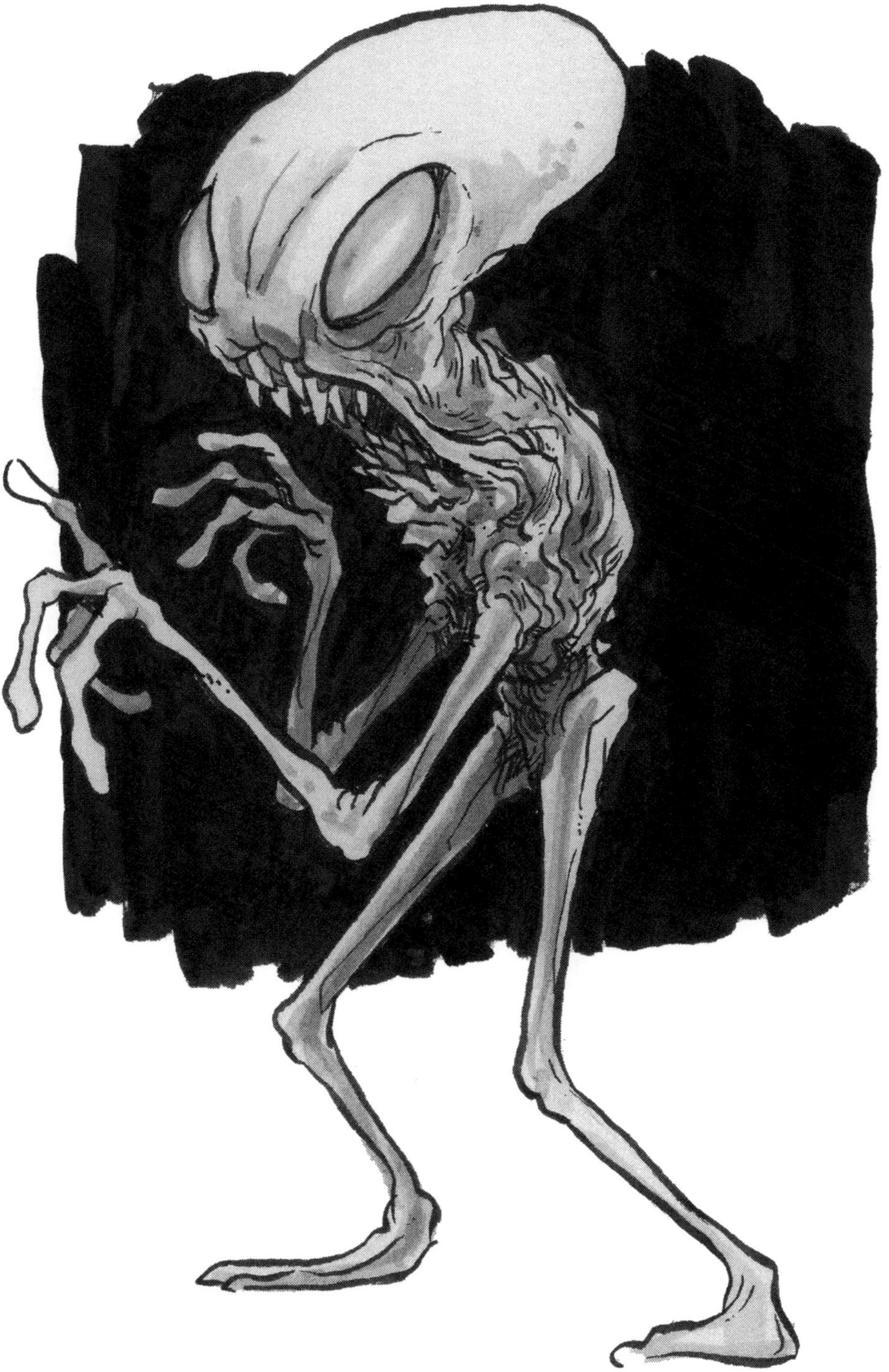

SUBJECT:
THE ORION PHANTOM

DATE: 1953 – Present

LOCATION: Sidney, Washington

They say someone died behind the screen while they were renovating the theatre. Others say that the theatre was just built on an aboriginal burial ground. Others claim that thing people have seen in The Orion theatre didn't show up until the screening of that "weird art film that magician brought when he rented the theatre in 1988". Either way it's been blamed for at least 12 deaths.

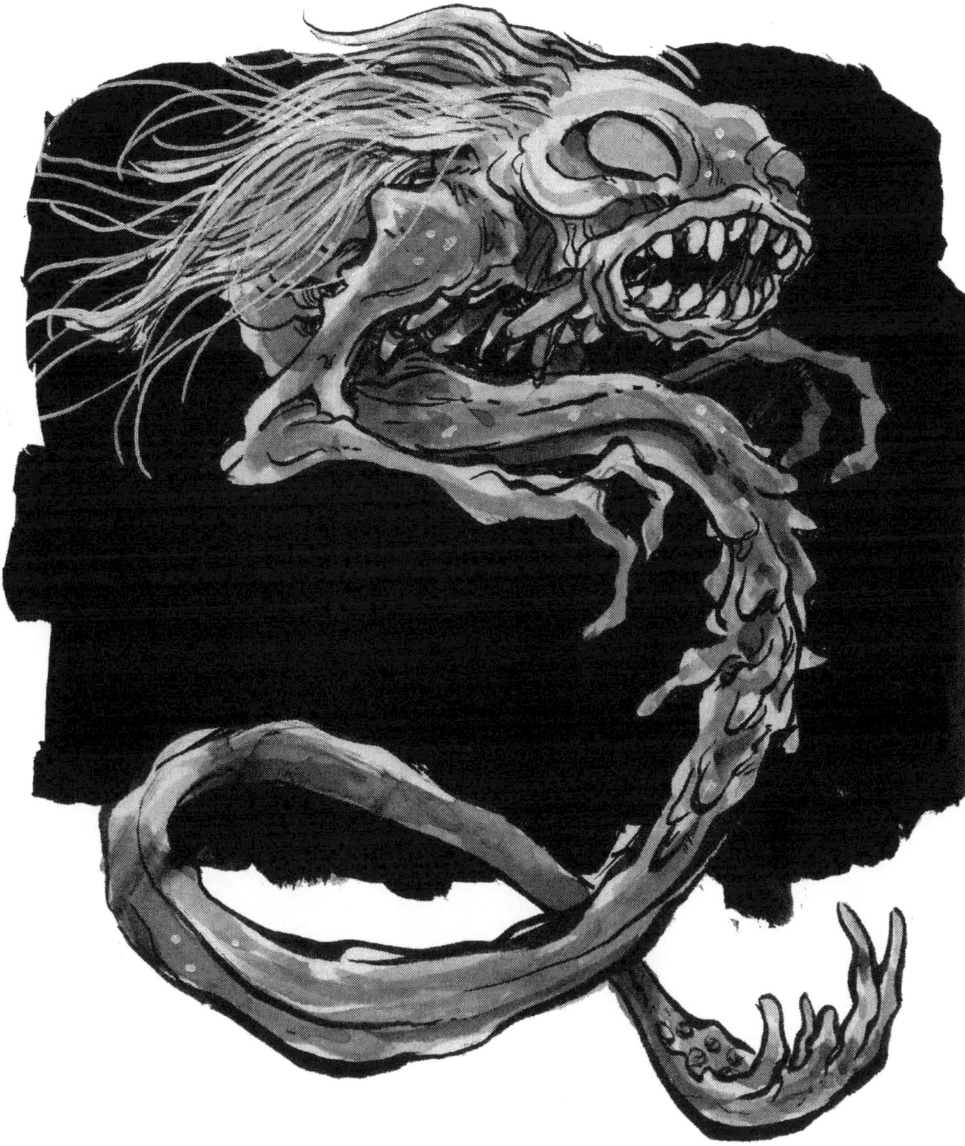

SUBJECT:
DEVIL OF HOWLING LAKE

DATE: 1899

LOCATION: Newsomme, Quebec

"It towered over me, legs and arms miss matched and angular. I saw no eyes on it's face but it seemed to stare up at the sun." Part of the statement of Jordan Waites, a man accused of the disappearance of five people who hired him to guide them in a caving expedition on Fifty Cave Island in the middle of Howling Lake near Newsomme, Quebec, in 1899.

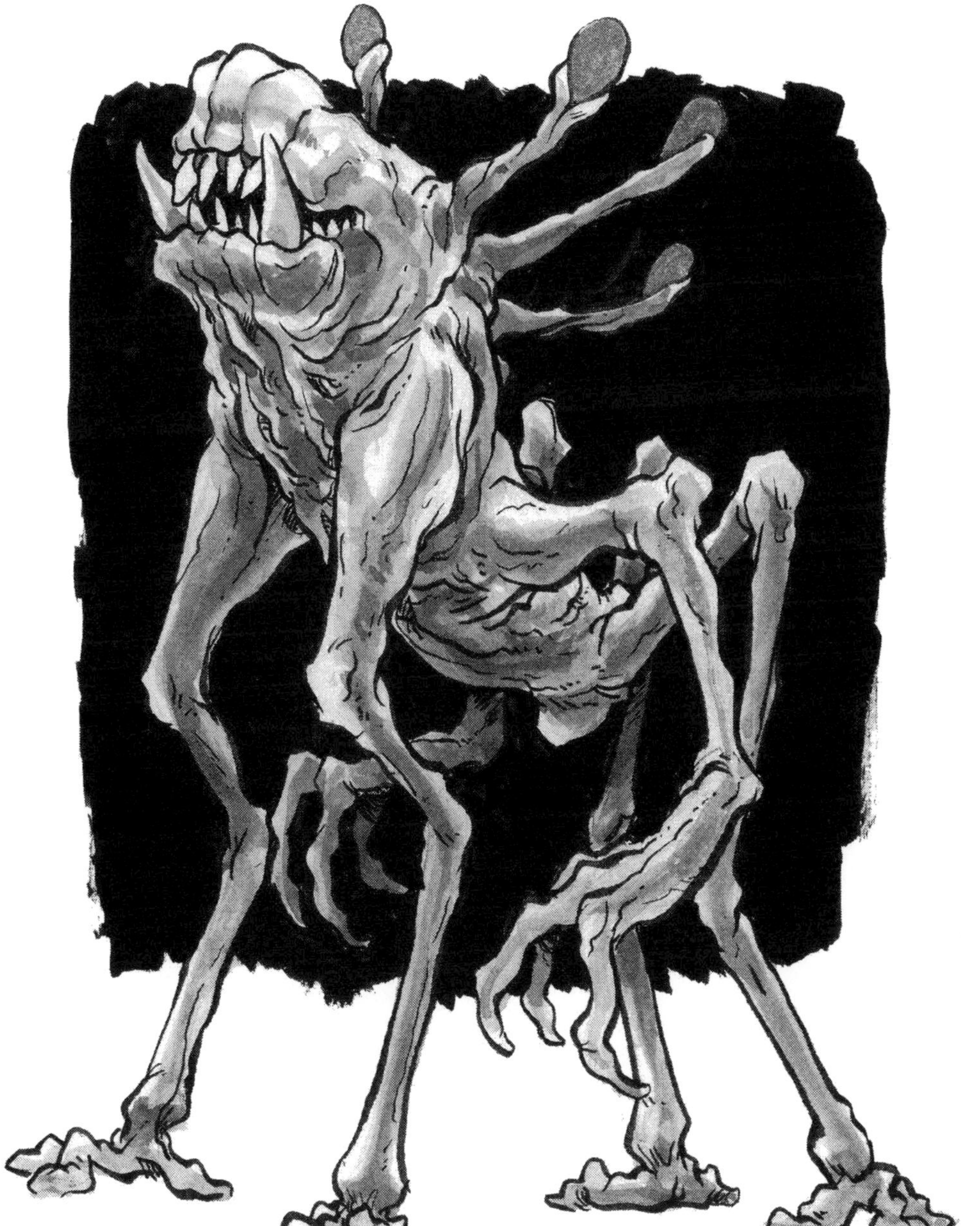

SUBJECT:
ROBO-SKELE-PIRATE

DATE: 2005

LOCATION: World wide

Long story short, it's a ghost.

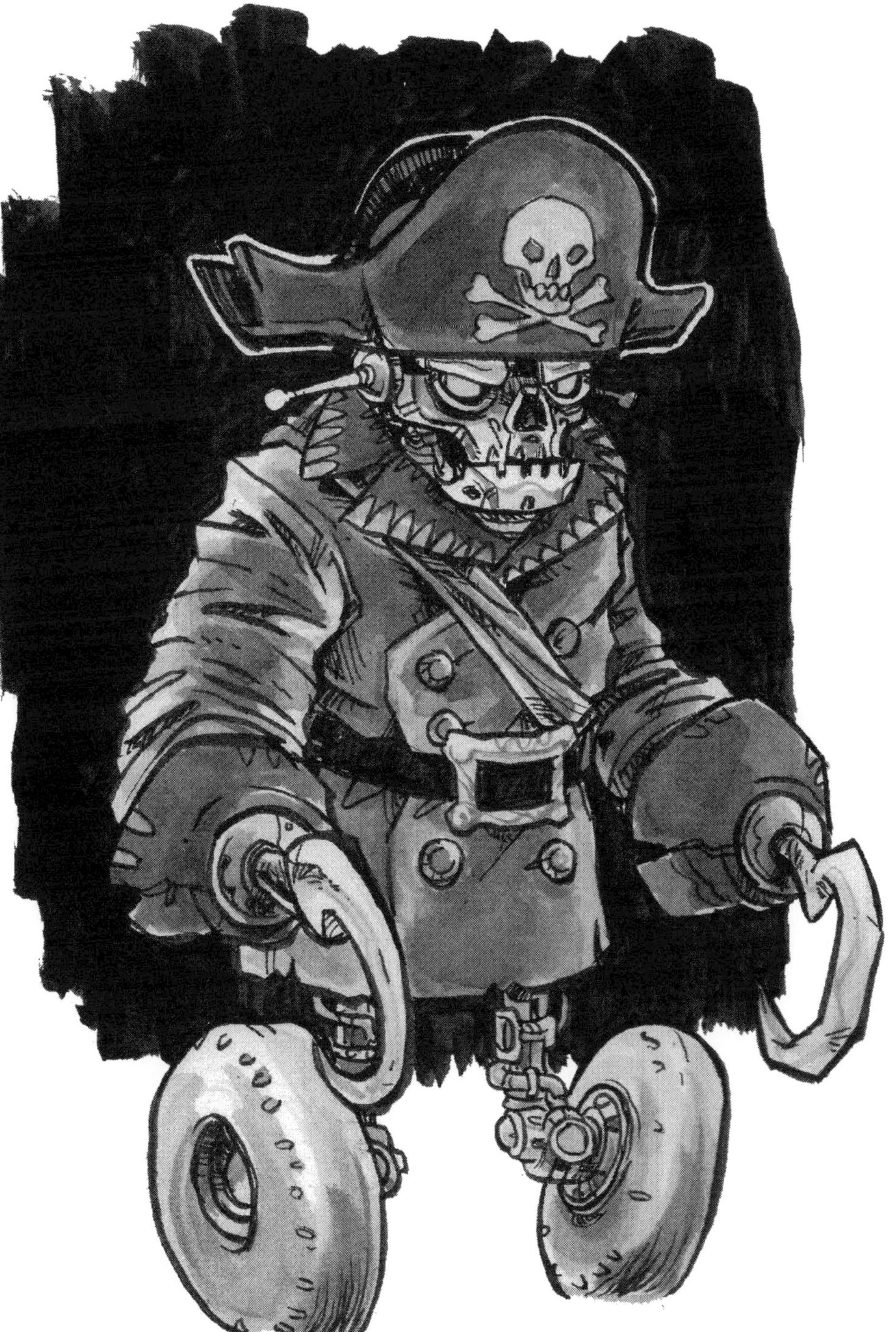

SUBJECT:
JOHNNY NOFOODORDRINK-INCOMPUTERLAB

DATE: June 3, 1983

LOCATION: Trout Lake, Saskatchewan

Thomas Mortleson (33) was driving through Clement, Ont. when one of his tires went flat. While preparing to change the tire he was approached by a creature who identified itself as Johnny Nofoodordrinkincomputerlab. Johnny engaged Mr. Mortleson in small talk, asking about the weather, where was the nearest amusement park, what Thomas thought of certain baseball teams, eventually offering to help change the tire. Once that was complete the creature slapped Thomas on the back, thanked him for his time and walked away. Two days later Mr. Mortleson realized his watch was missing.

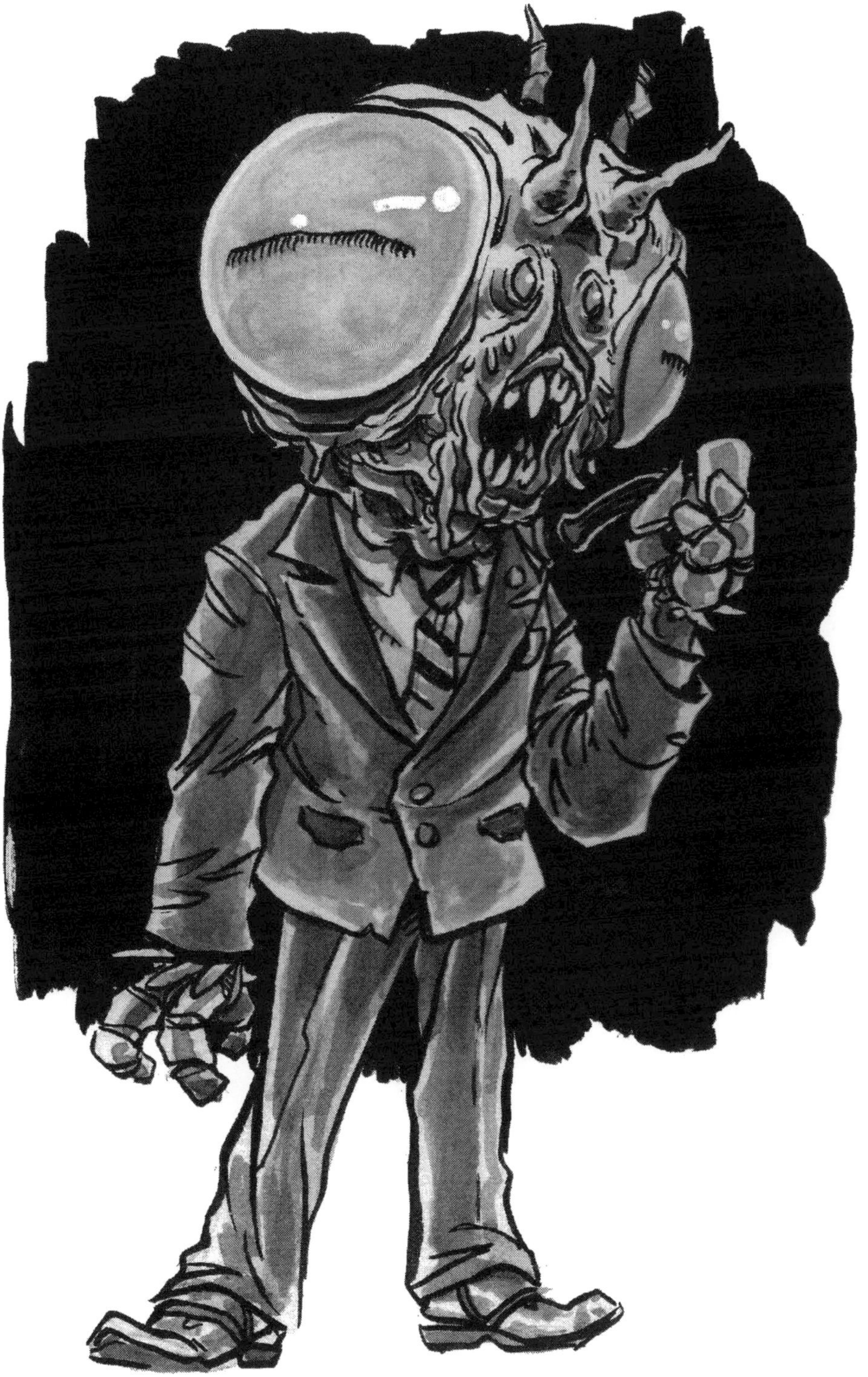

SUBJECT:
CRUMMLIN AMPHIBIANS

DATE: June 1, 1980

LOCATION: Crummlin, Ontario

While searching for frogs in a pond near his home, Tommy Forsythe (10) and his friends found a clump of strange amphibious creatures. The largest measured 36" long. Investigations into the strange illness that spread through Crummlin that summer might be linked to the town folk eating these creatures.

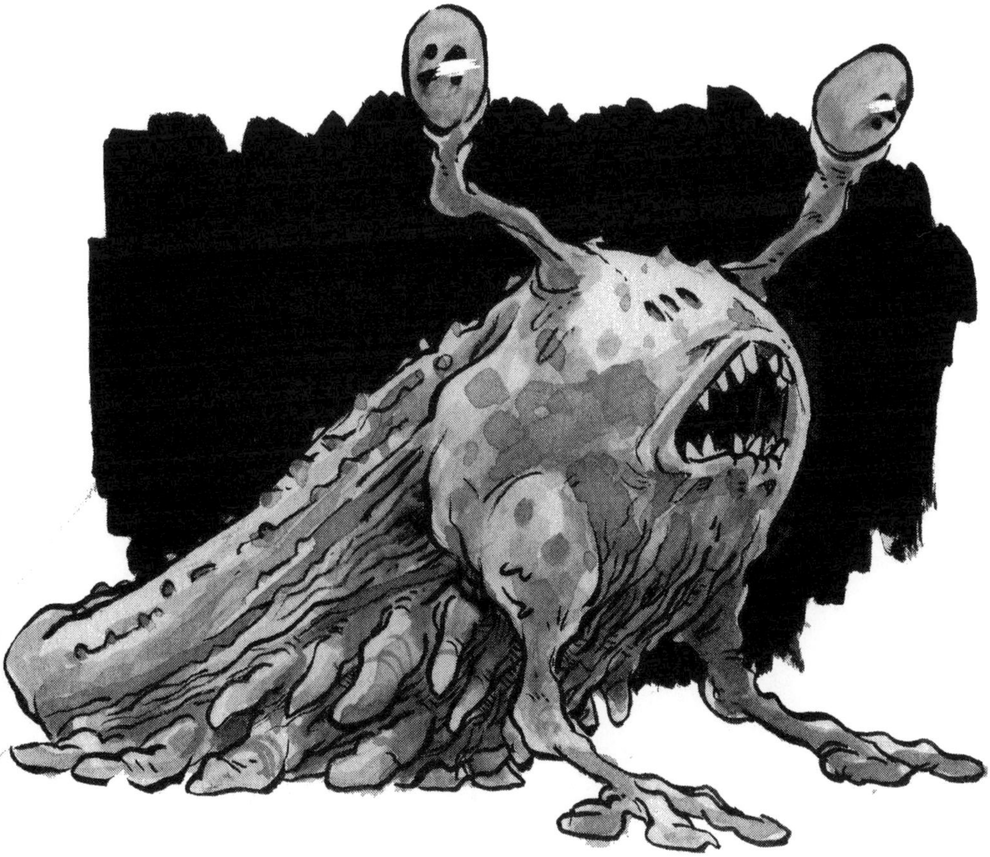

SUBJECT: GRAFTON MONSTER

DATE: June 16, 1964

LOCATION: Grafton, West Virginia

Robert Cockrell, a reporter for the Grafton Sentinel, was driving home when he spotted a large, white creature standing at the side of the road near the riverbank. After seeing it move Cockrell accelerated away.

He returned to the spot the next day to see if the creature was still there. The only sign that it had been there was the grass was flattened and a low whistling sound coming from the woods on the other side of the river.

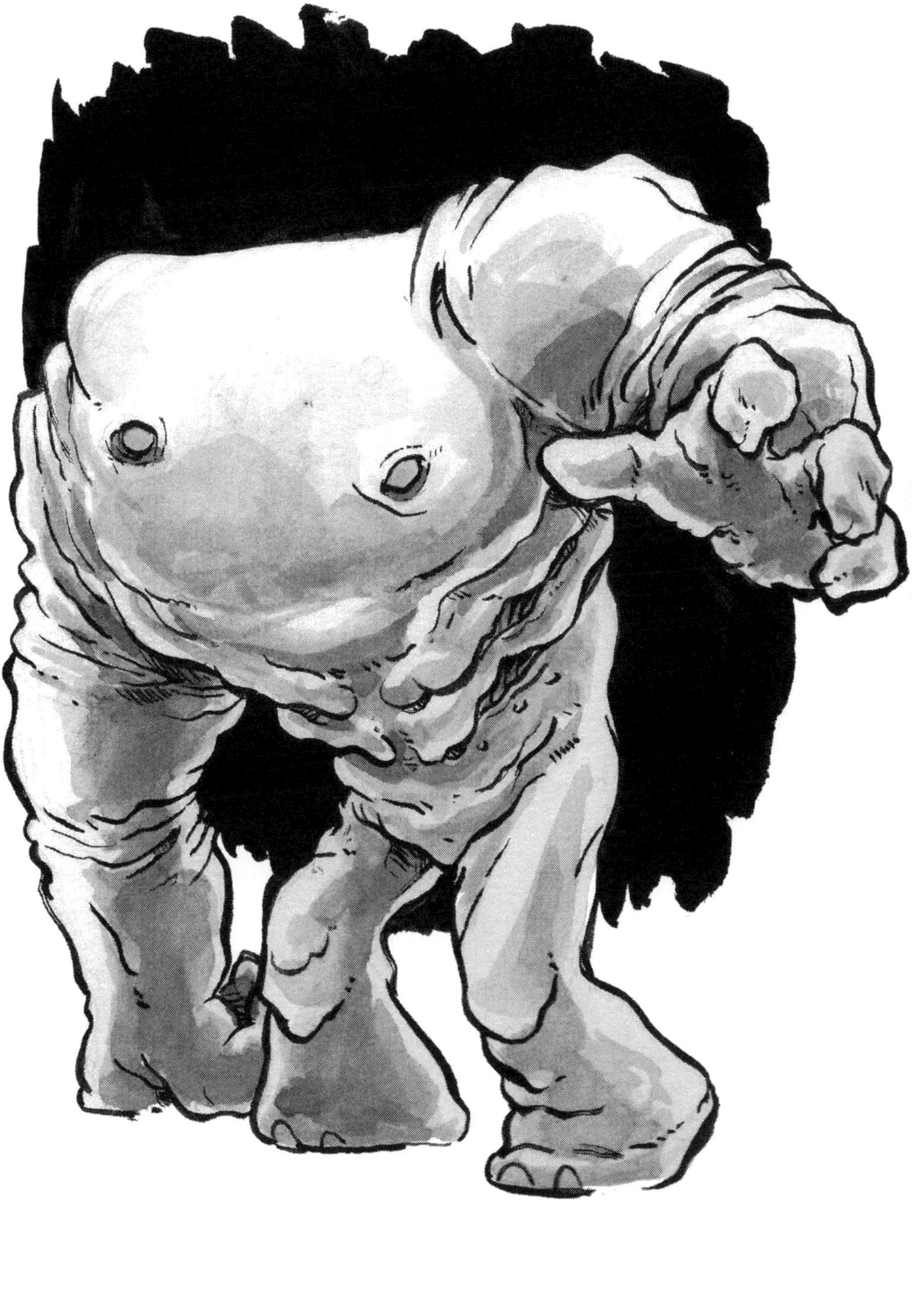

SUBJECT:
THE OBSERVER

DATE: March 4, 2019

LOCATION: Clearmont, Manitoba

While working at the Clearmont Observatory, Charles Whitmore (44) claims that on several occasions he saw a strange figure walking down a flight of stairs near the back of the building and entering a door leading to an unfinished portion of the building. He tried following them but always lost them among the unfinished equipment in the room. He claims that the sightings always corresponded with electrical storms in the area. Meteorologists say there is no records of storm systems at the times Whitmore claims.

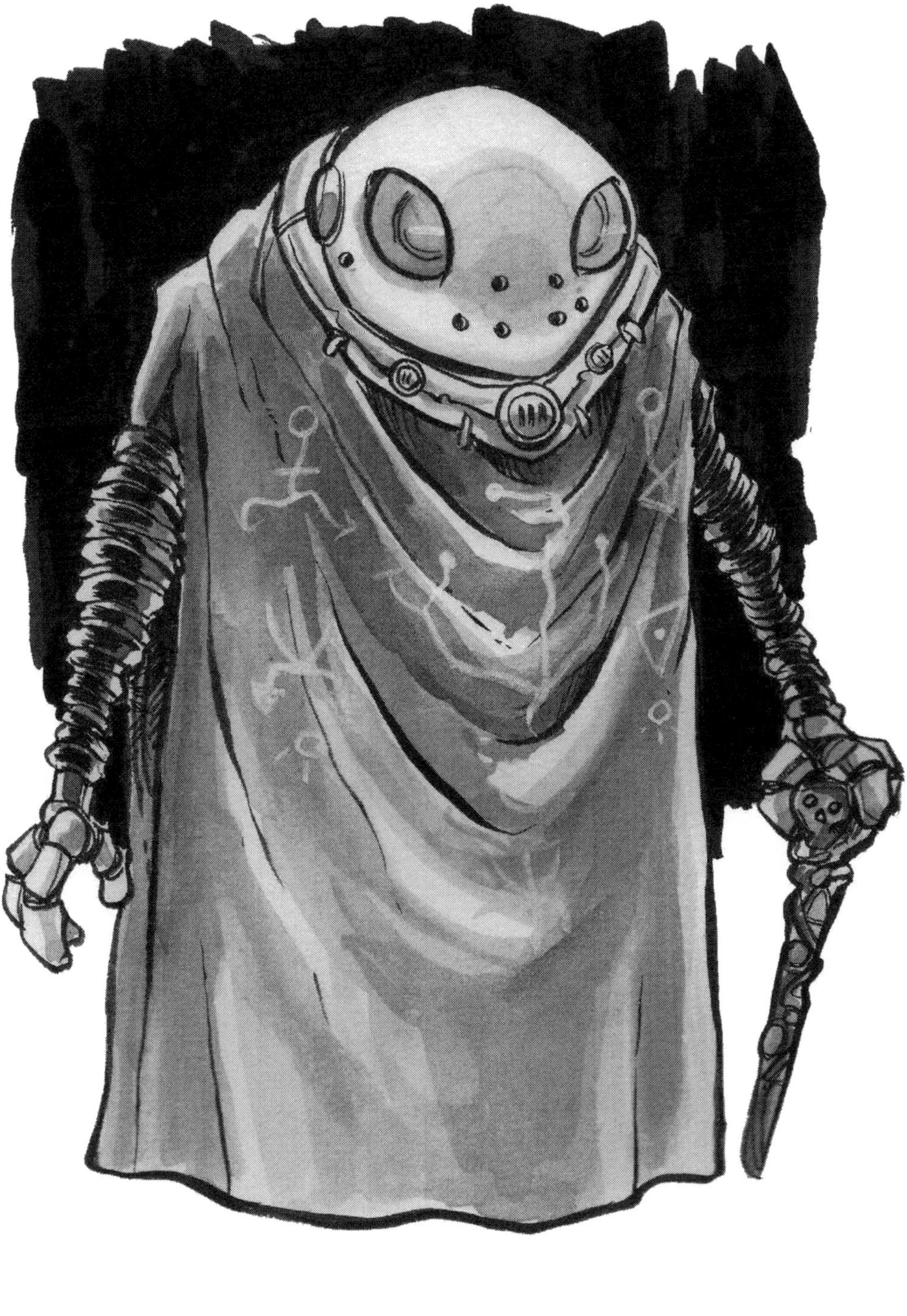

SUBJECT:
OZAMKI'S FIGHTING CHICKEN

DATE: 1965

LOCATION: Princeton, Wyoming

There were rumours that farmer James Ozamki (52), was performing strange rituals on his farm. Nobody was ever allowed to look in the big barn. But there were always strange sounds coming from there...

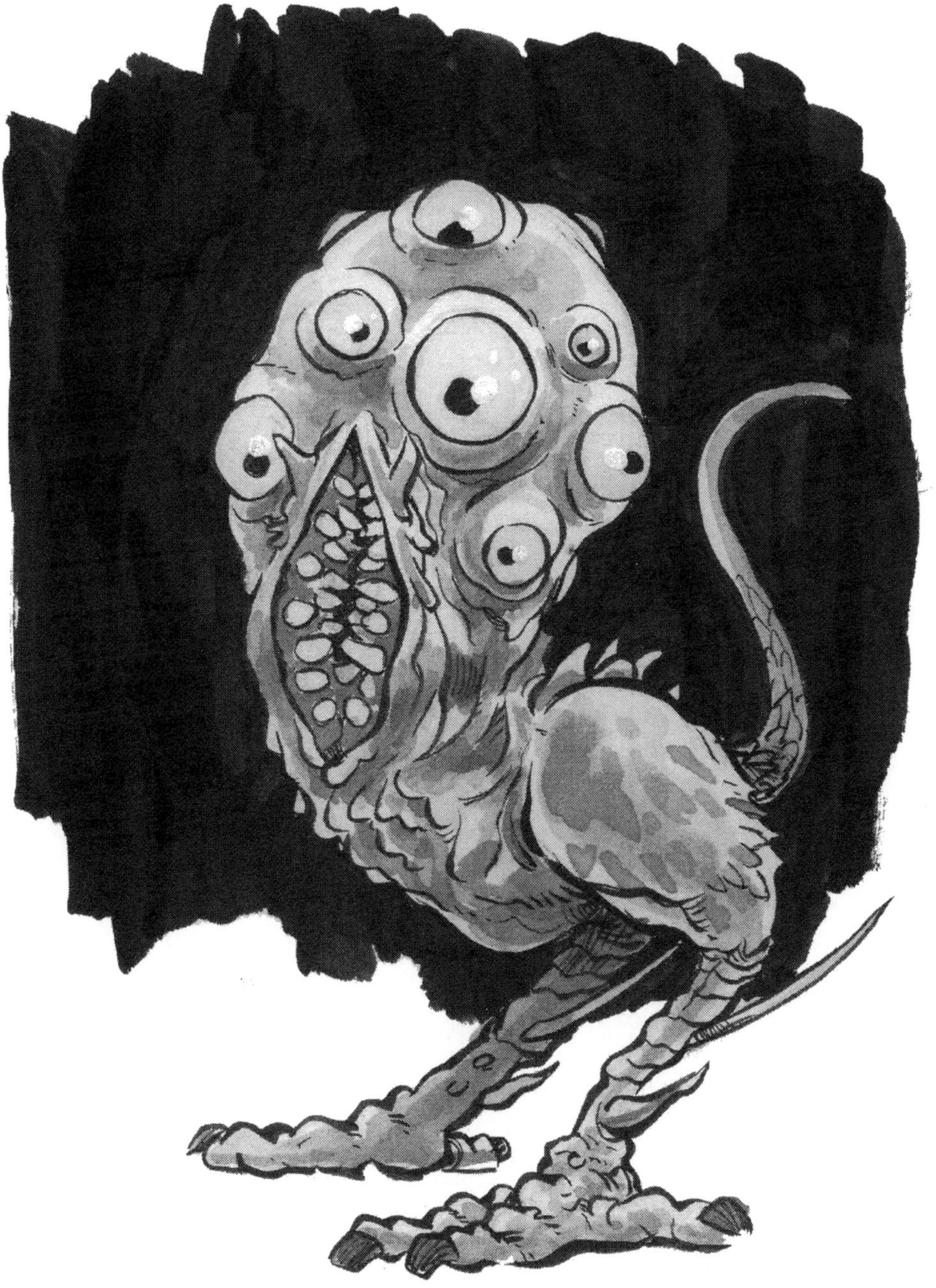

SUBJECT:
THE ORBEK HITCHER

DATE: 1955 – Present

LOCATION: Orbek, Ontario

People claim to have seen a strange creature apparently hitchhiking along the 401 highway near Orbek, Ontario. Sightings seem to coincide with the Perseid meteor shower every August since 1955.

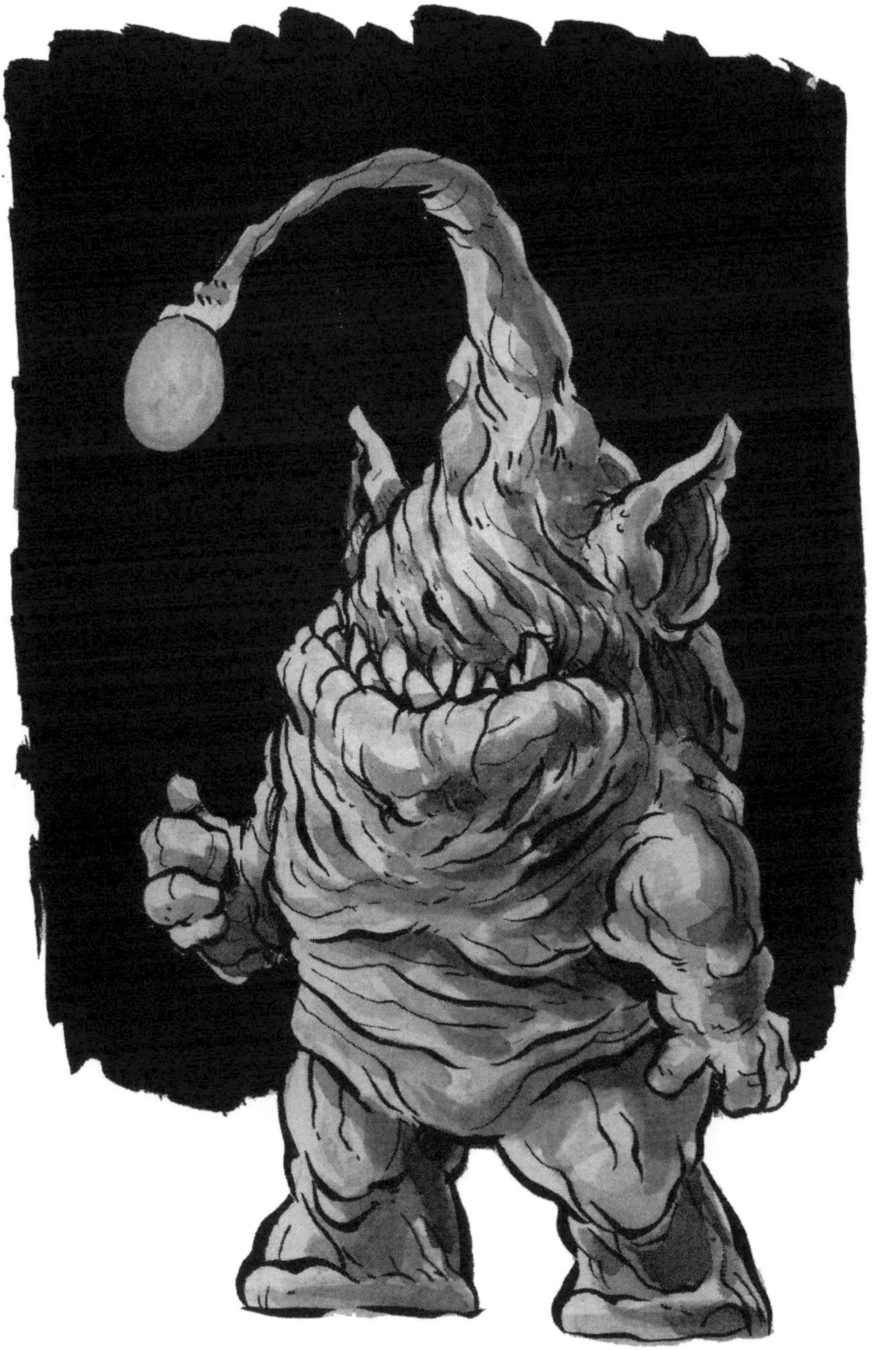

SUBJECT:
THE PUMIKIN LAKE BEAST

DATE: June 4, 2010

LOCATION: Pumikin, Ontario

Something weird washed up on the beach in Pumikin Ont. Residents claim the thing had be seen off and on for as far back as any can remember.

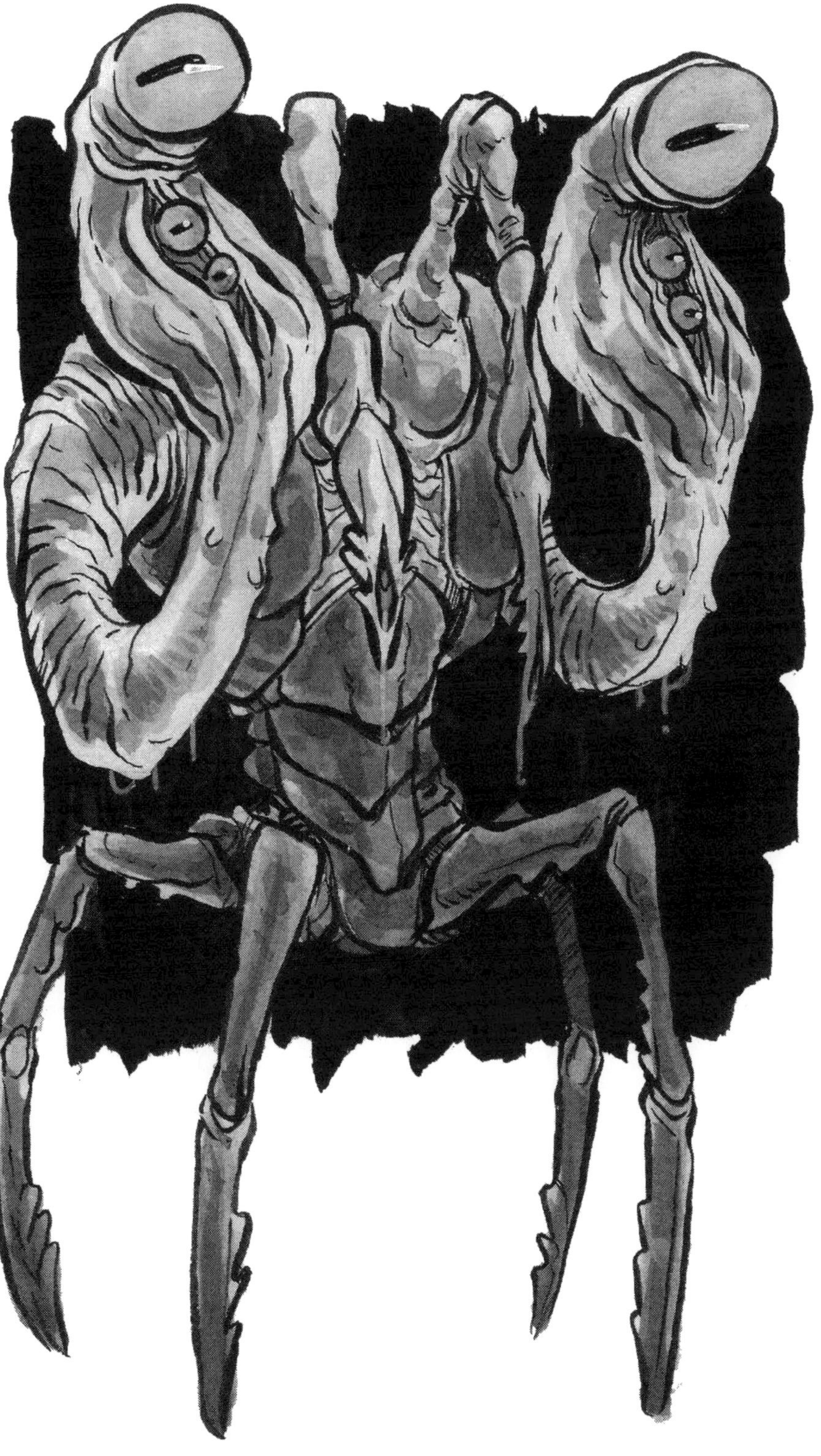

SUBJECT:
ALFONSE CRAMPOOR

DATE: July 3, 1965

LOCATION: Crangary, Alberta

Gossip was that Kezzie Crampoor's last pregnancy was unnatural, not just because of her age (88), but because of the fact her husband committed suicide around the same time. Few people have seen the result of the birth, most of the town shun the Crampoor farm, but Kezzie insists the child looks like its father.

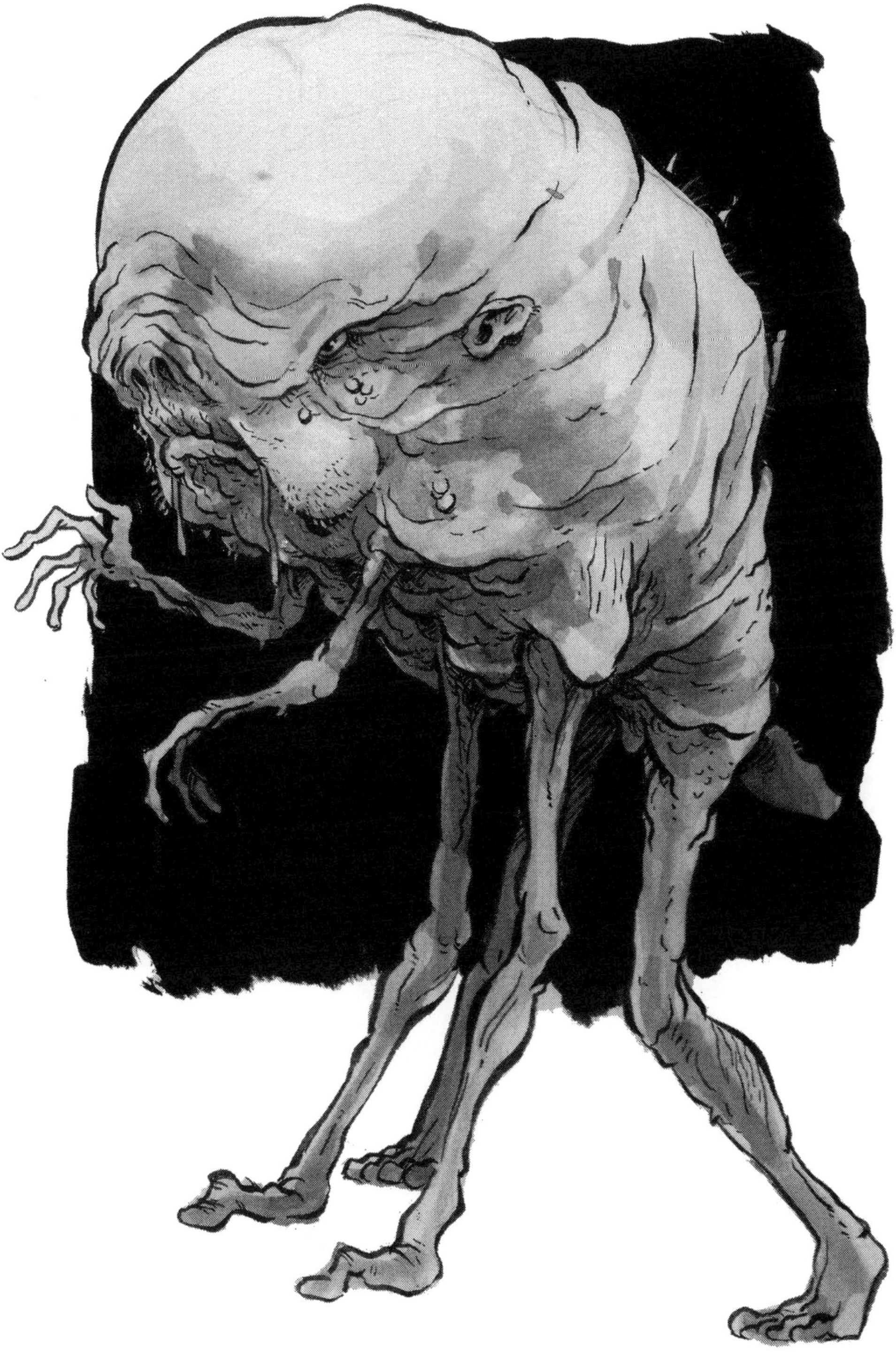

SUBJECT:
UNKNOWN

DATE: December 4, 2018

LOCATION: Niebling, Nova Scotia

Sanford Crumb (66) was working in his backyard forge when he noticed a strange pink light reflected in a window. He called the police thinking someone was breaking into his house. Police arrived to find the back door forced open and Sanford sitting at his kitchen table. Nothing was disturbed and Sanford had no memory of phoning the police.

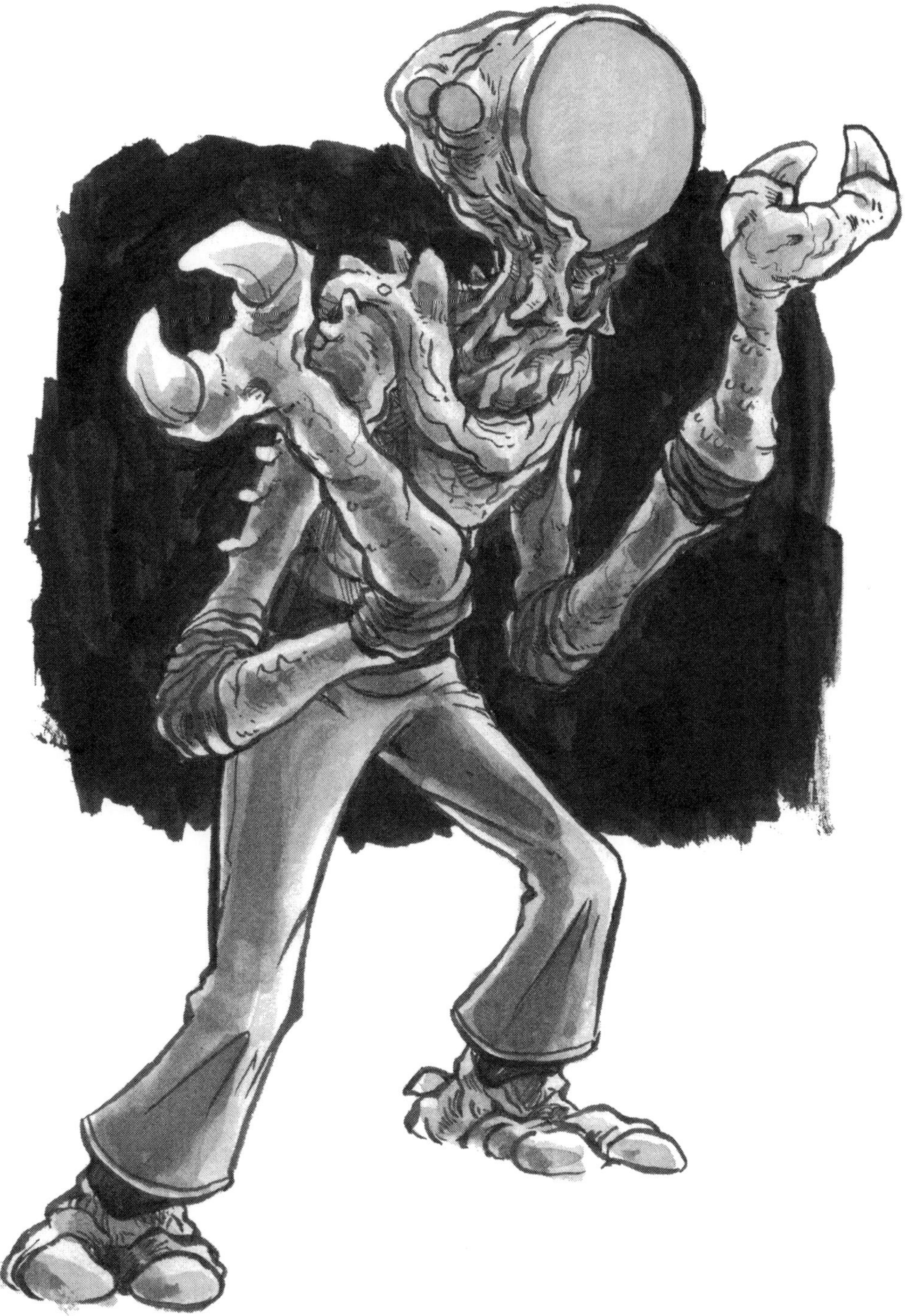

SUBJECT:
THE ARCHUM FIEND

DATE: June, 1985

LOCATION: Archum, Maine

Arthur Collins was arrested for the murder of his sister and three friends at a cabin they had rented for a weekend in June, 1984. To this day he maintains he is innocent. According to Mr. Collins they were attacked by something in the woods.

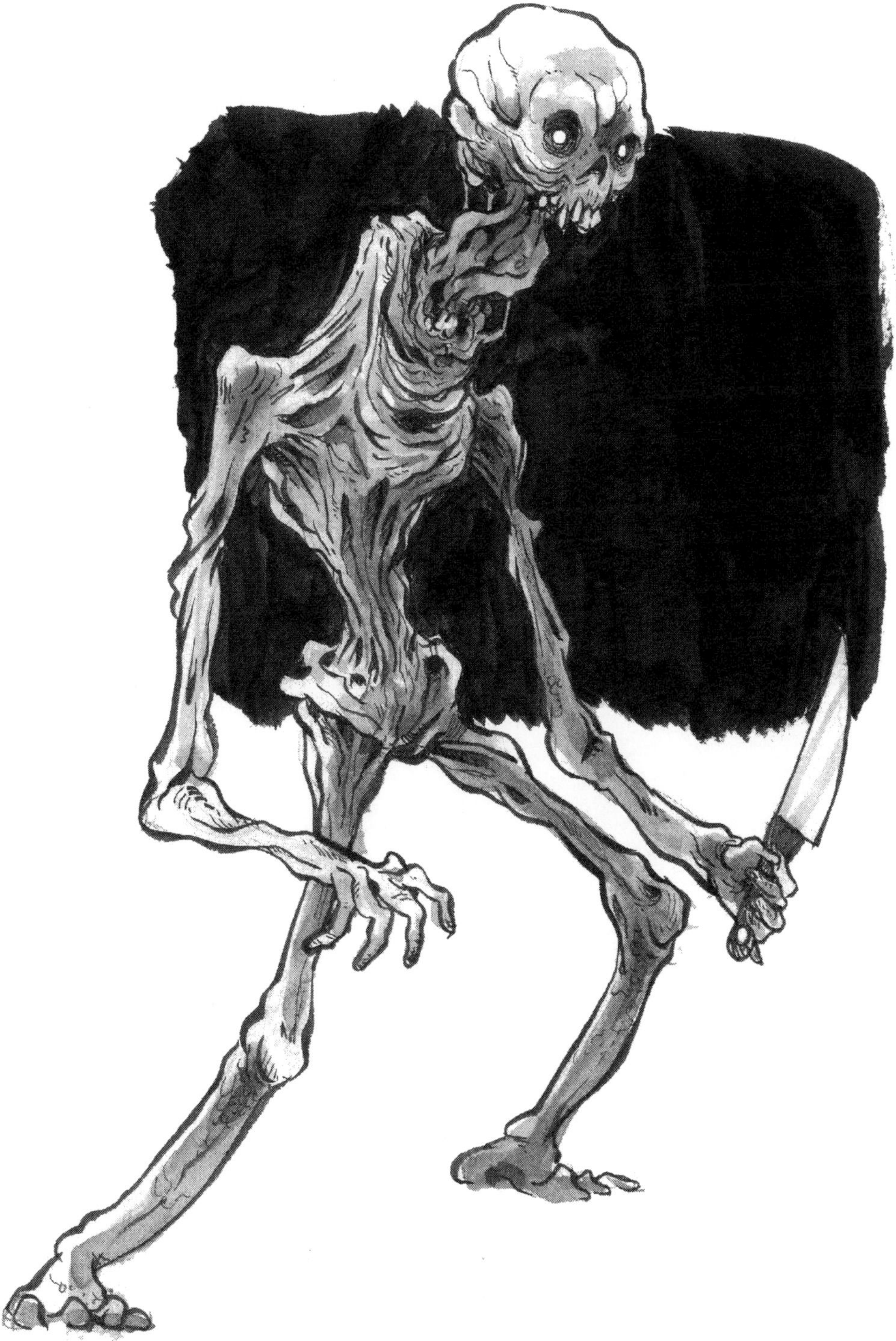

SUBJECT:
THE KNOCKER

DATE: 1950 – Present

LOCATION: Melville, Ontario

Everyone who has lived at 63 Chestnut Ave. claims that at 3:45 AM every day something knocks at their front door. It knocks six times, waits for 10 seconds, knocks five times, waits again, knocks four times. Occasionally small carvings will be left on their porch. They warn anyone who moves into the home not to answer the door. Neighbours and police refuse to confirm or deny these stories.

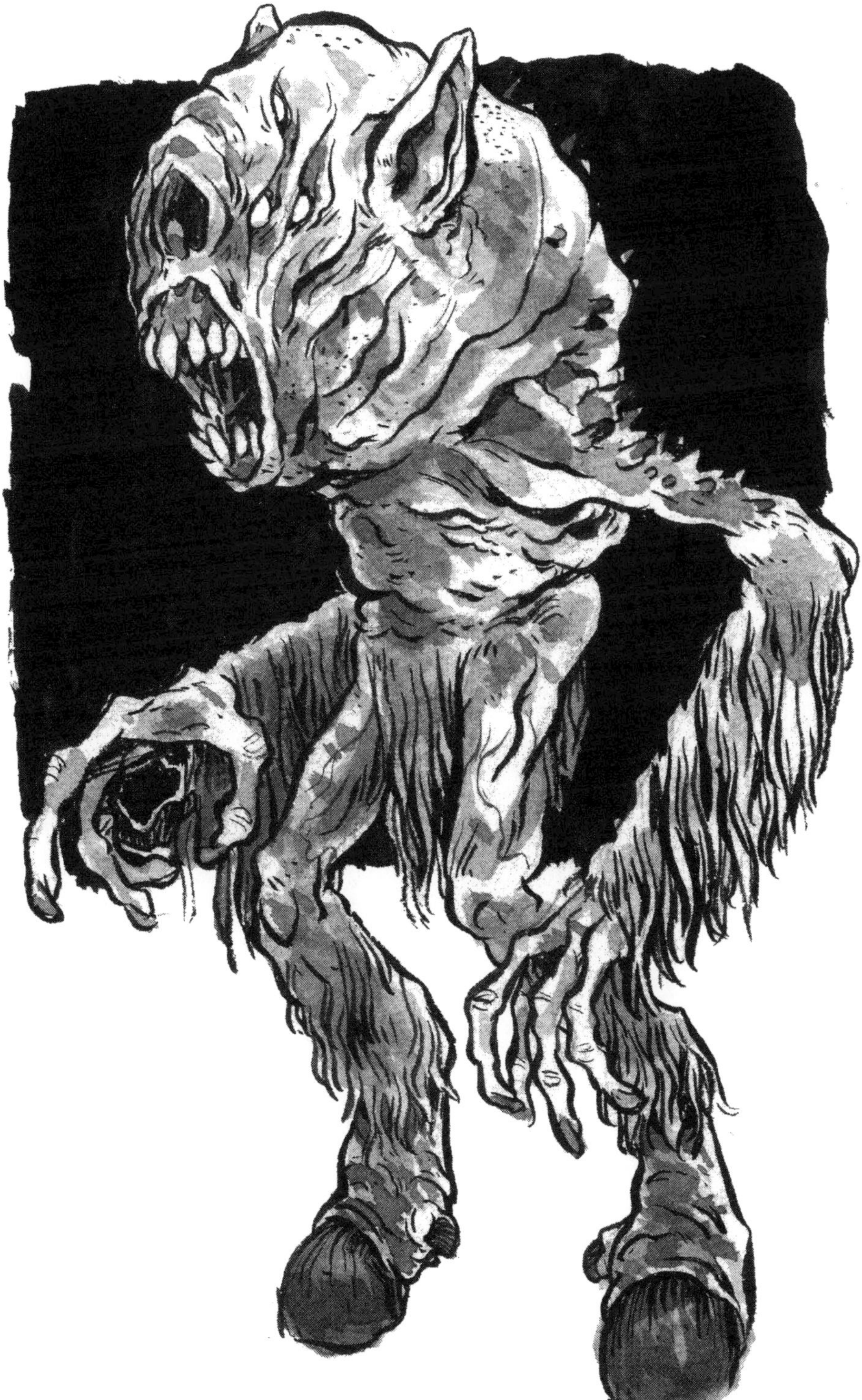

SUBJECT:
GOOSEY GOOSEY GANDER

DATE: 1983 — Present

LOCATION: Summervale, Prince Edward Island

Children dare each other to go to the basement of St. Lucan elementary, a school that was partially burnt down in the mid 1980s. Local legend says it is inhabited by a creature they call "Goosey Goosey Gander." Most townsfolk blame this creature for any misfortune around town.

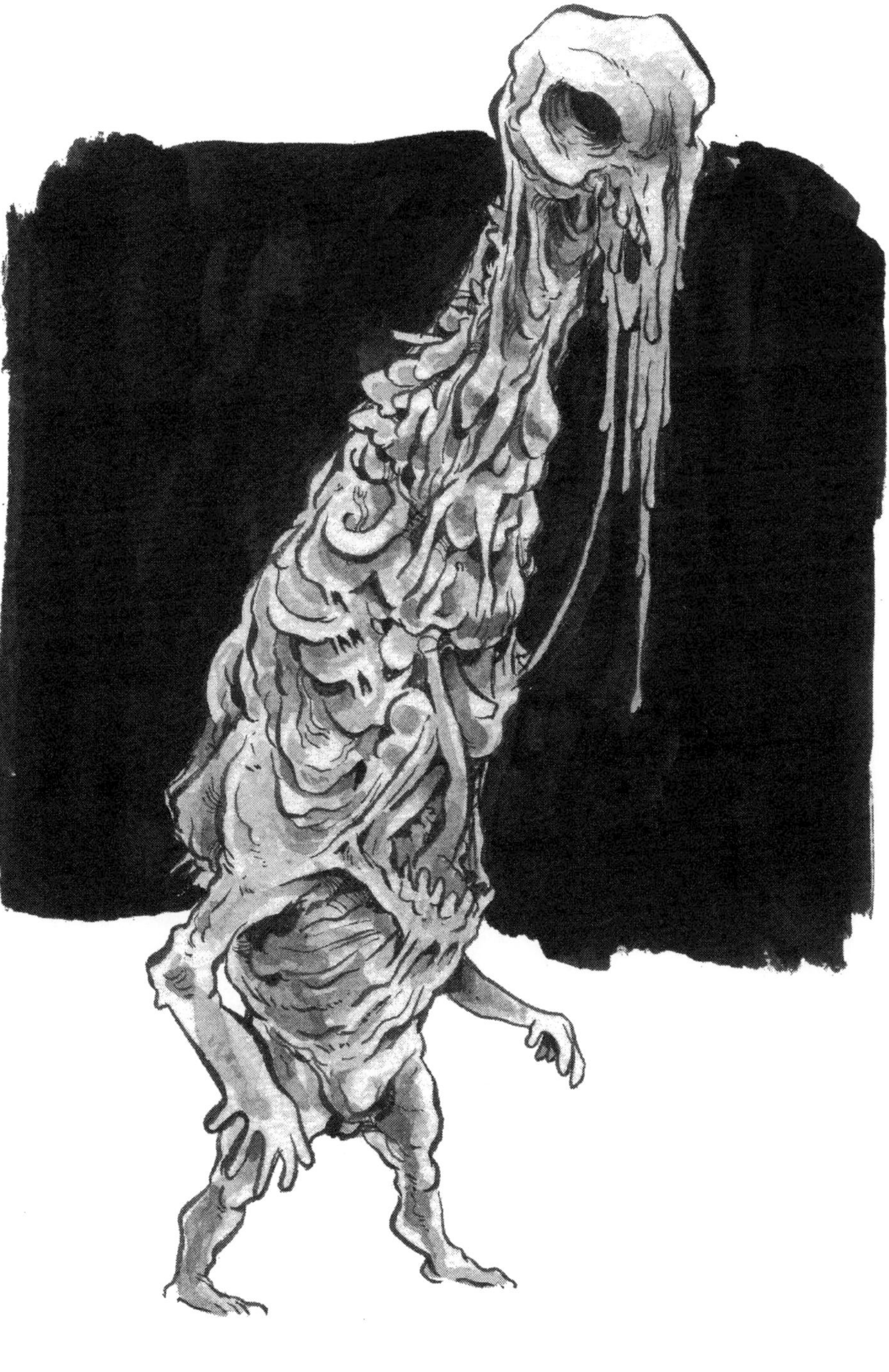

SUBJECT:
K'RZCREENGAL

DATE: Unknown – Present

LOCATION: World wide.

After a series of sightings of shelf elves and a strange deer like creature, the town of Morton, Ontario was visited by an unknown entity. Some people believe this may have some connection to the attempts to translate pages from the Notchordamnatchoz at the University. 60% of the inhabitants have not been accounted for.

> "It Knows when you are sleeping ...
> It Knows when you are awake ...
> It sees you where you hide ...
> The stars are right ...
> It is coming to town."

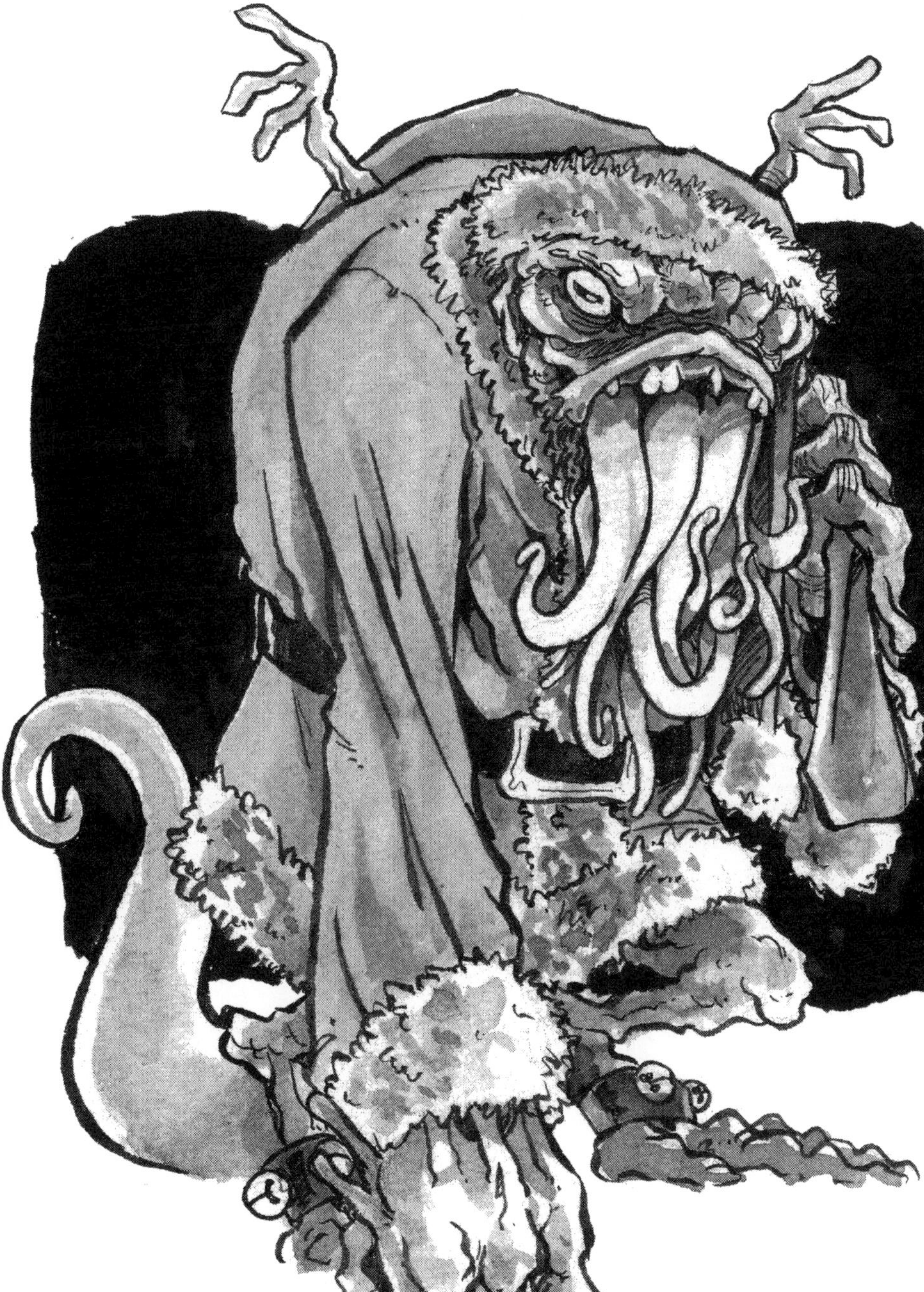

SUBJECT: UNKNOWN

DATE: January 2, 2019

LOCATION: Fallsview, New York

Edward Snythe (43) called 911 saying that an animal had gotten into his home and attacked his wife and 2 children. When the ambulance arrived they found the house on fire. There was no sign of the Snythe family.

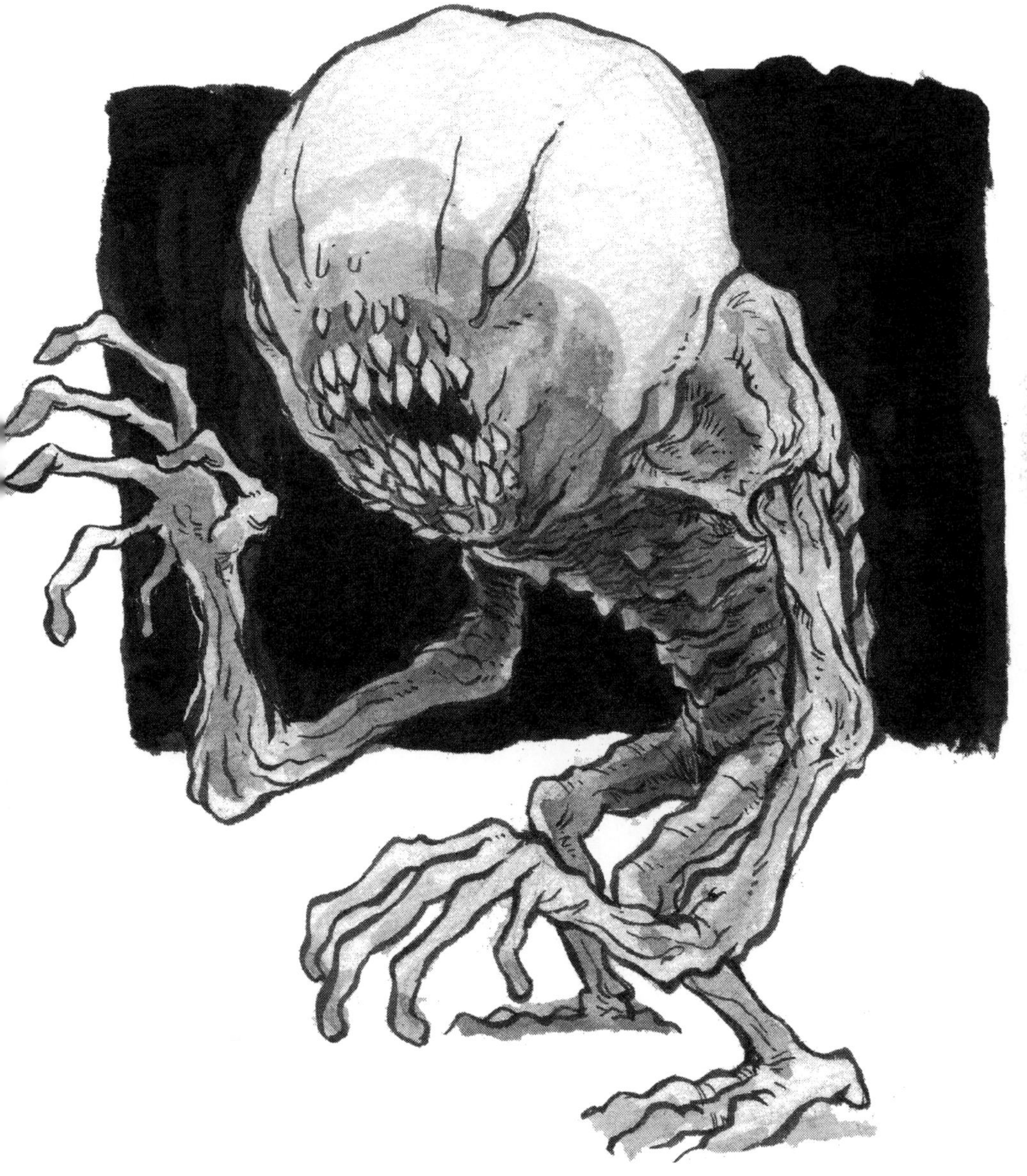

SUBJECT:
THE THUMBLESS SAINT

DATE: December 25, 2018

LOCATION: Fallsview, New York

Sarah Bringham (25), Keith Strode (26), and Dr. James Chow, PhD. (56) are arrested and charged with first degree murder and arson in connection with burning down the St. Felix church in Fallsview, On. The remains of 80 people were found in the remains of the church, many of them have yet to be identified due to the 'conditions of the skeletons.' In recent months there has been rise in the amount of graffiti in town. Most of it being the phrase 'The Thumbless Saint still lives."

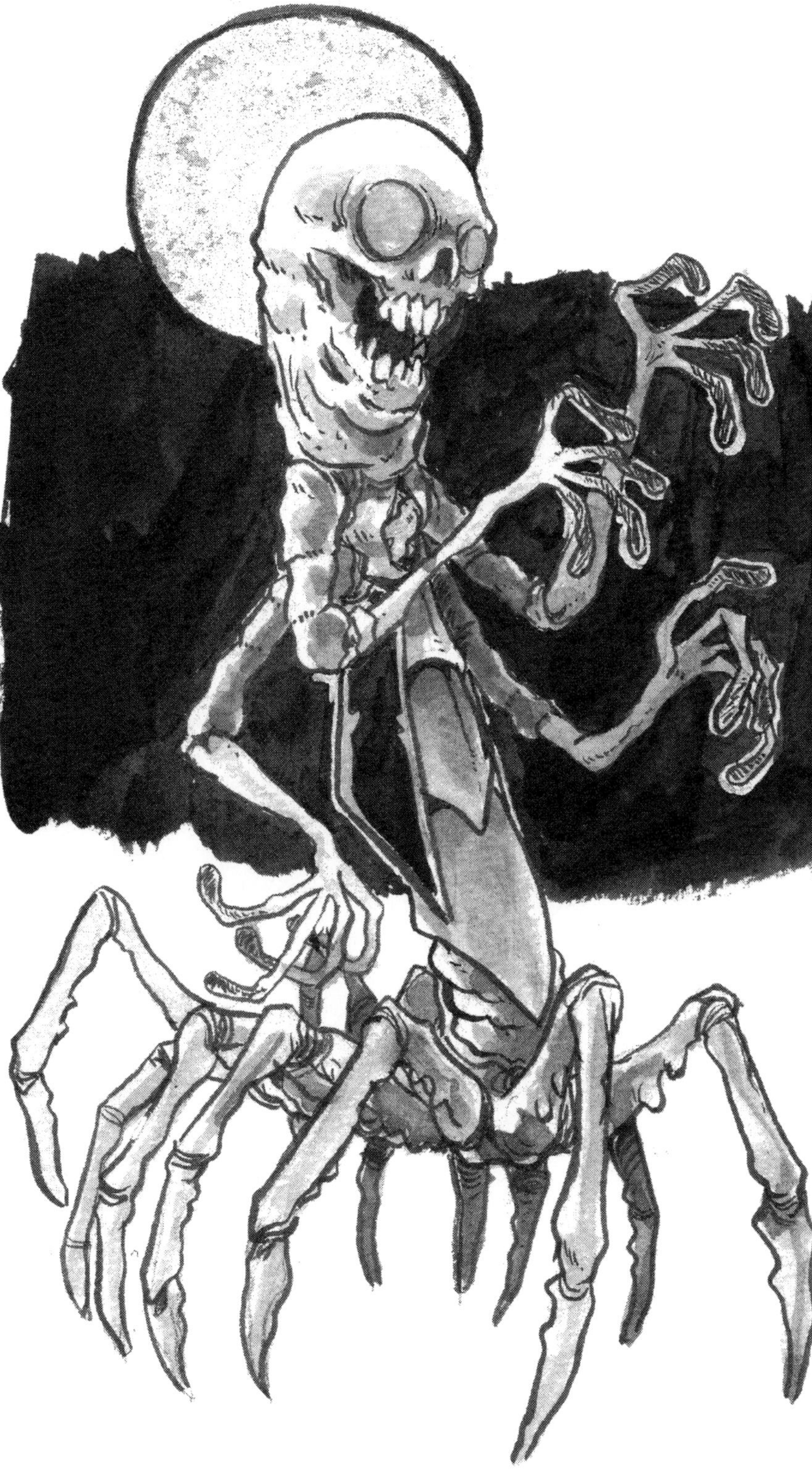

SUBJECT:
FRANKS' CAVES GHOULIE

DATE: March 5, 2010

LOCATION: Torrent, Illinois

Visitors to Franks' Caves see a strange creature shuffle out of one of the closed tunnels in the main cave. Shane Douglas (18) says staff at the caves have been told to stay away from that area of the park, especially on days when it has rained.

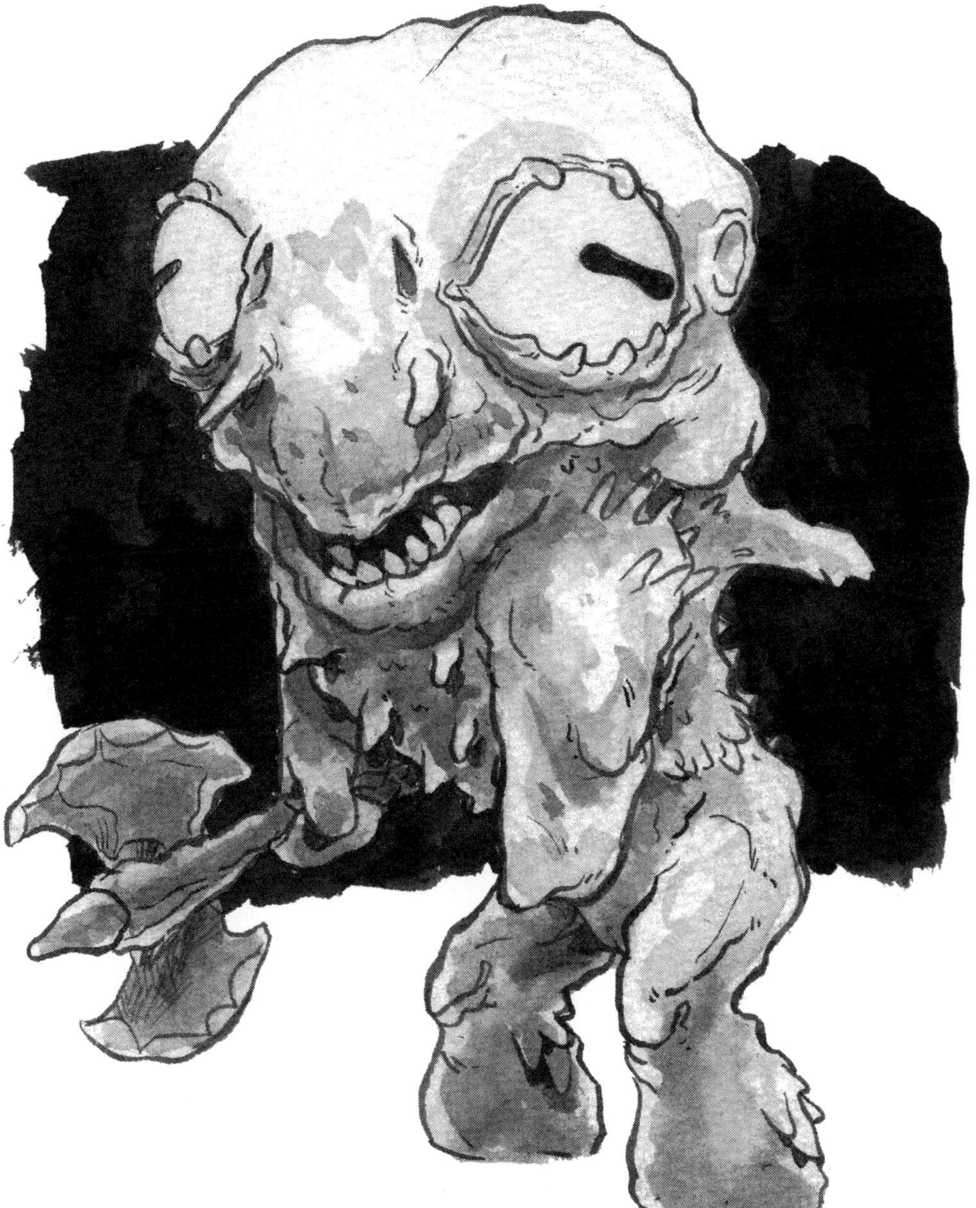

SUBJECT:
THE CRAWLER FROM THE GREEN STARS

DATE: 1976 – Present

LOCATION: Jefferies, Ontario

The small rural community was set up in 1976 by Anton Jefferies as a way to avoid persecution from his neighbours in Simone. All the residents follow a way of life based upon the book 'The Wisdom of Ib.' They claim their god, 'The Crawler from the Green Stars" lives in the church at the centre of town but no outsiders are allowed to enter the building unless they undergo the ritual of cleansing, which takes four weeks to complete. The community of Jefferies makes money by selling a very popular brand of wine they produce as well as pies.

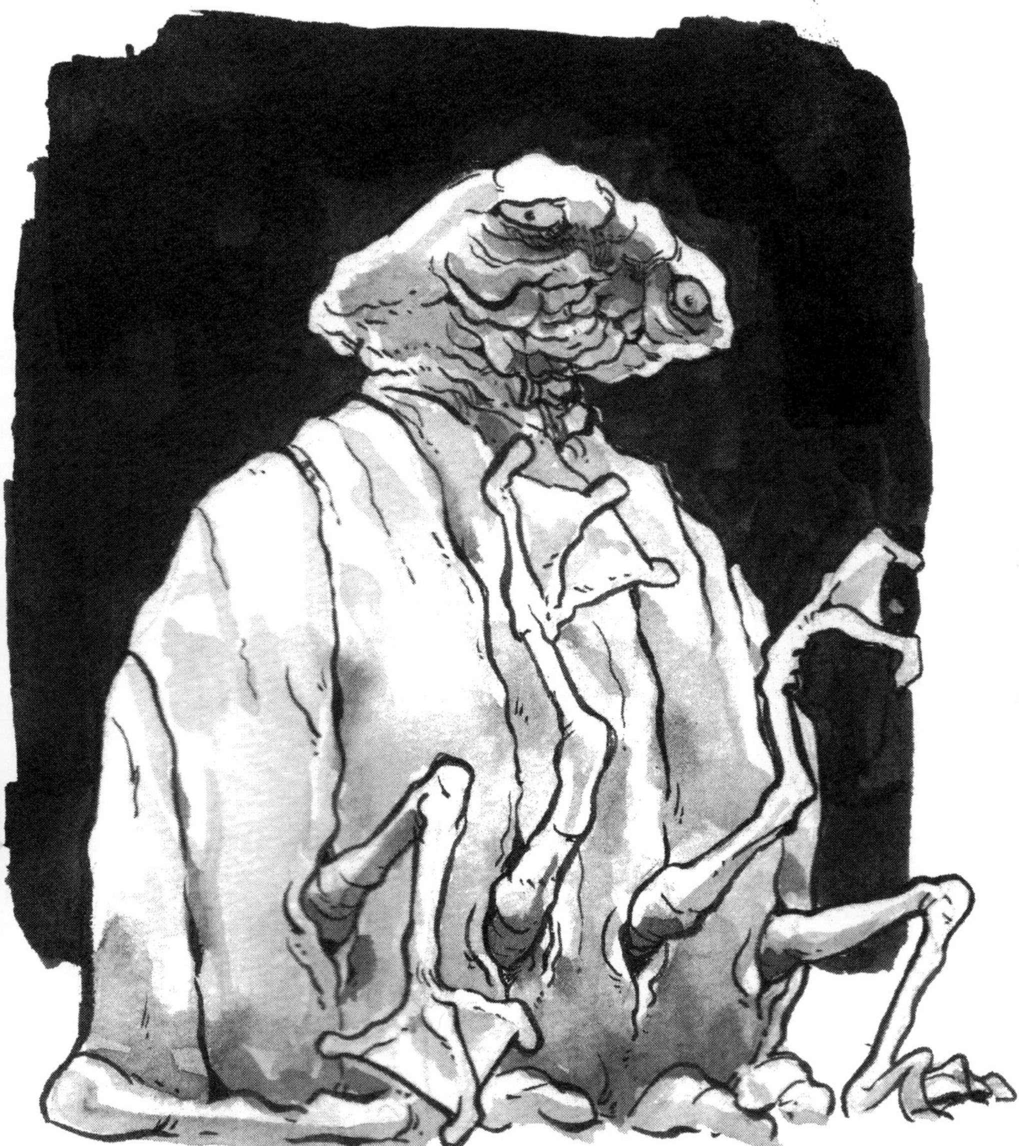

SUBJECT:
STRIPED DEATH FLAPPER

DATE: 2017

LOCATION: Ontario, Alberta

Since 2017 people have been reporting sightings of a giant bird. Authorities say the rise in reports of missing pets and people is just coincidental.

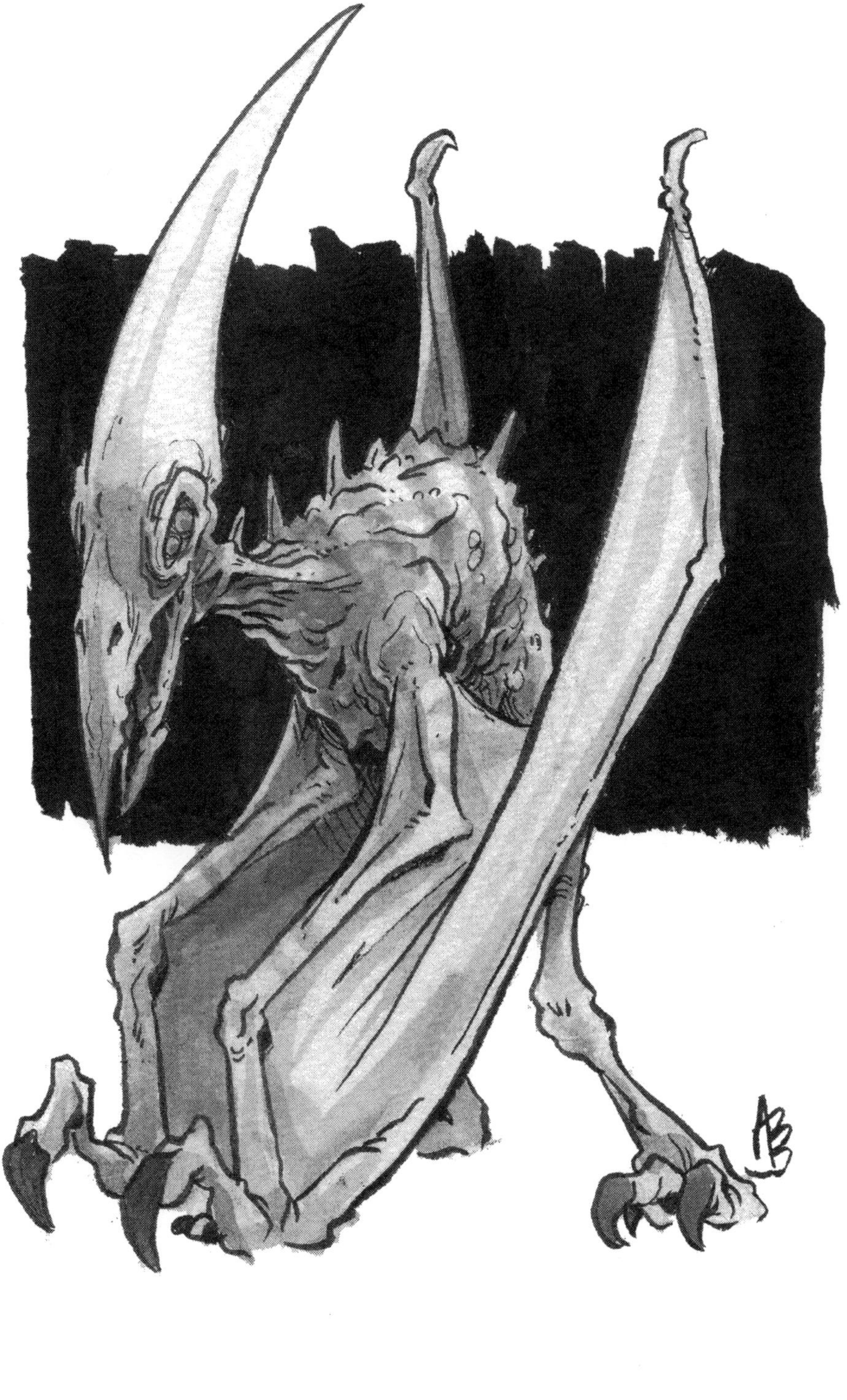

SUBJECT:
LORD HYDROX

DATE: 1983

LOCATION: Flank, Ontario

After three weeks of local crackpot, James Franklin (64), accosting people in the streets shouting about Lord Hydrox returning, the town was destroyed buy what authorities claim was a freak combination of a tornado and earthquake.

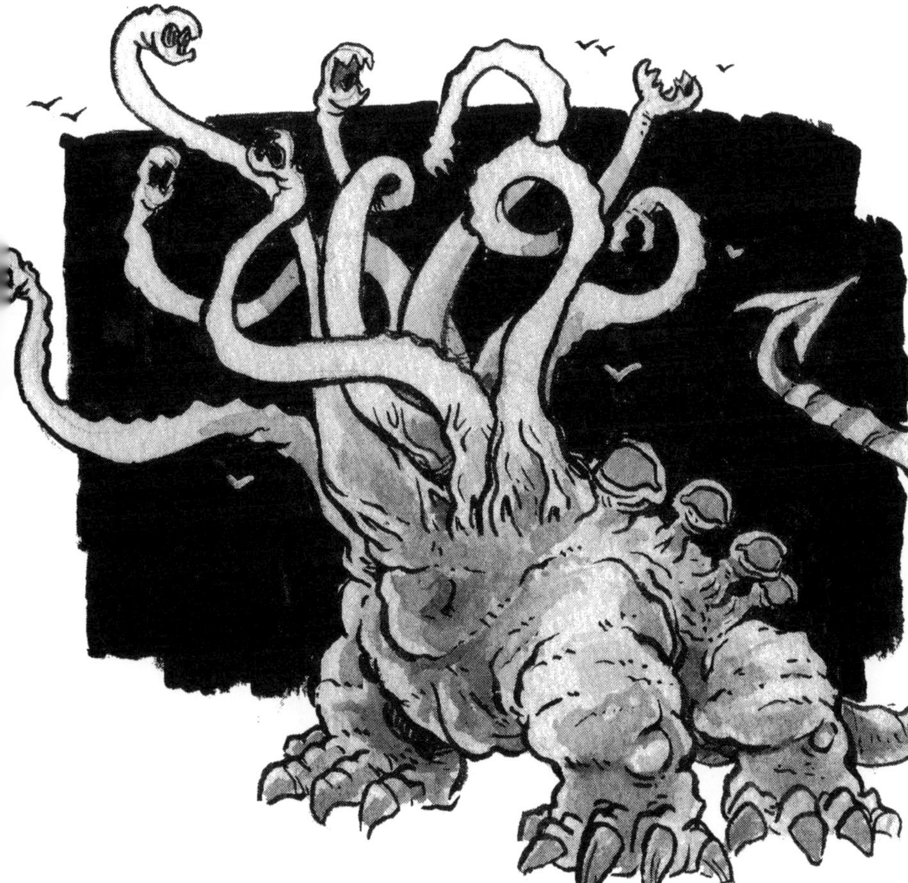

SUBJECT:
NUCLEAR TOURIST

DATE: January 12, 2020

LOCATION: Pickering, Ontario

Technicians at the Pickering nuclear power plant see something moving around the main containment structure at 6:45 am. Shortly after the sighting an emergency alert is issued. Security forces find no evidence of the 'visitor' and the alert is retracted.

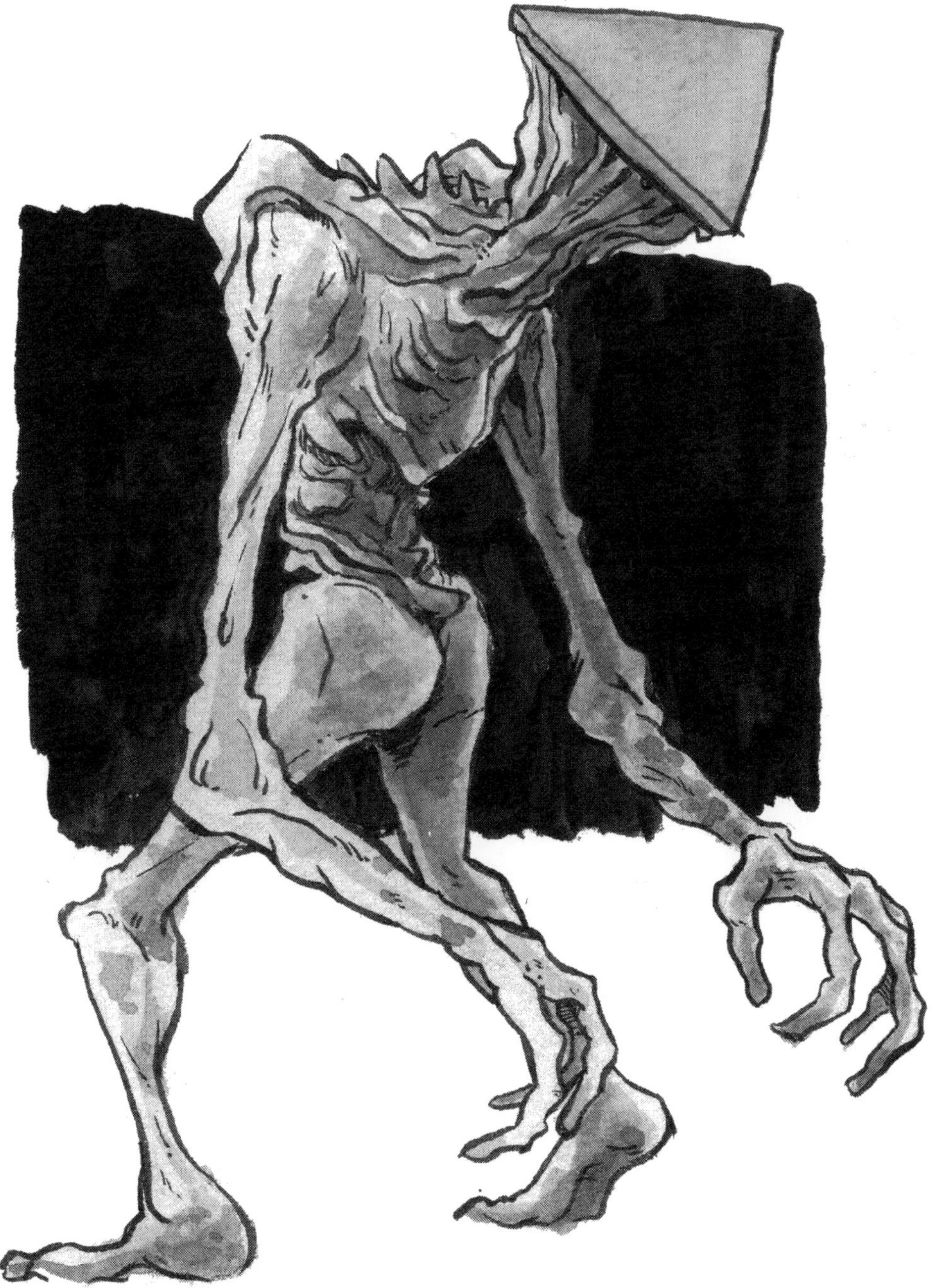

SUBJECT:
UNKNOWN

DATE: April 4, 1963

LOCATION: Shale, New Brunswick

While responding to a fire at the home of astrophysicist Prof. Wilmarth Blight, respondents saw something run out of the flames and into the nearby woods. "The weirdest thing about it was the small blue shorts it was wearing." Said Jim Gorgan(23), "I don't remember anything else about it, really." Prof. Blight has not been seen since.

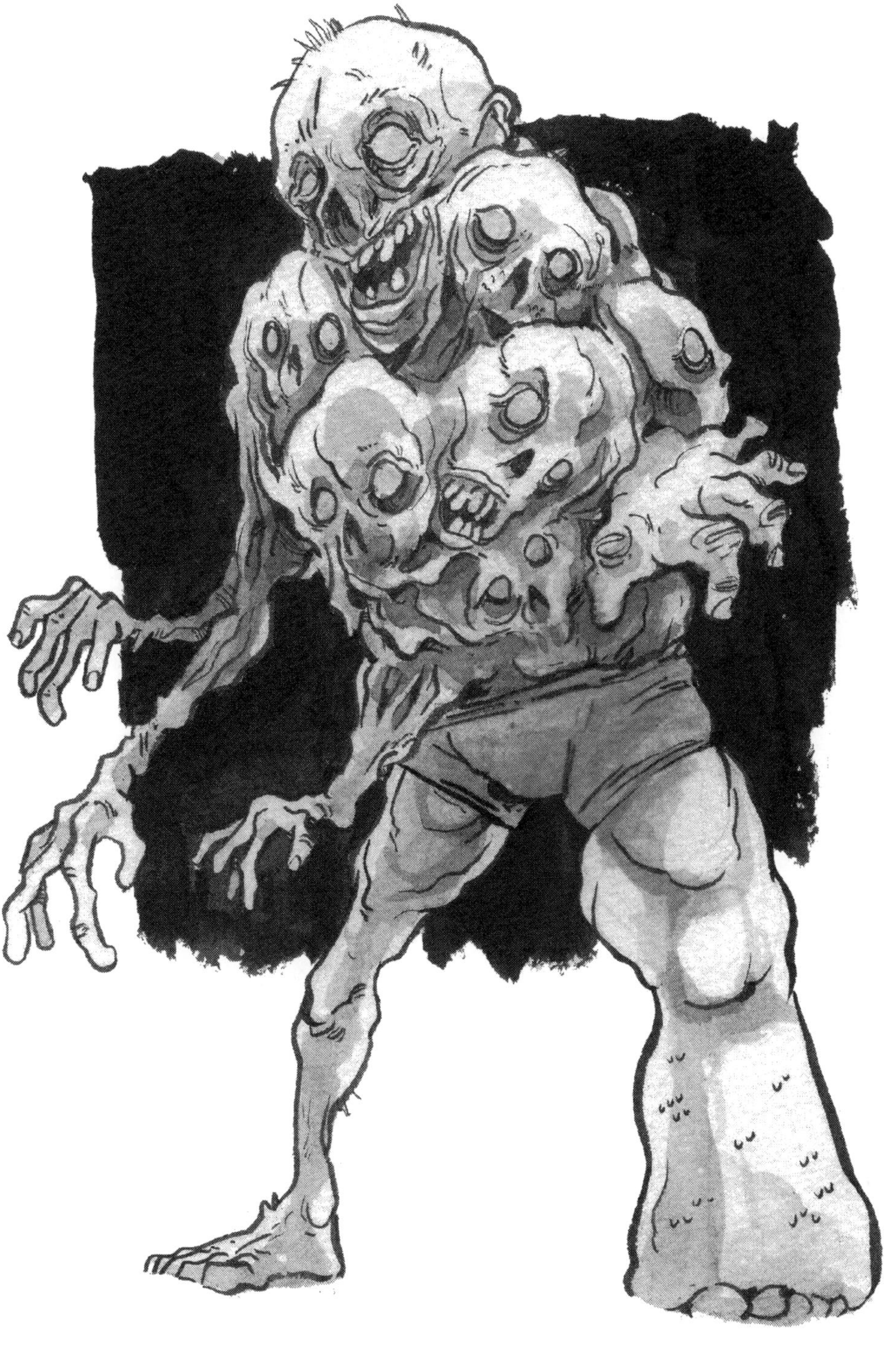

SUBJECT:
FLAT FRANK

DATE: 1967

LOCATION: Scenic, Nova Scotia

A strange outbreak of anaemia affected the entire town, including animals. Residents blamed it on the old folk legend of Flat Frank. A strange creature that surfaced every 20 years to drink the blood of people who don't believe and smells like Hot Dogs. Flat Frank can pass through any crack it can fit its head into.

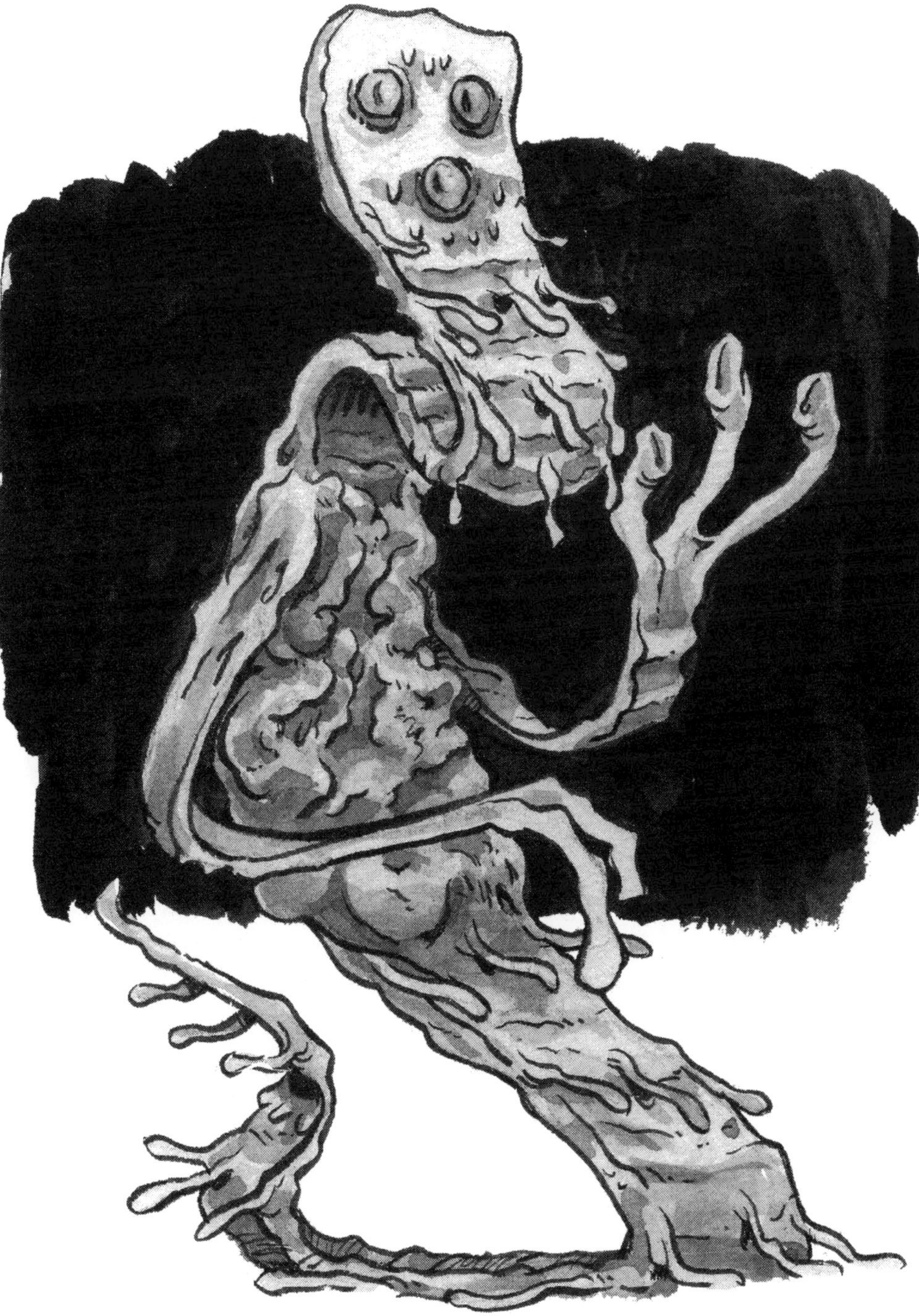

Printed in Great Britain
by Amazon